OPERATION BLACK KEY

Kim Hughes, GC, is an acclaimed public speaker and a trustee of the Victoria Cross and George Cross Association. Leaving the Army in 2020, Kim is the most highly decorated bomb-disposal operator to have survived the Afghan conflict. He was awarded the George Cross in 2010 following a gruelling six-month tour of duty in Afghanistan during which he defused 119 improvised explosive devices, survived numerous Taliban ambushes and endured a close encounter with the Secretary of State for Defence. His internationally bestselling autobiography, *Painting the Sand*, pathed the way in his transition to fiction writing. *Operation Certain Death* is the first thriller in the Dom Riley series followed by *Operation Black Key*. Each can be read as part of the series or as standalones.

Also by Kim Hughes

FICTION

Operation Certain Death

NON-FICTION

Painting the Sand

KIM HUGHES

OPERATION BLACK KEY

**SIMON &
SCHUSTER**

London · New York · Sydney · Toronto · New Delhi

First published in Great Britain by Simon & Schuster UK Ltd, 2021

1 3 5 7 9 10 8 6 4 2

Simon & Schuster UK Ltd
1st Floor
222 Gray's Inn Road
London WC1X 8HB

Simon & Schuster Australia, Sydney
Simon & Schuster India, New Delhi

www.simonandschuster.co.uk
www.simonandschuster.com.au
www.simonandschuster.co.in

A CIP catalogue record for this book
is available from the British Library

Hardback ISBN: 978-1-4711-8360-7
Trade Paperback ISBN: 978-1-4711-8361-4
eBook ISBN: 978-1-4711-8362-1
Audio ISBN: 978-1-3985-0156-0

Typeset in the UK by M Rules
Printed and bound in Great Britain by CPI Group (UK) Ltd, Croydon, CR0 4YY

MIX
Paper from
responsible sources
FSC® C020471

For my sons, Jack and Edward.

A SPECIAL FORCES MISSION SIMILAR TO THE
ONE FEATURED IN *OPERATION BLACK KEY*
DID ACTUALLY TAKE PLACE, MORE OR LESS
AS DESCRIBED. SEE APPENDIX FOR DETAILS.

AT THE REQUEST OF THE CRUISE LINES
THAT ASSISTED IN THE RESEARCH FOR
THIS NOVEL, SOME OF THE AT-SEA TRPS
(THREAT RESPONSE PROTOCOLS) HAVE
BEEN CHANGED FOR SECURITY REASONS.

PART ONE

ONE

'Target sighted. Cutting engine.'

Despite his near-whisper, Lieutenant James Varney's voice came over the speakers of the Special Boat Service's Mobile Command Centre truck with admirable clarity. The MCC was parked up on the pebbly beach near Herne Bay, the stretch of Kent coast where Varney and the men under his command had launched their Rigid Inflatable Boat on that night's training mission.

Inside the highly modified IVECO lorry, Staff Sergeant Dom Riley looked up at the pulsing red dot on the screen above the radio operator's head. This indicated the position of Varney's RIB, currently some six miles offshore, in the liminal zone where the Thames bled into the Channel. Back in the day, Riley had been out there himself, practising the same moves, pretending that hostiles had taken over the objective and had mined it, threatening to cripple the UK's vital maritime trade in and out of Tilbury. The fictitious target was one of the Maunsell Forts, Second World War-era structures that had once held anti-aircraft guns and now sat, decaying, forlorn and unloved, out in the estuary.

If he closed his eyes, Riley could picture the four units

making up the fort, which had once been linked by long-rotted walkways. Each sat on rust-streaked legs, standing like the aliens from *The War of the Worlds*, as if ready to stride ashore. With engines cut, the six SBS men would paddle the RIB through darkness — it was gone midnight, with March's new moon mostly obscured by clouds — to the largest of the four (there had once been five, but a careless Swedish ore transport had taken out one of the quintet). It was an unnerving approach for the men in the RIB, Riley knew. The metal giants groaned and creaked with the waves, as if they really were living, breathing entities. First time out it was, Riley had to admit, a spooky, sphincter-clenching sound.

Riley was in the truck purely as an observer, part of the MoD's new initiative to have more 'cross-fertilisation' between regular and special forces, to see if they could learn from each other. It was his role these days. Observing. His army-appointed shrink had recommended 'light duties' for him. What kind of fucking light duties does an Ammunition Technical Officer do? You're either making bombs safe or teaching others how to do it. Not standing on the sidelines, just watching, like some military voyeur.

Apparently, though, since the disappearance of his wife and daughter ten months previously, he was too 'unstable' and 'volatile' to be trusted with a live device. It was bollocks. Yes, in between shouts he might have a short fuse, but once he was at work, confronted with a real fuse and a genuine threat, his focus was only on the job at hand. And he needed to focus on something else right now.

He had to admit, though, that his attention was wavering that night, ever since he had spoken to his grandmother, Barbara Clifford-Brown, on the phone. She had said, cagily, that she might have a tentative lead on what had happened to Izzy and Ruby, his missus (well, strictly speaking, ex-missus) and little girl. Riley had pushed her for more, but she said it would wait until they could speak in person. Barbara was once in MI6 and she had her own ways of doing things. She'd probably prefer to communicate through dead letter drops. Open phone lines were certainly an anathema.

Riley had arranged to see her in London the following day. He had to remember to steel himself for disappointment. With the army's unofficial blessing, he had followed plenty of leads over the past few months while on his reduced duties. All had ended in a heartbreaking cul-de-sac. Ruby and Izzy had been taken by persons unknown after a gun battle on the streets of Padstow, of all places, that left one bodyguard dead and another badly injured. The police and MI5 – involved because Riley had worked alongside them during a series of terrorist outrages – had also drawn a blank. So any feeling of cautious optimism about Barbara's call was cut with a low hum of anxiety that it would be another dead end.

'Approaching access ladder.'

James Varney again. On board he had two almost-qualified ATOs, which the SBS was desperately short of, thanks to threats to tankers in the Straits of Hormuz which required the bomb-disposal experts out there. The trainee ATOs were backed up in the RIB by a team of regular SBS 'swimmer-canoeists', too bulked up with body armour, stun grenades, night vision goggles and Colt C8s to do any actual swimming. In a real-world situation, their job would be to take out the 'X-Rays', enemy combatants or terrorists on the fort, clearing the way for the ATOs to perform their task of neutralising any explosive devices. This time, at least, the IEDs were phoney, installed by a team of sappers from the Royal Engineers.

'Wish you were out there, Staff?' It was Joshua Kebede, the Special Boat Service Captain in charge of the exercise. He was from the outfit's specialist MCT – Maritime Counter-Terrorism – unit.

Riley drank the last of his now-cold coffee and binned it. 'What, freezing my nuts off in a blow-up boat in a fast-running chop, climbing some rusting ladder up into a dark, unsecured, rotting iron box that might actually fall into the bloody sea at any minute, while pretending to save the nation?' Riley waited a beat. 'Every time.'

Varney came back on. *'Hussein, Ricketts, you're on.'*

'Yes, Skip.'

'Liddy and Perring, you're covering.'

'Yes, Skip.'

Kebede and Riley turned to look at the MCC's speakers and waited for the next communication. No sound came for a while, apart from static and the odd electronic whistle. Riley was aware that the men out at sea had trained hard as a unit, so that most communication was by hand signals, nods and even winks. SBS men were tough fuckers for the most part, although Hussein and Ricketts, the ATOs, had been fast-tracked to bring the numbers up to strength. From what Riley could gather, the pair weren't as steel-hardened as the rest of the team. Yet.

Riley pictured them once again. If he had any sense, the bomb guy on point would be climbing gingerly, testing the rusted and pitted rungs and uprights of the ladder. It was a perfect place to leave a VOS, a Victim Operated Switch, a trip wire or pressure sensor, designed to detonate when a hand grabbed it or a boot sole pressed down in it.

'Hold it. Wire next to steel hatch.'

Riley nodded to Kebede. The ATO had found the first fake booby trap that the sappers would have put in place.

'False alarm. Clear. Checking rim of hatch.'

Good. By the book, thought Riley. The exercise was going smoothly. With a bit of luck he would make it home in the early hours to his 24-hour local and pick up a bottle. End the night as he normally did. At the bottom of that bottle. It was quiet and warm down there, with no nasty memories to taunt and prod him, a different world.

'Nothing. Lifting hatch.'

Riley heard it clang back with a noise that made him wince. Later, after the enquiry, he would discover that a plunger must have been placed on the floor where the rectangle of metal would drop. At the time, all Riley knew was that the command vehicle was filled with a roar that threatened to blow the speakers' cones apart.

A voice that might have been Varney's was just about audible over the racket. *'Fuck, fuck, fuck. Get out of here! Now!'* Then, a piercing, agonised scream, before comms went dead. Static filled the air. The red dot on the screen stopped pulsing and faded to black.

Riley sprinted along the length of the truck, throwing back the door, jumped down onto the beach and crunched rapidly towards the incoming tide that was hissing over the pebbles. He heard a new, terrible sound over the moan of the wind, a dreadful groaning, followed by the deep boom of another detonation. Then, Riley swore as he located the crimson glow on the horizon, like a beacon out at sea, marking the spot where good men were dying.

The horizon lit up with another flash, this one a searing white rather than red. As the rumble of the collapsing fort reached him, Riley heard Kebede approach and stand at his side, his breathing shallow and ragged. The man spoke for both of them when he asked: 'Fuckin' hell. What's gone wrong out there?'

It didn't require an answer, but Riley gave one anyway. 'Fuck knows.' Riley had no idea who or what could have caused this disaster out at sea. Nor could he possibly know that the events out there, many bleak miles from shore, would one day come back to screw up his life even further.

TWO

Helsinki. Three months later

Dom Riley had to admit that he had been incarcerated in the cleanest prison cell he had ever seen. Not that he was an expert on prisons, apart from a few hours in an MI5 detention centre and a night in the glasshouse at Colchester, sleeping it off after a drunken night on the town. But nothing he had witnessed in person or on TV came close to the room in which he had been locked up. The walls were a pristine white and graffiti-free, there was a privacy screen of frosted glass in front of the toilet. The opaque texture matched that of the panes in the porthole windows, high on the rear wall. There was a bed with duvet and (feather?) pillows, a desk, two chairs, and a comfy armchair. It was like he had been whisked off to a gaol built by that bloke from *Grand Designs*. Riley had no clear idea of why he was in this jarringly pristine Finnish prison. Espionage, the arresting SUPO officer had said.

Espionage?

What the fuck was he talking about? Riley had been following Barbara's lead, a painstakingly negotiated meeting with a Russian grandee, to establish if the abduction of his daughter and ex-wife was carried out by elements of the FSB or GRU or some other bunch of acronyms on British soil. Finland was not part of the deal. Just a convenient place for a face-to-face. Neutral territory. He was no threat to the security of the nation. It had taken a frustratingly extended period to set up the meet and now he was out of action, kept away from the hunt for Izzy and Ruby. *What a fuckin' waste of TIME.*

It was only after the final word bounced off the walls of the room that he realised he had blurted the sentence out loud. He filled his lungs. Breathed easy. Take stock, he thought. Be practical. Not the flake in Cell Nine.

The guys from *Suojelupoliisi* – the Finnish Security Intelligence Service aka SUPO – had ignored his protests. At least Riley still had on his own clothes, rather than an orange jumpsuit or whatever colour the Finns went for. They had, however, taken not only his shoelaces, but his boots too. Probably because they realised they had steel toecaps. There was a steel sole insert, too. Not that either would offer much protection if you stepped on a proper IED, but they gave some psychological support. And steel toecaps came in very handy for arse-kicking anyone on the team who wasn't doing their job. Not that he had had a team for some time. He was still officially an ATO on light duties.

But that could change any moment he wished, he was sure. He had made a concerted effort to mislead, or at least misdirect, the army psychologists. To stay calm in their presence, no matter how much they probed about his missing wife and daughter or his friend Nick, who had died in Afghanistan, a victim of an IED. To put a plug in the vent of the hot lava of anger that boiled inside him, always threatening to blow. To make them think that PTSD wasn't an issue. It was like fooling a lie detector. However, Riley had to be careful not to be too remote and unemotional. What man wouldn't be disturbed and outraged by the disappearance of his family? It was a balancing act, and so far he reckoned he hadn't wobbled too much.

Although there had been one notable stumble. In the aftermath of the Maunsell Fort fiasco – which, appallingly, was a piece of hazing, a prank, gone horribly wrong – and when no blame was attached to Riley or Kebede, a goodwill tour of the US had been arranged for him. He had lasted a few days before the feeling of inadequacy hit him – how could he put up with PR shit when his family was missing? – and it ended with him standing up an attractive Puerto Rican woman from the New York and New Jersey Harbor Authority at The Aviary bar on the Upper West Side and flying home. She probably thought he saw the price of the cocktails and bailed. Not big or clever.

Now he was away from the shrinks, he could let all the fury rise to the surface. Possibly punch a wall or two. But he knew that would be a waste of energy and maybe his carpal bones. He needed to get home. He needed to find out if Barbara's tame Russian was on the level. For crying out loud, he just wanted Izzy and Ruby back. Alive. Was that too much to fucking ask?

The metal door opened and Riley glimpsed the two SUPO men who had arrested him before a long streak of piss in a sharp blue suit ducked into his cell. The newcomer straightened up and adjusted his tie while the door clanged shut behind him. He was thirty or so, with a blond fringe of floppy hair, and the bulletproof confidence of his class.

'Staff Sergeant Riley. I am George Hutton of the Embassy's Legal Affairs Department. Do you mind if I sit?'

'Be my guest.'

With some awkwardness, the newcomer folded his long limbs into the armchair and put his briefcase down next to him. It was like watching a leggy foal make itself comfortable. Riley waited until Hutton had finished unbuttoning his jacket and smoothing his tie before he asked: 'What is this bollocks? Who sent you? And can you get me out of here?'

Hutton opened his case with long, bony fingers that suggested he could have had a career as a concert pianist and took out a slim folder. 'So, Staff Sergeant Riley. In a bit of a pickle, eh?'

'Not really. The charge is espionage, for fuck's sake. I'm innocent.'

'Espionage and, additionally, compromising the security of the nation.'

'Like I said, it's bollocks. Do I look like a spy? I'm just here to try and get to the bottom of—'

Hutton had flicked open the folder and was peering down at it when he interrupted. 'What happened to your wife and daughter, I know. I also know that you met with a Russian operative—'

'Former operative.'

'Don't be naïve, Riley,' he snapped, the chummy demeanour evaporating like spit on a hot griddle. Riley took another look at him. High cheekbones with a face just the right side of gaunt, a wide mouth that didn't open when he smiled and eyes that were a startling green. When he spoke, you got a glimpse of teeth that were a shade too white.

'There is no such thing as a "former" or "Ex-" KGB man,' he said. 'Their loyalties and service has simply passed to its various successors.' That slit of a smile pulled across his face.

The penny dropped with a loud clatter. 'Legal Affairs? For fuck's sake. You're Six, aren't you?'

Hutton answered with a noncommittal wave of those preternaturally long fingers. 'And you have, um, associations with MI6's sister organisation across the river.'

He meant Five. 'I think "associations" is a bit strong. I helped them out some time back. And if you know that, then you know *I am not a spy.*'

'Well, let's see, shall we? Can you start from the beginning?'

'Which beginning?' There were plenty to choose from. Afghanistan. Nottingham. Scotland. The Emirates Stadium. *Padstow.*

'Your meeting with . . .' Hutton allowed a flicker of distaste to show on his face. 'Colonel Brodsky.'

*

Dom Riley was not surprised that there was an Irish pub in Helsinki. They were everywhere in the world, as ubiquitous as Starbucks or Maccie Ds. He was taken aback, however, to learn that the Finnish capital could somehow support a dozen shamrock-and-stout establishments.

He was sitting in the latest addition to the list, Mary's Shebeen, situated not far from the Nordmann department store. Despite the name, it wasn't decorated like an illicit drinking den, but riffed on the classic Dublin pubs, plenty of dark wood, etched and stained glass, intimate snugs, signed hurling shirts and an ornate ceiling stained nicotine yellow in honour of the cigarette smoke it had never seen.

He was the sole occupant of a booth, distressed green leather under his arse and a ruinously expensive Jameson's in front of him. He took a sip of the whiskey, a few quids' worth by his reckoning. Part of him wanted to down it in one and order another. And then another. Numbing the higher centres of his brain, the ones that questioned the wisdom of meeting a man in an Irish pub in a foreign capital, a liaison that had taken weeks to set up, thanks to careful work by his grandmother, using the famous but mysterious 'back channels'. Helsinki was agreed as a venue because it was where the Russian said he felt safest. The UK was out of the question; he had history there, and he didn't want to be seen consorting with an agent of a foreign power on home soil. Finland, though, was acceptable to him.

Apart from the fact that Riley probably didn't have enough limit on his credit cards to drink himself unconscious at Helsinki prices, he had seen what alcohol had done to his mother's brain. He didn't want to inherit that particular family jewel.

Riley had been drinking pretty heavily before the incident at Fort Mansell. He had gone up a gear or two afterwards, while waiting for Barbara to put this meeting in Helsinki together. He knew full well the booze was a crutch, a tool designed to facilitate a retreat into a fantasy world. One where Izzy and Ruby were home and safe from harm, instead of . . .

No good ever came from that speculation. Plus he needed whatever wits he had left to deal with a retired KGB colonel. So, despite the temptation, Riley sipped.

There was a chance that the man he was meeting would have information on them. On who had taken them. They had been snatched in Cornwall, well over a year earlier. He felt constant guilt that it was his fault that they had been taken. That, because of his job and his history, Ruby had been kidnapped and . . .

No. They're alive. You know they're alive.

That was his old friend Nick, the ATO blown in half before his very eyes by an Afghan bomb, a less frequent visitor to his head these days. He was, at best, an unreliable source of information. Him being dead and all.

Yup. No wonder you need to see a shrink.

Riley flexed his left hand, trying to rid it of the pins and needles that sometimes invaded it. His body had recovered well from his exposure to a sarin-like nerve agent during his last proper

ATO assignment, but sometimes he got a neural reminder of just how lucky he had been.

He heard the squeak of the main door opening and the tap of a cane on the tiled floor. This could be his contact. But Riley didn't look. If it was his man, he'd make himself known. Riley was the amateur spy here. He would do well to remember that.

The metal ferrule on the cane tapped its way to the bar. A few minutes later a man of some bulk, dressed in an overcoat with a fur collar and a tall homburg on his head, struggled into the booth, wheezing. In his left hand he held the walking stick and in the right was a pint of Guinness. A moustache of creamy foam was sitting on his top lip.

'I got the taste for the black stuff in London,' the man said, once he had recovered his breath, putting the cane on the seat next to him and wiping away the froth from his mouth with the back of his hand. 'Of course, not as good as you can get at the Toucan Bar in Soho, but perfectly acceptable. Dominic Riley, I assume?'

Riley hesitated a moment before answering. 'Yes. You must be Colonel Brodsky.' Riley had asked Barbara how he would know Brodsky, but she had assured him the man would find him.

Pavel Brodsky examined Riley carefully and Dom returned the favour. The Russian was moon-faced, with few wrinkles, but with eyebags you could store handfuls of change in. His turkey-wattle neck and veined hands betrayed his longevity. If Barbara was right, he had to be well into his eighties. 'Thank you for meeting with me.'

'I am on holiday. That's all this is. A short break from my little house in St Petersburg. A chance to see some Finnish art. I am a big fan of Jorma Hautala and of Helene Schjerfbeck, of course. And to drink a Guinness or two. Do you know there are a dozen Irish bars in Helsinki?' His English was excellent, with barely a trace of an accent.

'So I've heard, colonel.'

'Former colonel. And call me Pavel.' He took a hefty sup of his pint. 'You are a bomb disposal man, I hear.'

'We call them ATOs. Ammunition Technical Officers. But yes. Was one.' *Am one?*

'Afghanistan?'

Riley nodded.

'You are a brave man, then.'

He wasn't sure whether the Russian meant because of his role as a soldier neutralising improvised explosive devices or just because he'd been to Afghan. He had had no choice in the latter, and he was good at the former. 'I'm not sure bravery comes into it.'

'Perhaps not. But we have something in common, I suspect. We never want to see Afghanistan again.'

Riley was more ambivalent than that about the country – true, half the population seemed to want you dead, but it had a rugged beauty and simplicity that he sometimes missed. In terms of not wishing to revisit the places where so many comrades lost lives and limbs, though, that was a given. So he just gave another incline of his head.

The Russian's features softened and his shoulders relaxed. It was as if Riley had passed some test. 'How is Barbara? Well? Bearing up, as you say?'

Riley knew he meant since the death of his grandfather, Henry Clifford-Brown. Murdered, Riley and others suspected, by agents of the Russian state. But now wasn't the time to bring that up. There was a little dance to be done first.

'Coping. I suppose she is as well as can be expected. The loss of both her husband and her home hit her hard. But she has a flat in London now. And she's a tough old bird.'

Brodsky's substantial and wiry eyebrows twitched towards

the brim of his Homburg. He took his hat off and placed it with the cane. 'I shouldn't let her hear you say that. She was quite a beauty in her day. But then I was handsome and dashing once.' He chortled to himself. 'Ah, Barbara. It was Henry I came across first, of course. In Bangkok. I met Barbara later, when Henry and she were in Moscow and Paris. And again in London. A remarkable woman.'

'She is.' It was only latterly he had begun to appreciate just how remarkable she was. On the outside, you only saw an elderly, slightly stooped woman with arthritic hands. If you could look into her past, you would find a very capable, very ruthless agent of Her Majesty's secret services. But enough of the skipping down memory lane, Riley thought. He needed to bring it back to the main purpose of his visit to the city. However, he was not the lead partner in this *pas de deux*. 'I'm grateful she got in touch and you agreed to help.'

'I am sorry about what happened to Henry. Death by lethal injection. Premeditated murder, I should say, given the way it was hidden under a nicotine patch. It was wrong. It was unnecessary.'

Unnecessary? Riley thought. But he didn't challenge him. Brodsky came from a world where murder was sometimes deemed very necessary indeed.

Brodsky supped once more and fixed Riley with a stare that might have been threatening. It was certainly uncomfortably intense. 'And it was rogue elements within the state security apparatus. The killing of your grandfather was not officially sanctioned. I think perhaps you should look closer to home.'

Riley's mouth kicked into gear before he could stop it. The words came out as a growl. 'Rogue elements? Isn't that what you people always say when your schemes go south?'

The Russian's head moved from side to side as he considered

this. 'There is some truth in that,' he eventually admitted. 'But it wasn't one of my schemes, you understand. The bombings. The murders. In my time such idiocy would have finished with a bullet in the back of the head.' He sounded like he missed the old days. 'Like your grandmother, I am retired. But like her, I keep some channels open.' From inside the overcoat the Russian extracted a magazine-sized guide to Helsinki. He laid it on the table and slid it across. 'Can you put your telephone on the table please? I want to be sure you are not recording this.'

Riley did as he was asked. Brodsky tapped the Home button to make sure it was off.

'Thank you. I'm assuming I don't have to frisk you?'

Riley opened his jacket. 'Be my guest.'

Brodsky nodded his satisfaction and tapped the magazine. 'In here is a piece of paper which contains all that I have discovered about the events leading up to the disappearance of your wife and daughter.'

'More than a year ago now,' Riley reminded him. 'Since then, nothing. No ransom demand. No blackmail attempts. No claims of responsibility.' Just the torture of silence.

'Once you have digested its contents, I would like you to dispose of the paper. By which I mean, I do not want it to leave this building. Understood?'

'Understood.' He was keen for the Russian to fuck off now and let him read the damn document.

Brodsky sensed his impatience, reached over and squeezed Riley's shoulder. 'Do not get your hopes up. It is not good news, I am afraid.'

Riley started to speak, but Brodsky raised a hand to silence him. He finished his pint and wiped his mouth for the final time. 'Tell Barbara if she ever wants to visit St Petersburg, she will be most welcome. I don't think she got across to the Hermitage when she was stationed in Moscow. It is a marvel.' He struggled to his feet and slid out of the booth, collecting hat and cane as he did so. 'I hope you find what you are looking for. I assure you, though, you have been searching in the wrong place.'

Riley felt a familiar fizz of anger and bottled it. 'So where is the right place?'

The Russian shrugged. 'That's not my job, son.'

It took a monumental force of will not to stand up and grab him by the throat. 'That doesn't help.'

A thin smile this time. 'I wish you luck, Dominic Riley. I know what it means to lose family.'

Riley found that no words would come. Not with a steady voice. He gave a nod as a farewell and Brodsky left, limping his way to the door. Riley would bet a fistful of roubles there was quite a story behind that gammy leg.

He waited a few minutes before he scooped up the guide and headed for the gents, only to be confronted with gender neutral toilets. All the cubicles were unoccupied, however, so he selected the farthest one and locked himself in. Then he flicked through the pages of the magazine until he found a single sheet of paper, with typed text on both sides. He had to read it several times before he could take it all in.

It had been called Operation *Reznya*. Carnage. An apt name. Its aim was to sow further confusion in the UK in the midst of the post-Brexit chaos. The public would begin to think society was breaking down, with bombing campaigns by the Muslim radicals, the far right and a resurgent IRA. As a bonus, the events would be a cover for taking out several Russian dissidents who had proved a thorn in Putin's side. It was instigated by something called Directorate 14 and given to the shadowy Unit 29155 for execution. The latter had managed to infiltrate two teams of three Russian agents into the UK completely undetected. One of them succeeded in recruiting a bomb-maker of Afghan origin, which was where Riley had come in, being an expert on that country's range of lethal devices.

According to the document, all of the Russian agents were exfiltrated when Carnage was deemed to have run its course. In fact, there was a feeling it had overstepped the mark and the agents were reprimanded. What did 'reprimanded' mean in Putin's Russia? Nothing trivial, he hoped. Maybe one of Brodsky's bullets to the back of the skull.

The last sentence was handwritten, probably by Brodsky. *There is no evidence that any of the operatives had anything to do with the subsequent disappearance of Staff Sergeant Dominic Riley's wife and daughter.*

What the fuck? These were the guys who exposed him to a nerve agent, leaving him with pins and needles, slightly out-of-whack tastebuds and a liver running at eighty per cent capacity. And they had taken Izzy and Ruby as part of the whole sick undertaking. *No evidence?*

He read the sentence again. Bullshit is what it was. It was the 'rogue elements' nonsense all over again – blame anyone rather than take responsibility. He tore the page into confetti and flushed it away, dumping the magazine among the used paper towels on the way out.

His fists were clenched as he crossed back to finish his whiskey. That familiar feeling of wanting to punch something was on him. Or someone. But the more rational part of his brain thought it best not to start with the man standing next to his booth.

He had mousy brown hair, with a fringe cut like he was auditioning for the part of Spock in yet another *Star Trek* reboot, and an oval face with a long beak of a nose planted dead centre. His grey eyes came with only one setting: suspicious. He was wearing a knee-length leather coat over a black polo neck and trousers. His friend Philip 'Scooby' Roscoe sometimes went for that look: Nick Fury, Agent of SHIELD as portrayed by Samuel L. Jackson. Except, in Roscoe's case, the eyepatch was the real deal. So, apparently, was his warning: *watch out for the Finns. The cops, the spooks. They're paranoid.*

Riley glanced towards the exit. There was another character there, also rocking the man-in-black look and big enough to almost fill the doorway completely. Riley guessed that doing a runner would be futile.

'Dominic Riley?' the one in front of him asked.

'Who's asking?' *Cop or spook?*

The man reached into the right-hand pocket of his shiny coat and produced a wallet, which he flipped open. 'I am Inspector Lars Wendell of the *Suojelupoliisi*.'

Riley looked blank. The dumbness wasn't an act. He had never heard of whatever they were called.

'SUPO,' Wendell said and the shortened version rang a vague bell with Riley. 'The Finnish Security Intelligence Service.'

'How can I help?' Riley asked.

'By making this as easy as possible. I am afraid you are to be detained under Article 579 of Section Five of the penal code.'

Riley glanced at the fridge-sized SUPO man blocking the exit. He hadn't shrunk any. And now he had pulled back his jacket to show the holstered sidearm clipped onto his belt. Glock 9mm. 'And what's Article 579?' Riley asked.

From his other pocket Lars Wendell produced a pair of Mil-Tec handcuffs and held them out. 'Espionage.'

THREE

Hutton had been taking notes while Riley spoke. He looked up from his pad when he sensed the story was done and said: 'Is that it?'

'Yes. Did the Finns arrest Brodsky too?'

'SUPO isn't stupid. They have to tread carefully. Russia is still a very unpredictable neighbour. Arresting the colonel would cause a diplomatic incident.'

'And I'm not a diplomatic incident? Innocent British bloke arrested for spying on trumped-up charges.'

'Well, I'm here, aren't I?' Hutton said, not too reassuringly. A junior MI6 officer hardly counted as sending a gunboat. 'Look, it's very difficult coming from an island as we do but imagine having Russia as a neighbour. Imagine seeing what it has done, with impunity in some cases, in Crimea, Georgia and Ukraine.'

'And Salisbury and Nottingham,' Riley reminded him. Russia didn't have to be right next door to cause a rumpus.

'And as you can imagine, after Crimea, the Finns are very nervous about another land grab.'

'And that's something to do with me?' Riley sighed. 'Why don't you just explain everything to SUPO. Sorry, misunderstanding.

Let me off with a slapped wrist and a warning not to talk to strange men in Irish pubs again.'

'I wish it were that simple.' He slid the folder back into his case, as if they were done.

'I need to get home.'

Hutton shook his head. 'You'll need to be patient.'

Not a strength, Riley thought. 'So, what's next?'

'SUPO has to apply for a detention order. Which means a court appearance. I'll sort you out legal representation. Don't worry, we have Finnish-speaking lawyers. Devil of a language, you know. I get by with Swedish. And I'll make sure you have an interpreter if need be. But most of SUPO have good English.'

Riley finally gave in to pacing, crossing the cell in three quick strides. 'How long can they keep me for? Before the court appearance? I have to get back. If what happened to Izzy and Ruby wasn't down to the Russians . . .' A surge of helplessness, a glance into the abyss, then gone. 'I can't stay here.'

'Four days, I'm afraid,' Hutton said, looking genuinely pained.

'Can I make a phone call?' Riley asked.

'To your legal representative, once I have assigned you one, probably. To anyone else? I suspect not. Not until the detention order is in place.'

He strode back and stood over Hutton. 'What? You have to be joking.'

'Well obviously, I'll see what I can do behind the scenes.' Hutton extricated himself from the chair and held his hand out. Riley didn't take it.

'But you could make a call for me.'

Hutton dropped the hand and pointed at the door. 'I had to surrender my mobile phone to the guards,' he said. 'Standard procedure.'

'Not now, you idiot. From the Embassy. You could call from the Embassy.'

'I could, I suppose. Did you have anyone in particular in mind?'

Damn right he did. Two people, in fact.

FOUR

'Do I look like the sort of person who would take a cruise?' Barbara Clifford-Brown demanded of the young man sitting across the computer-clogged desk before her.

'They're not as you imagine, Mrs Clifford-Brown,' Sebastian Virgo, the travel agent, assured her. 'Not at all regimented. The days of having to dine with the same people night after night are long gone. There's top notch entertainment. Very good speakers. And they are excellent value for money.'

She was in the cramped offices of Autry & Cole, a venerable travel company just behind Berry Bros & Rudd in St James's. It had survived in the twenty-first century thanks in part to the fact that the Intelligence Services often used it for non-sensitive travel arrangements. This visit, though, was for personal reasons. She simply fancied a holiday. The days of MI6 sending her abroad in the guise of a mere tourist were well behind her.

'I'm not bothered about that,' said Barbara firmly.

If she was, her next stop wouldn't be to the Dukes Hotel for her weekly £21 martini. 'I'm bothered about the company I would be keeping.'

'Ah, well, choose your ship carefully,' Virgo suggested.

'I'm going to carefully choose not to choose any ship at all. What else have you got?'

'Well, what about a safari? A luxury tented . . .' His voice trailed off as he caught the look on her face. He tapped his keyboard again, nervously this time.

'Rome?'

'Overcrowded.' Before he could add anything, she made a pre-emptive strike. 'Too many tourists. And that goes for Florence, Barcelona, Amsterdam, Venice, Dubrovnik and Porto. The latter has too many hills, as well. The same with Lisbon, of course.'

'Berlin?'

'Bad memories.'

The image of a young man with a hole in the back of his skull, the pillow under his head stained a deep claret, flashed before her. She batted it away.

'New York?'

Her face creased into a wistful smile. 'Ah. Too many good memories.' Harry Devonport. CIA. A handsome devil. Still lived in the city. 'Wouldn't want to spoil them.'

'What about China?' asked Virgo. 'Going in through Hong Kong?'

She couldn't keep the surprise from her voice. 'You are joking?'

'No. Why? There's no political unrest there at the moment, if that's what is worrying you.'

It wasn't. Well, not entirely. She reminded herself that this youngster, who was born after the Hong Kong handover, even if he was aware of the recent turmoil in the territory, would have no idea about the years when it was a hotbed of espionage. Her concern was a big wheel in the Ministry of State Security called Huang Jin who, when he was a mere field agent, had tried to have her kidnapped in Hong Kong and spirited to the mainland. It later transpired the idea was to trade her for one of their own who was languishing in an HK prison. She had had to hurt Huang to prevent that scenario coming to pass. The horrible man had lost a finger as a result of their encounter. She didn't want to be seen as unfinished business to him. So, even discounting the last few years' heavy-handed aggression that demonstrated a disdain for anything approaching democracy and transparency, China was definitely off the bucket list.

'The Caribbean?'

'Um.' She couldn't think of anyone she had killed, seduced or maimed in that part of the world.

'Bequia. Lovely little island . . .'

'You have any information?'

'I can email you some,' said Virgo, relieved at this break-through. 'Grenada and Bequia make an excellent combination.'

'Very well. And Jamaica, too. I hear good things.' Perhaps she would stay at GoldenEye. There was a pleasing irony in that, swanning around Ian Fleming's old place, a real spy in the home that helped spawn a fictional one. The writer had been a friend of Rory, her first husband, but she wouldn't let that darken the thought. She rose to leave and the young man said quickly: 'I'll add some cruise information on, too.'

She looked down at Virgo and he seemed to shrink into himself. A flash of pity stayed her tongue. 'Very well,' Barbara said, as she gathered up her handbag. 'But I shan't promise to read it.'

As she walked across to Dukes, Barbara thought of Dominic, out in Helsinki, meeting that old rogue Pavel Brodsky. Dom was on the trail of the *oprichniki* – most likely from Unit 29155 or similar – that had not only murdered Henry but seem to have taken poor Dom's ex-wife and child. Would Brodsky be truthful? Give Dominic an honest account of whatever he found? Well, Barbara had said that if he didn't, she would spit-roast Brodsky's privates over hot coals. She would like to think the Russian believed her. She put the meeting out of her mind for the moment. No good fretting about an asset running in the field until you had something worth fretting about.

Similarly she had spent many hours worrying, like Dom, about her great-granddaughter Ruby. She wasn't as close to the girl as she should be – her mother Izzy had always limited her and Henry's access, out of some sort of spite, she suspected – but the thought of the little girl coming to harm was distressing in the extreme. But the constant anguish had threatened her health. So now she coped by thinking of Ruby and her mother as operatives, missing on an operation. It helped her deal with the situation, to offer perspective and distance. Agents went missing. It happened in her day, it probably did still.

Once inside Dukes, Gilberto, the dark-haired, white-jacketed barman, ushered her through to the smaller, cosier section of the bar and, without having to ask her preference, went off to fetch the mixing trolley.

Would Henry roll in his grave – or, in fact, turn in his urn – if he knew how much the drink was going to cost? In all likelihood. In his later years he had become somewhat parsimonious, sometimes spilling over into tight-fistedness. But the buildings insurance after the fire that gutted Dunston Hall – collateral damage from the explosion that killed the oligarch who lived next door – and Henry's life insurance policy and astute pension arrangements meant she now had a robust bank balance.

She had imagined she would be bereft at the loss of so many keepsakes, books, furniture, paintings and sculptures in the conflagration. But she had found it incredibly refreshing to start again with a clean slate, as it were. Luckily, Henry had kept some sentimental papers and photographs – including his early letters to her – and important documents, such as their wills, in the care of Coutts. So, at least she had some mementos.

When she thought of Henry, his letters, she felt a sharp pain behind her breastbone. Acid reflux, she had thought the first few times, but eventually she had realised it was a physical man-ifestation of her loss. She missed him, his presence around the place, the heft of him, solid and reassuring, on the increasingly infrequent occasions when they shared a bed. But Henry didn't dominate her thoughts or actions. Barbara had always been her own woman, her own kind of spy, rather than part of a double act.

The chink of glass-on-glass heralded the arrival of the martini trolley. Gilberto set about coating the inside of the frozen glass with a graphene-thin layer of vermouth. 'How are you today, Mrs Clifford-Brown?'

'I'm well, Gilberto, thank you. Apparently I have reached the age where I have no option but to take a cruise.'

He gave a little chortle and a grin spread across his normally serious features.

'Is it that funny? A woman of my age escaping to sea? Is it a cliché? Do tell what's so amusing.'

She must have let a little vinegar leak into the last sentence, because Gilberto flinched. 'Forgive me, Mrs Clifford-Brown. I was just remembering. Reminiscing. I worked two seasons on a cruise ship. For Costa. You know it?'

She shook her head. 'Like the coffee places?'

'No, no. An Italian line. Big ships. It was fun.' That smile again. 'Hard work, but fun.'

It took her a few seconds to realise that the tinny music she could hear – the opening of Beethoven's Fifth – was coming from her bag. She looked at Gilberto, nonplussed. She could imagine

Henry, a prominent member of the generation who loathed mobile communications, tutting at the thought of her picking up the handset. *The only thing worse than taking a phone call in a public place is making one.*

'Answer it, Mrs Clifford-Brown, please,' said Gilberto, looking around to make sure they were alone. 'There's nobody to disturb.'

'Except you.'

'I'm here to serve, Signora,' he said, flashing the smile with his eyes this time. She could imagine what sort of fun the handsome young man had got up to on his Costa cruise liner.

She fetched the phone. Unknown number. It better not be someone asking if she'd had an accident that wasn't her fault. She was ready to give such people both barrels and follow it with a butt-clubbing.

'Hello?'

It was worse than an ambulance chaser. The words tumbled over each other on their way out. 'It's me. You've got to help. Please. I'm in big trouble.'

Barbara kept her voice steady and calm. 'What kind of trouble?'

'They've put me in prison.'

Barbara gave a deep sigh. This again? 'No, it's not a prison. It's the new home we found for you, sweetie.'

'They won't let me out, Mum!'

That's because you'll go straight to the nearest shop and buy a bottle of Gordon's. 'I'll come and see you first thing. I'll sort this out.' Rachel, her daughter, Dominic's mother, was suffering from a wicked form of alcoholic dementia known as Korsakoff's syndrome. When she moved back to London, Barbara had found a place for her in a decent care home in Amersham. 'I'll be in first thing. Is that all right, sweetie?'

Rachel's voice quivered. 'I suppose so.'

'I'll see you then. Promise.'

Barbara made a mental note to call the home and book a visit. After a succession of goodbyes and reassurances, she clicked off and felt the familiar stab of guilt at the fact that it was the child in the care home slowly losing her marbles, when it should have been her. But there was nothing to be done. The option of Barbara looking after Rachel at home, especially now she was alone, was out of the question. She had just turned her attention back to her rapidly warming martini when the blasted mobile rang again.

It was Kate Muraski of MI5, someone she had once underrated, if not actually disliked, but Barbara's frosty attitude had thawed somewhat toward her when the young woman had proved herself a capable operative. And she had looked after Dom in the wake of the Emirates Stadium incident. She now trusted Muraski enough to share her mobile phone number with her. 'Kate?'

'Yes. Barbara. Thank God. I've just had a call from a Six man in Helsinki. Hutton. He was trying to call you.'

'I was speaking to my daughter. Was it about Dom?'

'Yes.'

'Is he all right?'

'No,' said Kate. 'He's in prison.'

Barbara groaned. 'Christ on a bicycle. Not him as well.'

FIVE

Captain Harald Nansen stood on the quay at Southampton and watched the glass rectangle – nicknamed the Flying Carpet – move smoothly down the side of his vessel towards the dock. Inside was a group of travel writers who had just been given a tour of his liner (never referred to as 'cruise ship', in his earshot). The event had opened with a speech by Nansen, questions from the floor, followed by canapés and champagne and then, in small groups, a tour of *Rapide*, the pride of Anglo-American Lines. It held that position by default – it was actually the only ship that A-AL had, until its sister *Rapier* emerged from Nantes' Chentiers de l'Atlantique shipyards in eighteen months' time.

He watched with some pride as the transparent box – about the size of three shipping containers, joined end-to-end – kissed dry land. The door slid back and out they came towards the waiting coaches, a group of journalists, bloggers and influencers.

He looked up at *Rapide*, trying to see it with fresh eyes, to tap into what the writers must have thought on first encountering the ship. Perhaps, in comparison to his forebear (so family myth had it) Fridtjof's Nansen's *Fram*, his new vessel lacked a little elegance. But that was all relative – the engineers and architects had studied the great transatlantic liners of old, and clever design cues meant *Rapide* looked less like a floating office block or refrigerator than many of her contemporaries.

As the transfer coaches filled up with the assorted hacks and pulled away, heading for Southampton railway station, he heard a squeal of tyres as a car cornered at speed. It signalled the arrival of the captain's next appointment, one of the many VIPs A-AL hoped to attract to *Rapide*.

Onto the quay came a low, aggressive-looking sports car. Apart from the shout of money, the tyres were the only things that made a noise. This Koenigsegg had been modified to run on battery power and so proceeded along the dockside to the loading bay in near-silence. Nansen watched with a quiet envy, knowing he would never be able to afford any model of the Swedish hypercar. His brother in New York had bought a flashy Pagani once that was worth half a million dollars or more. But he worked for a company that was like something out of the TV show *Billions*. When there was a bull market, they all had obscene cars. Leased, just in case bull market became bear. Which was just as well, because with Jakob things had a habit of going bull-to-bear pretty quickly.

That reminded Nansen that he had promised to have a drink with Jakob in London, once *Rapide's* short shakedown cruise around the British Isles was completed. In his younger brother's books 'having a drink' meant getting what young people called 'wavy' and what he knew as 'completely pissed'. Nansen would try to make it a lunch. Jakob was more controlled at that time of day.

The electric car came to a halt and both doors opened at once. Nansen straightened his uniform jacket again and strode purposefully towards the vehicle. The young man who exited from the driver's side did not appear old enough to own a £1million-plus car. He looked like a surfer, with a mop of unkempt hair, a few days' carefully cultivated stubble and a face with an impish grin plastered across it, as if he had just thought of a filthy joke. He was dressed – as he always was in the many paparazzi-snapped photographs that regularly appeared in the print media and online – in jeans and a Supreme T-shirt, the company's logo written across his chest in gold.

This was Christian Ledgard, tall, scruffily fashionable, with a pair of classic Aviator sunglasses clamped onto his nose. In all the pictures Nansen had seen in the press and online of the man, the shades had never been off, even when surfing. The slacker image was a construct, however. Nansen had done his research. He had uncovered a Q&A interview in the Business section of the *Sunday Times*. In it the young man had emerged as one of those driven people who is up before 5am every day to check emails and hit the gym or drive to catch an early-morning wave.

The article had told Nansen that Ledgard's wealth came from cryptocurrency. Not necessarily from his own virtual money, Klondike, a version of Bitcoin that was as volatile as the original. No, in the wake of the fraudulent OneCoin scandal, most of his fortune came from designing legitimate 'mining' systems for others, such as Google and HSBC, which he then licensed to them. He had, apparently, turned down millions for the company.

One thing the article hadn't mentioned – something he had let slip with the cruise company's PR – was that this technocrat, for all his belief in toys of the modern world, was afraid of flying. Hence his choice to cross the Atlantic aboard *Rapide*.

A pair of long, tanned legs emerged from the passenger door, belonging to Christian's wife, Shelby Ledgard. She had the artfully cut blonde hair, smooth forehead, subtly exposed cleavage, pouty lips and honeyed skin of the selfie-ready social-media socialite. That was exactly what she had been, a woman who knew how to build a profile from thin air, and it had made her a perfect brand ambassador for any company determined to target millennials.

Nansen's reading suggested that, although she looked like a contestant on *Love Island*, she was far from shallow waters. She had a business degree from a Russell Group university and had managed to scupper the *Mail*'s suggestion that she was a trophy wife and gold digger by publishing her pre-nuptial agreement with Ledgard, forgoing all rights to any of his fortune in perpetuity.

He switched his attention back to the driver.

The young man was gazing up at *Rapide* with some admiration. He even lifted his sunglasses to get a better view. Nansen held out his hand as he reached the Koenigsegg. 'Mr Ledgard?'

He tore his attention from the liner and, with just a moment's hesitation, took the captain's hand. 'Yes.'

'Captain Harald Nansen. Welcome to *Rapide*.'

After they had shaken, Nansen turned to Mrs Ledgard and touched his cap in salute. 'Mrs Ledgard. You are most welcome. Would you like a look around?'

'I think that is rather the point of being here, isn't it?' she said flatly. Nansen had a sense that she would rather not be there. Not so much chilled, as permafrost. She pulled out her phone and began to tap on the screen, barely glancing at the ship towering over them. Then she looked up at him. 'You can get us to New York in six days?'

'We have to be there for the start of the Gumball Classic,' added her husband. This was, Nansen knew, a coast-to-coast 'rally' for the well-heeled.

'Because the *QM2* takes seven,' said Mrs Ledgard.

In fact, Nansen was well aware that the *Queen Mary 2* could do it in five, maybe even less, but it would roughly triple the fuel bill, which would ramp up the fares. Plus, a captive audience for a week meant more income from the passengers in bars, casinos, art galleries and concessions.

'Of course,' the captain assured them. 'Weather permitting.'

'You know I'm only considering this because Chris here won't fly? I mean, isn't it boring being at sea for so long?' Mrs Ledgard asked. 'Nothing but bad magic shows? And geriatric tea dances?' She flashed him a megawatt grin as insincere as it was dazzling.

Nansen couldn't help but think she was taunting him. 'We are a disrupter, Mrs Ledgard. This is a different demographic to more conventional ships. One that doesn't expect tired old cruise ship entertainment. No cheesy magicians. No novelty acts. No washed-up actors plugging their memoirs. People who want Goldie, Afrojack or Saz on the decks, rappers like Lord Apex or Louis Culture on stage and Spielberg introducing the films.' The latter was not quite true. The director had 'curated' a season, complete with filmed appearances, but they couldn't get him in person.

'It is also a generation that expects to be able to control everything from their phone. That's what the *Rapide* app is for. Everything from extending the balcony in the best suites – which you'll have, of course – lowering the blinds, running the bath, to booking spa treatments or asking for the wine to be opened before you go down for dinner at Rochelle Canteen or Gymkhana or The Breslin or any of the other seven restaurants. You can book time in the snow grotto, which has real snow, or the forest glade. There is even a "Bring Champagne" button. As it says, this a 5-Star-5G ship.' He was impressed at how easily the pitch was tripping off his tongue now. He hadn't been convinced that the attempt to attract a new market to cruising, Dalston or Williamsburg-on-sea, as he had cynically called it, was going to work. Now, Nansen thought he sounded positively evangelical.

Mrs Ledgard looked up from her screen, surprised. 'You have 5G?'

'Well, not while we're at sea,' Nansen admitted. 'What we are suggesting is that this is the most advanced, wired ship on the ocean. And Wi-Fi is free, unlike with most other companies.'

'Can we see the cabins?' asked Ledgard. 'There'll be four of us travelling, my co-driver and his partner. Amber X.' He said it in a manner that suggested Nansen should have heard of her. He made a mental note to do some research. 'They'll have a Twisted Land Rover. You have space?'

The captain was familiar with the "Twisted" version of the old workhorse – more power, more gizmos, a lot more money. 'The garage will hold twelve vehicles. We only have passage booked for four so far.'

'Excellent. Plus there's two mechanics, Jim and Reece, but they'll bunk in together. So. We'd like to see the cabins now.'

'Of course.' Nansen pointed towards the Flying Carpet. 'If you'll follow me.'

He set off, but Mrs Ledgard remained fixed to her iPhone, frowning down at the display. For a second, the captain recalled the old Norse superstitions about women on ships. He didn't subscribe to such nonsense. But this was a maiden voyage. And, traditionally, on those, ships needed all the good luck they could get.

'Shelby?' Ledgard asked.

'Yes, coming.'

*

Someone else was looking over the ship at that exact moment. Except he wasn't doing it in person. The man who had taken the *nom de plume* BaseHeart for his online work had pulled up the schematics of the liner for perhaps the two hundredth time. Thanks to the many VR renderings Anglo-American had posted on its website to entice clients, as he looked at the blueprints, two dimensions resolved to three and black-and-white gave way to technicolor. Bright carpets rolled out along the passageways, panelling appeared on walls, chandeliers glinted high above the atrium, tables were colonised by linen and flatware. The passengers appeared and he could picture himself walking the decks, the wind whipping at his hair, descending the gilded staircase into the main dining room, slipping into a hydrotherapy pool in the spa or catching a show in one of the three theatres.

He imagined the soft burble of self-satisfied conversations in the smaller, more intimate premium restaurants. The choppy, nervous rhythms of nu-jazz. The laughter from the Second City comedy franchise. The inevitable whale song creeping out from the spa treatment rooms. Then the stunned silences. Followed by the first stirrings of anxiety.

Did you feel that?

What was it?

What's that noise?

There it is again.

Oh my God.

Can you smell burning?

The first gasps of anxiety. The cold terror of hearing the alarm honk its warning. The crackle of the tannoy as the captain issues instructions, his voice robotically calm. The clatter of chairs overturned, the brittle noise of shattering china, the screams of children. The spread of panic, like a wildfire sparking through the ship. The slow tipping of the deck out of horizontal. The terrifying gush as thousands of gallons of sea water spew through the ragged gash in the side of the liner. The feral panic at the lifeboats, as a corrosive cocktail of survival instincts burn away the veneer of civilised behaviour. It will be a pack of beasts who clamber to safety.

Then *Rapide* slowly, almost elegantly, slides beneath the waves, ready to take its place on the rollcall of the wrecks on the bottom of the Atlantic. The lights flicker and fuse into darkness as the hungry sea runs through every electrical conduit. The stern lifts free from the water, the cracking and straining of stressed metal. The unearthly snap as the ship's back breaks. A last farewell, a giant belch of air as the sea embraces her. Then, only the oily black swell, the orange dots of lifeboats and the terrified wailing of the survivors.

BaseHeart chuckled to himself. Well, it might not come to that. But a man could dream.

SIX

The sleek, modern Finnish Church in London at Rotherhithe was a well-appointed house of worship. As well as a conventional space for services and prayer, with pews and an altar, it also housed a grocery store for homesick Finns to stock up on their favourite brands, cheap dormitory rooms for travellers, a sauna and a cafe. Barbara Clifford-Brown had considered choosing the sauna for her meeting with Mikko Salo, just to throw him off balance, but thought that might frighten her contact off. So she'd suggested they have coffee and took up her position in the blond-wood cafeteria fifteen minutes before the arranged time. Which was just as well, as the Finn was ten minutes early.

She recognised him right away. He was the spit of his father, the same stocky build and square jaw, identical piercing eyes that scanned the room before alighting on her, the same thatch of hair with a slight curl, although there was some grey in there. He was older than his father had been when Barbara had met him in the wilds of Finland.

'Lieutenant-Commander Salo?' she asked as he approached.

'Mrs Clifford-Brown.' His face split into a smile and he held out his hand.

'Barbara,' she corrected.

'Mikko, please.'

'Thank you for making the journey.'

'Ha. No problem. The *omenalörtsy* here are the best in the city.' Her expression conveyed her ignorance. 'Apple doughnuts. Would you like one, perhaps? And more coffee?'

'No thank you. You go ahead.'

He returned from the counter with a coffee and a pastry and sat opposite her. 'Do you know we Finns consume more coffee per capita than any other country in the world? Even the Italians.'

'I remember that everyone stops for a coffee break. Much like we stop for tea.'

'Coffee breaks are enshrined in labour law.'

The Finnish Military Attaché to Great Britain took a sip and Barbara fell silent. In his home country you don't gabble while a man or woman is taking their first hit of caffeine. It's rude. 'Hmm. The roast is a little light for me now. I am being corrupted by this country.' He put the cup down and as he gazed at her she had the strange feeling again that she was looking back through time at Captain Timo Salo.

'How is your father?' she asked.

'He is well, thank you. Lives about fifty kilometres outside of Helsinki now, on his farm. Still hale and hearty. He sends his best. He insisted I meet with you. He says they used to call you the *Rautu Nainen*. The Iron Woman.'

'Well, someone else purloined that nickname, or as close as dammit. And if I ever was iron, I'm busy rusting away these days.'

'Nonsense. You met him when? Sixty-five?'

'Six. Timo helped me with a tricky exchange, up at the Russian border, with my first husband, Rory.'

'He told me. The good old days, eh?'

'For some,' she said grudgingly. It wasn't an entirely happy memory.

'For my father. He loved sparring with the Reds. Excuse me.' He took a bite of the sugary doughnut.

Barbara fetched a small velvet pouch from her bag and slid out a military decoration. The silvery disc was attached to a black ribbon with red stripes, and the medal itself was embossed with the head and shoulders of a rifleman – or sniper – in action. She put it on the table and pushed it across so that the colonel could see it more clearly. His eyes widened slightly. 'A Winter War medal.'

The Winter War of 1939–40, when tiny Finland managed to fight the invading Russian army to a standstill, thanks in part to its sharpshooters, was their country's Rourke's Drift, Dunkirk and Battle of Britain all rolled into one. With the addition of snow and crippling cold.

'It's Henry's. My second husband.'

'Your husband fought in the Winter War?' There was surprise in his voice.

She wondered if he knew that a British volunteer force had gone to Finland to help thwart the Russians, a ragtag group which included the future *Dracula* actor Christopher Lee. The Finns had wisely taken one look at them and said: *thanks, but no thanks*. But Henry hadn't been part of that group.

'Not exactly.' While Salo continued to work on his doughnut, Barbara explained how, as a young man in late 1939, at the behest of the Ministry of Economic Warfare, Henry had resigned his commission in the Royal Artillery and travelled to bomb-damaged Helsinki as a civilian through neutral Sweden.

Meanwhile, the British clandestinely shipped First World War-era howitzers to Finland by sea. Henry's task, his first undercover assignment for the secret services, was to instruct Finnish gunners in the use of the weapons in the field and to help write an instruction manual.

'Henry got out by trawler from Liinakhamari in April 1940, just after the Germans invaded Norway. He was worried the Nazis would carry on across Finland and divide it up with Russia, as the pair had in Poland. But he had the job done by then. Arrived home terribly constipated, he said. Six months of living on reindeer meat, apparently.'

Salo smiled at that. 'So my country owes him a real debt of gratitude.'

'Well, Mikko, there might be a way you can help repay that debt. You being a SUPO man.'

He didn't argue. Everyone knew that the military attaché in London was an intelligence posting. 'Henry is still alive?'

'No. But his grandson is. And he's currently cooling his heels in a Finnish prison.'

Salo frowned. 'Ah. I see. And you want my help to get him out?'

'You have my word that he's done nothing wrong. He is a military man, in the army, that much is true. But he is no spy, Mikko. It's bound to be a misunderstanding.'

The attaché took a final, thoughtful bite of his doughnut, leaving a nub on his plate, and wiped his fingers. 'For the widow of a Winter War hero, I'll see what I can do.'

She breathed a sigh of relief. 'Thank you.'

'On one condition.'

Barbara bristled slightly. She hadn't come to *bargain*. She had come to get Dominic Riley out of a foreign gaol by playing the I'm-an-old-friend-of-your-father card. 'What's that?'

'My old man told me to ask you exactly what happened on the border with Russia that night back in 1966.'

'Really? He was there.'

'Yes. But he says he never knew the whole story. Why what happened took place.'

She considered the request for a moment. Few people still alive knew how that particular mission ended. But perhaps it was ancient history that had lost its power to shock. And if it freed Dom . . .

She took a breath, keen to answer before she over-thought it, and almost blurted her next two words. 'Very well.'

And, taking her time, smelling the pine forests and feeling the bone-numbing chill off the lake, she began.

'It was 1966. We were running agents through Finland that year . . .'

SEVEN

They waited until Riley got to his room at the top of the Grand Finlandia Hotelli before they went for him. His attention was distracted by his anger at his detention by SUPO and then the sudden release without explanation. Or apology. Or offer of a lift. He assumed Hutton had pulled strings as requested, but there was nobody to meet him when he was turfed unceremoniously onto the wet pavements of Ratakatu, near the Design Museum.

His best guess was that Hutton had, as Riley had requested, managed to get a message through to either Kate Muraski of MI5 or Barbara Clifford-Brown, late of MI6, and one of them had set the wheels in motion that had sprung him. Most likely Kate, he thought.

Riley had just slid his keycard into the slot and pushed down on the handle when he was aware of a rush of air as two men burst out of the door to the stairwell directly behind him, flinging their combined weight at him.

It should have worked a treat but for the fact that he had swiped the keycard incorrectly. The idea was obviously that the three-person package would crash the door open and take the trio inside, probably winding Riley, or worse, on the fall.

It didn't happen like that.

The breath burst out of Riley all right and the door bulged, but it didn't give. He used his arms to push back against the pair, who clearly had expected to be on the carpet by that point. Riley was no expert in unarmed combat, but his righteous fury had been bottled up for so long, he could almost taste it.

He spun around, fists flailing, a bellow issuing from his mouth that must have made half the inhabitants of the nearby Hietaniemi cemetery restless in their graves.

He saw the next few moments as if in a strobe light, brief flashes of an image, then darkness. Elbow. Nose. Blood.

Good.

Assailants: one short, one tall. And broad. *Get the big one.* Steel toecaps. Shin. Balls. A hoot, like a ship's siren.

Thumb. Eye. Squeeze. Yelp.

All the time, Riley knew he was taking hits. But it was as if there was a disconnect between the skin and muscle receptors and the nerves tasked with carrying the pain message to his brain. He could sense the pressure of contact, on his kidneys, his ear, his jaw, but nothing registered as hurt. Not yet. So he rode every punch and kept taking the fight to them.

Palm. Up. Chin. Crunch of teeth. Blood in the mouth, with a bit of luck.

And then he saw the pistol.

It was the shorter of the two who had yanked it from his jacket. Riley figured the big 'un was probably still wondering if he'd ever be a father after the steel in his boot had made intimate contact with his groin.

The gunman was waving the weapon in the vague direction of Riley's midriff.

Careful, now. You don't want to get gutshot, pal.

No I fucking don't, he thought. I saw enough of that in Afghan.

Riley stepped in closer to stymie any clear shot from the gun and did the most stupid thing imaginable: he grabbed the pistol with his left hand.

He got in two good smacks into the man's face – this was the one with the already busted nose – and tried to twist the pistol from his hand. He felt his opponent's finger tighten on the trigger.

As an ATO, it was his job to know his guns. This one was big and weighty, not one of the modern polymer jobs like a Glock. A cannon in comparison to those. But maybe you needed something that could take down a moose in Finland. The analytical part of Riley's brain, the one that wasn't busy seeing red, pinged a message, telling him it wasn't a striker pistol. It would have an external hammer. He slid his hand along the top of the barrel, past the breech and found the hammer just as it was arcing forward. He jammed his thumb in it.

He stifled a scream. Clearly the mental pain-dampening mechanism didn't extend to pierced thumbs. He used all his strength to twist the pistol from the man's grip and throw himself backwards, giving himself enough room to jerk the hammer off his thumb, lock it back and swing the weapon round to face the men. The pain was pulsing up his arm and his vision blurred in and out of focus in unison with the throbs. He blinked several times and the world steadied.

The pair of goons stood there, unsure of themselves now. Less than a minute had passed and somehow they were on the wrong side of the gun barrel. Just to press this home, Riley raised the weapon and held it out in a two-handed grip, feet well apart, core engaged. They would know from his stance that he had fired pistols plenty of times before. Just to convince them further, he let them know he was fully aware of what he had in his hands.

'Browning Hi Power,' he said between deep breaths. 'Belgian.

Thirteen rounds. Nine millimetre. Muzzle velocity? Three-fifty metres a second as I recall. That'll stop you dead.'

The two men did a quick calculation of the odds of them both making it out of the hotel corridor alive and fled back to the stairwell as quickly as they had come. Riley was happy to let them go. A fresh wave of pain came flooding over him almost immediately, as if his body was keen to get rid of the backlog. He gasped as a fire started in his lower back and ran up his spine, like flames along touch paper. Blood was running from his nose and one ear had a full-on tinnitus attack.

He staggered a little and placed one hand against the wall to steady himself, trying to ride the stabs of agony, each one more intense than the last. He was busy trying to make sense of what had just happened and who was behind it when he heard a gasp of horror and looked up. One of the cleaning staff, an elderly woman, was along the corridor, her mouth formed into an 'O' of shock. How much had she seen?

'What sort of hotel are you running here anyway?' he managed to ask.

She beat it back to the lift. No doubt to fetch the cavalry. Or, more likely, just the manager. He picked up his key card and tried the door again. It opened on the third attempt. What was wrong with a bloody key? Riley locked it behind him.

Who were those clowns?

Nick, his old and very dead pal, always there to ask the questions Riley couldn't answer. But he was right: they were clowns. He hadn't just taken down two stone-cold killers. His ego might like that to be the case, but had they been the real deal he'd be hog-tied on the bed by now, telling them his mother's maiden name.

It was possible he'd just had a brush with a couple of rent-a-thugs, albeit ones with a very useful pistol. It was just a shame he couldn't get it home. The Browning was big enough and ugly enough to set off every alarm at the airport while he was still in the taxi outside the terminal. He would have to find somewhere safe to stow it, though. If the housekeeper had called the police and told them he was armed and dangerous, he would claim she must have been hitting the *Kilju*.

So it was just a mugging?

Maybe. The timing was interesting, given he had just been released by SUPO, but it might just be a coincidence.

Yeah, right.

'Later. I'll think about it later,' Riley said out loud.

He tossed the gun on the bed, walked through to the bathroom and examined his face. The nose wasn't broken, even though it felt the size of a muffin, and he'd have a black eye. There was also a cut on his cheek, probably caused by a ring. And his throbbing thumb was swelling up to Looney Tunes size.

He moved back into the bedroom and stashed the Browning where it would never be found, short of tearing the room apart. One problem solved. And the other pressing one? Basically Nick's question: who the hell would bother sending hired help to rough him up? He put that to one side for now, parking it for later, just like the pistol. He might not know who his attackers were, but one thing he was certain of: it was time to get the hell out of Dodgski.

EIGHT

BaseHeart knew that communication was the key. If his scheme was to work, he had to have hour-by-hour knowledge of what, exactly, was happening on board *Rapide*. However, he certainly couldn't rely on normal comms — radio, internet, mobile phones. Once the shit hit the watery fan, any captain worth his salt would shut down all but the most secure channels to the outside world. Except to those who could help him. BaseHeart looked at the yellow legal pad on his desk, filled with acronyms in boxes and lines drawn between them. He had spent many hours over the past few days combing through the possibilities, in between making sure his team were all aware of their roles. All the scribbles on the yellow pages before him led to one name sitting at the centre of the crazed spider's web: COBRA.

The government's crisis management committee was bound to meet. It would be kept up-to-date with what was happening out at sea. It would recommend a response. It was there he had to place his listening device. Not that he could get a bug into the room, not even the tiny, sophisticated, sweep-proof ones he had at his disposal. No, his eavesdropper had to be human, just like his carefully cultivated agents on board *Rapide*. Getting a person into COBRA was not exactly simple, but it would be easier than planting anything electronic.

It hadn't been difficult, given his day job, to find out who was likely to be at any given COBRA meeting. But one only had to read a book by Frank Gardner or Gordon Corera to get the list of the great and the good: representatives of MI5, MI6, the FO, the Cabinet Office, the Met, plus government ministers. Most of them as impregnable as the room where they met.

But there was always one.

He leaned back in the chair and popped the ring pull on a can of Diet Coke. The weeks of sitting in front of screens in that windowless basement, chugging back junk food and fizzy drinks and the odd lager had piled on some unwelcome pounds. His face in the mirror was softer, blurred where it had been well-defined, and he had the beginnings of a paunch. When he was in Switzerland for a two-day conference, someone had said he was looking 'content'. A euphemism for chubby. Time to cut back. He looked down at the small picture of his daughter, taken on a school skiing trip, and mouthed an apology. He had let himself go.

He had come up with a list of potential names in COBRA, and the organisation known as Oktane, part of which functioned as a sort of online bazaar for information, had trawled the darkest recesses of its virtual medina and produced the photograph that was on the monitor before him. An older man lying on a large Chesterfield-style couch, face slightly turned away from the camera – but not quite enough to prevent him being recognised – busy being pleasured by a much younger woman, her head buried in his crotch. A second girl – eighteen? nineteen? – was standing behind the sofa, clutching a glass of champagne. She was at the very least topless and her rather gormless grin and glassy eyes suggested she was either very drunk, very high, or both.

BaseHeart reached in and pressed the mouse several times and a sequence of similar images flashed up, seven in all. He had paid Oktane a lot of money for them and they were of varying quality, but they left the viewer in no doubt that they were witnessing some sort of sex party – an orgy one might say, although that word gave it a veneer of conventional respectability it didn't deserve – that had taken place in the relatively recent past. And that one of the men indulging himself with the women on offer was the married and respectable Clive Greggs, now of the Cabinet Office, part of whose brief was liaising with COBRA.

Perfect.

NINE

She was waiting for Riley airside at Heathrow, just before baggage collection. He could see the concern slowly develop on her face, like an old photograph in a bath of chemicals. When he reached her, Kate Muraski of MI5 reached up to touch his face and then stopped herself. Her fingers hovered millimetres from his cheek for a second. For a brief moment he found himself wishing she would make contact and sod the pain. *Just friends.*

'Jesus, you look like you went ten rounds with Tyson Fury.'

'Good to see you too, Kate.'

He had history with this particular MI5 agent. They had met across an interrogation table when Muraski suspected that he was somehow behind a bombing in Nottingham. Of course, he wasn't, and she eventually accepted that, to the point he became a *de facto* bomb disposal man for the security services. She ended up being with him when he was exposed to the sarin gas in the shout at the Emirates Stadium. Since then she had kept him abreast of what he considered MI5's often rather half-hearted attempts to find his ex-wife and daughter.

Still, thanks to her prodding, Five were doing much more than the Devon and Cornwall Police, who seemed to think putting up posters in the streets of Padstow appealing for witnesses was a Sherlock-calibre investigation. Riley had told several police inspectors and a chief inspector that to their faces in no uncertain terms. Terms that eventually got him banned from the force's HQ in Exeter.

'It looks worse than it feels,' he said. It was almost true. The multihued bloom around his eye shouted that it must be agony, but as long as he didn't touch it, it was fine. Problem was, he couldn't stop touching it. His thumb, too, was still incredibly tender from playing stop-the-hammer-falling. At least the swelling had gone down.

'What the hell happened?'

'I'll tell you later. What did you do to get me out?'

She dodged that one. 'Is that all you have?' she asked, pointing to his holdall.

'Yup, hand luggage.'

'Okay, follow me.' She strode off and he followed. Muraski was a junior officer at MI5, but she still had the swagger that came with the job, having authority and the credentials that could get you through any door in the land.

So Muraski whisked them through an anonymous entrance that the general public couldn't access. He found himself in a room full of customs officers, some of them watching unsuspecting passengers through one-way glass.

'Thank you, gentlemen,' she said to nobody in particular as they strode through. 'And ladies.'

Riley caught a few admiring glances from the male contingent directed at Muraski. He broke stride and glared back at them. Not that he had any proprietary over her. Not that anyone did. But she was *his* friendly Five agent, not Border Security's. She had made it clear one drunken night after he had recovered from his exposure to the gas that she had recently ditched one boyfriend to clear her career path. She certainly didn't need a damaged ATO obsessed with his missing family and a dead pal in tow as a replacement. It was a fair point, well made. *Just friends, then?* he had slurred. *Just friends*, Muraski had agreed.

She glanced over her shoulder to make sure he was keeping up and flashed him a smile that dimpled her cheek. She had let her previously cropped hair grow out a little and, in her suede jacket and tight jeans, he could appreciate why she was attracting those looks. Not that he would tell her that. *Hashtag, keep these thoughts to yourself.*

He caught up with her as they exited the HMCR room and stepped into an anonymous corridor. 'So, Hutton got through to you?' he asked her. The MI6 man's expression at the request to call someone from Five was as if Riley had asked him if he had ever had Harvey Weinstein on speed dial. But he had agreed to do it.

'He did. Took his time about it.'

'And what did you say to get me out?'

'I didn't actually say anything. Barbara did. She has friends in high places in Finland, apparently.'

'And almost every bloody country in the world. Did she say why I was pulled by SUPO?'

'Someone told MI6 that you were treading on their toes.'

'Me? How the hell did they figure that?'

'You are MI5. Domestic only. Not meant to go sniffing around near the Russian sphere of influence.'

Riley stopped. 'But I wasn't working for you. This was personal. I'm not a fucking asset.'

She smiled and that cheek dimple appeared again. 'Ah, but you're tainted. Your reputation forever besmirched. You slept with the enemy. Metaphorically, I mean. It might have been a one-night stand, but in Six's eyes you're ours now.'

It was true, he had been, briefly on Five's 'books', but it was hardly a career choice. They resumed walking.

'So who in Six would try and mess with me? And why?'

'Barbara is asking those questions. And what about the battle scars?' she asked, pointing at his discoloured eye. 'How did you pick those up?'

He touched his face again with his fingertips and winced. He had to stop doing that. 'I'm not sure what was going on there. The bruises aren't from a SUPO interrogation, if that's what you're thinking. Couple of heavies tried to roll me. I have no idea why. Or who. Would SUPO do that? Or Six?'

Muraski shrugged. 'I wouldn't put anything past those slippery bastards at VX.' She meant Vauxhall Cross, Six's much-mocked HQ on the Thames. 'I've never met Hutton, but I didn't like the sound of his voice.'

'He looks like a fuckin' cockroach.'

'Sounds delightful.' She frowned. 'But using local heavies doesn't sound much like Six either.'

'Fair one. So maybe they were locals who thought I was a rich tourist.'

She gave a laugh of disbelief. 'Riley, you really don't look like a rich tourist, even when your face isn't messed up. Did you get any joy with your Russian?'

'I'm not sure.'

They burst through a door into the sudden brightness and bustle of landside. He hadn't even shown his passport. Maybe he'd take Muraski with him every time he flew.

'Not sure about what?'

'Anything he told me. I'm out of my depth with ... these people.' *You* people, he had almost said. Spooks. Especially old Soviet spooks.

'That's why I brought someone who isn't. Someone who is an expert debriefer. Better than me, anyway.'

He followed the direction her finger was pointing, over to one of the concessions, where a woman was sitting, a tall coffee cup before her. She raised a hand in greeting when she saw him.

It was Barbara Clifford-Brown. His grandmother.

*

Riley was physically and emotionally exhausted when he finally stepped into his rented flat near Paddington and turned the lights on. Nothing had changed since he had left it. Nobody had been in and done the dishes or vacuumed or made the bed. The takeaway cartons were still on the table in the kitchen and had attracted a cloud of attentive flies. He scooped the packages up and binned them, before realising there was no liner in there. He'd have to fish the cartons out. That could wait.

Keep busy, pal.

He filled the kettle with fresh water, then changed his mind about tea and took a bottle of beer from the fridge. In the living room he switched on the TV and slumped onto the sofa. It was almost ten o'clock. He would watch the news, maybe a movie, reluctantly turn in and try to unscramble his thoughts tomorrow. Barbara had certainly done a number on his brain.

From the airport they had been driven to a safe house in Chiswick. There, Barbara had listened to his account of the meeting with Pavel Brodsky, interrupting only to ask something about the Russian's tone or body language at a particular point. She had also taken charge of the recording of the meeting. Brodsky had been correct – Riley's phone hadn't been on. The voice-activated listening device was actually located in the iPhone's chunky case.

Barbara's initial feeling was that Pavel Brodsky was telling the truth. Carnage had been an unofficial, unsanctioned operation run by operatives within Moscow's Unit 29155, probably intended to curry favour with superiors at the Kremlin. However, it had raged out of control, as politics and the personal had become as hopelessly entwined as Japanese knotweed. Izzy and Ruby were collateral damage, their abduction probably arranged by the now dead Afghani bomber. They were not taken by any operatives of 29155.

Riley had protested that Brodsky might be lying to cover up Russian involvement.

Barbara promised to listen carefully to the tape. Kate suggested she then have it stress analysed using Mendacious, a new, albeit beta-stage, algorithm for detecting when a subject is lying.

But you have to be prepared to face the worst, Dom, Barbara had said as the session wound down, placing a hand on his knee.

And what's that? he had asked.

You know very well, the voice in his skull had chipped in.

Yes, Nick, I do. That he would never discover what had happened to his ex-wife and daughter. That they were dead. That he would never know where the bodies were. Never get to mourn properly. Never get to hold Ruby again, see that smile. A lifetime of what ifs, whys, hows. Torture for the rest of his days.

The frustration of the past few months broke over him like a wave. As it receded it left a feeling of emptiness, of total desolation. Never to see his daughter again? Never? How could that be?

He threw the bottle of beer against the wall. It hit with a deep thud, then fell to the floor, spewing out its contents onto the carpet like it was losing blood. The stain would add to the collection he had made over the past few months. A giant Rorschach test. Any shrink reading it would probably demand he be locked up immediately. He was fine as long as he kept moving, kept busy, focused on finding his family. Even in Helsinki, in that cell, he'd felt he was being proactive in the hunt. Someone had to be. Apart from Kate Muraski and Barbara, he felt Izzy and Ruby were fading from authority's consciousness. Disappeared in all senses.

What was the next step? he asked himself. Up to now he had always had a Plan B. But the disappointment of Helsinki had pulled the carpet from under him. So that had to be the immediate plan: come up with one.

From the corner of his eye he saw a familiar vehicle on the TV screen, a police Land Rover. Riley used the remote to crank up the volume. A female reporter was in the middle of a piece to camera, with the Land Rover just behind her. It was not a standard police vehicle but an EOD – Explosive Ordnance Disposal – 4x4.

'The New IRA claimed to have planted a bomb discovered under a police officer's car in County Tyrone earlier today,' the reporter said. *'It was discovered by the police officer during a routine under-vehicle check in the car park of his gym. The dissident Irish group issued a statement saying,'* – the woman cleared her throat – *'"We were unlucky this time, but the Police Service of Northern Ireland's luck cannot hold forever."'*

Riley leaned in closer to the TV. The only thing that could temporarily distract him from thoughts of Izzy and Ruby was this one, his other life, lived in the moment where one wrong decision meant oblivion.

The reporter continued: *'Police then called in bomb disposal experts . . .'*

Good call. You don't want to call in bomb disposal amateurs. They never last long. Riley watched as an ATO in a bomb suit began that lumbering walk towards a device of unknown origin, unknown potential to kill, and he felt sweat begin to pool around his neck, as if it was him in that bloody outfit.

' . . . who rendered it safe. The bomb is believed to be the work of the New IRA. This organisation emerged in 2012 via a merger of several groups opposed to the

peace process, including the Real IRA. Police believe it has several hundred active
supporters, a mix of former Provisional IRA members, new recruits and the unit
known as Bráithreachas—'

His phone rang. Number unknown. He answered it and waited
for the caller to speak first.

'FAP?'

A heartbeat of hesitation. 'Fuck, yeah.'

TEN

Dom Riley was having a beer with Robert De Niro, Clint Eastwood and Woody Allen. He waited until they had all had their say, and then he said, 'Scooby. Knock it off.'

Philip 'Scooby' Roscoe was about to say something witty, in character. He had about fifty to choose from, including the entire roster of Hanna-Barbera, Looney Tunes and obscure TV shows and movies Riley had never heard of.

'Stop it,' said Riley.

Scooby glared at him with his one good eye and then nodded. Riley had tried to tell him many times that what was hilarious at fifteen didn't always play out in the adult world.

Actually Riley thought Roscoe was a pretty talented impressionist. Had been since they were at school, when it was his go-to get-out-of-jail (or a beating) card. Riley also thought there was a time and place for it, which Scooby Roscoe didn't always appreciate. It was partially because Riley was one of the few people he could practise his art on. His day job was far too serious for riffs on the cast of *Family Guy*.

They were sitting in The Lamb on Lamb's Conduit Street, one of Roscoe's favourite pubs. The acronym FAP he had barked down the phone meant 'Fancy A Pint?' The approved answer was always 'yes'. Especially when Riley felt the dark clouds of depression looming.

Their arrival at The Lamb had coincided with that of a gaggle of tourists, all of whom wanted fish and chips. They could hear evidence of an overwhelmed kitchen and they were slowly being hemmed in by excited, talkative Americans.

'You doin' all right for money, mate?' Roscoe asked as Riley insisted on buying the first round. 'You must be burnin' through the cash running around Europe.' In the early days, when there were regular police appeals for witnesses, there were plenty of sightings of Izzy and Ruby, from Newquay to Nuremberg. To begin with, Dom had gone chasing after the more credible ones. It took a while for the truth to penetrate his grief that it was always a fool's errand. 'Did you buy those shares I recommended?' Roscoe asked.

Riley shook his head. 'That's all a mystery to me, Scoob. I can render any IED safe, no problem, but stocks and shares make me come out in a rash.'

Roscoe shook his head in mock dismay. 'It's easy money. One pound invested gets you nine to take out.'

'Less commission and fees.'

'Well, yeah,' his friend admitted. 'Still, a tidy profit these days.'

'Money isn't my problem these days. The army still pay me. I got something in my grandfather's will. It's the next step that worries me. In that I haven't got one. Maybe I'll go and knock some more heads together in Exeter.'

'That,' advised Roscoe, 'is a daft idea.'

Riley gave a thin smile. 'I have a lot of daft ideas.'

Roscoe slapped his stomach. 'My only daft idea is to feed this beast.'

A group of the Americans at a table nearby began braying at a dog-eared story one of them was telling. The guy, who must have been in his seventies, wore a London Fog windcheater, plaid shirt and a white flat cap that belonged in Miami. 'When we first met, I told her I worked with animals. Not that I was a butcher, though.' Hoots of laughter. 'So, anyway . . .'

'The missus has me on a diet, but I'm off the leash tonight. You hungry?' asked Roscoe over the din.

'Could be,' said Riley. Apart from tea and some biscuits, he hadn't eaten since the plane from Helsinki. 'Not here, though,' he added, nodding to the visitors.

'Italian over the road?' suggested Roscoe. He tapped his belly again. 'Could always have a salad.'

'I'm not sitting with you if you order a salad, Scoob. People'll talk.'

They drained their pints and Roscoe took the empties to the bar, unable to resist a Schwarzenegger-ish 'I'll be back' to the long-suffering landlady.

As they crossed the road, Roscoe asked: 'You remember the Johnson Brothers?'

How could he forget? Max and Martin Johnson. Identical twins who shared every characteristic, including their single brain cell. They were the school's premier bullies when he and Roscoe were fourteen and made Beavis and Butthead seem like a pair of Stephen Frys. By the time they had targeted Scooby full-time – nobody knew why or how they selected their victims, it was part of their mystique, like never knowing whether it was Max or Martin hitting you – Dom had grown and filled out enough to be a serious obstacle for them. Then he took a day off school – something to do with his mother going AWOL, he recalled – and the Johnsons had pounced on Scooby. He was in hospital for the best part of a month. When he came out, he hit the gym and took up kick-boxing. Finally, the bullying stopped.

'I remember them,' Riley said. 'Why?'

'I thought you might have heard. They died. Drug deal gone wrong in Leicester. Shotgun discharged in the face of each of them. Really couldn't tell them apart then.'

'Shit. Not sure they deserved that.'

Roscoe shrugged. 'You weren't the one with the ruptured spleen.'

'That's true.'

They strolled into the old-fashioned Italian 'tratt', sat and ordered a bottle of Gavi and pasta.

'How is Lisa?' Riley asked as they waited for the wine. He was referring to one of Roscoe's private PPOs – Personal Protection Officers, one of the businesses Scooby was in – who had been wounded trying to save Izzy and Ruby. She was lucky. Her partner Jackie had been killed.

'Yeah. Okay. She took a couple of months off. She's got a daughter, you know. Younger than yours. She still feels terrible about what happened.'

'I know. She wrote to me. It wasn't her fault. It was all out of her league.'

Scooby froze, the glass of wine halfway to his lips. He placed it back down, slowly, purposefully. His one eye was really glaring now. 'You saying it was mine, Dom?'

'Fuck, no, pal.'

Roscoe didn't look convinced.

'*No*,' Riley emphasised. 'I just meant, the opposition were trained killers. Someone walks up and starts shooting, there's no PPO in the country who could respond. Not against a bloody FSB hit squad.'

'That's what you still think?' his friend asked. 'FSB?'

'I *did* think that. Now I'm not so sure.' Riley ran him through the rendezvous with Brodsky. 'I'm just waiting for Barbara to listen to the tape of the meeting. But she thinks the Russian might be on the level.'

'So do I.'

That sideswiped Riley. 'What? Why?'

'I know it's tough on you about Izzy and Ruby. Christ, I don't know what I would do if anything happened to Evie.' His teenage daughter. She and Ruby had been friends for a while, at least on social media, but Evie had hit puberty harder and faster and had accelerated away towards adulthood. There had been a falling out. 'But I have skin in this game too, Dom. A dead operative. And Lisa. I feel guilty about them, too. Losing Jackie that way—'

'Get to the point,' Riley snapped. Scooby gave him a withering look with that single eye. 'Sorry. On edge.' Always on fucking edge. 'Go ahead.'

'You seen the news?'

'About the bombs in Ireland?' What else could he mean?

'Yeah. You heard them mention the *Bráithreachas*?'

Riley thought back. His linguine with clams arrived and he kept silent until the waitress had left. 'I think so.'

'The word means brotherhood in Gaelic. It's made up of former Big Daddies and their sons and, in one case, a daughter.' Big Daddies were veteran bomb makers for the IRA. Riley had had dealings with one such person just before the incident with Ruby and Izzy. The 'dealing' involved threatening to blow up the guy's dog. But MI5 had checked to see if there was a connection between the aggrieved Irishman and the abduction, but could find no link. 'There has been talk of a job done in England, recently, just like in the old days.'

'Talk?'

'You know what those fuckers are like. Someone has been boasting to boost their standing in the *Bráithreachas*.'

Roscoe's penne arrived. 'How do you know this?'

'Jesus, Dom, it's my job. Well, one of my jobs.' As well as supplying PPOs, Roscoe sourced high-tech equipment for organisations such as the Metropolitan Police and Her Majesty's Customs and Excise. 'I used to have a contract to supplying surveillance gear to the PSNI.' The Police Service of Northern Ireland. 'I've still got friends there.'

'Christ. Is George O'Donnell involved?' This was the allegedly retired bomb-maker whom Riley had got to talk by strapping his Airedale into a (fake) suicide vest. They hadn't parted on good terms. Were they acrimonious enough for O'Donnell to target Riley's family? The IRA certainly knew how to bear a grudge and how to cause pain by 'disappearing' loved ones. Had he really been looking in the wrong place all this time? Riley reminded himself yet again that Five had firmly dismissed an Irish connection. But maybe MI5 had been wrong.

'That I don't know,' said Roscoe, signalling for some extra parmesan from the waitress.

Riley twirled a forkful of pasta and shovelled it into his mouth. When he had swallowed, he pointed at Roscoe's dish with his fork. 'Eat up, pal.'

'Why?'

'We've got work to do.'

ELEVEN

The wild boar burst out of the undergrowth a few hundred metres from Kate Muraski. She instinctively shouldered the Barrett MRAD Centrefire rifle, squinting down the sights, tensing for the recoil from a weapon that looked as if it belonged with a SWAT team. It was chambered for the .300 Win, a cartridge that could stop an elephant, let alone a wild boar. The animal skidded to a halt, looked around with its black beady eyes, and, having registered the MI5 agent as a threat, began to charge towards her, kicking up whorls of dust as it did so. Muraski thumbed the safety off.

'Patience, sweetie.' It was Barbara, standing next to her on the raised podium that felt as if it would offer little protection from a hundred kilos of galloping porcine rage. 'Remember, you need a shoulder shot to take it down cleanly.'

Muraski's mouth was suddenly dry, watching the boar barrelling towards her, a snarling mouth showing teeth and tusks, as if this was something personal. 'Now?' she asked.

'Soon.'

The beast let out a low, guttural growl, far deeper than the squeal she was expecting. 'Christ.'

'When you are ready.'

Muraski squeezed the trigger just as Russell the gun tech had demonstrated and winced at the kick in her shoulder. The cartridge bounced next to her feet and wisps of propellant fumes stroked her cheek.

The boar kept coming, growing larger with each stride. A miss. 'Fuck.'

'Second shot. Plenty of time,' said Barbara coolly.

Muraski changed her stance slightly, planting her feet more firmly, squinting down the barrel. Oh, for a scope. But, she had been told, that was unsporting. As if using a bullet that could knock out a tank was somehow fair odds.

The animal made that primeval noise again and she pulled the trigger. The boar shuddered under the impact, the head went back, the left front leg collapsed, and like a belly-flopping bomber, it skidded to a halt in the dust. There was a plaintive, high-pitched squeal and the boar breathed its last. Blood glistened among the coarse bristles on its neck.

'Jesus, that was realistic,' said Muraski, lowering her weapon and clicking the safety back on. 'I think I need a fresh pair of knickers.'

They were in the 'shooting cinema' in the sumptuous lodge of Holland & Holland's hunting estate, a hundred and fifty acres sitting in the triangle formed by the A40 and the M1, dedicated to any sport involving firearms. The cinema allowed participants to fire at projected clips of various quarry, using specially modified weapons which interacted with the screen and its computers, so that the animals behaved as they would in the wild when shot at. It was like an ultra-realistic video game.

'Go again?' asked a voice over the loudspeakers.

Muraski looked at Barbara. 'I need some fresh air,' she whispered.

'Thank you, Russell,' announced Barbara. 'I think we'll try some clay pigeon.'

'Right-o. See you out there in ten.'

The lights flicked on and they took off their ear defenders. 'Do you know *Jurassic Park*? Or are you too young?' asked Barbara.

'They re-made it,' Muraski said. 'Lots of times.'

'Really? Well, Henry was a friend of Dicky Attenborough. He told us that when they were looking for a scary noise for the T-Rex, they used recordings of charging wild boar.'

'I can well believe it.'

As they left the cinema, Muraski handed the fearsome rifle to one of the gun techs. They walked out past the copper-topped bar and the climate-controlled glass cabinets holding bottles of Chateau Canon, Berliquet, Lafite, and Leoville-Barton and other eye-wateringly expensive wines. Across the room was a walk-in humidor. Muraski very much felt as if she didn't belong in this world of claret and cravats. Particularly as she didn't much care for shooting living things, even in virtual reality. Or fine Bordeaux and cigars come to that.

They emerged into sunshine, a light breeze and the muffled thud of shotguns being fired.

'Why did you invite me here, Barbara? We could have talked over the phone.'

'Well, as I said, they have an arrangement here where time at the facility counts towards your Continuing Professional Development.' Even MI5 and MI6 agents were subject to the madness of corporate speak. Those agents who were firearms trained were obliged to keep themselves sharp and up-to-date. Quite why bagging wild boar counted was beyond her. But she'd happily pocket the CPD points.

'Barbara,' she admonished quietly. 'I am familiar with your

games by now.' They had only known each other for a little over a year, since the incident that culminated in Dom losing his family, but a grudging respect had grown between them, the young MI5 agent and the seasoned (almost) retired woman from Six. At least, Muraski hoped so.

Barbara smiled. 'Games?'

'The ability to never give a straight answer, honed to perfection over a lifetime. That sort of thing.'

'Forgive me. I wanted to ask you a few questions in person. I prefer it that way. For one thing, I needed to know what that Mendacity programme revealed.'

'Mendacious,' she corrected. 'Like I said, I would have told you over the phone. Nothing. It was inconclusive.' The algorithm hadn't been able to make up its mind whether the KGB man in Helsinki was lying or not.

'Hmmm.'

'You have different thoughts about Brodsky?'

'Possibly.'

'More games?'

'Be patient, young woman.' A little flash of steel in the voice. 'I'm very set in my ways.'

'Let me ask you another question. How did you get on with finding out who tipped SUPO about Dom being in Helsinki?'

'Well, that's rather odd, Kate. Nobody seems to have. Nobody from VX, anyway.'

'You certain?'

'As I can be,' said Barbara cagily. 'Dom is hardly on its radar.'

'Unless someone else is trying to mess up his life. Someone other than Six, I mean.'

'Hmmm.' Non-committal again. 'Have you heard from Dominic recently?'

'No. Not for almost a week now. Have you?'

Barbara sighed. 'A phone call. He told me he had applied to go back to work. Bomb work. He's been tackling his issues with a psychiatrist, he said. I cannot decide whether that is healthy or not. Why does he do it? The bomb thing? I've asked him a hundred times. Never a clear answer.'

'He once told me that the only analogy he can think of is with extreme mountain climbers and other athletes who can't ignore the voice in their heads. It's a calling.'

'One normal people are deaf to.' Barbara pointed at a side path. 'Clay pigeons is over here.' They swerved to the right. 'And he also has it in his head the Irish are behind the disappearance of Izzy and Ruby.'

'We discounted the Irish. Twice.'

'I'm fully aware of that.' Haughty now.

'Are you worried about him? Do you think he might do something stupid?'

'I doubt it. No, I just wondered if you felt any special concern for him.'

Muraski laughed to hide her embarrassment. Did she think she and Riley were an *item*? Sure, she had grown ... fond – what a feeble word, but it would do – of him. But to imagine anything else was ridiculous. 'Special concern? What does that mean, Barbara?'

'Nothing. Just being a silly old woman. I wondered if you would help me help him. And perhaps find out what happened to poor Ruby.' Muraski noticed the ex-wife didn't get a mention. 'Off the books.'

Off the books. Muraski didn't like the sound of that. 'How exactly?'

'Tell me, Kate, do you have any leave due?'

'I might have,' she replied cagily. 'Why?'

71

'I'm thinking of taking a cruise. I thought you might agree to come with me.'

'A what? You can't be serious.' I'm several decades too young for that purgatory, she almost added.

'They're not too bad these days, apparently. My first husband loved them, pre-war of course.'

'What first husband?' Muraski thought the late Henry Clifford-Brown had been her one and only love. She certainly acted that way. But they were at the clay pigeon shooting area and Russell was already selecting weapons for them. She asked the question again, but Barbara was apparently struck by an attack of the deaf 'uns. Clearly, business would have to wait.

'Just remember this,' Barbara said. 'Clays are not like wild boar. Shoot early to avoid disappointment, that's the rule. Now, shall we make it more interesting with a little wager?'

*

The terraced house was covered in scaffolding. The upper windows had been smartened up with brand-new wooden sashes. Downstairs, the frames had been taken out but not yet replaced. The roof was being re-tiled. There was a strong smell of paint coming from the open front door. Riley tapped on it and a workman appeared, dark hair flecked with plaster. 'Yes?'

'Hi. Sorry to disturb you,' Riley said. 'I'm looking for Mr O'Donnell. Lives here. Or used to.'

'Why?' asked the painter.

He wants to cave his skull in, said Nick, less than helpfully.

But not untruthfully. Riley was dressed in Edwin jeans, his steel-capped boots, polo-necked jumper and a waxed jacket. In the long poacher's pocket of the coat was a length of steel pipe. The last time he had seen George O'Donnell, the man was furious with him. But had he been enraged enough to go after Riley's family? That's what he needed to find out. The pipe was just a precaution, in case O'Donnell or the dog still bore a grudge.

'I just want a word with him. A personal matter.'

'No O'Donnell here,' the painter said in his thick accent. 'Missus!' he yelled over his shoulder and down the hallway.

A slightly harassed women in her early thirties appeared. She was wearing paint-splashed dungarees and a baby was bouncing on her hip. The kid looked cheerier than its mother. The work-man left her to it and went back to work.

'Thank you, Gabriel,' she said over her shoulder. Then, to Riley: 'Yes? Can I help?'

'I'm sorry to bother you. I'm looking for a Mr George O'Donnell. He used to live here. I mean, I guess he has moved out.'

'Yes, a while back. Six months? We're just . . .' She pointed to the scaffold. 'And it's . . .'

'Lots of work to do?'

'Well, it was sold as a doer-upper.' She gave a world-weary smile. 'We just didn't realise how much doing-up it needed. Are you a friend of his?'

If he was a friend, he would know he had moved. 'No,' he said. 'Not really. We worked together. I wanted to return some books he lent me that I have in the car. On Irish history. But I can post them if you have a forwarding address.'

She nodded. 'I have. Somewhere. Give me a minute.'

She disappeared and came back without the child. In her hand was a sheet of sticky-backed address labels. 'It's a solicitor's office, I think. Take one.'

He ripped a label from the bottom of the sheet, backing and all, and glanced at it. County Tyrone. Was it coincidence that bombs had reappeared in that very county, shortly after O'Donnell, a

Big Daddy – chief bomb-maker – of old had re-located over the water? Possibly to his old stomping ground? Maybe, maybe not. It wouldn't stand up in court. But then, nothing about this was going to make it to court.

'Great,' he said. 'And good luck with the refurb.'

She gave another long-suffering smile and pulled a stray lock of hair off her forehead. 'Thanks.'

So, Riley thought, that was one thing decided. As soon as he was back to full operational status, he'd put in for a transfer to Ireland.

TWELVE

Having unpacked the Range Rover and moved the luggage into what he called the cottage – to anyone else it was a substantial and extended farmhouse of honeyed Cotswold stone – Clive Greggs of the Cabinet Office and COBRA, announced he was going to see Fiamma.

Jessica, his wife, smiled indulgently, and kissed him on the cheek. 'I should be jealous, you know. Italian beauty and all that.'

Greggs wrapped his arms around her and pulled her in close. 'You are my one and only love, Jess, you know that.'

She nodded against his chest. There was something of the Italian beauty about Jessica herself, all that long dark hair cascading down to her shoulders, the flashing brown eyes.

She untangled herself from his embrace. 'I'll start dinner then. Xanthe won't be here before nine. Can you pick her up from the station?'

That meant no red wine for a while. A small sacrifice for his lovely daughter, who was (whisper it) the child he was most proud of. Not off 'finding herself', as his son Max was doing in some armpit of a South American country, but with her eyes on the prize. Medicine. A heart surgeon, no less, was the stated ambition. Not stuck in airless committee rooms or roaming shabby corridors like her old man. But making a real difference to people's lives. He swore he could feel his own heart well in his chest when he thought of her. 'Of course.'

'Shall I unplug the phone? Mute the mobiles?' Jessica asked, one eyebrow arched in query.

'No. I told them not to bother me unless it's war.'

'Let's hope it doesn't come to that,' she said in a way that made it sound like a threat. Of late, his wife had been struggling with his working hours. In truth, so had he. Insomnia was now a problem, which meant he was tired all day and even more exhausted by the time he got home. The house in the Cotswolds was a welcome escape, but he knew he would have to come up with a permanent exit plan soon. He couldn't carry on this way for much longer. He'd be needing the services of his heart surgeon daughter if he did.

Greggs walked down the gently sloping garden (although 'meadow' would have been closer to the mark) through the last of the hazy daylight towards the barn. The exterior suggested a nondescript, careworn farm building that had seen better days. But this was actually cladding, over a purpose-built, climate-controlled garage with room for four cars. At the moment, there was only one in there and some gym equipment – bike, treadmill, a rack of free weights that Jessica had installed in the hope of rediscovering her formerly svelte husband.

Fat chance, as he liked to say. Not until he was out of politics.

Greggs unlocked the outer doors and swung one of them open to reveal the smaller gateway set in the larger metal double doors. That way he could access the inside without throwing the bigger panels open and revealing to the outside world what sat within the 'barn'. He punched in the code and stepped through, clicking on the lights and admiring the sheen on the vehicle before him.

Jerry, the mechanic from Chipping Norton Ferrari charged with looking after the car, had already been in and removed the dust cover and given it a polish. Greggs liked to see his pride and joy undressed and ready for him, rather than having the exertion of pulling off the shroud himself. Like a lover in her boudoir, in repose on the bed, ready for her man to appear.

He admired his prized possession for a few moments before he lowered his frame – he had to try to stop groaning as he did so – into the driver's seat. He adjusted it so he could reach the pedals more comfortably – Jerry had a good four or five inches on him – went through the elaborate start procedure and fired her up.

It caught first time, that glorious burble filling the cabin, his aching bones vibrating in unison with the V8. It sounded and felt wonderful. There was a button which would mute the throaty exhaust, but who in their right mind would use that?

Fiamma was an F430 Coupe, with a 4.3 naturally aspirated (Greggs loathed turbos) V8 and it could do 0-60 in 3.8 seconds. Never mind that a service cost enough to fund a small wing of an NHS hospital, it was his indulgence. It wasn't as if he kept race-horses or racy women like some of his old colleagues in the City (many of whom kept both). Nor did he play golf or hanker after a yacht or a collection of vintage wines. Besides, he no longer had to cover exorbitant school fees for Xanthe and Max – they could pay back their own student loans – so the damn thing was almost free. He had christened the car Fiamma after one of Enzo Ferrari's mistresses – a little joke between himself and Jessica. While he had a metal mistress, he wouldn't countenance a flesh and blood one. At least not on a permanent basis. There had been the odd unfortunate slip up in the past, but those days were behind him now.

He would take the car out tomorrow, Saturday, a run through the lanes, maybe to Daylesford Organics, which was like an unofficial car rally for high-end marques on the weekend. As Clarkson had said, this was one Ferrari that was happy in every environment, from motorways to twisting B roads and even in traffic, it kept its cool.

His phone rang, breaking into his reverie. He pressed the button to kill the engine. It was Jessica, from the house. 'Dinner already, darling?' he asked

'Bloody hell, no. Who do you think I am? Nigella with her brigade of assistants?' Snappy, he thought. But then, he always liked the acerbic side of her. His wife had spirit. 'Another hour. Although you could come and open some wine.'

'I'll be up in a minute. Is that why you called?' She was more than capable of choosing a good bottle and getting the cork out.

'No,' she said. 'There's a special delivery for you. I had to sign for it. It says urgent. On the weekend, Clive. The weekend. You did promise.' The last word was said with an acid sharpness that could blister paint.

She wasn't the only one annoyed by the intrusion of Westminster into his country life. 'I know, I told them. Sacrosanct, I said. Nothing short of war. But sometimes . . . you know it might be something to sign or briefing papers for Monday. Nothing too taxing.' And not, he hoped, a COBRA being convened.

Greggs clicked off, not knowing yet that it was neither a document requiring a signature nor briefing papers. Nor that it would turn out to be very, very taxing indeed.

Nor that it was from someone calling himself BaseHeart.

THIRTEEN

'I brought you this,' said Scooby Roscoe. From his inside pocket he fetched a folded, glossy catalogue. 'I was at that security show in Geneva. Some gear in there for you blokes.'

'You blokes' being ATOs, Riley assumed. He took it and flicked through it. 'Chinese?' There was still an informal embargo on the army buying security kit from mainland China.

'Taiwanese. Above board, as far as I can tell. Anything you want, give me a shout. They are giving stuff on spec. You know, if you like it, you tell your superiors to buy whatever it is.'

'I'll have a look.' ATOs were allowed to customise and supplement the standard-issue equipment, within reason, although some of the electronics in the booklet were doubtless beyond the army's budget. And he wasn't sure he could stretch to his own personal robot. But if they were handing out goodies for review, he'd take that.

They were sitting on the steps below Granary Square in King's Cross, overlooking the canal. It was mid-morning and a blustery day. They had the steps to themselves. All around them, though, jackhammers and piledrivers burrowed into the earth, building the next stage of the regeneration. The last time Riley had been in Kings Cross it was with a bunch of squaddies when he was in his twenties. Half the lads had wanted to go to an infamous strip club, which offered what was known as 'afters', the other half to a rave in a former cinema. Riley had chosen the latter. The queue at the Medical Officer's surgery over the following few days confirmed it had been the wise choice, life-threatening hangover notwithstanding. At least, he thought at the time, he'd die with his dick on.

'George O'Donnell has left the country,' Riley said. 'I went to his old place yesterday. His house is busy being gentrified by new owners. So I need to find him.' He took out a piece of paper with the forwarding address in County Tyrone and laid it on the table.

Roscoe lifted the eyepatch as he read the address, as if he didn't quite believe what his good eye was seeing. 'The idea was to pass the info on to Five or Six.'

'Yeah, those bastards have done me proud so far, haven't they?'

'And you'll do what?'

'I don't want you involved, Scooby. Just get one of your people to find out where O'Donnell's mail goes after here. Is it forwarded? Or does he pick it up? I'll do the rest.'

'I dunno . . .'

'Scooby.' Riley's tone wasn't friendly. There was to be no argument over this.

'The exploding dog trick won't work twice.'

Riley knew he was never going to be allowed to forget what he had done to O'Donnell's dog. 'What I do is up to me. None of your people will be on the frontline because of me ever again. Not after Jackie and Lisa. But me? I'm going back in.'

'Into what?'

'I spoke to my CO this morning. If I pass one more psych test, I can return to being an ATO on active duty. There's simply not enough of us for them to be picky.' He thought back to the two good SBS bomb guys killed by idiocy – a prank gone lethally wrong – on the Maunsell Forts when he was an army observer. The waste had made him furious. He hardly felt less angry about that stupidity now. 'They need me, Scoob. I give it a few weeks, ask for a transfer to Northern Ireland. I've done two tours, they're sure to say yes, given what's going on – bombs in the north, new republicanism rampant in the south. I'm a safe pair of hands.'

Roscoe shook his head at that questionable statement but said nothing.

'I'll do my own sniffing around,' said Riley. 'Fuck Five and Six. And Seven, Eight and Nine if they exist.'

'MI9 certainly did—'

'Scooby, I don't fuckin' care. Just get me that link to O'Donnell.'

'But, Dom, if it's them, if it's IRA, then—'

'I know, Scooby. You don't have to spell it out.'

They've been shot in the back of the head, buried in an unmarked, shallow grave.

Roscoe slid the solicitor's address into his top pocket. He produced the harsh tones of a Northern Irish character Riley could barely recall. The Reverend someone. 'How about a drop of the devil's buttermilk? The breath of Satan upon us.'

Paisley, that was it. Riley looked at his watch. A bit early for him. Still, he had just asked for a big favour from his old pal. 'Just the one.'

'Splendid.'

*

Barbara Clifford-Brown spent two hours with Sebastian Virgo, the young man at the Autry & Cole travel agency in St James's. He was delighted that she had changed her mind about a cruise and was impressed by the routing she had chosen. In the end, they had narrowed it down to two options, both ships leaving from Southampton.

'I'm a bit worried about fellow passengers,' she said as he pulled up images on screen.

'How do you mean?' Virgo asked.

'Well, you know ... Cruises as God's Waiting Room and all that. The age. The agility. Will it all be Zimmer frames at dawn? Colostomy bags at dinner?"

'Not at all,' the agent quickly assured her. 'I'd be lying if I said it was full of Millennials, but there'll be the sort of people you can relate to.'

'I do hope so,' she said with a smile. 'Because if I do get on board and find it is a floating hospice, I'm going to come back here ...'

'Mrs Clifford-Brown, I have already booked several people on both these cruises. None of them fit into your ... categories.'

'Prove it.'

'I beg your pardon?'

'Show me I'm not going to have to push past the Grim Reaper to get to the bar.'

'How?' he asked.

'Tell me who you have booked. Show me their profiles.'

Virgo pushed back in his chair, as if she had threatened to strike him. 'I can't do that. Data protection. Customer confidentiality.'

Barbara said nothing, simply fixed him with a stare.

'I could lose my job,' Virgo said softly.

'Tell me, Sebastian ... Is that right? Sebastian?' The young man nodded. 'Do you know the history of this company? Its, um, unique role in the defence of this realm.' As MI6's preferred travel agency, she meant.

'Well ...' he began cagily.

'Of course you do. I was one of your best customers at that

time. Right through the Cold War. And although you might doubt it by looking at me, I have security clearance up to the highest level.' No longer true, but still. 'Such petty regulations do not apply to me.'

Virgo frowned and rung his hands, a picture of indecision.

'Shall I perhaps speak to Miss Cole?' This was the formidable granddaughter of one of the founders.

'No,' Virgo snapped back quickly. He looked and spoke like a condemned man. 'Just between us? You promise?'

She hit him with her most sincere expression. 'Of course.'

Thirty minutes later, Barbara Clifford-Brown left the offices of Autry & Cole with the profiles of five potential fellow cruisers in her handbag, narrowed down from a baker's dozen. She crossed over to Dukes and ordered her usual martini from Gilberto, making sure to establish early on that she was not in the mood for chitchat.

Left alone she sorted through the printouts. She discarded the two men in the pile immediately, they were a mere smoke screen. Of the three women, one was in her fifties, far too young for what she had in mind. The second was a relatively well-known author who had once troubled the bestseller charts with family sagas set in and around the factories of the Black Country. Barbara suspected she might attract a fan club.

The third, though, was the right age, slightly younger than Barbara, a widow who listed her hobbies as the cinema, crime novels and ballroom dancing. Perfect so far. Barbara looked at the scan of the woman's passport and tutted to herself. Sebastian Virgo really shouldn't have given her this. If she was his boss she would reprimand or perhaps sack him. Still, she had put him in an impossible situation.

Barbara squinted at the poorly reproduced passport photograph.

Promising. But she needed to see her in the flesh, to establish if they had even a passing resemblance to each other. Otherwise her plan might flounder. Luckily the woman lived in Hampstead, so it wouldn't be difficult to get eyes on.

She sipped her martini and shuddered in pleasure. For a second she even thought the cruise might be bearable. The feeling passed, replaced by a sense that needs must. Grin and bear it, woman. It wouldn't be the first time. She looked at the photo again. Edith Rankin, she thought, I just hope you pass muster for Queen and Country. And little Ruby.

FOURTEEN

Captain Harald Nansen was wrong about his brother going easy at lunchtime. When he arrived at The Ned, the converted banking hall that was now part of the Soho House empire, Jakob was sitting at one of the many bars, finishing off what might or might not have been his first drink of the day. Observed from a distance, Jakob looked tired, almost as drained as his glass. Women and money troubles were not good for the soul, the blood pressure or, in Jakob's case, the liver.

Nansen wasn't sure about The Ned. The Lutyens-designed building made for a great flagship for a bank, but carved into an upmarket food hall with a bandstand at the centre, he felt he was always battling against the boomy acoustics, especially when the live music started.

However, Jakob had booked them into the quieter enclave of the complex, the grill room named after the building's architect, and they were ushered to padded green seats and plenty of precision-folded napery, crystal glasses, cherry wood panels and stained glass.

Jakob's backside had barely brushed the cushion before he ordered another martini in the Americanised accent he now sported. The captain settled for a single gin and tonic.

'You okay?' Nansen asked his brother.

'No,' Jakob replied, already looking around for his drink with twitchy impatience. 'I'm being double fucked. My wife has her dick up my ass and the financial regulators have one in my ear, all because that fuckin' fucker Peterhouse has fuckin' fucked up.'

Peterhouse was Jakob's company's star stockpicker, the one he had chosen to launch his company's investment fund in London. From what he could gather, the man seemed to have lost his golden touch. The captain, though, didn't really understand high finance, just the high seas. He preferred it that way. Despite what was often said, the sea was nowhere near as cruel as the markets.

'Meaning?' asked Nansen.

'He's gated the fund.'

Nansen shook his head and smiled. 'Again ... plain language, please.'

'He's suspended all withdrawals from his Equity Income Fund. Frozen it. Some city or other asked for their two million back and started a run. He couldn't let every schmuck empty the fund. A lot of the stocks are illiquid.'

Nansen was fairly sure it wasn't really the done thing to call your clients *schmucks*, even in the world of investment funds. 'Why did they ask for it back?'

'The fund has been down about eleven per cent over the past year. The FTSE All-Share Index is up by six per cent.'

Jakob leaned back as the drinks arrived and took a large bite out of his cocktail.

'Cheers,' said Nansen, raising his own glass.

'Yeah. Cheers. Sorry. Well the *FT* did this piece ... well, it doesn't matter. Fund hasn't performed the way it should have. Look, change the subject, Harald. Have you spoken to Mother?'

'Yes, I've invited her on the ship. She said she would wait until it was going somewhere warm. Why do you ask?'

'Nothing.'

'Jakob . . .'

His brother began to study his knife, polishing it with his napkin, as if he had found a blemish. Jakob took a deep breath and jumped in. 'I persuaded her to put some money into Peterhouse Equity Income Fund.'

Nansen banged the table. 'Jakob! I told you. Rule one. Do not involve family in your get-rich-quick schemes. How much?' The last sentence was almost snarled. Jakob flinched a little, as if expecting to be struck. Harald Nansen was physically far more imposing than his brother.

'Half a million krone.'

Nansen tutted loud enough to attract a waiter, who thought he was complaining about service. The captain waved him away. 'For God's sake, Jakob. That's nearly all her savings.'

'It's not even half, Harald. Not with the house. I can get it back for her. She'll be first in line when it unfreezes next week. And if not, I can cover it from New York.' Jakob put his hand on his heart. 'I swear it.'

'You better,' the captain growled.

'I will. No question. Relax.'

Nansen could hear blood thumping in his ears. Not a good sign. He took some long, steady breaths and leaned back, out of the confrontation zone. 'Dad would have killed you.'

'I know. Bloody *Reptilicus*.'

They both burst out laughing at the old childhood reference, instantly cutting the tension. Their father had been a strict disciplinarian and, one drunken evening, they had admitted to each other that when he died of a heart attack, the sorrow was

leavened with something close to relief. It was a guilty teenage secret they had never shared with anyone and they hadn't
spoken of it since, except obliquely. It was a code word to indicate
their father was on the rampage. For a couple of years *Reptilicus*
saw lots of action.

They ordered Hereford steaks and Nansen stopped Jakob
going for a third cocktail. Instead he ordered them a mid-list
bottle of wine.

'How did the shakedown voyage go?'

'Good. They loved us in Liverpool. Same in Belfast, Cardiff,
Portsmouth.'

Nansen wondered how much to tell Jakob. He was a loud-
mouth. Of course there were snags. Just like in a new home. One
of the stabilisation pumps had failed. A replacement was being
fitted as they spoke. A routine glitch. It was better it happened in
the Irish Sea than out in the Atlantic. The pump was one of the
weapons against the relentless swell, and sometimes worse, that
the ship would encounter in the northern waters.

No, the main problems were human, getting the staff up to
the quality the owners were – quite rightly – demanding. He had
already been forced to let half a dozen crew go.

'So, you head for the Big Apple when?' Jakob ran a hand
through his hair as he spoke. Twitchy. Back on the coke? No, he'd
have been to the bathroom twice already if that was the case.

'The maiden voyage proper is in three weeks,' he replied. 'After
a goodwill visit to France. Le Havre. Come along if you want.'

'I might.' He drained his glass, smacked his lips and winked.
Jakob nodded his approval as the wine was displayed. He waited
while the cork was eased out, the wine poured and sniffed and the
waiter dismissed, 'I have a present for you,' he said to his brother.
'A bon voyage gift.'

'Really? Not another surefire, money-making tip?'

Jakob looked hurt. 'No. A *present* present. The kind you can hold.'

'That's very thoughtful of you. What is it?'

'Too big and too scary to bring to the table.'

'A dog?'

Jakob whooped at that. 'Yes, just the gift for a sea captain.'

He was clearly bursting to reveal all, so Nansen prompted him. 'Tell me. I hate surprises.'

'It's a harpoon.'

Nansen laughed. 'A harpoon? You think I'm going whaling?'

A sly grin spread over his brother's face as he came in for the kill. 'From the *Fram*.'

'The *Fram*? How on earth ... I mean. Wow. How can you afford that?'

'It's not a full-length one. The shaft has been shortened. It's the real deal though. I had it checked. And I know you always fancied yourself as a whaler. All that javelin you threw at school. You wished you were on a Nantucket sleigh ride, eh? Am I right?'

'Yes. Not something I'd admit to these days, of course. Greenpeace would have me run off the ship. But ... thank you, Jakob.' His brother beamed in pleasure. He was a simple soul, thought the captain, and, despite his sometimes hare-brained schemes, he did love him. 'That's very thoughtful of you. I'm touched. I'll mount it in my cabin.'

'Great. So, tell me, Captain Nansen, who have you got on board?' Jakob's eyes took on a hungry look as he narrowed them. Harald knew what that meant. He was hunting for gossip, the more salacious the better. 'I don't mean the riffraff. The movers and shakers. Did you lure Rod Stewart away from Cunard?'

No, he hadn't, disappointingly, but, glad to be off the subject of money, Nansen told Jakob the big names they were expecting to be on board.

The captain would come to realise, eventually, that being so candid was unwise where Jakob was concerned. In fact, as he would later declare when the truth about his brother's intentions emerged, it was a fucking disaster.

PART TWO

FIFTEEN

Three Weeks Later

During the Second World War, the Luftwaffe dropped upwards of 30,000 tons of high explosives on the UK. By far the majority – estimates hover around eighty per cent – of all bombs released over Britain were *Sprengbombe Cylindrisch* 250 or 500s, which conformed to the image the general public have of what a bomb should look like: a tapering cylinder with fins at the rear. They were filled with HE (High Explosive) – either Amatol, TNT or Trialen 105, a mixture of 15% RDX, 70% TNT and 15% aluminium powder.

Over the course of the war the Germans had used many different types of fuses in these bombs. As the conflict went on they became more complex, with integrated anti-tamper devices to target the EOD operatives tasked with defusing a UXB. The most dangerous of these was the Y fuse, aka *Elektrischer Sonderzeunder EI.Z (50) Y*, which came with three mercury tilt switches that would detonate the bomb if it was moved or rotated. It wasn't until 1943 that one was successfully disabled without the loss of life, by John Pilkington Hudson, using liquid oxygen to freeze everything solid, for which he was awarded the George Medal.

Dom Riley thought of all this as he crouched down in the rear garden of a house in Sandgate, Kent. New owners had decided to build a kitchen extension and, while preparing the footings, the workmen had discovered an unexploded bomb, probably close to eighty years old.

Police had evacuated the surrounding homes and thrown up a cordon. The engineers had come in and built a Hesco blast wall and put three hundred tons of sand around it. Once constructed, it was down to Riley to enter the blast zone. Now, if anything went up, he would be the first to know the good news.

Riley slowly brushed away at the muck on the casing. It reminded him of 'painting the sand' in Afghanistan. But what he was uncovering over there were improvised explosive devices assembled in people's homes, the most basic of bomb circuits — though no less deadly for that.

The *Sprengbombe* that the Royal Engineers had uncovered for him was far more sophisticated than Afghan IEDs. But given this was eight decades old, it was just as unpredictable. Sometimes the lightest brush of a spade could set them off. Others you could sling on the back of a truck and take away for harmless detonation in a disused quarry or similar.

The key to staying alive was knowing which type you were dealing with.

In this case, *in situ* detonation was out of the question. The bomb was big enough to take down a whole row of terrace houses. The neighbours to the rear would gain unexpected sea views. Riley's instinct was that this Nazi bastard had to be castrated on the spot.

He hesitated and massaged his thumb, still a little sore from the pistol hammer strike. 'Okay, Staff?'

It was Jeff 'Smiffy' Smith in his earpiece. Smiffy was his number two, in charge of all the gear, the robot and explosives and would be watching him through binoculars. Of course, you didn't need robots with a Luftwaffe bomb. But Smiffy had set up a sophisticated listening device on the metal casing, a sort of EOD stethoscope, which he was monitoring for signs of activity within the UXB. Like ticking.

Other than that listening bug, rendering a vintage UXB safe hadn't changed much since Hudson's time. They still basically used Second World War kit. Riley's job was to disable the fuse. If that couldn't be done, there was the option of introducing steam into the casing and 'sweating' out the explosive.

'Yeah, Smiffy.' He brushed some more. 'Just doing some bed-time reading.'

He was revealing faded paint marks. This bomb had been 'dec-orated' before loading onto its Heinkel or Dornier, either at the munitions factory or, more likely, by the bomber crew. Illegible now, but he could make out a caricature. Possibly Mr Churchill. It would probably have said something like 'Greetings from Berlin'.

He carried on brushing away the soil.

Riley had been back on the duty roster for two weeks. As he had hoped, it had been surprisingly straightforward to be wel-comed back to active service. A few sessions with Ms Carver, the shrink, and another with an army doctor and he was passed fit to return to ATO duties. He hadn't yet put in his request for a tour in Northern Ireland. He didn't want to seem too keen. People might suspect that he had an ulterior motive. Which of course he did: track down O'Donnell and wring the truth out of his scrawny neck.

Back to the world, Dom. Don't drift off. You have something there. Look.

Nick was right. The brush had uncovered a stamp on the casing. A few more strokes revealed the letters SC and then the number 250. A general purpose 250kg device. Now he bit his lip as he dusted the suffix. The earth was compacted, so he rooted around in his various boxes of kit and found his secret weapon for such situations: the wire brush used to clean suede shoes. It was a step up from a paintbrush, but not as crude or rough as a traditional wire brush. It worked a treat. The long-covered letters appeared as a ghostly trace.

LZZ.

'It's a *LangZeitZünder*,' he said to Smiffy. It meant a long-time delay fuse. It was a simple electrical-clockwork system that could be set to detonate anywhere between 13 and 135 minutes. They could be fitted with anti-handling devices, sometimes a simple spring-loaded detonator that activated if the fuse was removed, known as the Type ZUS 40 mechanical anti-withdrawal fuse. It might also have the Type 50 or 50B, which the British EODs called the Type Y, after the letter stamped on the top of the fuse. That was the one with the mercury tilt switches. They were tricky bastards, the Nazi bomb designers. They sometimes used left-handed threads, so that the fuse could only be unscrewed by turning it clockwise, the opposite way to normal. An operative could waste a lot of time before figuring that out.

'I'm just going to move a bit more earth. I think I know where the fuse is.'

'Take it easy, Staff.'

As if there was any other approach to rendering an SC250 safe. He found the head of the fuse under a clod of earth. With a few deft movements he cleared the dirt using the suede brush, then switched to the paintbrush, until he could see the whole cap clearly.

No Y.

He checked again. Using his phone, he took several pictures of it.

'If it's got an anti-handler, I think it must be a ZUS 40.'

'Roger that.'

'I'm going to use the salt,' Riley said. There were various ways to stop the detonator working. Saline solution was often used during the Blitz to jam up the clockwork elements. Later, a urea-formaldehyde formulation was developed that would literally clog up the works. The Americans had developed an aerosol-sprayed 'Gunk', a modern waterproof resin that almost instantly rendered all moving parts completely static. He didn't have any Gunk to hand – the Americans were being very secretive about the formulation – so it would have to be the saline.

First he had to drill a hole in the fuse casing before squirting the solution in under pressure from the pump he carried in his kit. He began to sort through his drill box. He stopped short. He'd been whistling. Like he was happy. Sitting on top of 250 HE and he was whistling some stupid pop song. As if messing with UXBs was somehow *fun*.

It is. Welcome back, Dom.

It was misdirection, of course, his brain trying to distract him from why he was back working as an ATO in the first place. Not to start messing about with ancient explosives. To get to Ireland. To start on the trail of his ex-wife and child. But he couldn't rush that. Softly, softly catch the bastards who . . .

Stay in the moment, pal.

Riley took a breath.

Nick was annoying, but right. He couldn't get to Ireland if he was blown to the four winds. He had to remind himself that this was all part of the plan – he needed to be patient.

Riley set up the cordless drill and got to work on the top of the ancient fuse. Low revs, just enough pressure to produce neat curls of greyish metal. Easy does it.

'Skip,' came the voice in his ear.

'What?'

'Stop what you're doing,' commanded Smiffy.

Riley instantly took his finger off the drill trigger.

'Fuck.'

'What?' Riley asked.

'I think it's ticking. No. It's whirring.'

Ticking or whirring. Neither were good. He cocked his head towards the casing. He couldn't hear anything, but Smiffy's microphone was more sensitive than his ears, which had taken a battering thanks to years of controlled – and otherwise – detonations. 'Shit. You sure?'

'Positive. Best out of there, Skip. Let her blow.'

Riley looked back at the way he had come in. How long would it take him? Ten seconds? Fifteen. Even clearing the Hesco might not save him. This was a big, ugly bastard of a bomb that was going to make quite the crater. And he had no idea what delay was set on the fuse.

Maybe short enough that there was no time to get the saline in.

Riley turned the speed up on the drill, selected hammer and, against every rule in the book, leant his full body weight on top of it, praying the shaft wouldn't snap.

The bit squealed as it penetrated the corroded metal and the whole drill twisted out of Riley's hands with a kick like a mule as it went chuck-deep into the fuse.

He fell backwards, put his arms behind him to break his momentum and sat, his chest heaving, staring at the fuse and the wisps of smoke rising from it. Smoke from the drill? Or from whatever was inside? Had he miscalculated? Time slowed, congealed, thickened some more and then stopped. In this state of temporal stasis he thought of Ruby, that holiday when she lost her favourite toy rabbit in the sand dunes in Cornwall. How he had contrived to get a replacement posted from London and then buried it in the sand to be discovered by Ruby. Only recently had she told him that she had known it was a copy: the eyes were a different shade of blue. But she hadn't wanted to hurt his feelings. At seven, she was already worried about him. He closed his eyes, feeling the Cornish breeze on his face, enjoying the ghostly echo of his child's laughter.

A little creak from within the casing brought him back to the moment. It was like waiting for God to make up his mind. Heads or tails? It wasn't that difficult, Almighty, either that little fit of pique with the drill worked or it didn't. He lived to fight another day or his day was done. He was getting to the point where he didn't care which option came next.

'Well?' Riley asked eventually.

There was a short silence before Smiffy spoke. 'I think it's stopped. What did you do?'

'I jammed the internal cogs with the drill bit. I'll make a new hole and put the saline in. Just to be on the safe side.'

Smiffy laughed. 'You sure you know where the safe side is, Staff Sergeant?'

'Fuck off.'

Twenty minutes later he walked out between the blast walls, his parched mouth craving a pint. A lieutenant of the Royal Engineers waited until he drew level before he asked: 'How did it go, Staff?'

Riley shrugged. 'Like clockwork.'

*

'I'm not some body-for-hire to be farmed out,' Muraski snarled at Paul Oakham, her line manager at Thames House.

'Nobody is saying you are.'

'So why would you agree, behind my back, to me going along with Barbara's scheme?'

Oakham fiddled with his cufflinks. He was dressed, as always, like a mannequin from Gieves & Hawkes' window display. No dressing down at work for Mr Oakham. He probably slept in a tailored suit or, at the very least, bespoke, monogrammed pyjamas. She killed that image immediately.

'I haven't. I simply told her we had no objection to you taking some time. You are due it, you know. No prizes for never taking a break.'

Muraski reckoned this was the first time those words had ever been spoken within Thames House. 'She wants me to go on a fuckin' cruise.'

There was a sparkle of humour in his eyes. 'She wants you to go on a *fuckin' cruise* for a very good reason. She suspects her old KGB pal is lying.'

'I think she's wrong. It's wishful thinking. Or an excuse to get back into the old life, playing at spooks again.' Muraski leaned back in her chair and let out a long sigh. 'I won't do it. If you insist on me taking leave, I'm going to book a flight to Jamaica.'

'As you wish.' He paused for a moment and interlaced his fingers. 'You do owe Barbara Clifford-Brown a debt, though.'

'What kind of debt?'

'The tribunal.'

Muraski's heart sank. There had been, of course, an internal MI5 inquiry into the events leading up to the destruction of Dunston Hall and the deaths of a group of Russian dissidents, as well as the bombing of a Nottingham shopping mall. As the enquiry had proceeded, it was obvious a convenient scapegoat was needed. And that Kate Muraski was it. Tethered to a stake waiting to be torn limb from limb. The mandarins of Five had recommended that Muraski face a disciplinary tribunal to establish if she had withheld vital information during the investigation and put her own career before the good of MI5 and the country. This was the problem with Five and Six: when things go well, both were invisible to the public, their good deeds unnoticed and unsung. But when something goes awry, questions are asked. Such as: why didn't they keep us safe? They do, every day, but even the best goalkeepers let one in now and then. And whose fault is that?

'You said that completely absolved me from any responsibility,' said Muraski. 'Clean slate. No blemish on my record.'

'Only after Barbara intervened.'

'What?'

Barbara Clifford-Brown, Oakham explained, had demanded she be allowed to address the tribunal before it gave its verdict. She had gone in all guns blazing, praising Kate and coruscating the management structure of MI5. Words such as mediocre, sclerotic, amateur, myopic and even turds-for-brains were sprayed around the room like machine-gun fire. She reminded the panel that MI5 had only just been released from the humiliating 'Special Measures' that the Investigatory Powers Commissioner's Office had imposed on it. Handling data of any description seemed a task too far for the security service.

She had gone further with a *mea culpa*. Had she and Henry been more forthright, and less conditioned to be obstructive, then when Muraski approached them, she said, the whole Gordian knot of which bombers were at large in the UK and their motives might have been untangled that much quicker.

'To be frank, before her performance, you might have been looking at a transfer to the paperclip-supply department in Staines.' He chuckled. 'I thought "turds-for-brains" was a nice touch.'

'Why wasn't I told this?'

'She insisted it all be *in camera*, as it were.'

'Does anyone ever say no to that woman?' She feigned even more irritation.

'Kate, she is up to something, that much we can be sure of, given her destinations on that voyage. I think both ourselves and Six would like to know what. You can be our eyes and ears.'

'Since when have we played footsie with Six?'

'Since you became the only person in either organisation to have a relationship with Barbara Clifford-Brown.'

'Relationship?'

'She likes you.'

'She likes beating me at clay pigeon shooting. And taking my money.'

Oakham sighed, as if irritated at having to explain his motives to a junior. 'Look, her beloved husband is dead.'

'Her second husband, apparently.' Muraski hadn't got any further with that, apart from establishing there had been someone before Henry.

Oakham acknowledged Muraski's interruption with raised eyebrows. 'And her grandson's family is missing, presumed ... anyway. We both know she wants to help Dom find his daughter and she's not one to sit on her hands, believe me. We just don't want her causing any international incidents. She needs babysitting. No, wrong term,' he added hastily. 'She needs surveilling.'

'That's a word, is it?'

Oakham ignored her. 'She's a combination of loose cannon and national treasure. Six thinks that if we try and stop her going on this jaunt, she'll give us the slip, might do something rash.'

'Really? She's not Villanelle. She's a hundred and bloody ten or something,' said Muraski.

'Which means she has three times your experience. At least. Eyes on, Kate.'

'Is that an order?' she demanded, her voice flinty.

He reached into his desk drawer and produced a pink form, which he pushed across to her.

'What's that?'

'An OEC.'

'What?'

'Overseas Expenses Chit. Rarer than hen's teeth in Five. Have a nice cruise, Kate.'

SIXTEEN

Captain Harald Nansen loved the moments before a ship finally eased itself from the dock and, after all the bureaucracy and prep, actually did what it was made for and set sail. Even if, sadly, no actual canvas triangles were involved in the process, as they had been on Fridtjof Nansen's *Fram*.

Soon, he would be the master of the ship in more than name only, once the pilot had departed the bridge. That feeling of open sea and open opportunities might be illusory – maritime rules and protocols were more rigid than ever before and he had to abide by the United Nations Convention on the Laws of the Sea – but the fiction that he was his own man made him feel a tangible connection to his forebears. Fridtjof must have felt the same fish-jumping-in-stomach excitement as an expedition began, as would his ancestors, going all the way back to the unknown Vikings whose blood ran in the modern Nansen family's veins.

His phone beeped. A good luck message from Mette, his wife. She had wanted to leave the children with her mother and come on the inaugural voyage across the Atlantic. He had dissuaded her. Not out of any superstition about captains' wives being on board but because he was going to be so busy on this crossing that he would end up neglecting her. And Mette did not like to be ignored. He had promised her a trip on board when the crèche was fully operational and they weren't facing the Atlantic during hurricane season.

He had also said no to his brother. *Take the plane, Jakob. Please.*

Why? he had asked.

Because we aren't carrying enough booze.

Jakob had managed to drain the Bilge Bar, the drinking den for all hands apart from officers, almost bone dry on *Rapide*'s goodwill crossing to Le Havre. And he was worried about his brother. He had a feeling he was deeper into a financial mess than he cared to admit. And he had dragged their mother into his fiscal maelstrom. He made a note to confirm a meeting with Jakob once *Rapide* docked in New York. He needed to sort him out once and for all.

There was a buzz in his ear and he pressed the 'receive' button on the breast pocket of his jacket. It was Jason Truluck, his number two, telling him that everything was ready for departure.

Nansen spoke into his lapel mic. 'And the weather?' he asked for the tenth time in the past hour. The meteorological reports were not promising a mill pond by any means. The European Centre for Medium-Range Weather was the most pessimistic but the US National Weather Service was suggesting *Rapide* would be able to skirt around any problems. Anglo-American used a proprietary company called All Weather Solutions, AWS, to collate reports from all the major meteorological providers, along with its own monitoring stations. There was nothing building, it had concluded, that was unusual for that time of year. That, also, cheered him.

'AWS suggests it might be a bit frisky once we pass Brow Head,' said Truluck. The tip of southern Ireland. Nansen tried to decode what 'a bit frisky' meant. Truluck was a former Royal Navy man and prided himself on that service's phlegmatic understatement. It might mean anything from a light swell to twenty-five metre seas. He'd check for himself. He just hoped rough weather wasn't some sort of Atlantic tradition for maiden voyages. The *QM2* had hit not one but two cyclonic storms on her first leg. And there were other ships, one in particular whose name would remain unspoken, that had fared even worse.

The band on the quayside struck up, playing the *Star Wars* theme. A cheer erupted from the passengers at the rail. There were fewer of them than he had expected. The day was fine – you could smell salt water on the breeze, albeit cut with notes of tar and diesel from less green vessels – so there was no need to be cowering inside. But he had noticed something that had crossed his mind even at the concept stage of *Rapide* and was confirmed on the sailings to Liverpool and Belfast and Le Havre with invited passengers. With everything controlled by an app plugged into a closed Wi-Fi circuit on the ship, most clients spent an inordinate amount of time looking at their screens and not the scenery. Still, that was the modern world, he guessed. He let out a long sigh. Nansen sometimes thought he had been born a decade or two too late.

He went inside and called the elevator that would take him up to level twelve, from where he could access the bridge.

That was a modest amount by modern standards – the *Rapier* would have sixteen public decks, the *Rialto*, still on the drawing board, twenty. Nansen feared that by that stage any of the sleek lines and architectural motifs that echoed the passenger ships of old would be long gone, replaced by the brutalist shape of a floating housing project.

As he emerged from the lift, he was confronted with the Ledgard party in one of the two hot tubs. Ledgard himself raised a hand in greeting. He still had his trademark aviator sunglasses on. Hot tubs were something else Nansen disapproved of. The ship's medic had summed it up perfectly. *How would you feel about getting into a bath after fifty others?*

The four in the tub were Ledgard and his wife Shelby, his co-driver Ben Clark and his partner Amber X, who, according to Nansen's Google search, was some sort of minor but rising pop star. She certainly looked the part, with lustrous dark hair cut in a long, severe bob and flawless skin, as if she had been Photoshopped to remove any blemishes.

Two passengers he hadn't seen before were sitting nearby. From the look of them, they were the mechanics Ledgard had told him about. Hired help, hence their not being in the tub. One of them kept turning his head from side to side, as if watching a very slow tennis match. He wasn't. He was scanning for trouble. He was broad, gym-buff, dark-eyed and Nansen understood that, although he might know his way round a socket set, that one was more than just a mechanic. Ex-services by the look of it. This was no grease monkey. The guy was a bodyguard.

Ledgard tapped his expensive, waterproof watch and mouthed. 'You're late, Captain.'

Which they were. By about thirty seconds so far. He was about to shout something back when the horn blew its mournful note on the stack. He gave a thumbs up and walked over to the keypad that, once he had punched in the code, would allow him to open the heavy security door and go up the ladder to the bridge.

As he tapped in the sequence he heard a loud squeal from one of the women, Shelby or Amber X, he couldn't be sure. 'Oh, be quiet, you deadshit bitch,' one of them said, so loud it could probably be heard in the engine room. And it hadn't been said in a jokey tone. There was venom in there.

'Fuck off. I really don't need your negatons today,' came the reply. The captain had never heard the word negatons, but he could guess the meaning.

There came the sound of slopping water as someone got out of the hot tub with Ledgard placating, 'Ladies, ladies, please.'

Nansen sniffed the air. There was definitely a storm coming. And, he suspected, not only out there at sea.

*

The weather system that would eventually intercept *Rapide* originated as a tropical disturbance over Africa. Satellites picked up the unstable weather system in mid-September and the National Hurricane Centre tagged it as a potential threat. It was tracked moving westward, across Senegal, where it strengthened, with winds of 45-50 mph. Off the coast of Africa it paused in the Atlantic, as if girding its loins, and morphed into a tropical storm/cyclone. Advisories were issued to all shipping and aircraft.

The storm moved north, still building in intensity. When it hit the Cape Verde islands, it was a minimal hurricane, just edging into what the Saffir-Simpson scale classified as a Category 1. It was named Hurricane Marshall, the thirteenth of the season. Influenced by the westerlies, it shifted again, heading for the Azores. There was some debate at this point whether it was still a hurricane or should be classed as a large scale (synoptic) low pressure, or extratropical, cyclone. Whatever its status, it caused a private plane to lose visibility and crash off the Azores, killing the pilot and two passengers.

Now it deviated once more, heading northwest, deepening, and progressing to a Category 2. It then moved due north, and the NHC and Met Éireann, the Irish National Meteorological

Service, issued storm warnings for Ireland, before Marshall started pushing westward, expanding into a true extratropical cyclone, thus sparing Ireland its worst hurricane since Debbie in 1961.

SEVENTEEN

The crime scene marks had gone, washed away by the rain, but in Riley's mind they were as bright as the day they were sprayed onto the asphalt and pavements of Padstow. He stood outside the Red House, facing a big-sky vista of the Camel Estuary. Clouds were doing that thing that people called scudding, hurrying inland as if they had an appointment to keep, driven by the winds off the Atlantic. The low sun was playing peek-a-boo with them. On the shoreline there were turnstones, curlews and oystercatchers to be admired.

Riley, however, was mainly looking down. It was his seventh or eighth – perhaps more – trip to the Cornish coastal town, the last known sighting of Izzy and Ruby. It was an itch he hadn't just scratched, he had raked it until it bled. Each time he hoped the site would speak to him, tell him where they had gone, what happened to them. But there was only ever a pinched silence and a man with a broken heart.

This would be the last time for a while, he told himself. Soon, he would be over the sea, in Ireland. His request had been granted. He had already done two tours over there, so he was seen as a safe pair of hands who knew the ropes.

He leant back against the flint wall of the Red House and

surveyed the road in front of him. In his mind's eye the flagstones glowed with circles of fluorescent yellow, each with a small, numbered plastic triangle standing next to it. They marked where the cartridge cases from an automatic weapon had fallen. He could also see the debris – glass and carbon fibre and paint – where Jackie had tried to ram herself out of the roadblock when she had been sandwiched by two vans, the blood stains that dripped from her head wound after they shot her behind the wheel and she staggered out of the car, the outline of a human where she fell in the gutter.

There was more blood on the opposite pavement, from Lisa, the second bodyguard, who had been beaten around the head and shot in the leg as she fought tooth and nail to protect her principals.

Of those, his family, there was no sign. They had disappeared from the crime scene as if they had played no part in it. Izzy and Ruby were like wraiths, a phantom presence, haunting the junction of Dennis Road and Sarah's Lane, and he had trouble bringing them into focus.

He looked up at the house. It had been sold recently, for more than a million, so he heard. Probably to a developer who planned to tear it down and build more Lego-block flats. It certainly had a commanding position, and it had been a good choice by Lisa and Jackie as a safe house for Ruby and Izzy. Except it turned out to not be so safe. What had happened wasn't their fault. Outnumbered and outgunned, they stood no chance. It was only by a miracle that Lisa had survived.

'I thought you might like a cup of tea.'

Riley jumped, startled by a voice. It was a neighbour, a woman in her fifties, and her dog. 'I've seen you here before, haven't I?'

He nodded as he took the tea. 'Thanks, that's very kind. Yes, sorry, I have been here before. I hope I'm not disturbing you.'

'No, not at all.'

He could sense her steeling herself to say something about why he was standing on her street examining the flagstones. 'Terrible what happened here. Gunshots in Padstow! What's the world coming to? You . . . you're related? To the poor people involved?'

Another nod. Riley was frightened his voice would break if he replied with any fuller explanation, so he drank some of the tea.

'We put flowers out sometimes. On the fence. I took them down only the other day.'

Riley cleared his throat to make sure the words came out steady. 'That's very nice of you. Thank you.'

'Has anything . . . Does anyone know . . . ?' Her words faded away.

'No.'

She put a hand on his arm. 'It must be awful. I hope you get some peace.'

Only when the people who did this are dead.

If all went well, starting with the Big Daddy bomb maker himself, George O'Donnell. As the days had passed, Riley had grown more convinced than ever that the Irishman had to be the answer to all of this. Had to be. And with that certainty came a resolution – that he would kill to find out.

EIGHTEEN

Even when they were on the M3 heading for Southampton docks, Kate Muraski could not believe that a) she had agreed to go along with Oakham's scheme, b) she had said yes to a *cruise* and c) the amount of stress that had ensued from that decision. She was not a great one for fancy wardrobes. Most of her shopping was done online, in the knowledge that more than half of the items would be sent back. The majority of her in-person shopping was very much mid-market, Arket, perhaps, or J. Crew. The thought of formal evenings and cocktail parties on board a ship filled her with dread. Such a waste of time, the whole charade. What had she done to deserve this?

Barbara had arranged a car to take them to Southampton, a rather plush Mercedes that was a cut above the Ubers or Kapitans Muraski used. She was glad of it, though. Barbara seemed to have been equipped for a voyage to Australia with two large suitcases and various ancillary bags. Muraski had one Tumi, and a very modest one at that.

Barbara was in a chatty mood on the way down, having drawn up the privacy screen to make sure the driver couldn't hear. Not that she was spilling state secrets. She was mainly talking a lot about Henry. Muraski couldn't escape the thought that Barbara would rather be going with him. Well, of course she would, she scolded herself. They were together . . . how long?

'I heard that I owe you a thank you. For the tribunal. You spoke up for me.'

'Oh, that was nothing. You were being treated unfairly. Anyone would have done the same.'

'In this business? I don't think so. I really am very grateful.'

Barbara squeezed her knee, perhaps a little harder than mere affection demanded. 'Change the subject, dear.'

In for a penny, thought Muraski. 'At that shooting range . . . You mentioned that Henry wasn't your first husband.'

Barbara made a little huffing sound that might have been annoyance. 'Ah, therein lies a story.'

'We still have sixty-odd miles to go.' She looked at her watch. They were running a little late. Part of her hoped that they would miss the bloody ship. She wasn't sure how she would cope with all the costume changes. Or the seasickness. She got nauseous on pedaloes, something Barbara had dismissed as psychological and easily cured with drugs. Maybe they would see the liner sailing off into the distance and have to settle for a week on the Isle of Wight.

'Yes, Henry wasn't my first husband,' Barbara eventually admitted. 'Poor old Rory sometimes gets . . . what's the word? Airbrushed. Airbrushed out of history, like they used to do in the Soviet bloc.'

'You and Henry always seemed as if you had been together forever.'

'Not quite. I made an error. I married his best friend.'

'Oh.'

'Rory was more . . . dashing? More outgoing than Henry, certainly. I didn't realise it but Henry had inner strength. While Rory, well, he had an instant charisma. He was even older than Henry.'

'Was he . . . a spy?'

'Of sorts.' Barbara didn't expand on that, just leant forward and opened the wooden cabinet in the bulkhead in front of them. It disguised a mini-fridge and there was a half-bottle of champagne sitting in there. She took it out and handed it to Muraski. 'Will you do the honours?' She held up her left hand, the knuckles swollen by arthritis. 'My grip isn't what it was.'

Muraski started to remove the foil. 'I do want to know about Rory,' she said, as the cork eased out of the neck with the merest *pfffft*. She poured a glass – actually a plastic flute – for Barbara and passed it across. 'I enjoy hearing about . . .' She struggled for the correct phrase.

'Ancient tales?'

'People's time in the service.'

Barbara leaned forward and pressed the button that lowered the privacy screen. 'Peter, is it all clear?'

'Yes, ma'am, nothing untoward. Have you seen something?'

'No, just a feeling of eyes-on. Like someone walked over my grave.' She gave a little shudder. 'Thank you.'

She put the screen up.

'This is a company car?' Muraski asked.

'Yes,' she said with a satisfied chuckle. 'The old Firm do look after me.'

'And Peter is a driver for Six?'

There was a moment's hesitation before she answered. 'He is.'

'And you think we're being followed?'

'Just an old spook's paranoia. Come on, drink up.'

Muraski had the feeling she was being guided away from the previous subject. That she had just been a victim of misdirection. 'What happened to Rory?'

'Pardon, dear?'

Muraski tried but failed to keep an undertow of impatience from her voice. 'What happened? You married Henry. So did you divorce Rory?'

They both drank to fill the silence. 'Well, in a manner of speaking,' Barbara said eventually.

The champagne made Muraski bolder and blunter than she would usually be with the old spy. 'You're being more than a little obtuse again.'

Barbara laughed. 'Of course I am. Force of habit. He died, actually. Some other time, perhaps.'

What other time? Muraski tried to supress the frustration she felt building. Slippery didn't even start to cover this woman. 'Fine. Then answer me this. Despite everything, you think Brodsky lied to Dom?'

Barbara turned in her seat. 'Well, that's why we're here, isn't it?'

Muraski was just about to press her further when her phone rang. Speak of the devil. It was Dom Riley.

NINETEEN

'A cruise?' Riley couldn't keep the incredulity from his voice.

'Yes,' said Kate Muraski. 'A cruise. Very fashionable now, apparently.'

'Really?' he asked, his voice rich with disbelief. 'Where are you now?'

'In a car. Not far from Southampton. Didn't Barbara tell you?'

'No,' he said, trying not to sound hurt. 'My grandmother said she was going on holiday, but . . .'

'Not with me?'

'No.'

There was a silence that threatened to consume all further dialogue. Then Riley laughed.

'What?'

'I can't see you on a cruise. Isn't it all tea dances and the shuffle-whatsit?'

'Wish you were here, too.' She softened slightly. 'I'll give you a call when I get back, eh?'

You won't be here, will you? Tell her. Go on.

He ignored Nick's less than sage advice. 'Sure. Have fun. Don't do deck quoits with any strange men. Say hello to Barbara.'

'Will do.'

The line went dead just as there was a knock on the door of his billet. He opened it to find a lance corporal holding a large cardboard box. 'You've got mail, Staff. This is bloody heavy, what is it?'

'A dog,' Riley said.

'Ha ha.'

It wasn't that far from the truth. It was a special delivery from Scooby, a machine that Riley had ordered from the catalogue of devices he had given him to peruse. Kit that might just make the life of an ATO a tad easier. Riley relieved the lance corporal of his burden and was about to kick the door shut when the lad remembered something else.

'Oh, and the CO wants to see you at fifteen hundred.'

He nodded his thanks and closed the door. That would be details about his Northern Ireland posting. There had been two more car bombs and a truck bomb. He hadn't been lying when he had insisted they needed all the help they could get, ATOs being rarer than tits on a bull.

Told you.

What?

Told you that you wouldn't be here when Kate gets back.

He placed the parcel on his desk, pulled the blade out of his pocketknife and replied out loud. 'Nick. Shut The Fuck Up, mate.'

TWENTY

On the second evening out of Southampton, *Rapide* hit the first fallout from now ex-Hurricane Marshall. Nansen spent the afternoon on the bridge, alternating between watching the sea, the radar, a bank of screens that would not have shamed NASA, and the weather printouts. He also had to cope with a constant stream of mostly minor niggles from passengers and crew, nearly all of which he passed along to the appropriate department – being so tech-heavy, there were bound to be teething troubles. He also decided they needed to tweak the command structure. Some of the more trivial complaints should never have reached his ears.

Outside, the ocean had grown petulant. The sky had lowered a tin-coloured lid on them, the bow was beginning to dip below the waves, and as he listened to weather updates from other ships entering the Atlantic, he decided he had better address the passengers.

'Ladies and gentlemen, and those who choose not to be gender-specific, this is Captain Nansen speaking. Some of you may have noticed a distinct lack of sunshine on the voyage so far. And yes, we are in for some of the weather the Atlantic is famous for. It is the tail end, and I stress that, the tail end of Hurricane Marshall, which is now slowly blowing itself out to the south of our route.

I want to assure you that *Rapide* is an ocean liner, not just a cruise ship. It is designed for weather like this. It welcomes it. We have the most advanced stabilisation systems on the high seas. I would only ask that for the next forty-eight hours you take care when on deck and please respect any out-of-bounds notices. It will be windy and some decks will be wet and, therefore, slippery and we'll have to make them out of bounds. We will have to close the outdoor pools and hot tubs for a while. But the inside entertainment pro-gramme will continue as planned. You will get weather updates in your daily schedule, delivered to your cabin and by email every morning. If you have any questions, please do not hesitate to ask me or any member of my crew. Thank you for listening, and I wish you a pleasant afternoon and evening.'

As he put the intercom down he could sense another change in the swell. The boat took on a more lethargic motion as the sea seemed to have thickened. The waters outside had transformed into salty porridge, its movement slow and sluggish. Rain splat-tered on the windows. The giant wipers began to describe smooth arcs, leaving momentary clear spaces that were soon covered in liquid buckshot.

Nansen was not frightened by the sea. What he said about sta-bilising systems was true, but like traction control on inherently unbalanced supercars, he thought it was cheating. Oh, it was absolutely necessary for the passengers' comfort, but part of him would like to take the ship through a storm without any techno-logical assistance. The Old School way. Sadly, he had come into the job far too late for that. Which was why he planned to cross the Atlantic by yacht with a group of friends, whenever they could all find a window. It would be back to basics. Not quite navigating by the stars, but with minimal technology. Unlike *Rapide*.

The captain called down to Karun Roy, the chief engineer.

Although he could see it on the display in front of him, he wanted to be sure the systems didn't lie. 'Is the Flying Carpet stowed and locked, Karun?' The glass-bottomed lift feature could be withdrawn from its exposed position jutting out over the side of the ship and turned into a pop-up cocktail bar.

'Yes. And extendable balconies overridden.'

'Good,' said Nansen. *Rapide* was getting ready for anything the weather had up its sleeve. Again, double-checking the information the computer was feeding to the bridge he asked: 'All the fins deployed?'

These were gyroscopically controlled lateral extensions from the hull that helped dampen any excessive roll. 'Yes, Skip,' Roy replied. 'You want me to start the hydro pumps?'

Rapide had a secondary stabilisation system whereby water could be pumped up into the side of the ship when it was about to roll, making it heavier than its counterpart. Computers controlled just how much water was needed and whether the port or starboard tanks needed filling at any given time. It was one of these stabilisation pumps that had failed during the sea trials and had to be replaced. 'Not yet. Let's keep them in reserve for an hour or so. I want to see how good the fins alone are.'

'Okay, Skip.' *You're the boss*, his tone said. *And the buck stops with you.*

Nansen looked out again over the bow of the ship. The ever-restless Atlantic had transmuted yet again, and thin flumes of water were breaking over the bow with caps of white speckling the once uniform grey. He checked the time. He would have to go and change. The captain's table awaited.

TWENTY-ONE

There were many people with their eyes on *Rapide* as it made its passage away from Ireland, heading, in a relatively straight line, for the New World. Many of them were using a website called Cruise Mapper, which enabled anyone to pinpoint exactly the position of a ship anywhere in the world.

A second system, Marine Tracker, brings up a map of all the world's cargo ships. At first sight it seems that the planet's oceans are clogged with vessels, that you can walk from one continent to another by hopping from deck to deck. Some areas of the globe are nearly like that – the English Channel, the east coast of the US, the Straits of Hormuz and Malacca (both dense with oil tankers) and parts of the China Sea are all 'chokepoints'. But zoom in on the Atlantic or Pacific Oceans and great swathes of untroubled sea open up. Human activity is not quite as ubiquitous as it at first appears.

The person known as BaseHeart was in London studying the progress of *Rapide*, cross-checking between cruise and cargo traffic. BaseHeart knew that the time wasn't right for him to send the message to Anglo-American. That might be another twenty-four or forty-eight hours away, when the ship was committed to the lonely northern course. Other cruise ships dipped south hunting for warmer weather, calmer seas. *Rapide*, like Cunard's *QM2*, went high up in the Atlantic, into more unpredictable waters, and he admired her for it. But it would also be her downfall.

He looked at the weather map. He was no expert, but he suspected *Rapide* was in for a roughish night or two, and then she should catch something of a break. Big seas still, perhaps, but the wind would have dropped. Hurricane Marshall would be long gone, possibly heading to molest the Carolinas or the Caribbean, more likely losing its shape and blowing its last breath before landfall.

'Still, there'll be some up-chucking on that tub,' he said out loud, addressing the thought to the photograph of his lost daughter. 'And even more in Whitehall when they get the email.'

He pulled up the message for the fiftieth time. When he pressed send it would bounce around the world like a global pinball – Reykjavik, Oslo, Copenhagen, Moscow, Bangkok, Sao Paulo, Seattle – obfuscating its origins with each leap from server to server. The first statement was concise:

> *Attention Anglo-American. There are several bombs that we have planted on your liner* Rapide*. All are well hidden and fitted with anti-handling devices. They can be triggered remotely. And they will be within twelve hours. In order to receive information about the location and exact layout of the devices, we will require action by yourselves and certain people on board. More follows.*

He added one more word at the end: 'Charitable'. His finger hovered over the 'send' button, but he hit 'save' instead. Not yet. Wait until *Rapide* was a solitary speck in the swell of the deep Atlantic, beyond help. Then tell them their ship is rigged to blow.

TWENTY-TWO

Their steward — the poor guy who was tasked with sculpting towels into witty animal shapes every night — had told Kate and Barbara that most guests were keen to bag a slot on the captain's table. They could enter a prize draw, apparently. It was, he said, the ship's Golden Ticket. So, as perverse as ever, Barbara declared that they would eat in one of the more intimate restaurants, *Il Lupo Affamato*, which translated as The Hungry Wolf. Like all the 'speciality' dining on the ship, it cost extra — in this case, one hundred and twenty dollars (the universal currency of cruising) per person with wine pairings.

The dining room was decorated with murals depicting various classic — or clichéd — views of Italy, including the inevitable Venetian gondolier and Vesuvius erupting. It was early, the seas were rough so there were only four other sets of diners, which meant they could talk without fear of being overheard.

As they sipped their champagne (another extra; Barbara had declared she hated the 'mouth feel' of the proffered Prosecco) Kate Muraski waited for an opportunity to steer the conversation back to Barbara's first husband, Rory. Before they had left London she had gone over the files concerning Henry, Barbara's second husband, but there was no mention of Rory. Yet Barbara had suggested the man was in the espionage business, so he damned well should be in there somewhere. Perhaps Barbara's implication that he had been airbrushed from history wasn't far short of the mark. Yet Kate couldn't help but feel that Rory was the key to understanding the remarkable and infuriating *grande dame* of SIS.

Barbara took a decent sip, just shy of a gulp, out of her drink. 'You know what Chekhov's dying words were? "It's been a long time since I drank champagne." I decided when Henry went, that I would never be in a position to claim that on my death-bed. Cheers.'

Muraski raised her glass and drank. It was the good stuff, rich and biscuity. Ah well, there were worse assignments than this, she thought.

'You know there's an art auction tomorrow morning.'

'You have to be kidding,' said Muraski.

'Why?'

'Have you seen the art? It looks like Technicolor vomit.'

'Some of it's not bad,' protested Barbara.

'The stuff that isn't bad is fuckin' awful.'

Barbara gave a sly smile. 'One wouldn't have it in one's own house, I suppose.'

'Not without a gun to your head.'

'Quite.'

The ship gave a little shudder along its length and Muraski felt the world move out of true. She looked around, but realised, for the first time, that they were in a windowless room. She felt a sudden panic about not being able to see the horizon. A bloom of hot sweat prickled across her forehead.

Barbara reached over and put a hand on hers. 'Concentrate on me. You'll be fine.'

Muraski gave her best brave smile.

'How about after this we go and try our hand at some dancing?'

Muraski couldn't help herself. She let out a low groan of despair.

*

Kate Muraski watched as her elderly companion foxtrotted around the small dancefloor as if she were fifty years younger. It helped that she was in the arms of a tall, dark, handsome stranger – well, dark with silvery streaks – who danced with commitment and precision. In fact, he glided. As if he had hidden wheels embedded in his patent leather shoes.

She had the feeling the man could even make her look good. Muraski was sitting at the semi-circular bar, looking out over an area that was clearly designed for the more mature cruisers. A lively four-piece was playing songs from the Thirties and Forties. A sheath-dress-clad singer with a gardenia in her hair was taking occasional vocal duties. Seven or eight couples shuffled about – several of them women partnered with the same sex – while a small audience sat at round tables at the edge of the dance floor, applauding politely as each number ended.

Help, I'm trapped in Strictly Come Dancing for Geriatrics.

Muraski grabbed the glass containing the last mouthful of gin as the boat rolled again. She looked down at the seasickness wristband that Barbara had insisted on buying after dinner. She didn't know whether it was that, the drugs or the alcohol, but the ship's motion was no longer bothering her. It did, however, cause the dancers to do some very fast footwork to stop themselves sliding off the floor.

The music finished with a drum roll, there was applause and Barbara shook hands with her partner and then came over to the bar.

'My knees won't thank me for that tomorrow,' said Barbara, still catching her breath. 'Maurice is a very good dancer. Well, he should be, I suppose. It's in his job description, after all. He was telling me that they aren't paid to be on board. In fact, once upon a time, back in the days of the great liners, the men paid the company to be on board, such was the generosity of their clientele.'

It took a second for the tumblers to click into place. 'Like gigolos?'

'Gigolos who could do the cha-cha-cha, yes. But these days, they just do it for a free cruise, cabin and board, so Maurice was telling me. Right, I am going to ask that woman if she would like to dance.'

'Which woman?'

'Edith.'

Muraski looked across. Edith was another willowy woman with short grey hair, that looked to be about Barbara's age. In fact, on closer inspection, they could be related. Muraski had a feeling, one she couldn't quite explain, that this was no coincidence.

'For Chrissake, Barbara. You really are the limit. How the hell do you know her name? Who is she?'

This was met by another of Barbara's enigmatic smiles. 'She's going to be our new best friend.'

*

Riley went into town for a drink. He didn't want to be in the mess, not tonight. He wanted to be alone, that precious resource the army rarely allows you. He had almost forgotten how it felt to be surrounded by hundreds of men, busy bantering, troughing, shitting, pissing, farting or wanking. Normally he just saw it as army life. For some reason, tonight, he wanted no part of it.

The pub he chose was away from the main drag. The faded

patterned carpet was sticky with beer, as was the ancient dog lying against the brass foot rail under the bar. There was no TV, no jukebox, no slot machines. The only music was the soft burble of someone his grandfather had liked. Not Sinatra, but similar. Dressed in mundane civvies, he barely warranted a glance from the other customers. The majority were solitary men, all over fifty, apart from an entwined younger couple in the corner, the thrill of the illicit crackling between them like static. As the lovers doubtless assumed, Riley was fairly sure he wouldn't run in to any familiar faces in the Bull and Last.

He ordered a Guinness and a Jameson's from the amiable if slow-moving landlord. His phone rang while the stout was still waiting for its top-up. He moved to the corridor that led to the gents. Unknown number. But he knew who it was.

'Scoob?'

'Yeah.' No silly voice this time. 'How you doing?'

'Good. Yeah. Good.'

'You sound like you aren't sure about that.'

Riley let out his breath, the first time he had fully emptied his lungs in over an hour, it felt like. He needed to get some of the tension out of his body. A drink now, a long run in the morning. 'I got the transfer. The old man agreed. Northern Ireland, within the week, so he says.'

'That's good, isn't it?'

'I reckon. Just ...' Riley struggled to articulate what he was feeling.

'I know,' said Roscoe. 'Another path to follow. You don't know where it will end. But you gotta take it, pal.'

'Yeah.'

'I got the address. I know where he is. Yer man. I'll Google Map and satellite it to confirm and send it over before you go.'

'What do I owe you?' Riley knew Roscoe would have had to get someone over there to do the donkey work.

'On the house, mate. I pulled a few favours, that's all. There's one problem, though.'

'What's that?'

'He's in the south. Not far from the border, but still south. Gives you less room for manoeuvre.'

Once fully operational, Riley could more or less move with impunity around the north but crossing over into Eire stripped him of any official status. 'We'll cross that border when we come to it. Thanks, Scoob. And for the sniffer,' he added, having almost forgotten the parcel that had been delivered to his billet. 'You're a pal. I mean it.'

Scooby laughed, probably at the uncharacteristic sincerity and gratitude in Riley's voice. 'Anytime. You take care, Dom. Speak before you ship out. Be safe, eh?'

'And you, mate.'

Riley went back to the bar, where his two drinks stood waiting for him. It occurred to him he had unconsciously ordered a brace of Ireland's national tipples in celebration of his transfer over there. He downed the whiskey in one, shuddering at the burn, and followed it with a soothing draught of the black stuff. He felt the knotted muscles in his neck and shoulders release a little. Riley held up the glass to the light and quietly spoke to the cream-topped dark liquid within.

'Don't worry, Ruby, Izzy. Stand fast. I'm coming for you.'

TWENTY-THREE

Tim Purcell, the duty operations manager of Anglo-American, sat in the head office in Southampton, typing out an urgent request for yet another stabiliser pump to be flown out to New York from Germany. He had spent fruitless hours trying to locate one in the US, but nobody had the exact model needed. Why had it failed a second time? He had already asked this question of the engineering department of the designers, but nothing had come back. It might be that the German company was in the habit of supplying faulty pumps, but Purcell somehow doubted that. It was more likely to do with the feed to it – an installation problem.

He pressed send and heard the *swoosh* of an email streaking away. Well, *Rapide* would have to do without some of the stabilisation tanks. There were six in all, three on each side, and with that pump out of action, the chief on board would switch off its opposite number to starboard. They were effectively sealed units, so it was virtually impossible to repair a faulty unit while at sea without specialist equipment. It wasn't the end of the world, but it was a shame that on its first transatlantic crossing, and hitting heavy weather to boot, it was not as plain sailing as it might have been.

He was about to get up and make a coffee when his computer pinged. He hoped it was the pump manufacturer. It was actually someone called BaseHeart. He hesitated, then opened it. He read the contents and frowned. He looked around the office, to see if some joker was winding him up. But he was alone.

He read it again and felt his stomach churn. He could taste the hastily consumed curry from earlier in the evening. BaseHeart. Would they be able to trace it? This was a malicious prank, some spotty oik in his bedroom who alternated cyber-mischief with porn.

He scanned the message a third time and something told him that wasn't the case. It wasn't a hoax. Or, at the very least, it was something they couldn't afford to treat as if it were a prank. BaseHeart was bloody serious.

'Christ,' Purcell said to himself.

He could feel panic rising in him along with his chicken korma. He took a breath. He wasn't paid to panic. He was paid to respond. Which meant contacting the Crisis Management Team. From the bottom drawer of his desk he took out the blue folder marked Emergency Protocols. What would it be under, this sort of email? Blackmail? Bombs? No, it would be under 'T'.

For terrorism.

TWENTY-FOUR

As he made his way back to the bridge, Captain Nansen mused that, despite the rough seas, the first formal evening had gone well. On his table, the Ledgards were mainly concerned about losing time due to the storm, but Amber X had turned out not be a pop princess diva, as her rather glacial expression in photographs suggested, but a gossipy young woman who entertained them all with scandalous tales from backstage at TV talent shows.

The two mechanics – Jim and Reece – had dined on another table, Nansen only too aware of the sweeping stares of the former, making sure his charges were safe. As Nansen had suspected from the man's build – broad of shoulder, square of chin, bulging in all the right places – and his hypervigilance, Jim was what Ledgard called his 'security advisor'. Reece, on the other hand, was just billed as someone who could service their vehicles blindfolded.

The only sour note of the evening was when Karun Roy informed the captain that the replacement stabiliser pump had also failed and that he had no spare parts to fix it. Well, the only sour note that was, until Mrs Ledgard intercepted him before he reached the elevators.

She was clutching a glossy brochure under her arm and her expression was far from benign.

'Do you have a minute, Captain?' she asked sharply.

'Of course.' He steered her towards the Ronnie Scott's at Sea Jazz Lounge, which he could guarantee would be pretty empty at that time of evening, and they sat at a table with Stan Getz sliding smoothly out of the speaker above them. 'Drink?'

'No, thank you.'

'Was the meal to your satisfaction, Mrs Ledgard?'

'The meal was fine.' She pushed back a stray lock of blonde hair. She was wearing something floaty and semi-transparent with a halter neck which left little to the imagination and, as he had made sure he had done all night, he kept his eyes fixed on hers. 'You know my preference was to fly? But Christian isn't keen on planes. Irrational fear of crashing. But I have to say I am generally very impressed with your ship.'

'Thank you.' He asked the waitress for a glass of sparkling water. 'But . . . ?'

'But this, this is surprisingly crass. This is, after all, meant to be a leisure trip.'

As he was wondering if people like the Ledgards had ever truly embraced the concept of down time, she put the brochure she had been carrying on the table in front of him. He swivelled it around and read the name emblazoned across the cover. He felt himself redden slightly with embarrassment.

'Does everyone get one of these invitations slid under their cabin door? Or is it just those of us with what it calls "liquid assets"?'

'I—' he began.

'And the pop-ups on the ship's internet server? Really? I didn't expect such pound-shop tactics.' She sounded very disappointed but there was something about her expression that bothered him. She was attempting to frown but her forehead wasn't having it.

Botox? At her age? He could hear Mette whispering in his ear not to be so old-fashioned.

Nansen picked up the sales booklet and flicked through it. One name kept leaping out from the pages. He felt a short, sharp stab of anger. 'This, Mrs Ledgard, is not company policy. I shall have to get to the bottom of it. As you say, such a hard sell has no place on board *Rapide*. May I keep this?'

'We certainly don't want it. What on earth made anyone think that we would get involved in something so ... so ... twentieth century?'

'I don't know. Leave it with me. You won't be bothered again, trust me.'

'Thank you, Captain.' She stood and smoothed out her dress. He was a half second behind her getting to his feet. 'Have a good evening.'

'And you, Mrs Ledgard.'

After she had left, the music switched to 'Kind of Blue', the *lingua franca* of jazz. Nansen sat once more and ordered a single shot of Balvenie Double Wood.

Have a good evening? That was unlikely. The six-course meal and the champagne had already curdled in his stomach. Nansen could feel the first stabs of heartburn. He hoped the whisky would settle him. If not, he had antacids in his cabin.

Nansen looked down at the slick brochure once more and its promises of unearned wealth without risk. Peterhouse Investments. Not the gated fund, but one of the others still trading. Now he knew why Jakob had been keen to know which VIPs were going to be on board *Rapide*. And he had spent all that time in the crew bar on the trip to Le Havre doing more than just drinking. He had managed to turn at least one, probably more, of the crew to his stupid schemes. Probably by invoking Harald's name. *Of course my brother, the captain, knows all about it. All you have to do is slide a prospectus under certain doors. And perhaps insert a few pop-ups onto the* Rapide *homepage.*

Fuck you, Jakob, he thought. Fuck you, my reckless, feckless brother. That's the last straw.

*

The Emergency Protocols book had told Tim Purcell of Anglo-American to phone Special Branch, which then contacted the Counter Terrorism Command and MI5. In turn, the message was passed to the MoD, who pulled George Pearman, Minister of Defence, out of a dinner at the Army and Navy Club. Pearman's response was to convene an emergency, augmented meeting of the Cabinet Office Briefing Room A (COBRA). In fact, the gathering would be in meeting room C in the windowless basement of 70 Whitehall, just to the rear of Number 10. Unusually, Pearman would chair the gathering, with the PM to be briefed about any decisions.

Apart from Pearman, in attendance were representatives of the MoD, the various branches of the armed services, including Special Forces, the security services and the anti-terrorism branch of the Met.

There was also Clive Greggs from the Cabinet Office, which had responsibility for supporting and advising the National Security Council and the Joint Intelligence Organisation. Greggs would also be responsible for handling the media, should any press wrangling be required. The camera liked him and his bluff pronouncements, and he shared the ability of the current generation of MPs to obfuscate, bluster and bullshit till the cows came home and settled down for the night.

The gathering was completed by Hugh Chamberlain, co-CEO

of Anglo-American Lines, the only non-government individual present.

'Thank you all for coming at this late hour,' said Pearman. 'I'll get to the point.'

Pearman gave the signal for the first image of the PowerPoint and a copy of the email from BaseHeart came up. There were mumblings around the table as those not yet privy to its contents digested the message. Then, silence.

'Thoughts?' prompted Pearman.

'Is it genuine?' This was Chamberlain. There was more hope than doubt in his voice.

'We have to assume so,' said Quentin Cobb, MI5's Director of Anti-Terrorism. 'Especially in light of the word "Charitable" at the end. It is this month's code word at Five, to be inserted in an otherwise innocuous communication or conversation as a warning that the operative is in danger. This is someone who knows that, telling us not that he is under threat, I suspect, but that he is a serious actor. I am fully aware this suggests he is someone within the security services or, more likely, knows someone within them. Then there is the second email, which suggests we'll know soon enough if this is a real threat. Like the first one, it's been processed through servers across the globe. GCHQ reckon they could trace it. Eventually. We don't have eventually, of course.'

Pearman gave the signal to change the image on screen. Chamberlain had not seen this yet and he let out a groan.

Expect a demonstration of intent within the next three hours.

'What does that mean?' he asked.

'I think they're going to show that they aren't bluffing.' This was Commodore Stavely, in charge of Naval Special Forces.

'Thank you, Commodore,' said Pearman, with just a trace of sarcasm in his voice, suggesting they had all reached that conclusion.

'Has the captain of the vessel been informed?' asked Sir Keith Millner, the National Security Advisor.

'Not yet,' replied Chamberlain. 'It was decided to wait until after this meeting, so we can perhaps offer more than "there's a bomb on board" by way of guidance.' His dismay had turned to tetchiness now. All these well-decorated and highly promoted minds around the table and they were hardly coming out with acceptable strategies. Or, in fact, any kind of strategy at all.

Pearman had the next slide brought up. It was a deck plan of *Rapide*.

'Do we have any theories as to how they might have got it on board?' asked Penny Wiltshire of the Foreign and Commonwealth Office.

'I think we can worry about that later. Our priority now is to find out *if* there are any devices on board, if so, *where* they are and then, *what* to do about them.' The Met's Salvini underlined her emphasis with a Morse-code tap of her pen on the desk. Her gaze around the desk was as steely as her short, sharp crop.

'Do we have any idea what this BaseHeart wants?' asked Cobb.

'Money,' said Sir Keith. 'It's always money at the end of the day.'

Carlyle of Six shook his head slowly. 'Don't bank on it. What if it's ISIS or al-Qaeda? What if they want some of their men released in exchange?'

'It is possible,' said Sir Christopher Blaine, Chief of Defence Staff, with only a hint of superciliousness. 'What about this name "BaseHeart"? Is it some play on Braveheart? Could he be Scottish? SNP, perhaps? I suggest we get the cryptanalysts at GCHQ to think about it. Most people choose something significant as a nom-de-plume, even if they don't realise it.'

'When I was a young boy,' said Sir Keith quietly, 'Nanny used to let me watch all sorts of American rubbish on TV. Against Mother's express wishes, I might add. *The Invaders, Lost in Space . . .*'

'Sir Keith,' Pearson began.

The NSA raised a hand in a let-me-finish gesture to show he hadn't gone entirely off-piste. 'Different spelling I think, but one of the shows featured an actor called Richard Basehart.'

'And what was that called?' asked a somewhat exasperated Pearson.

Sir Keith hesitated, as if unsure of the wisdom of what he was about to say. '*Voyage to the Bottom of the Sea.*'

*

The committee took a short break for tea and coffee after Sir Keith's comments. The idea that they were dealing with a fan of 1960s sci-fi would be passed along to GCHQ. Just because it was outlandish didn't mean it shouldn't be considered a possibility. After all, it was unlikely they were dealing with a rational personality. It could be a Scottish nationalist with a liking for submarine shows.

'I suggest we take an in-depth look at all passengers and crew,' said Pearson when they had reconvened. 'Just in case this BaseHeart is hiding in plain sight. You can get us a manifest?'

Chamberlain nodded. 'Of course. Although all the crew members have recently been vetted.'

'Not like the security services vet,' said Carlyle, dryly.

'Fucksake,' Salvini muttered. She was well aware that COBRA meetings were unminuted. She thought it a blessing. 'Is there anyone qualified on board to tackle some kind of explosive device?' she asked.

Chamberlain shrugged. 'There's a head of security. Formerly with the South African Special Forces I believe.'

Stavely gave a grunt. 'That doesn't mean he knows one end of a bomb from another. Unless he's throwing it.'

'Where is the ship now?' asked Clive Greggs.

Pearman clicked his fingers and a chart appeared on the screen. 'This is real time,' he said. 'As you can see, she is quite far into her voyage. The nearest landfall is probably one thousand miles away. The weather, incidentally, is still deteriorating.'

'Nothing in the vicinity? No other ships?' asked Wiltshire.

'There's nothing in the immediate vicinity, no,' replied Stavely. 'The *QM2*, which sails a similar route, is berthed at Southampton. And if there was, what could they do? Take an extra thousand people on board?'

'More than a thousand,' muttered Chamberlain. 'If we include the crew.'

'Submarines?' suggested Greggs.

'Same problem,' said Stavely. 'And we don't have ATOs on them anyway.'

'And we don't give out the position of our SSNs under any circumstances,' intoned Sir Keith, as if he was reciting a holy text. The acronym was shorthand for a nuclear sub.

Stavely nodded his agreement. 'We will, of course, ask the closest ships to re-route to the immediate vicinity, just in case. There are two tankers and a container ship heading for Halifax. One Norwegian, one Japanese and one Kuwaiti. There will be a CQD sent out. That's "Come Quick, Danger", one level below SOS. We'll tell them that *Rapide* has a potential engine failure crisis. Which isn't far from the truth.'

'Bloody hell, it really is just like the *Titanic*,' muttered Wiltshire.

'No it is not. That does not help. Has anyone got any sensible solutions here?' Pearman demanded. He then fixed his stare on Stavely. 'And please, no suggestions that years of defence cuts mean we aren't prepared. That might wash in the Gulf, but not in the mid-Atlantic. I can't imagine a situation where we had frigates and EODs on standby out there at any point in the past fifty years.'

Cobb twirled his pencil. He looked down at what he had been sketching in a pad and then at Stavely. 'You can drop SBS people into water, can't you?'

'I said the weather was deteriorating,' Pearman interrupted. 'The backwash from a hurricane.'

'Yes, we have that capability,' said Stavely, ignoring the minister for the moment before glancing back at him. 'Within reason.'

'And you have Ammunition Technical Officers in the SBS?'

'We do,' Stavely said, nodding his head so that his jowls wobbled. 'Although a training accident some time ago has left us very short-handed.'

'But we only need one, don't we? I mean, how many bombs can there be?' Carlyle said.

'But the majority of Royal Marine, SAS and SBS ATOs are in the Gulf with Special Reaction Force 20,' said Stavely. 'Checking oil tankers for limpet mines and the like.' Everyone round the table knew why: there had been another round of attacks on tankers in and around the Straits of Hormuz. It was an A1 priority for the British that the straits remained safe and secure with oil flowing freely. It was, although nobody would voice it, more important that the oil got through than saving a cruise ship in the mid-Atlantic. 'We could never get them back in time to be useful.'

'We have EOD units,' said Salvini. 'In the Met. With the equivalent of ATOs.'

'Do you train your Explosive Ordnance Disposal teams for low-altitude, low-opening parachute jumps over oceans?'

Salvini frowned. 'I'd have to check.'

'Don't bother, the answer is no,' said Stavely curtly, adding, 'With all due respect to the Met. This is a specialist situation.'

Salvini either didn't notice the disdain in the naval man's voice or chose to ignore it. 'What about the Americans then? Could they help?'

'I'll check,' said Wiltshire, scribbling in her notebook. 'Although is it a good idea to go cap in hand to the Yanks again?'

'Needs must. As I am sure you know, most Navy SEAL units are based out of San Diego,' said Stavely, 'And, again, the active units are mostly in the Gulf. And I agree, given our lowly status at the moment, it might be best if we look self-sufficient. No harm in briefing them, though.' He turned to Wiltshire. 'It'll be faster if I go direct. Let me have a word, Penny, will you?'

'Of course.'

Pearman's impatience suddenly showed. 'Ladies and gentlemen, I have to tell the PM something in fifteen minutes.'

'I suggest we inform the captain of the situation,' said Clive Greggs. 'It's ridiculous to keep him in the dark.'

'Agreed. He absolutely needs to know. But what kind of lifeline will you throw him?' asked Carlyle.

'And this must not get out to the general public,' added Chamberlain, looking at Greggs, who had responsibility for the media. Greggs stared back as if that really didn't need saying out loud.

Commodore Stavely suddenly spoke with a booming authority, as if he were addressing his men on deck. 'I suggest we put together a combined SAS and SBS team. This is a Deep Blue Op, so SBS will take the lead, agreed?' There was no argument. 'Put them all in a C-130 and fly them over there, it'll be quicker than any ship. See if the Americans can help us with comms, they'll have something relatively near that can overfly, give us a good connection between ship and aircraft and London. Failing that, they could re-route a satellite. They have plenty looking for Russian intruders up in that neck of the woods. But it would be a UK operation, as it is a UK ship.'

'Registered in the Isle of Man,' muttered Chamberlain.

'Close enough,' said Carlyle.

'They can parachute onto a moving ship?' asked Wiltshire, a hint of disbelief in her voice.

'Not in those seas, no,' Stavely replied. 'But they can get themselves near enough to be picked up by a tender. It means finding at least one ATO who can jump into the Atlantic without getting himself drowned.'

TWENTY-FIVE

Dom Riley dreamt of Izzy and Ruby most nights. Often, it was reliving the ambush in Padstow. Even though he hadn't been there to witness it, the scene played out as if he had been a spectator — the discharge of weapons, the screams of the victims and he could smell what most people called cordite, even though it was years since that had been used as a propellant.

This time, though, it was more benign, less painful. A trip to the beach, near Aldeburgh. Benjamin Britten country, so Izzy had said. He had asked her to whistle some of the great man's tunes and she had laughed.

In the dream Ruby was about ten, but in reality she had been much younger when they had crunched down over the shale to watch the grey, grubby sea rake through the shingle. Ruby was fascinated by the beach detritus, the old twine, bits of driftwood, the egg cases. 'Put it down!' Izzy would yell. 'You don't know where it's been.'

'It's been at sea,' Ruby replied, as if her finds were voyagers returned from adventure.

After their cheeks had been blasted to apple-rosiness, they walked into town. Fish and chips. A pint at the White Hart in the high street. Happy families. In reality, it was already all beginning to fall apart. Lots of glum silences, no arguments while they were with their daughter, but tension you could take an axe to. And did they really take out a rowboat in the very strange little town of Thorpeness?

Dom put his back into moving the oars, pulling like he was training for the Boat Race, but the edge of the lake never seemed to get any closer. Now people were hollering and pointing: 'Get in, man, get in.'

The buzzing became even more urgent. He was aware of something rising from the waters, a vast shape, water cascading off it to reveal—

Dom awoke with the sheen of exertion on him, a film of sweat over his entire torso. He threw back the covers, reached out to the light and switched it on. The wasp-in-a-jar noise hadn't stopped with the dream. It was his phone. The work one, making the buzzing sound and dancing a little jig on the bedside table.

He picked it up and tried to blink away the film of moisture covering his eyes. What had the shape been, the one coming from the water? The features remained vague, just out of focus.

Just a dream, Dom.

He looked at the number on the screen. It wasn't one he knew. 'Yeah? Riley.'

'Dom. Sorry to disturb you.' It was the CO.

Riley cleared his throat, hoping to sound sincere. 'That's okay, sir. What can I do for you?' *In the middle of the fucking night.*

'Am I right in thinking you did a low-level release parachute course a few years back? A LALO?'

Yes. For a bet. Well, also so he had another string to his bow, but really it was a couple of blokes geeing each other up, daring their mate to have a pop at it, never thinking they'd be allowed to go through with it. Thing about the army, you can never predict how they'd react to bollocksy stupid ideas. Go ahead, they had said. Apparently Maersk and some other shipping lines had suggested that it might be a good idea if the army, as well as SBS, had at-sea capability within British territorial waters. It wasn't an experience he enjoyed or cared to repeat. And they had never needed to use their skills, the Royal Marines and the Boat boys having dealt with any situation that had risen.

Until now.

And it was on his file. It was useless denying it. 'Yes. But it was a long—'

The CO steamed in to cut him off. 'Thought so. Get your shit together, Staff.'

He had the feeling of his fingertips touching something solid before it spun out of his grasp. Ruby and Izzy. 'What about Ireland?' he demanded, trying to keep his voice level. 'I'm due to deploy over there.'

'It'll still be there when you get back. Get a move on, Dom. You've a plane to catch.'

TWENTY-SIX

It wasn't a plane that Riley ended up catching, but a bloody helicopter. Not his favourite form of transport, not since his time riding Chinooks in Afghan. This one was a Eurocopter AS365 N3 Dauphin, and it was waiting for him at the barracks helipad as soon as he got dressed and pulled all his kit together.

The brief before take-off had been just that – brief. He had been told the rush-rush, hush-hush job was an 'at sea' incident and that it was a situation that needed delivery by parachute of an ATO. It was not a drill. When he had done the low-level parachute drop over water, he had mostly practised scenarios where North Sea oil rigs had been taken over by terrorists wearing suicide vests and conventional chopper landings were impossible. But it wasn't that, he was told, it was the other one they had rehearsed – boarding a moving vessel. None of it filled him with great cheer.

Riley was bundled aboard the chopper by Ray the Tortoise – shortened to Torty – a too-cheery corporal, given the hour, who stowed and strapped down his kit. 'Good luck, Staff,' he said with a grin.

'Fuck off, Torty.' He was still seething at Ireland being snatched from him for this 'at sea' gig. Whatever the 'at sea' was, it was screwing him up big time. But this was the army. This was his job.

He had to swallow it, like a cup of cold sick. It was a delay, that was all. The sooner he dealt with the emergency, the sooner he could be back onto the trail of Ruby and Izzy.

Torty laughed. 'Enjoy your flight, Staff.'

Bastard. He knew Riley didn't like flying without reassuring fixed wings. He buckled up and was passed a helmet and comms by the co-pilot. They exchanged thumbs ups. The guys upfront, he knew, would be men of few words while on duty. The Dauphin could seat twelve people. There was only one other passenger, a civilian. He held out his hand. 'Staff, thank you for being ready at such short notice. Gregory Obi. I work for Foreign Office as liaison for the DSF.'

The Director of Special Forces.

'Dom Riley.'

A politician then. Riley looked him up and down. Obi. What was that? Nigerian? The man had no accent, he sounded like he went to the same school as the Rees-Moggs. How old? Tricky. His face was smooth and unlined, with baby cheeks of the kind that mothers loved to pinch. He could be thirty-five or fifty. Riley reckoned closer to the latter, that he wore his years lightly. He wondered if they could say the same about him. Not last time he looked.

'You here to brief me properly?' Riley asked. 'Because what I have is sketchy as fuck.'

'No, next briefing is . . .' He stopped as the twin-engine began to turn the blades and a whine filled the cockpit, almost enough to blank out conversation even over comms. They waited until it had reached the high point of its crescendo and then the Dauphin took off, leaving Riley's stomach behind.

It might be unmarked with only a civilian registration on the fuselage, but this was a Blue Thunder, one of the choppers used by the SAS when they wanted to move around with some degree of stealth. As well as not looking like military transport, its transponders could be switched off, so it wouldn't appear on most radar screens or on flight tracking apps. The pilots of the Special Forces Air Support Squad, which included both passenger helicopters and an Apache gunship, were among the best in the world, which reassured Riley. The downside was they liked to prove it.

After the faster-than-a-speeding-elevator take-off, the Dauphin assumed a slight nose down attitude and headed off into a night as yet untroubled by dawn. His stomach settled back into its usual position and the noise in his ears abated.

'They picked me up first,' Obi said. 'In London. Quite a trip, I can tell you. Probably scared the shit out of a few drivers on the M40.' See, Flash Harrys the lot of them. So much for keeping a low profile.

'What do you know?' Riley asked.

'One of our ships is missing. Well, not missing, but under threat. By parties unknown.'

'Naval or civilian?'

'It's a cruise ship.'

It didn't entirely surprise him. Jihadists had used planes, trains and automobiles. It was only a matter of time before ships got on the list. And cruise ships were huge, often with three thousand or more passengers. Then, a jolt of concern struck him. Weren't Kate and Barbara holidaying at sea? Although what were the chances of it being the very one targeted? Slim was the answer. 'Okay. Where exactly is it?'

'Mid-Atlantic.'

'Fuck,' Riley said. 'That's a big place.'

'Quite. We'll be told exactly when we reach our rendezvous point.'

Riley realised that in all the speed of getting showered, dressed and packing two large bags of kit, he hadn't asked where they were actually going on this first leg. Not out to sea in a Dauphin, he reckoned. The army always told you the SP eventually. But sometimes it liked to keep the information back, delivered to you all wrapped up in a bow. Especially if it was a destination that might cause some concern. Like the bloody North Atlantic. If this was a seaborne operation, he assumed Poole, home of the Special Boat Service, would be the next stop. After all, it would be their shout. And he knew from bitter experience that they were down a couple of ATOs, their lives and skills wasted out on the Thames Estuary. 'That's Poole, is it?'

'No,' said Obi. 'We're going straight to RAF Brize Norton.'

Fuck. Riley felt his heart sink. He had, of course, suspected this the whole time, but refused to face up to it. Brize Norton. Home to his second least-favourite mode of transport. The fucking C-130.

TWENTY-SEVEN

Captain Nansen gathered his people together in the wardroom. All had received the emergency message on their radios. The single word, *Dominion*, meant there was an issue of Category One severity. Nansen sat at the head of the table and waited as they filed in. Jason Truluck, his staff captain, was the first to arrive and he had brought with him a steaming mug of coffee. Nansen suddenly realised he needed one – he wouldn't be getting any sleep that night – and got up to make his own. He didn't want any stewards around for this meeting.

He braced slightly as he operated the machine. The sea wasn't particularly high but it was unsettled, as if it couldn't make up its mind which direction to flow. It made for an unpredictable motion which, he knew, many passengers would find equally unsettling. He had been informed that there had been a rush on wrist bands and pills, even at that hour.

Truluck came and stood at his side while the machine gurgled. 'All sorted, Skip. We'll be letting a couple of crew members go in New York.' A euphemism for having fired them on the spot. 'Meanwhile, they've been relieved of duty.'

'Thank you.' Suddenly his brother's grubby little scheme didn't seem so important. But he was glad his number two had got to the bottom of it, found the culprits who had helped Jakob turn *his* ship into a two-bit brokerage firm. It was probably harsh to sack the culprits, but it was best such schemes were nipped in the bud. Cruise ships were notorious for the little rackets that were run, most of them harmless enough. But it fostered a particular Jack-the-Lad ethos on some ships that he wasn't going to tolerate on *Rapide*. But for the moment he had to deal with something else he wasn't going to countenance. A bomb threat.

'There's another little problem,' said Truluck wearily, as if disappointed by his fellow human beings. 'One of the CCTV operators has been pulling images off the surveillance cameras. You know the sort of thing.'

Nansen did. A female passenger déshabillé in a passageway as she tried to get her cabin open; some discreet topless sunbathing; a man with a woman, not his wife, making out in what they mistakenly thought was a quiet corner.

'He'd got some, um, juicy footage of a couple having sex below decks. I've had it wiped. And reassigned that entire shift to other duties. I'll give you a list of the changes later.'

'Well done.'

'But there's also been a burnout in one the CCTV router systems.'

Nansen didn't like the sound of that. 'What sort of burnout?'

'Electrical fire of some description.'

Nansen swore softly in his native tongue. 'Same as the stabilisation pump?'

'I don't know,' Truluck admitted. 'Might be the same company did the wiring.'

But Nansen doubted the shipyard cut corners on such things. There was another, more likely, explanation. 'And it might be someone who doesn't want us to see something.'

'Like what?' asked Truluck, puzzled.

'I'll explain in a moment. Can you get it repaired?'

'Of course. There's two sparks on it now.'

When Nansen returned to his seat there was almost a full complement. Jos Swart, Head of Security; Rashmi Fonseka, Jos's deputy – known as the Guest Security Supervisor; firefighter Team Leader Lazlo Dvali, a tough Georgian from Tbilisi; and Jon Cappelli, the Passenger Safety Officer. The Chief Engineer, Karun Roy, was the last to arrive, mumbling apologies. A streak of oil on his tunic showed he had been working. Now they were seven altogether. He wondered how long before this magic circle expanded. Quite soon, he imagined, as the crisis evolved.

'Thank you for coming at this hour,' he began. 'I know you all either had beauty sleep to catch up on or duties to perform. Or some of you were on duty in the disco.' He glanced at Jon Cappelli who, on a previous posting, had a reputation for making some passengers safer than others. There were a few knowing chuckles around the table, but Cappelli just shrugged.

Nansen cleared his throat. It was, he supposed, a rather flippant start to what was a serious situation. There would be no further laughter. Once the nature of the emergency unfolded, he knew he would be expected to exude a glacial calm, typical of the clichéd image of his countrymen. Inside he was boiling like the famed Saltstraumen Maelstrom. *How* dare *they target my ship. Who the fuck do they think they are?*

However, he betrayed none of this when he finally spoke. 'I have just had a conversation with Hugh Chamberlain who is, as most of you know, co-CEO of Anglo-American Lines, and another with Tom Peszek, Chief of Operations.' He cleared his throat. 'A few hours ago the office in Southampton received an email claiming there were bombs aboard the ship.'

He waited to gauge the response. Everyone remained impassive. Fonseka's smile shrank back slightly.

'At this point, you think I am going to tell you this is a drill. It isn't. This is a genuine alert.'

Now the babble of voices burst forth with questions and exclamations. Several of his people shook their heads, as if they couldn't believe what they were hearing.

'Bombs? Plural?' Capelli yelled above the din. There was an audible undertow of panic and fear in his voice. He wasn't alone. Even those who had remained calm on the outside had a slightly hunted look in their eyes as they ran through the possibility of an explosion or explosions at sea.

Nansen held up his hand. 'You will know what I know. The email is, so far, untraceable. We do not know their demands. We do not know if it is terror-related. Or indeed a hoax. We have been promised a demonstration that they aren't bluffing within' – he glanced at the wardroom clock – 'well, less than three hours from now.'

'Shit.' It was Cappelli again. 'How did they get bombs on board?' He looked at Swart, as if he bore personal responsibility. 'All the luggage is X-rayed. So it couldn't be in the passengers' cases.'

'It is impossible to make any ship totally secure,' replied Swart. 'Determined individuals will always find a way. Ask the airlines.'

Cappelli went to answer, but Nansen jumped in. 'I don't think speculation helps. If this demonstration of intent involves a bomb, then we must locate it. Most passengers will be asleep by now. We have to search the ship.'

'Cappelli is right about one thing,' said Swart. 'It would be difficult to get anything on board in luggage. So we must assume some other method. With the food and beverage perhaps. In my experience any device might well be hidden in plain sight.

Galleys, for example. A while back there was a device at Arsenal's stadium in London. It was disguised as a catering trolley. That's what we might be up against. There are protocols for this sort for thing. I'll find the relevant one and make sure you all get a copy.'

Nansen nodded. 'And please, do not share it any wider than strictly necessary. I suggest we get started. You can each pick a team of six members of the crew you trust to keep this quiet. Do not tell them the full details.'

'Is that all we can do?' asked Fonseka. It was what most people were thinking. Their calmness, Nansen knew, was but a thin crust on top of bubbling anxiety.

'No. I have been informed that a team is being flown out from the UK. It will deploy into the sea. We'll have to pick them up and bring them on board. Among their number will be a bomb disposal specialist.'

'I think the passengers are going to notice that,' said Fonseka.

'I know,' said Nansen impatiently. He could already sense his maiden voyage being tarnished by this turn of events, no matter what the outcome. 'We'll tell them it is an exercise.'

'That won't wash, will it?' said Reeves.

Jason Truluck answered for his captain. 'It'll placate some passengers. Probably not others. But, Fonseka, I think we'll have to make sure nobody starts tweeting or emailing or Instagramming. Can we do that?'

Fonseka nodded. 'I can kill the internet, obviously. Although expect a passenger mutiny.'

'They'll live,' said Truluck.

'I'm not so sure.'

'And the apps that control everything?'

'They're backed up on Bluetooth. They'll still work in the

closed circuit we have.' She twirled a finger to indicate the whole ship. 'So they'll still have their toys.'

'Right,' said Nansen abruptly. 'Let's get to it. A bomb hunt. Jos, can you split the ship up into inspection areas?' He knew damn well he could; he had read all the security scenarios and a stem-to-stern search was among them. He just wanted Swart to take control of the inspection.

'It's already done, Skip,' Jos Swart replied. 'Part of the protocols. I'll assign each person a zone for his or her team to clear. One thing.' He paused to look around the table, making sure he had all their attention. 'If you find something that you even think might be an explosive device, *do not touch it*. Most IEDs have anti-handling tricks up their sleeves.'

'Boobytraps,' said Nansen, just in case anybody wasn't clear.

Swart nodded his solemn agreement, then looked over at the captain. 'Permission to break out firearms?'

Nansen shook his head, more reluctantly than it appeared to his colleagues. The thought of hunting down these jokers with automatic weapons had a certain appeal.

'Not yet. I know you are trained in weaponry, Jos, but most of the searchers won't be. And consider this: we don't know if there is a bomb on board as yet. Nor do we know if the bombers or blackmailers – I assume there will be a demand eventually – are on *Rapide*.'

'Tasers?' Swart asked, not wanting to go about this business totally unarmed.

'Tasers and nightsticks, yes.'

'Thank you.'

Nansen stood, keen to speak to London again. He needed to know how long before the experts dropped from the inhospitable skies. 'Any questions?'

'Yes,' said Fonseka quietly, as if embarrassed by her query. 'How on earth will we know a bomb when we see it?'

Cappelli had an ancillary query. 'Do we think this is an inside job?'

Suspicious glances were exchanged around the table, but nobody had an answer to his question.

*

After the COBRA meeting finally spluttered to an end, Clive Greggs had made the call as instructed, using one of the increasingly rare public phone boxes. He chose one in Pimlico, just next to the pub he was going to bolt into the moment this was done.

He dialled the number and waited. It connected with a series of clicks, whirrs and beeps. It took him back to the old days of modems.

'Mr Greggs.'

The voice crackled electronically. There was obviously some technology interface involved. It sounded inhuman, like dealing with a Dalek.

This was the first time he had actually spoken to the man calling himself BaseHeart. All the other directions had been on a pre-recorded tape that he had been told to dial into. Instruction one: attend COBRA as normal. Two: report the proceedings back to BaseHeart. Three: or else.

'Who the hell are you?'

Silence on the other end, but for a low hum.

'Hello?' he shouted.

'We had an arrangement, Mr Greggs. A simple transaction. As I said in my covering letter, do not ask questions. You will not get an answer.'

'We didn't have an arrangement,' he snapped. 'I got a set of demands. It's blackmail. Where did you get that stuff? It's all fake, I can assure you.'

'Please. I am running out of patience already. The photographs are not fake. I paid good money for them. I have had them professionally appraised. Should you choose not to proceed, then they will be released. And believe me, I know what it means to lose a family. Goodbye.'

'No,' he yelled. 'Wait.'

Another lengthy pause, before BaseHeart spoke again. 'Tell me what happened at COBRA today.' It was not a request.

Greggs looked over at the inviting lights of the pub, his throat constricting at the anticipation of the comforting warmth of good whisky on his gullet, the first of many.

'Mr Greggs?'

'Very well.' And to his shame, he did exactly as he was told.

TWENTY-EIGHT

The four-engined Lockheed C-130 Hercules is the long-distance workhorse of the British armed forces, as familiar to the troops as the Chinook helicopter. Its name was aptly chosen, Riley thought, because the inside always smelt like the Aegean stables before the Greek god managed to flush them out. It was a potent mixture of sweat, fear, bodily fluids, vomit, aviation fuel and, more often than not, the bleach some fool had used to try and get rid of the stench.

The RAF operates three squadrons of the cargo plane out of Brize Norton, so Riley's guess that he would be boarding one was spot on. He was now sitting halfway along the fuselage, comms headset with built-in ear defenders clamped on, hoping his fillings didn't shake loose as the machine climbed through the clouds sitting over the Irish Sea. You could just about have a one-to-one conversation in the rear of a C-130, but group briefings would be liable to send the speaker hoarse, hence the earphones/mic. It wasn't the one they would deploy with – for the mission the comms were built into special SBS-issue neoprene hoods.

The briefing that Obi had mentioned had been given before take-off by two Green Slimes – military intelligence officers – and to say it was sketchy would be an insult to sketchers. Boat, bomb, blackmail. They had decided on a small team, rather than swamping the boat with Special Forces. The ship's owners had asked for the operation to be as low-key as possible, and the government had agreed. Riley thought this a mistake – the situation had surely moved beyond not spooking the passengers – but as he was there in a tactical rather than strategic role, he kept his opinion to himself. To his surprise, Gregory Obi had come along for the ride on the Herc. Now dressed in green overalls, he was swiping through a document on an iPad, frowning as he did so.

Also present, sitting in their respective canvas bucket seats, were Captain Joshua Kebede and his sergeant, a Geordie bruiser by the name of Bill Capes, and an SAS sergeant and corporal, Mike Tremaine and Rogan Norwell. Riley liked the look of Tremaine. The SAS sergeants and warrant officers were the backbone of the Regiment, far more so than the officers, who generally did a three-year tour. NCOs were in for the duration. Tremaine was short, stocky and dark-haired, like a troglodyte come to the surface.

Norwell was the opposite – tall, blond and willowy, unusual for a Blade. Rogan wasn't his real name. That was Josh, apparently. But Joshes, Tristans and Tobys don't fit in the SAS, not unless they were Ruperts. So Josh had picked up a nickname riffing on a popular Persian/Kashmiri dish and a staple of Indian takeaways across the UK. Rogan Norwell was electronic counter-measures and comms. He would make sure they could talk to each other, the ship's captain and London on a closed circuit.

The final figure present was a twinkly-eyed jump- and loadmaster of Bengali descent called Monty Ghasak, who was addressed by his nickname of 'Breezy'.

Riley remembered Kebede, of course, and vice versa, from the Maunsell Fort incident. They had exchanged nods which conveyed more than the small movement suggested, but they had no time to reminisce about the Thames Estuary fiasco. Getting airborne had been the priority. They had a lot of kit, including parachutes, the latter being Breezy's domain. These were going to be interesting. When Riley had made his 'wet jump', as they called ones over the sea, he had been using a PX chute. The technique involved ditching the reserve chute at around sixty metres above the waves and undoing the leg harness so you could shrug off the straps in the water and not be dragged down. It was even trickier than it sounded.

On this jaunt they were using more advanced Low Level Parachutes than the PX Mk 4, the Irvin GQ400 Static Line LLP, which came with audible and visual warnings when it reached the requisite sixty metres above sea level. It was programmed, using an Automatic Altitude Detection System, which used barometric pressure and pulsed lasers to calculate height, to then automatically release the leg straps.

Their kit would be tethered to them by a length of webbing, all of it stored in neoprene-wrapped Bergens, which were fitted with self-inflating flotation sacks. It was an improvement on the metal canisters with their own chutes that Riley had used in training, which often ended up a long swim away from the jumper.

As they levelled off and the din receded, Obi worked his way up to the cockpit. When he came back, he stood, one hand holding the webbing for support, his folder in the other, and spoke to them through his headset mic.

'Gentleman, I can now give you full details of the mission, as sanctioned by the Director of Special Forces, most of which I have gone over with Captain Kebede. Some of this you heard from intelligence, but I can now identify the vessel involved. We are heading out to the mid-Atlantic, where the cruise ship *Rapide* is currently heading to New York. Some hours ago, the company that owns and operates the ship received a threat that there were bombs – note the plural – there were bombs on board. We do not yet know what the perpetrator's demands are. As you know, at the moment there is a search of the vessel underway by the crew.'

'I hope they've told them not to touch anything suspicious,' said Riley.

'Of course.' Obi nodded at him. 'The perps have announced a demonstration of some description within the next few hours. To avoid panic the passengers are not yet aware of the threat. Nor will they be told unless absolutely necessary. We don't want word of this getting out.'

Good luck with that.

Keeping any operation under wraps had become exponentially more difficult since the days of, say, the Libyan Embassy siege. Mind you, Riley supposed security was easier when you were in the middle of the Atlantic. Far fewer passers-by with smartphones for one. Plus, presumably you could control comms with the out-side world. Sooner or later, though, this *Rapide* was going to have to dock and the story would flash around the globe.

'Your mission is to assist with the search of the ship. And, of course, render safe any devices.' He glanced at Riley as he said that.

'Do we know if the X-rays are actually on board?' asked Tremaine, using the common term for unknown enemies.

'We do not,' said Obi.

'What's the weather like over the jump zone?' asked Bill Capes.

'We'll update you once we have an accurate picture,' Obi replied. 'In the old days we would have sent a Nimrod out to help co-ordinate the mission.' This was the RAF's long-range maritime reconnaissance plane, based on the old De Havilland Comet, which had been retired in 2011. 'We haven't got any

Nimrods. A number of its replacement, the Poseidon P-8A, are at RAF Lossiemouth, but they are not yet fully operational.' Obi's eyebrows signalled some exasperation at this. There had been well-publicised problems with a software update. 'Now, the Hercules does have advanced satellite communications, but there's nothing like eyes in the sky. So ... we have a US Navy P-8A out of Jacksonville, Florida, heading to intercept us. It will provide weather updates and ship-to-plane-to-London contact if required. Norwell, you'll set up the links?'

The comms man nodded.

'I'll leave it to Captain Kebede to go through the technical aspects of the jump. Then I think you should try and get some rest. We should be over the drop zone in around' – he checked his watch –'three and half hours. Just in time for sunrise.'

'But not for the promised demo,' said Riley.

'No,' admitted Obi. 'We are at their mercy on that one.'

Kebede moved position when Obi had stopped speaking and slotted himself next to Riley. He didn't use his mic, just leaned in close enough not to have to shout. 'Staff, I think you should jump with me. You're the Golden Ticket on this one.'

Riley just nodded. He knew what the SBS man meant. Everybody else's skills could be duplicated. Only Riley was equipped to deal with explosive ordnance. 'Did you request me?' he asked.

'Not exactly. I just didn't object when they said they were bringing an outsider in and it turned out to be you. Normally I wouldn't allow it. But ... well, we have history, don't we?'

'I guess we do. And if that idiot Varney hadn't rigged up some flash-bangs, I wouldn't have to be here. You'd have two ATOs of your own.'

'I'm well aware of that. I was there, remember. It just seemed fitting it was you who got the call. But I don't like having non-swimmers on my team.' He meant anyone who wasn't with SBS. 'I'll tolerate the Blades,' he nodded at the SAS. 'But you . . .'

'Not much we can do about it up here.'

Kebede fished in his pocket and handed a padded envelope to Riley. 'What's this? My cyanide pills?' If so it was a bloody big one.

'Take a look.'

Riley extracted a watch from within. It was an Omega Seamaster 300, with a rubberised NATO strap. On the caseback was the SBS motto: 'By Strength and Guile'.

'Not the latest version, I'm afraid.' He showed his timepiece, a newer Planet Ocean, 'but it was all I could rustle up at short notice.'

Riley took off his own watch, a Stowa Marine, and put it in the padded envelope. He fastened the Seamaster on his wrist and admired it in the dim light.

Kebede slapped him on the shoulder. 'Welcome to the Special Boat Service, Staff Sergeant Riley.'

*

There was a row of twenty cabins that had not been sold because the plumbing was faulty. Rather than delay the voyage, Anglo-American had decided to seal them off and forgo the revenue. The bomb sat on a table under the window – this was not a suite, but one of the budget cabins, so there was no balcony.

Jos Swart held his breath as he examined the device. It was a straightforward set-up. It looked something like the old Teasmade his parents used to set for their weekend cuppa. His father was Afrikaans but his mother was as British as cream teas. She had tried to bring a little bit of the Home Counties to Tokai. The Teasmade always sounded terrifying, like a steam engine that was about to blow, but she thought it was marvellous. His father, a die-hard coffee drinker, had tolerated it as one of his wife's homesick foibles. Swart wondered if Teasmades still existed outside his mum's bedroom.

Such a simple set-up, he mentally repeated as he traced the circuit again. Timer, in the form of a Casio digital watch, the Seventies type that had enjoyed a hipster-led revival of late. Detonator. Pack of explosive. Isolate the timer from the circuit, which was what the toggle switch was for, and it was just a piece of inert wire, steel, plastic and RDX. So, flick left for unarmed, right armed, timer initiated.

Do we think this is an inside job? that idiot Capelli had asked. Hell, yes. How else could so much have been achieved?

Here we go, he thought. Swart flipped the toggle switch to set the device counting down, which was, he had been told, set to a ten minute delay to give him time to get clear. His nervous system almost had time to register the blindingly, bright light blooming in front of him – and a fragment of the thought that he had been lied to – before the detonation transition swept all consciousness away in a blitz of screws, nuts and bolts.

*

The ship might be relatively new to Captain Harald Nansen but he already felt a keen familiarity with its rhythms and its cadences, even when it was nosing through roller-coaster seas. High on the bridge, six storeys above where the bomb had exploded, he felt a tremor run through the fabric of *Rapide*, transmitting through the soles of his feet and up his spine. He looked at the status screen as an alarm sounded, screeching until he hit mute. On the schematic of the ship, a section was pulsing red.

A noise continued to screech in his head until he managed to smother it. Blind panic wasn't going to help. Think. It could only be a detonation. The demonstration that had been promised by some maniac.

The watch officer came across. 'What was that?'

'It was something,' Nansen said as calmly as he could manage. 'In one of the empty cabins by the look of it.' Nansen picked up a radio and switched to emergency channel. 'Lazlo?'

'I see it. I'm on my way,' said the Georgian.

Jon Cappelli, the safety officer cut in. 'Lazlo, if there is no fire to be put out, do not enter the cabin.'

'Why?'

'If that is a bomb, there might be secondaries. Another device. Designed to kill the next guys in . . .'

'Shit, yes, not thinking straight.'

'Nobody do anything,' interrupted the captain. 'I'm on my way down. Jon, can you get the area sealed off? Tell any passengers in the area a Nespresso machine backfired or something.'

'They might not believe it when they see the smoke. I'm looking over the rail now. It's taken the window out.'

'I'll be two minutes,' said Nansen, already heading for the ladder and the lift.

When he reached the passageway in question, Lazlo was there wearing breathing apparatus. The two assistant firemen were in the doorway, having hosed down those flames that the sprinklers had missed. Lazy tendrils of smoke were drifting out of the cabin. Lazlo took off his breathing gear. 'You have no need to look. It wasn't a big bomb by the look of, but it must have killed him instantly.'

'Who?'

'Swart.'

His head of security? They had killed his security guy? He

realised he knew little about the man. Was he married? Children? He couldn't recall. He imagined trying to write a letter to his dependents. Nansen felt blood drain from his face and his world swam a little. There was a nausea deep in his guts, an echo of the seasickness which, thankfully, he no longer suffered from. The next few weeks fast forwarded, spooling before him. It was a nightmare.

He forced himself back to the present. 'What happened?'

'I don't know,' Lazlo admitted. 'I don't even know how the bomb was triggered. Could have been someone opening the door or him trying to move it. Or defuse it.'

'Is he really . . . ?'

Nansen went to step round the Georgian but the big man put a hand on his arm. 'Captain, I only recognised him by his clothing. It looks like he took the full force. Not pretty. There was metal in there. Projectiles. What do you want me to do, Captain?'

Nansen shook his head, trying to clear it of fog. He ran through his options. What if there was a second bomb, timed to go off just as they tried to shift the debris and take Swart's body to the morgue?

The word morgue was like a bucket of cold water to the face. He had a dead man, a murdered man, a crew member on his watch. Is that what he would be remembered for? 'Seal it up,' he said forcefully. 'Hammer a panel over the door. It's a crime scene. They'll need to sift through it.'

Do we think this is an inside job? Nansen looked round at the men in the corridor. Could it be one of them who did this? Who murdered Swart? Or any his crew? The thought was untenable. But he would have to face it sooner or later. There might be a killer, a traitor, on his ship.

'And what about Jos?' Lazlo asked.

'Leave him there until this bomb expert gets here.'

'When will that be?'

The captain studied his watch, his usual decorum momentarily deserting him. 'The sooner the fucking better.'

*

BaseHeart ran through the progress of the operation so far. As usual it had followed the old *Art of War* maxim: no plan survives contact with the enemy. It was when you showed your mettle. Initially, a scheme like the one involving *Rapide* was scored like a mighty symphony, with the right players and a fine conductor. The latter being him, of course. But even before *Rapide* set sail, the repertoire switched from the tightly scored classical world to the much freer musical landscape of jazz. Improvisation became the key word.

Take Swart. A very foolish man. You don't bullshit a bullshitter and you certainly don't blackmail a blackmailer. Or threaten to expose the whole enterprise unless your share is increased. The South African had decided he was worth double the original fee. So it was Swart's own actions that decided what type of device he would be asked to prime. The one that went off the moment you armed it. If he hadn't been so greedy, he might still be alive. But once BaseHeart realised what kind of man he was, how unreliable, he had to act. BaseHeart valued loyalty above all else. So Swart had to die, by his own hand, as it were.

Still, on a positive note, the death would make them take BaseHeart seriously. He had been very careful to make sure no link between him and Swart existed. Files had been purged, hard discs dunked in acid. Belt and braces, the best way. 'Brought it on himself,' he said to his daughter's picture.

167

He looked at the screen before him, showing *Rapide* making half-decent progress towards New York. As if she could outrun him, outrun the fate that awaited her. Not with another team still in place on board she couldn't.

TWENTY-NINE

Kate Muraski didn't go straight to her cabin and her bed after leaving Barbara to her new dance partner. She needed to blow away some foggy cobwebs first, she thought, as she stepped out on deck. The wind had abated, and although the sea was still churning, the waves weren't as tall as they had been. Still, it could have been worse: Barbara could have chosen something really stormy, like an Atlantic crossing. She gripped the rail, enjoying the cold and wet after the over-heated, stuffy interior. She watched goosebumps rise on her forearms; she was underdressed for a stroll on deck. But the chill felt invigorating.

She could see lights on the horizon, but she realised she had no idea how far the liner was into its voyage. *Thetis*, their ship, had made one stop so far, some remote point on the tip of Denmark called Skagen, but Barbara had not wanted to get off. Pretty red-roofed houses, windswept beaches, lots of birdwatching: she had read out the blurb from the Daily Bulletin in a voice dripping with ennui. 'Let's wait until Helsinki, dear,' she had said. 'That's a real destination. And on the way back, Copenhagen. A lovely city. Or Tallinn, which has its own charm. Besides, we'll have the ship to ourselves if we stay put this once.'

It seemed attractive at the time, the ship emptied of other

passengers, room to breathe and find a sense of uncrowded space on board. Now, of course, she was wondering if there was some other reason Barbara had kept her on board rather than going ashore. Was this the world Six inhabited, where nothing was ever played straight? Good Lord, Five was pretty good at dissembling, but she had a feeling the old lady had been – or maybe still was – a world champion at obfuscating. What on earth was she doing dancing with this Edith? Maybe with Henry gone she was free to explore a repressed sexuality. No, it wasn't that. She was momentarily forgetting how Machiavellian Barbara was. Edith was yet another pawn in her schemes. Muraski was certain that Barbara knew that poor woman would be on board.

Muraski felt someone standing behind her and caught the smell of lilacs on the breeze. It was Barbara, hand on a wall to steady herself against the motion of *Thetis*, one of her very occasional cigarettes between her lips. She removed it before she spoke. 'Not thinking of jumping?'

'It's not that bad an option,' she said, turning back to the rail.

'She's very nice. Edith. You'll like her.'

'I think I have it figured. She's a decoy isn't she? Same age, height, colouring.'

The older woman gave a smirk. 'She's a *potential* decoy.'

'You knew she would be here?'

'And that she was a widow, too. And that she liked ballroom dancing.'

'How on earth?'

'SOP.' Standard Operating Procedure.

Muraski felt like stamping her foot, like a little girl refused a pony for her birthday. She spun round to face the old woman. 'Barbara, you are the most annoying woman I have ever met. No, let me correct that. You are the most annoying *person* I have ever met.'

'Should I take that as a compliment?'

'No,' she spluttered. 'Why would you?'

Barbara tossed the cigarette over the rail and Muraski turned to watch the spark spiral away, lifted briefly by the wind until the waves extinguished it.

'I'm sorry. It's in my nature. What do you want to know?'

Muraski took a deep, calming breath. At bloody last, she thought. She had to be careful not to sound too greedy. She knew from recent bitter experience it would be all too easy to trigger another shutdown or pointless diversion from the old woman. 'Let's start at the beginning. You never told me you were married before Henry till recently. There was nothing I could find about an earlier marriage in your file. My guess it has been purged. Why? Tell me about Rory.'

'It's a long story.' She blinked as a spray of seawater swept over them. 'Shall we go inside?'

As she pulled open the door to the warmth of the ship's interior, Muraski said, 'He died, you said. Rory.'

Barbara turned and fixed her gaze on Muraski, almost staring her down. 'He did. Although strictly speaking, I murdered him.'

*

In his cabin, Nansen read aloud the announcement he would make over the public address system at around seven o'clock.

'Ladies and gentlemen, and those who prefer not be gender specific. I am sorry to interrupt your breakfast or beauty sleep.' He crossed the last two words out and inserted 'slumbers', then reverted to the original version. *'We have received a rather unusual request from the British government. Some of you may have witnessed the first part of this, in the rapid firefighting response training exercise undertaken during the night. I hope that didn't disturb too many of you. That routine test of our capabilities was very successful. However, as you will be aware,*

there has been an increase in maritime incidents and the UK government has asked if we would co-operate in an exercise by Special Forces, who want to run a scenario where they have to board a cruise liner out at sea. I have agreed that Rapide *would be available for such an exercise. I had confirmation during the night that Special Forces are en route. In order to facilitate the rendezvous, we will be cutting speed at some point, although not for too long, I hope. I will let you know when the troopers are expected to arrive, although, at the request of the British Ministry of Defence, I would ask that you do not take any photographs of any part of the exercise. These are highly trained elite forces who would rather not find themselves on Facebook or Instagram. I am sure you understand. Just to make sure nothing leaks out, I am afraid the internet will be taken off for a few hours starting immediately. I will update you as soon as I know more; in the meantime enjoy your morning.'*

He read it through again. *Bullshit*, it seemed to scream. Still, it was meant as nothing more than a sticking plaster. He had had terse conversations with Chamberlain of Anglo-American Lines. He was concerned about the impact of a dead security officer on the future of the company. A collapse of passenger confidence, even in the short term, would be disastrous. The fact that a man had died seemed to be a secondary concern to the co-CEO.

Nansen had told him the *QE2* had had a bomb scare and survived for another twenty-five years. Of course, nobody died during that incident. He would have to write to Swart's parents when this was all over. Not a nice task. But better than receiving the news that your son has died, as they eventually would. The thought of a body sealed in a cabin weighed heavily on him. As the captain, responsibility for the death stopped with him.

He had spoken to Mette, his wife. She had been surprised to hear from him.

'Is something wrong?'

'No, darling. Why should it be?'

She had laughed. 'You never ring mid-voyage.'

'Everything is fine. But if you hear anything, please don't worry.'

'Ha! Now you're worrying me.'

'There's just some publicity-seeker at work. But if they get wind of it, the press will blow it up.'

'It's not your brother?' she said, acerbically.

No love lost there. 'For once, no. How are the kids?'

'At school, where they belong.'

'Give them a hug for me when they get home. I love you, Mette.'

'Harald . . .' Her concern was palpable.

'I have to go. I'll call again soon.'

As always, he was left feeling as if he had not said the right thing. Like he had made matters worse.

There was a tap at the door of his cabin and Truluck's head appeared. 'Sorry, Skip. Two things. There's a personal call for you on bridge satphone.'

Chamberlain again? Not so soon, surely. 'Who is it?'

'Your brother.'

Jakob, with impeccable timing as always. Maybe Mette had a sense about these things. 'Is he still on the line?' Burning money on expensive phone calls.

'No. He asked you to call him back.'

'Call him and tell him I shall speak to him in New York, not before.'

Truluck nodded, having expected that response.

'What else?'

'London has been in touch. They've had a confirmation of the ransom demand.'

Nansen folded the draft announcement and slipped it into his pocket. 'I'll be right up.'

THIRTY

As always when he needed to relax before an op, Riley had plugged himself into his phone and, rather than the usual Radiohead or Nirvana, he listened to an audiobook. It was never a novel. He didn't trust much made-up stuff and hated the twisty murder mysteries that seemed so popular. The last one he had listened to ended up with the villain slicing the nipples off the female investigator. He had seen enough body parts in his time to not need gratuitous and titillating descriptions of mutilation. And a large number of them seemed to concern missing children, something that, given his own situation, made him sick to his stomach. It was as if the authors were exploiting his grief. So he was drawn towards military history books, events he could be sure really did happen.

This time he had chosen *Vietnam* by Max Hastings, narrated by the author who, as a young journalist, had actually covered the conflict. He had just reached the debacle at Da Nang when he was aware of movement in front of him. He opened his eyes. The cargo bay was bathed in red light. The 'on your marks' signal for the drop.

It was Kebede standing in front of him, one hand gripping the webbing as the Herc bucked in mid-Atlantic turbulence. Riley pulled out his earbuds.

'Okay, Staff?'

'Yes, Skip,' he said. 'How long?'

'About forty minutes to run. You need to double-check anything?'

Riley glanced over at Capes, Tremaine and Norwell, all of whom had assault rifles or pistols on their laps. It was a tic among elite forces; for these guys, a personal weapon can never be cleaned or put through their paces often enough. As at least two of them would have his back – in Norwell's case, he'd probably be on electronics duty most of the time – it was a habit Riley approved of.

'I'm good,' he said to Kebede. Riley would go through his gear once they were on the ship. Which was, of course, the main mountain to climb as far as he was concerned – getting onto *Rapide*. He was impressed by how calm Kebede looked, on the outside at least. Maybe, like Riley, he was compartmentalising the thought that in less than an hour they would be falling through the sky into a very hostile environment – the Atlantic in a less-than-welcoming mood. There, he had done it now. Opened the door to that cupboard in his brain. 'How's the weather at the drop zone?'

Kebede's mouth tightened, briefly, into a grimace. 'There's a Yank up there,' his eyes rolled to indicate the sky above the C-130. 'Giving us the SP.'

'Let me guess. Bright with sunny intervals?'

Kebede laughed, but there was no humour in it. 'It sounds like one of the gloomier Radio 4 shipping forecasts.'

'The ones about dogging and biting Germans?'

'You should stay off those kind of porn sites, Staff. Seas are moderate to rough, which means waves up to eight metres, although they are currently below that, wind gusting up to 30 knots and the cloud ceiling is about 80 metres.'

'Eighty metres? We'll be jumping blind?' The lowest safe height for a LALO in poor conditions with unpredictable wind was about 250 metres, although it had been done as low as 150. Either way, they would have to exit the plane and deploy above the clouds, without being able to see the target.

'At the moment, yes. This crate has a SIGMA Thermal Imaging system in a Titan 385 turret under the aircraft's nose. It'll give us a good picture of the ship. But as you know, nothing beats a proper visual.'

Which they wouldn't have as they were falling through space. Riley put his weight against the open door in his cerebrum and tried to close it. It wouldn't budge. Snapshots of himself lost in a dark, oily sea, with only towering walls of water for company, came through the portal, unbidden. The plane shuddered in sympathy and he felt his stomach rise as the Herc dropped though an empty pocket of sky. 'If we land too far from the ship . . .'

Kebede nodded, indicating he was well aware of what being lost in an Atlantic chop meant. He wasn't about to dwell on that. 'We'll be fine. I'll give you the signal to get into the dry suit in ten.'

'Roger that.'

'Oh, and Obi told me they finally have the ransom demand.'

Riley looked around for the DSF man. He was obviously up front with the pilots. 'What do they want?'

'Something called the Black Key.'

PART THREE

THIRTY-ONE

On board the Hercules that was powering at close to its maximum speed across the Atlantic, Riley struggled into the dry suit. As he pulled up the over-sized watertight zip, Obi swayed across to him. Both held on to grab handles and rode the invisible cobbles the C-130 was bumping over. 'Staff, a quick word,' said Obi. The DSF man took off his comms and indicated that Riley do the same, then he led Riley to the rear of the fuselage, standing on the ramp that would soon open like a toothless maw to release them into turbulent skies.

He had to shout over the racket of the Herc's engines, but even so Riley doubted his voice reached the others. 'There's something that Captain Kebede didn't tell you, because the situation wasn't clear. As threatened, a device has detonated on board *Rapide*.'

'Shit.' Well, they had promised some kind of demonstration to show that they weren't bluffing. Riley groaned internally. Deep down, he had hoped this was all some elaborate hoax. He could wrap it up, get home, get on with leaning on O'Donnell in Ireland. *He was wasting time.*

A modicum of professionalism returned. Whatever the situation was, he had to deal with it before he could get back home. 'Damage?'

'It was a small bomb. Mostly confined to a single cabin.'

'Casualties?'

'One fatality.'

Riley shook his head in annoyance. 'Civilian or crew?'

'Crew. The security officer.'

'Don't tell me. Thought he could do my job.' It had happened a lot in Afghan. Regular soldiers who had watched *Lethal Weapon 3* or DVDs of *Danger UXB* and thought they didn't need an ATO to make a device safe. They were almost inevitably wrong.

'We don't know,' said Obi. 'All we do know for sure is, he's dead.'

'What's the status of the site?'

'The captain ordered the cabin sealed. With the victim still inside. He's waiting for specialist advice.' He pointed a finger at Riley. 'That's you.'

Riley nodded his approval. He felt sad at a needless death, but they should probably have sealed the cabin and piled mattresses up against the door the moment they discovered something. 'This isn't public knowledge?'

'No. If nothing else, the news of a bomb threat, explosion and murder on board could kill the cruise industry stone dead. Travellers are very fickle these days. And shareholders.'

Riley wasn't overly concerned about the health of the cruise business. He was worried about what the fuck the perps were up to. 'Anything else from the people doing this?'

'Just that they want action within' – he checked the time – 'about six hours. Assuming you are on board within the hour, that gives you . . . almost no time at all. Not on a ship that size.'

'Do you know what this Black Key is yet?' Riley asked.

Obi shrugged. 'It's not really clear. But as far as we can tell, it's a way of accessing all the money in the world.'

'All?'

Obi smiled. 'Well. A big chunk of it. It's something to do with cybercurrency. It's immaterial to us right now. Our job is to nip this whole thing in the bud. If we can.'

It sounded to Riley like they had already moved beyond that stage. A man was dead. The bud was already flowering.

THIRTY-TWO

COBRA met again in the bleak, early hours of the grey London dawn to discuss the latest developments in the *Rapide* crisis. As he waited to be called in, Clive Greggs sat in the anteroom, fiddling with his Mont Blanc pen and cursing his bad luck and poor life choices. Previous PMs looked down on him from the walls, all apparently damning in their judgement. His slide into ignominy and despair at the hands of the sadist calling himself BaseHeart had begun when he had accepted an invitation to a 'discreet' party at a country pile near Northampton. It had been put on for a TV personality who had managed to duck Operation Yewtree, an American Silicon Valley millionaire and a Qatari prince, the very one who had given him the F430. Nowhere on the invitation did it state that it was going to be a cross between a Berlusconi bunga-bunga party and one of Jeffery Epstein's 'soirees'.

This was before Greggs was in the Cabinet Office, but there was no statute of limitations on being a fucking idiot, he thought.

One photo. One stupid photo.

It could ruin a career. Ask US Senator Al Franken, scuppered by a picture of him apparently about to fondle the breasts of a sleeping woman. Never mind the 'victim' had a flak jacket on.

Ignore the fact it was a reference to a skit the pair had performed on a USO tour. Career in the toilet and flushed.

Okay, so his photograph was more graphic. And rather than comic intent, it was serious action. And it turned out there was more than one; a whole catalogue of them, in fact. And video tape, now transferred to digital. How was he to know she was fifteen? Christ, the thought of it brought prickles out on his forehead. The headlines. The devoted wife standing by her husband (would she?). The dazed children – young adults now – dealing with a very public scandal. The chances of a lucrative post-political career in the City? Zero.

'Mr Greggs?' A fresh faced young aide, not much older than Xanthe, was standing over him. He pushed his concerns to the dark corner where they lived. 'They're ready to start now.'

*

In the absence of the Minister of Defence, who was attending the much-delayed launch of the Navy's latest aircraft carrier, COBRA was chaired by Sir Keith Millner, the National Security Advisor.

As well as the usual suspects, two naval communication technicians were also present, sitting behind Sir Keith, leaning over laptops, headphones in place as they monitored communications from the ship, the circling Pioneer and the Hercules.

Sir Keith called the meeting to order, although in truth nobody was in a particularly talkative mood at that hour, and he ran through the events of the night. 'So, to summarise, we have one casualty and we have a ransom demand for this Black Key. I'm waiting for details on what exactly it unlocks and we have a response almost in place.'

'This is still not public knowledge on *Rapide*?' asked Carlyle of Six.

'No,' said Sir Keith. 'There is a blackout on all comms on the ship, apart from the bridge and the radio room.'

'What response to the ransom demand?' asked Stavely.

'The captain is in discussions,' said Sir Keith. 'Our recommendation to him is the usual one. No monies to paid to terrorists or criminals.'

Sir Keith turned to the DSF. 'How long until your people are in position?'

The DSF frowned. 'Not too long now. But listen to this.' He caught the technicians' attention. 'Play the recording, please.' Then, back to the table: 'You are about to hear secure communications between Major James Olsen, who is piloting a Poseidon P-8A long-range maritime reconnaissance plane above the incident area, and Group Captain Collinson of 47 Squadron at the controls of the Hercules.'

The tech pressed buttons and voices came over the loudspeaker.

'Jackdaw Five, this is Freebird One-Twelve again. Over.'

'Jackdaw Five receiving you. Go ahead Freebird One-Twelve. Over.'

'We are tracking you, Jackdaw. Estimate twenty minutes to your DZ. Over.'

'Confirm that. Over.'

'I wish I could tell you that things got better, weather-wise. We have the target on our instruments. But no visual. Repeat, no visual. Cloud ceiling estimated below 200 feet now. Over'

'Roger that.'

'Too low, eh? Over.'

They heard Collinson laugh. *'That's not really my decision. Do you have contact with the target? Over.'*

'Yes. We can patch you straight through. Over.'

'Appreciated. I'll take a look before we do anything. I'll let you know our thinking. Over.'

'Understood. Freebird One-Twelve out.'

'Our problem here,' said the DSF, 'is that the cloud base is very low for a LALO over water. With the winds and waves so unpredictable, there are real risks.'

'What are you saying?' asked Sir Keith irritably. 'That this is Mission bloody Impossible?'

'Not at all,' countered the DSF. 'More like Mission Not Everybody Might Make It.'

'We'd best make sure the ATO makes it on board that damned ship,' said Stavely grimly, 'or it's all been a waste of time.'

'And money,' said Greggs, mainly to himself.

They were pondering this when the door to Room C opened and a flustered looking Quentin Cobb, Director of Counter-Terrorism at MI5, entered. 'Sorry I'm late, ladies and gentlemen.' His head swivelled to take in the assembled bodies. 'What do you think?'

'Of what?' asked Sir Keith.

Cobb composed himself, realising he had knowledge the others didn't yet possess. 'I've just had a call from Frank Gardner at the BBC asking for a response to the crisis on *Rapide* and rumours of the death of a crew member. It's common knowledge now, apparently, at least among journos like Gardner. Which means it'll be all over the media soon.' He sat down at a spare place, poured himself a glass of water and drank. He examined each of his colleagues in turn, trying not to look too accusatory. 'Gentlemen, we have to face facts. COBRA has sprung a leak.'

Luckily for him, nobody around the table noticed the colour draining from Greggs' cheeks.

THIRTY-THREE

Nansen invited the Ledgard party to breakfast in his cabin to discuss what he described to them as a highly sensitive matter. Apart from Christian Ledgard and his wife Shelby, there was the ever-taciturn Ben Clark (but no Amber X, it being explained that the hour was unholy to her) and Jim, the Ledgard's security advisor, but no Reece as there was no call for the mechanic at this meeting.

With the RAF plane closing fast, *Rapide* had throttled right back. It meant that she was even more at the mercy of the waves and she was moving with a pitching, wayward movement, like she had drunk too much the night before. There were horizontal rain streaks on the panoramic windows that looked out onto the uncooperative ocean.

It was Shelby Ledgard who spoke first, her husband's attention momentarily held by the harpoon from the *Fram* that Jakob had given him, which he had had mounted on a shelf. She was devoid of her usual make-up, the hair was pulled back into a ponytail and her lips, now devoid of lipstick, looked less like inflated inner tubes. Nansen thought she appeared more attractive than the buffed-up model, but this stripped-back version probably wouldn't translate into 2D phone screens quite so well. And being 2D-friendly was important in this modern world. 'That was bullshit, wasn't it?' she said.

'What was, Mrs Ledgard?'

'All that PR bollocks over the tannoy. The exercise that is taking place. What the fuck is going on?'

'I think the captain is trying to keep a lid on a difficult situation,' said Jim quietly. 'Perhaps to avoid panic among the passengers?'

Nansen welcomed the less hysterical tone. He confirmed the diagnosis with a nod.

'You know my first duty is to protect my principals?' Jim added, nodding at the Ledgards.

'And ours is to protect all passengers,' said the captain.

'We're not going to make New York in time, then?' asked Ledgard. He had taken off his sunglasses and his eyes looked small and porcine. When Nansen didn't answer, he said, 'For fuck's sake.' His fist hit the table, spilling coffee. 'I'll sue your bloody shipping line.'

'Jesus, Chris,' said Clark. 'Let the man speak. We can always leapfrog a stage or two. It's just a stupid car race. It's not the end of the fucking world.'

Ledgard gave a petulant sneer and took a bite out of a pastry. 'Come on then,' he said, showing Nansen a mouthful of partially chewed Danish.

'This was received by the Anglo-American office about an hour and a half ago.' Nansen pushed a piece of paper across to each of them in turn and let them read it. There was a rap at the door. 'Come in.'

It was Truluck. He showed surprise at the gathering and appeared lost for words.

'Yes?'

'Alpha tender ready to launch.' This was the most powerful of the lifeboats, with two 170 hp diesels, which could manage 8 to 10 knots, still bright orange, still pretty unsinkable, but shaped like a more conventional cutter. Unlike the other lifeboats, it came with a fridge usually stocked with champagne. It was designated as the preferred transfer vessel for VIPs. 'On your mark.'

'I'll be on the bridge shortly. Thank you, number two. Anything else?'

'Your brother.'

'I told you, do not bother me with him. Not now of all times.'

'Yes, Captain.'

Truluck disappeared. The captain turned his attention back to the group at his table. Nobody was touching their breakfast now. It seemed blackmail was a great appetite suppressant.

'You have to be shitting me,' said Shelby Ledgard.

Her husband simply shook his head.

'Doesn't make sense,' offered Clark.

'You understand this, Captain?' Jim asked.

'Only superficially.'

The bodyguard read out loud a section of the ransom demand. *If you wish* Rapide *to reach New York in one piece, you will instruct Christian Ledgard to hand over the four code sequences that make up the Black Key.*

'And the Black Key allows access to your money?'

Ledgard snorted at his ignorance. 'You can't be fuckin' serious? Is this a joke?'

'No joke. I need to know the answer.'

'You know the Winkelvoss twins?' asked Clark.

'They invented Facebook and Zuckerberg stole it?'

'That's the reductive version. They hired him to do some coding on a prototype, which he turned into The Facebook.

Eventually they received a sixty-five-million-dollar settlement, part of which they put into Bitcoin, the cybercurrency.'

'I think I knew that.'

Clark nodded. 'They rode the ups and downs of Bitcoin; at one point they were billionaires. Probably are again, now it's bounced back in favour. But in order to resist the temptation to bail when the going got rough, and to thwart hackers, they split the code to their wealth into four sections, buried away in electronic vaults across the world. Chris here did something similar. But the Black Key isn't just virtual money. It's the instructions for mining more Klondike.'

'I see,' said Nansen, although he didn't quite. He knew what Bitcoin was, but Jakob had once tried to explain blockchain to him – this from a man who almost invested in OneCoin, which was a glorified Ponzi scheme – but it remained as opaque as coal. 'And can't you just change the code?'

'No,' snapped Christin Ledgard, as if he had just been asked a particularly stupid question. 'Klondike is not set up like that.'

'How is it set up?' asked Nansen.

'The Black Keys, together, form a particular algorithm to generate a series of equations. You need supercomputers. Lots of powerful supercomputers to solve the equations that the codes generate. Once they do, you can mine more of the currency. It also gives access to existing reserves. In theory, you could be very rich. In practice, we could find out who is doing the mining and where the new Klondike comes from, know what I mean? There's digital fingerprints all over it, if you know where to look.' He stuck out his lower lip. 'Anyway, they can fuck right off. I'm not giving anyone the Black Key.'

Shelby Ledgard put a hand on her husband's forearm. 'No key is any good to you at the bottom of the ocean.'

Ledgard looked a little green and began to chew his lip. Nansen realised the man wasn't really afraid of flying. He was afraid of dying.

His wife fixed Nansen with a penetrating gaze that said: *don't lie to me.* 'Tell me, Captain, how hard would it be to sink this ship?'

'All ships can sink,' Nansen said. 'It is foolish to think otherwise. But you'd need a very big bomb. She would need to be ripped along one side.' Like the *Titanic*, he thought. But that sank because of poor quality rivets that allowed the hull to peel open like the skin of an orange and flood six 'watertight' compartments that had transverse bulkheads which weren't high enough to be effective. None of this applied to *Rapide*. But it didn't pay to be cocky – as he had said, all ships were vulnerable in one way or another.

'Even if we didn't sink,' he continued, 'which I believe we wouldn't, limping into New York harbour with a hole in our side would devastate this company and the cruise business in general.'

'Your point being?' Jim asked.

'That I hand over the locations and combinations to build the Black Key, just to keep your shipping line afloat?' said Ledgard, in a manner that suggested he would do no such thing.

'My point being, that it is in all our interests that we find any bomb on board and make sure it doesn't go off.'

'And we do that how?' asked Clark.

Nansen stood. 'If you'll excuse me. The very best hope we have of success is about to drop from the sky.'

THIRTY-FOUR

It was a strange moment to be thinking about Kate Muraski. Izzy and Ruby, yes, because he was well aware of the deep well of guilt he felt that he had temporarily abandoned the search for them. It was no good telling himself this jump was his duty, that it was for the greater good. He should be in Ireland. Those two were rarely far from his thoughts. In fact, he sometimes had to remind himself that Izzy was his *ex*-wife. He was having trouble recalling why they had separated in the first place.

But as he held onto the webbing, an image of Muraski came to him unbidden, lying next to a pool on the cruise ship, sunglasses on top of her head, a cocktail and as yet untouched paperback on the deck beside her. She was busy rubbing suntan lotion into already brown legs. He blinked the image away.

Friends, he reminded himself.

Breezy stepped in front of him and did up and tightened the straps of his chute. He gave him a thumbs up. 'You're good to go, Staff.'

With dry suit and the chute on they were all too bulky to sit in the bucket seats. Three last things to do. They had yet to put on the neoprene hoods, then they had to attach their Bergens to their ankles with a cord and finally hook up the static line that would deploy their canopies. They had one shot at this. Given the height, Kebede had explained, it was pointless carrying a reserve. Anything went wrong with the main canopy and they were going to hit that water with a force that would break every bone in their bodies.

But the light was still red, not green. So, they put off the final rigging. Riley was aware the Herc was circling and he could feel the airframe twisting as winds buffeted it. They were obviously directly over the drop zone. To say he wasn't looking forward to that ramp opening was an understatement.

He heard Obi's voice in his ears. 'Gentlemen, the captain would like to address you. We're patching him though now.'

'This is Group Captain John Collinson from the flight deck.'

He had those plummy tones you expected from a British Airways pilot at the controls of Speedbird One. For some reason, it was the only time that a public-school accent was welcome to Riley. Too many old war movies on wet Sunday afternoons growing up with his grandfather, listening to the laconic, stiff upper lips of Kenneth More or Richard Todd, perhaps. In most cases such RP accents made him think 'Rupert'. But from upfront of a Hercules it was oddly reassuring. Even if they were unlikely to fly into a flock of ME-109s or bomb the Möhne dam.

'As you may know, we've got a friendly eye in the sky above us. They've been keeping us informed of conditions which, to be frank, are not ideal.' Riley laughed at this downplaying of the hazardous conditions. *'We have another slight problem. Our thermal imaging is slightly on the fritz.'*

Riley watched as eyes rolled. Every man would be familiar with fancy kit which arrived late, over budget, and then didn't work as described. Everything from the latest night-vision goggles up to the RAF's F-35B Lightning had suffered from CAFFU – Cost A Fortune and it's Fucking Useless – syndrome. The gear nearly always got fixed eventually, but only after more time and money was ploughed into 'tertiary development'. Or what they would call snagging in the building industry.

'We can't stabilise the image. But even if we could, I'm reluctant to rely solely on remote sensing on this one. I am proposing to go down through the cloud cover and take a look. This will involve a parabolic dive. Which is a way of saying steep dive and ascent. My aim will be to repeat this for the actual jump, opening the ramp on the way back up so that you, uh, simply fall out of the rear of the plane.'

Simply fall out?

'Just make sure every bit of kit is tied down. That includes you. I don't want any flying toolboxes or people, okay? And I wouldn't be telling the truth if I didn't say there is some risk to the integrity of the airframe, given the forces involved.'

'What's the worst that can happen, Skip?' asked Capes, voicing the question everyone wanted to ask but didn't want answered.

Collinson gave a mirthless laugh. 'The bloody wings could come off.'

*

Nansen listened to what the Hercules pilot had to say and signed off, wishing him good luck. He told Truluck to stand by for pick-up and glanced down at the sketch he had done of what the squadron leader proposed. Yet again, he was pleased he came from a family of seafarers, not aviators.

He looked out of the window at the flat, low cloud and the restless waves. He had long given up cursing the weather when it didn't behave as required. It was a rookie mistake to feel that the sea or the sky had any personal gripe against you. They were neutral; you didn't register. To try to conquer the elements was all part of humankind's hubris, the sense that everything, even the tides and the winds, could be bent to its whim. It didn't take a particularly lengthy apprenticeship at sea to realise the folly of such an attitude.

He moved over to the starboard side of the bridge. This was

where the aircraft would appear, once the pilot had prepared the on-board team for the manoeuvre. He should probably make another announcement, giving notice of what was about to unfold.

After consultation with Hugh Chamberlain and with the various agencies that made up COBRA in London, it had been decided to ask Ledgard to make a series of bogus codes that could be substituted for the real Black Key. Ledgard was insistent the blackmailers would be expecting such a move, but London said if he didn't do it they would get GCHQ to examine Klondike in depth. The subtext being it would strip the secrets out of the cybercurrency, perhaps even make them public. The phoney Black Key ciphers, the spooks argued, would at least keep this BaseHeart busy while they tried to establish who he was.

So, at that very moment, Christian Ledgard was busy coding.

Whatever that meant.

Nansen grabbed the binoculars and stepped outside, bracing himself as the wind swirling around the superstructure tugged at him. He leant against the rail and put the Zeiss bins to his eyes. Above the roar of the elements he reckoned he could make out the thrum of the C-130's engines. He decided not to make any more announcements to the passengers. Those who caught the event would do so by accident rather than design. Probably. He had asked for no photos to be taken, but he knew that human desire to record every moment on a phone overrode all other considerations.

He heard the engine pitch change. A thrum became an impatient rising scream. He imagined the nose of the Hercules dipping, the throttles being pushed forward. What on earth was it like being on board a dive-bombing transport plane?

*

Riley thought he was going to be sick. He really didn't look well. There was a definite green tinge to his skin, as if to say: I didn't sign up for this. Riley, like all of them, was strapped to the webbing that lined the cargo area, jammed against the ribs of the metal fuselage and holding on for grim life. He gave the Kermit-coloured Norwell a thumbs up. It was more a question than a statement. Norwell managed a nod and a thin smile. Yup, thought Riley, the guy is definitely going to puke.

And they hadn't even begun the dive yet.

When it came, it announced itself with a sudden lurch, a screech of engines, the rapid tilt of the floor beneath their feet and then the certainty that they were all going to die. Riley felt himself forced backwards. It was a strange sensation. They were falling, yet if he let go he would be flung to the rear of the plane.

'Jesus fucking Christ,' someone said.

Riley reached up and clicked off the comms, just for the duration of the parabola the plane was performing. He had his own cursing and blasphemy to be getting on with. He wondered how Obi, up front with the pilots, would be faring, as the giant transport headed for the clouds like a Stuka bomber. He hoped the man had his eyes closed.

And then he was weightless, his feet heading up towards the ceiling. He tightened his grip. His restraining straps straightened and dug into him.

The floor came up again and the engines gave a metallic gasp of relief and the plane levelled out. Riley let out the breath he had been holding in. He took in a fresh lungful as the four Allison turboprops began to growl once more, and the plane tilted again, the nose lifting, the tail dropping, making Riley's stomach perform confused somersaults.

The fuselage began to shudder as maximum power was applied

and Riley had the sensation they were going backwards, sliding back down out of the sky.

Norwell vomited.

Riley pressed himself against the curve of the plane's skin as the mixture was propelled down the cargo bay and splattered like wet hailstones against the rear bulkhead.

And then they were levelling off again, the madness subsiding, the plane seemingly panting with relief, like a sprinter after breaking the tape. Riley switched on the comms once more.

'—and you can clean that mess up, you dirty bastard.' Breezy seemed to have lost his sense of humour.

'*Group Captain Collinson here again from the flight deck. Apologies for any discomfort just then. You'll be pleased to know the old girl held up well. Rapide was exactly where we expected. The good news is, I reckon we can get you within easy pick-up distance. The bad news is we've got to do that all over again. For real, this time.*'

THIRTY-FIVE

Nansen felt someone beside him at the rail. Sajiv, the Officer of the Watch. Technically speaking the OOTW should not be outside but a few metres away on the bridge, but Nansen was well aware that they were about to witness something special. Even over the wind they could hear the engine noise shift and a screaming, banshee wail that built and built until the sounds of the sea were swamped by the howl of stressed mechanical systems.

The enormous plane didn't so much dive through the clouds as simply appear, as if it had deactivated one of those cloaking devices from a sci-fi movie. Sajiv gasped as it materialised in front of them, if not close enough to touch, near enough, it felt, to be hit with a well-aimed rock.

Now the racket of the Allison engines felt like it might scramble their brains. It also appeared the Hercules was doomed, plummeting towards waves that were reaching up to grab it in a fatal embrace.

And then the nose lifted, the plane gave an enormous shudder, as if it were reluctant to break out of its suicidal trajectory, and, at first agonizingly slowly, then, for the last few degrees, more rapidly, it finally straightened into level flight.

Nansen could just make out a few ragged cheers from those

passengers who had braved the cold and wet to see what all the fuss, and racket, was about. But it was a congratulations too soon.

The note from the four turbo-props increased once more, from a relieved drone to a roar, like they were in pain. The front of the C-130 pointed heavenward, the tail drooped, so low it was within striking distance of the bigger waves, and, as if pulled on a string, it was jerked up into the clouds and disappeared. The engine noise faded behind the grey blanket.

'Good grief,' said Sajiv.

'I know,' said Nansen, turning to go back in and speak to the pilot. 'At this precise moment, I've never been more grateful to be a sailor.'

*

The SBS and SAS men on the C-130 were, by any definition, brave men. Some might say Riley was, too, given his day job involved making explosive devices safe. But every man in that cargo hold, including Breezy, the jumpmaster, looked pale and shaken.

Riley tried to think of something witty or eloquent to say. In the end he managed just two words. 'Fuck me.'

'You know what, Staff?' said Capes. 'I think I would fuck you, rather than do that again.'

But they did have to do it one more time. With the ramp door open, looking out into empty space. Riley shook his head, trying to clear the image. Christ, it was exactly the same feeling as standing on the high dive board at his hated boarding school, pupils and teachers yelling at him to dive: *you coward, you chump, you spineless tub of lard.* From up there, it looked as if it was possible to actually miss the postage stamp pool. It felt like he was on that edge for hours, when in reality it was probably less than a minute. In the end, the taunts echoing around his skull, he had closed his eyes, convincing himself the board was much lower than in reality. And he had done it, after a fashion. Not just a nose-holding jump like most of his classmates, but a proper dive. He was no Tom Daley, but it had won him a round of grudging applause. So, he had to treat this parachute jump as a repeat of that. With, he thought, one bonus. *There's no way I can miss the sodding Atlantic.*

Riley sensed the plane banking. They were coming around again. Breezy was already out of his harness, issuing each man with a lightweight helmet with quick-release strap. 'We really need these?' Riley asked.

'We can't guarantee you won't bang your head on the way out,' said Kebede, in a voice less steady than before the dive. 'Not in the middle of our little party trick.'

'Put it on over the neoprene hood, please,' added Breezy. 'You can ditch it once you are clear of the plane if you wish, but it will offer some protection if, say, your Bergen lands on your head. Or someone else's does.'

'Fair one.'

'Flight deck again. Hope that wasn't too uncomfortable. It worked fine for us. We'll go again. Once we change Jocko's shorts.' Riley assumed Jocko was the co-pilot. At least, being in a windowless cargo bay, they were spared the sight of the cold Atlantic filling the windshield. *'We reckon we can get your DZ within a few hundred metres of the ship, so you shouldn't be drifting round for too long. They're launching the tender as we speak. So, kit up, clip on and get ready.'* The light turned from red to amber. *'Good luck, everyone.'*

Kebede moved them down the interior to where the enormous rear cargo door hinged onto the main fuselage of the Hercules. They clipped themselves onto the metal wires usually used for the static line and then onto the post that would prevent them dropping before they were ready. On a high-altitude deployment

(HALO) the jumper free falls and pulls their chute at the appropriate height. On this jump there wasn't the time or height for fancy skydiving. One less thing to worry about. He made sure the straps attaching his ankle to his kit bag were clear, free from any potential entanglements. Behind him he was aware of the others taking their places.

The SBS captain tapped him on the helmet as the plane's engines began the urgent growl of descent. Riley gave him a thumbs up.

They both braced as the Herc tipped over, as if they were in a car at the top of a rollercoaster. The same butterflies, the same lurch in the stomach. But no fairground ride ever vibrated like the diving C-130 as it dropped through the sky. It seemed every rivet was dancing in its housing. Riley's teeth began to chatter in unison. He clamped his jaw shut as the weightlessness hit him and he felt his feet lose contact with metal.

Kebede looked over as he, too, floated free. His face was impassive. Riley tried to keep his equally neutral. He wasn't sure he succeeded.

Then gravity hit again and the plane began to shudder as the pilot pulled the big beast away from its suicidal plunge. It bucked and twitted, as if trying to free itself from an unwanted grip. The engines screeched in protest too, but eventually it levelled out and the Allisons gave a roar of triumph. Riley felt like joining it. That gave them a few precious seconds of respite. Riley tried to relax his neck and shoulder muscles, to get some saliva back in his mouth. They had a brief window of respite before the climb began.

Riley let out his breath. If he was going to die, then . . . Fuck it, he wasn't going to die. He still had things to do.

The nose lifted and Riley had to steady himself again. A new mechanical sound and the huge rear flap that was the cargo door inched open. The wind came then, swirling in, plucking at them, as if greedy to pull them out. As the gap widened he could see the iron grey of the ocean below, a featureless sheet of burnished metal from that height.

The ramp dropped a few more metres and now the sea was disappearing behind whips of milky fog as they entered the cloud base. The angle of ascent steepened, so that the plane was almost standing on its tail. The fuselage was twisting under the torque, the panels groaning as if in pain. The amber light turned green and began to flash. They were dangling vertically. Kebede unclipped them both from the post and Riley was sliding feet-first through the air, and he was spat out into space, struggling to orientate himself, get his arms out, legs straight. Kebede was below and slightly to his right, perfectly streamlined, head up, shoulders back, the lines holding his kit stretched out behind him, falling like he was in a fucking Marvel superhero film.

Riley, closer to an ironing board than Iron Man, managed to stabilise so that he was in a controlled fall, although as the wind slapped at him he felt like he was being hit by invisible rubber hammers.

The long static line finally tensioned above him and he felt the chute jerk out of its case. He watched Kebede's deploy, from folded handkerchief to bell-shaped canopy in an instant. Riley felt the straps dig into his crotch and he seemed to rise up, as if the parachute wanted to take him back to the Hercules.

Then, that euphoria that he had cheated death, that his equipment had saved him, plummeting through the sky into the ocean.

Immediately below was the cloud. He checked his altimeter and the pulsing green light that showed him the auto-release mechanism for the straps was working. The cosseting silence that envelopes every jumper, all sounds muffled as if in snowfall – the transient peace that kept people going up and jumping out of small planes – was quickly broken by an alien noise cracking across the sky. He pulled a line to spin the chute.

Behind him, to his left, he heard another foreign sound, the brutal noise of metal ripping as if it were paper, followed by the shriek of mechanical distress. He moved the chute again, too roughly this time, and he swung like a human pendulum, back and forth. Against the wild buffeting of the wind, he managed to turn his head and take in the hell unfolding above him.

THIRTY-SIX

Nansen stepped outside once more, binoculars at the ready to watch the Hercules do its stuff for real this time. The wind had dropped slightly and was no longer whistling mournfully around the superstructure. It meant he had a clearer sense of the aircraft's engine pitch, and it was already at its dive volume. This time the sound of the propellers appeared to envelope the ship. Was it above him? Would it suddenly appear over his head? He wasn't going to recommend a medal if the idiot took off the stack and masts. Nansen could see the Alpha tender working its way towards the presumed drop zone. As it made its yawing progress, it gave scale to the size of the waves. Nansen wouldn't want to be jumping into them.

Then the amorphous racket shifted and focused to off the starboard side. The Hercules poked its bulbous front through the cloud more gradually on this run, as if he really had found a set of airbrakes. Nansen used the binoculars to scan the plane as it punched a hole through the clouds, juddered, and then swooped into its last-second recovery, pointing its nose skyward once more.

Nansen scanned the space from which the C-130 had

disappeared with engines screaming. Any second now he knew he would see the first two 'sticks' of parachutists appear.

The next sound he heard was like twigs snapping. Then a screech of tortured metal. Something emerged from the clouds, but it wasn't human. For a brief, hopeful fraction of a second he thought the long cylinder with the whirling disc on the top was a large drone. But even before it hit the waves, sending up a perfect circle of white spray that looked like a watery crown, he knew it was no unmanned surveillance machine.

It was an Allison turboprop engine.

The rest of the C-130 followed in a nightmare played out to Nansen in scratchy black and white, as if he was watching some old film footage, like the fiery death of the *Hindenburg*. Maybe that was some sort of self-protection. This is historic, ancient. Not happening now. The fact that it was real and current kicked in while he studied the doomed plane, which appeared belly first, spinning like a giant metal sycamore seed.

As the entire airframe cleared the clouds, Nansen could see that one of the wings, the one missing the turboprop, had folded up, vertically. The rear cargo door was open, sagging like a boxer's broken jaw. There was no way any pilot could save the stricken monster.

A cry of anguish came from Nansen's mouth. He imagined he could hear a matching chorus of dismay, this one a low, collective groan, from below him as unlucky passengers witnessed the terrible scene.

The cargo door caught the water first, was torn off and sent cartwheeling away. Then the Hercules belly-flopped with the sound of a flat hand slapping water, followed by a loud squeal of metal. It settled and wallowed, still afloat, but sinking fast as the rear compartment flooded. The sea was taking her.

Already the Alpha tender was steering a course towards it. Nansen put the binoculars to his eyes once more and scanned the length of the shattered plane. It had fractured in the centre, broken its back, revealing a deep fissure. Nansen remembered reading that hitting water wasn't dissimilar to hitting concrete at that speed. The damaged wing flopped down, as if its bones had fractured. The fuselage began sinking, stern first. It was a hell of an impact but it was possible that someone had survived. The windscreen was cracked and crazed to opaque, but if the crew had been strapped in . . .

That's when the first pockets of the plane's JP-5 fuel, which had vaporised on impact, exploded, setting the sea ablaze.

*

Beyond the edge of his canopy Riley could see the C-130 still faltering, like one of those swinging-boat fairground rides that had reached the pinnacle of its arc. The props bit bravely at the air but seemed to have lost their grip. It was also slipping sideways, the nose dropping. With another ripping sound, the inner engine on the starboard wing detached itself, like an escape pod abandoning ship, the whole nacelle and propeller plunging away.

Riley screamed in disbelief. Now the sounds of a doomed aircraft filled his ears, the stuttering engines, the screech of distressed metal.

He scanned the skies, in case he had missed the others exiting. But there were no more red canopies to be seen against the icy-blue backdrop.

'Come on!' he yelled in useless encouragement. 'Get out of there!' But the aircraft was rotating faster and faster and he could imagine the men still in the cargo hold pinned to the fuselage. Still, he prayed for the figures to appear, but there was only Kebede and himself, dangling helplessly, left to watch the neutered giant spiral into the clouds and disappear.

*

Twenty minutes later a phone call interrupted the glum proceedings of the COBRA meeting, the loss of the plane having cast an even deeper pall over the table. It came through on a secure handset, the ring more like an insistent chirruping noise. George Pearman, the Minister of Defence, now returned to take charge of the crisis, eyed it suspiciously before reaching for the receiver. Probably the PM, he decided. Not a man for detail – Pearman suspected he couldn't sit still for a whole COBRA session – but he liked to know the broad brushstrokes. Pearman rehearsed his opening line. How would, *This is the biggest cock-up since Brexit* go down? Not well. Especially as they'd had bigger cock-ups since then.

The others watched as a brief expression of surprise flitted across the minster's face as he listened, followed by a furrow of his brow. 'Of course, patch him through.' There was a few seconds' pause. 'Marvin. Yes, thank you. Terrible. No, we have no real idea exactly what happened just yet. It was a risky manoeuvre. But not unprecedented.'

Pearman listened intently, lips pursing and unpursing, as if imitating a goldfish.

'I see. Yes, yes, of course. We would be very grateful, of course. Yes, we'd do the same for you.' He gave a mirthless chuckle, as if he had just heard an inappropriate joke. His neck reddened. 'I will inform the PM. Yes, and the captain. There will be comms through the Poseidon, I assume. Excellent. Well, I don't quite know what to say. Thank you, Marvin.'

He slammed down the receiver into the cradle so hard, something in the casing cracked with a loud snapping sound.

'Fuck, fuck, fuckety-fuck, FUCK.'

The COBRA members waited. He would tell them the news in his own good time. Several hoped that, given the crimson tinge to his visage, he would do so when his blood pressure fell. He took a deep breath, as if practising an anxiety-defeating technique and slowly the redness faded.

'That was Marvin Esposito, the United States' Secretary of Defense.'

From the nature of the conversation, they all knew it was more than just a sympathy call.

'There is, apparently, a US Navy C-2 some forty minutes' flight time from the *Rapide*. On board is a troop of Navy SEALs that Marvin says they managed to "rustle up" plus an ATO trained for Explosive Ordnance Disposal. This ATO has never jumped over water, but will be strapped to the SEAL commander and jump in tandem with him.'

'Did we know about this?' asked Stavely, jowls wobbling with his frustration. 'Did anyone know about this?' he regarded his colleagues with suspicion. 'Is this something the PM cooked up without mentioning it to us? It has the hallmarks of one of his Special Relationship stunts.'

'Nobody knew. The Joint Chiefs of Staff over there approved the mission.'

'Forty minutes away?' asked Clive Greggs, scribbling notes on his yellow pad. '*When* did they approve this?'

'The C-2 has been in the air some time, with in-flight refuelling on hand. It was deployed just in case, as Marvin so delicately put it, "we needed our asses pulled out of the fire". Prick.'

'So yet again,' said Sir Keith Millner. 'We have to go cap in hand to the Yanks.'

Sir Jeremy made a *harrumf* sound. 'Worse than that. Don't you see? The fact is they sent up their plane before our lads reached the drop zone.' He banged the table for emphasis as he uttered each word, with an extra hard blow on the third one. 'The Americans *expected* us to fail.'

THIRTY-SEVEN

Why me? Nansen thought as he watched three tenders, tossed by the aggressive waves, as if the sea did not want to give up its dead, running through their established search grid. *Why on my watch? What have I done to deserve this? Have I been really bad in this life or another? Is it somehow all my fault? Or is blind fate just dealing me bucket-of-shit cards?*

Of course, he didn't speak such self-pitying sentiments out loud. The captain had to maintain his dignity after all. But a giant plane crashing out of the sky, the stuff of many people's nightmares, was not something he could ignore or gloss over. So he had told his passengers the truth. That it was not an exercise. That there had been some genuine security concerns on board. And that brave men had died trying to keep them all safe.

Fortunately, thanks to a message from COBRA, he had been able to tell the passengers and crew that there was backup in place. A second bite of the cherry, little short of a miracle he thought, but he didn't mention that. The Americans were coming, a dozen of them, apparently, well trained in anti-terrorism searches. Whoever had the foresight to order them up deserved his thanks.

Nansen lowered the binoculars. He and Sajiv exchanged rueful glances. No matter what happened, Nansen was fairly sure his career as captain of *Rapide* – or any other liner – was over. Not that any of the events were his fault, nor could he see how he might have behaved differently. But a life at sea remained a life of superstition, where bad luck and good luck were almost tangible entities. You could be a lucky skipper or an unlucky one. A Hercules consumed by flaming waves had tipped him over to the latter.

'Fuck it!' He thumped the rail in anger and then looked around to see if anyone had witnessed the sudden flare of petulance. Nobody had. He rubbed the reddening edge of his hand.

Stupid behaviour. He took a breath. He had a whole ship full of traumatised passengers, and he had to set an example. They were allowed to panic, to fret. Not him. And some certainly were doing just that. Dr Courtney, *Rapide*'s medical officer, had just reported a surge in requests for Valium, painkillers and beta blockers. Nansen had cancelled that evening's captain's dinner, as it would be an ordeal for everyone involved, with all the jollity of a last supper. He checked his watch. He had ordered another muster drill, just in case. He doubted it would do anything to calm passenger nerves, but it would make him feel better if all on board had a good idea how to get off safely.

On a positive note for the owners, bar sales had gone through the roof. As had shoplifting from the concessions.

He wondered what Jakob would make of all this. *Hey, brother, I'm meant to be the family fuck-up.* Nansen really didn't want to challenge for that crown, but the Hercules had made him a pretender to the throne at the very least. But Jakob would know from the inevitable news headlines that he was in serious poop. Maybe that was why he stopped phoning. He could rely on his brother to make himself scarce when trouble loomed.

He scanned the decks below, picking out a grim-faced Ledgard with his muscular shadow, Jim, at the rail. They were having a heated conversation, no doubt about how best to protect Jim's principals in the aftermath of the failed SBS mission. The absolute fucking *debacle* of the failed SBS mission, he corrected.

He wondered if this BaseHeart would have been more amenable if he had been given the codes . . . Perhaps he should have strong-armed Ledgard. Demanded he hand over the Black Key. Then, perhaps the whole sequence of events that culminated in men dying in a hideous crash might have played out differently. A happy ending? But something told him anyone mad enough to put bombs on a ship would not behave rationally, even if his demands were met. Still, it was a sobering thought that a tribunal might find he was too soft on the surfing millionaire. What would they expect him to have done? Flogged Ledgard with the cat o'nine tails? Jim might have had something to say about that.

The words from Capelli came back to haunt him once more. *Inside job?* But who? Truluck? He was Royal Navy, a military man. He had seen conflict, sailed on warships. Probably witnessed death up close. Was he as shaken by the Hercules crash as he might have been? Or was he just being professional in his calm communication? What about Karun Roy, the engineer? Surely he would have the skills to plant, maybe even make, bombs. And the opportunity. Access all areas. But it could equally be a waiter or steward, they often moved around the ship as if invisible.

A voice from the bridge's loudspeaker broke through his ruminations. 'Captain. Alpha tender here, over.'

It was Jason Truluck. He felt a stab of guilt about his suspicions. Nansen scooped up the handset. 'Yes, Jason. What is it?'

'We have another body, Skip.'

'Who?' They had already recovered what they thought was either the pilot or co-pilot.

'Can't be sure till we get him on board, but it looks like one of the jumpers.'

THIRTY-EIGHT

Helsinki hadn't put on its best face for the early-morning arrival of *Thetis*. The islands that should have greeted them like a guard of honour on either side of the ship as they headed for port were wreathed in a damp mist. No sun penetrated the cloud base to burn it off. Instead, the sky was producing a fine, penetrating drizzle.

Barbara shrugged off both the weather and the shore excursions that were on offer. While the bulk of the passengers were coached off to the Sibelius monument or boarded ferries to tour the mighty Suomenlinna fortress 'built in the eighteenth century when Finland was under Swedish rule', as the sales pitch had it, she had other plans.

Instead, Barbara marched Kate Muraski along the waterfront to the restored Helsinki market. She led the way to the central atrium and ordered them both scrambled eggs, smoked salmon and caviar. She took the tray to the window seat and they sat. 'I remember when this was very run down, nothing but fish and vegetable stalls, bad coffee and herring rolls if you were lucky. They've done a wonderful job of giving it a lick and polish.'

'You were here when?'

'Oh, must have been sixty-six.'

'With Rory? Or Henry?'

'Oh, both. But I don't want to talk about that. It'll spoil the mood. Eat up.'

'Both'? What did that mean? A *ménage a trois*? Surely not. She had never doubted that Barbara Clifford-Brown was anything other than a formidable woman. Now she realised hanging on to that life, still being regarded as a ruthless femme fatale, was a cornerstone of her self-image. Disregard her rather startling career and she would just be another lonely elderly woman, loitering on the stoop of death's door. It was probably why she was drip-feeding Muraski snippets then darting away, like an elusive stickleback. Did she really murder her first husband? (Once she had made the revelation that she had killed Rory, Barbara had feigned exhaustion and sloped back to her cabin, leaving Muraski like a frustrated bride on an unconsummated wedding night.) Did she have two men on the go simultaneously? Muraski determined that she would make sure the truth would out before the damned voyage was over. If not, she was pretty sure she would end up tossing the old woman over the rail and have done with it.

Muraski tucked into the plate of food. She was enjoying being off the ship, on solid earth and surrounded by regular people. She decided to park the Rory/Henry question for now. The old spy was expecting her to pursue it. No doubt she had her deflections lined up, like ducks in a row. So let her stew for a change.

'Aren't you worried about SUPO?' she asked Barbara. 'After what happened to Dom? We're both affiliated to intelligence agencies after all.'

Barbara looked around the market and out through the windows at the sodden umbrellas of the exterior stalls, as if searching for suspicious characters. Then she shook her head. 'I'm retired. Nobody would give me a second glance. And I doubt you've popped up on any alerts. Spooks rarely arrive by cruise ship. And you're Five, purely domestic.'

'Didn't stop them giving Dom a tug.'

Barbara gave a wry smile. 'Ah, but we're not on our way to meet any old school Russian heavies in an Irish pub, are we?'

'I can never tell with you.'

'Well, I can tell you, we aren't. But it is why I insisted we leave our phones behind, just in case SUPO tags us. There'd be incriminating material on there.'

'Maybe. But I still feel like I've lost a limb.' A sensation that began when the ship's internet went down the previous day for some unknown reason.

Barbara smiled. 'More like a crutch, dear.'

Muraski cleared her plate and started on the coffee, which was very good. The daily bulletin that was delivered to the cabins in the morning had declared Helsinki's booming caffeinated drinks scene as a 'must try'. It certainly put her local Costa in the shade. 'What are we going to do here in Helsinki then?'

'Well, there's something I'd like you to put your mind to.'

Muraski braced herself, feeling that, yet again, the rug was about to be pulled from under her. 'What's that?'

'I need to get a gun on board the good ship *Thetis*.'

THIRTY-NINE

Jason Truluck ordered the tender be brought round to move alongside the body that was busy playing peek-a-boo with the waves. He needed to get closer so they could hook the corpse. The inflated dry suit kept it bobbing on the surface, although he could see no sign of the kit that was meant to be tethered to the jumper's ankle. The flashing light on the shoulder of the suit kept up its mournful blinking. Spread over the nearby ocean, like a dead jellyfish, was the canopy of the 'chute that had probably deployed as he had exited. He – or the automatic system – was meant to have released that over the water; clearly the auto-undo had failed and he had been unconscious during the descent.

It took several frustrating attempts to snag a boat hook under the straps on the man's back. As the crewmen pulled him near, Truluck leant over and cut the cords of the silken shroud free. Other hands helped him manhandle the body onto the deck of the tender.

Despite his waterproof gear, Truluck felt soaked through by the spray breaking over the gunwales, but he was also sweating from the exertion. He bent down and rolled off the poor man's neoprene hood, which had been gashed open by some sort of trauma. There was blood on the face underneath and he wiped it way with a towel.

The man's skin was pale and mottled, but his expression was benign, as if death had been no great surprise. His gaze was fixed on infinity, but Truluck didn't try to close the lids. He could leave all that to the doc, whose morgue was about to be far busier than usual. Truluck stood, steadied himself against the yawing motion of the tender, and turned to the man in the thermal blanket behind him, the one they had pulled out alive some twenty minutes previously. 'Well?'

'That's Josh Norwell, SAS. My Beep,' said Dominic Riley quietly.

*

Rapide had a deployable platform for water sports, a panel that slid out to enable Seabobs and jet skis and the like to be launched and docked from the hangar-like space (known as the 'toy garage') just above the waterline. Normally it would be stowed and the watertight doors sealing the deck locked into place, especially given the current sea conditions. But it was opened now to allow the Alpha tender to be berthed and Riley, and the two bodies, to be brought on board.

Anxious and curious faces stared over the rails as they approached. Riley could read fear and concern in the nearest ones. What now? they all seemed to be asking. What now indeed? Was he the only survivor?

'Anyone else make it?' he asked Truluck.

Truluck didn't answer directly. He pointed out at the distant dots that were other tenders. 'Still searching. What the hell happened out there?'

Before he could answer, Riley felt his throat constrict and he began to cough. Something slimy filled his throat and he spat over the side. He could still taste the fuel oil in the water that had engulfed him as he dropped into the greyness, smell the smoke from the fires that had all but gone by the time the automatic release had pulled away his lines and canopy. He had hit the water hard, gone down and down, feeling that the kit bag on his ankle would take him to the bottom. Lungs burning, eyes squeezed shut, he had struggled to find direction. He was kicking, clumsy and awkward in the dry suit, but was he heading up or down?

As he had thrashed around, the piercing cold and pressure began to work on him. His ribs were being squashed, compressing his burning lungs, his brain screaming that he should take a breath. The ice-cold water was penetrating him like an animal with steel claws.

Riley had felt something bump him, something with heft. A shark, he thought, for a panicky moment. Are there sharks in the mid-Atlantic? He reached out and touched man-made material. His kit bag had built-in buoyancy pockets. It was floating upwards, past him. He tried to hang onto it. It knew which way was up. Then, just as the crush in his chest was becoming unbearable, the flotation panels in the dry suit began to gain traction against the momentum of his plunge. He began to rise. Then he broke the surface and that oily black wave came . . .

'Sir?'

It was Truluck. 'I said, are you okay to climb out?'

The tender was bucking and banging but three crewmen were standing on the sports deck, reaching across to help him.

'Sure. Thanks.' He shrugged the space blanket, stood, wobbling as he tried to keep balance against the unpredictable motion. Truluck put a hand in the small of Riley's back and heaved. The crewmen grabbed his arms and as they did so, he was aware of a new sound, above the wind and waves.

As he got his two feet onto something relatively solid and

steady he looked up at the passengers leaning over the rails, staring down at him. He could see instantly where that fresh noise was coming from.

The passengers were applauding him.

FORTY

'What happened?' asked Dr Courtney, echoing Truluck, as he shone a light into each of Riley's eyes in turn.

'To the plane? I'm not sure,' he replied. He had been asked that question a dozen times so far. He was no closer to having an answer.

He was sitting on the examination couch in the Medical Centre, with the well-groomed Courtney examining him. The doctor's hair and beard were extremely neat, his skin smooth, and he smelt vaguely of citrus. Riley was rather less fragrant. He had been stripped out of the dry suit and allowed a hot shower and fresh clothes. Then, a quick session with the medic, before a full briefing from the captain or Truluck, the number two. But the stench of the disaster was still on him.

Riley looked at his watch, which had survived unscathed. Twelve hours had been the bomber's deadline. It had taken more than three hours to assemble the team in the UK, another three and a half to fly out against the headwind. It was now just over ninety minutes since the Herc went down. He shivered involuntarily, just thinking of that grey, unforgiving ocean.

'All right?' the doc asked.

'Yeah.'

Four hours until BaseHeart's deadline ran out.

Plus, of course, there had already been a detonation, to show he hadn't been bluffing. Riley had a lot of work to do.

'Looked to me like an airframe failure,' he said eventually. He knew what the doc and many others would think: that there had been a bomb on board the Herc. What he recalled of that terrible break-up suggested some form of metal fatigue. 'An accident.'

The image of a black wave breaking over him as he tried to blow a whistle to attract attention reared up behind his eyes. He blinked it away. There was no time to waste on flashbacks. They could wait.

'Well, I have some good news. Two pieces of good news. One is that I got word before you arrived that you were not the sole survivor.'

Riley felt a surge of relief. 'Who? Who was it?'

'I have no idea till he gets here.'

'And the second bit of news?'

'Apparently an American SEAL team is on its way.'

Come to help the Brits out of another snafu, no doubt, and rub our noses in it while they're at it. Ah well, he couldn't blame them. He'd do the same if they'd fucked up this badly. But he didn't want the Yanks waltzing in and taking over the whole shebang. 'How am I, Doctor?'

'How do you feel?'

'Mostly good. But all I can taste is seawater. With trace notes of burnt fuel. It's not nice.'

'Can't do much about that. It'll pass. Try a Fisherman's Friend. Not much gets past one of those.'

'First time I heard a medic suggest that. I can go?'

The doctor nodded. 'As far as I'm concerned, you are physically fine. But you've had quite a traumatic experience. I'd recommend—'

Riley held up a hand. 'I've seen your passengers, Doc. They look like hunted animals. They clapped me when I came on board because they think I'm about to pull a rabbit out of a hat. They don't know I haven't got a rabbit or even a hat yet.' Riley thought about those who hadn't made it. The look of deathly calm on poor Norwell's face when they pulled him out of the drink. Christ alone knew what their final moments on that plane were like. The horror certainly wasn't reflected in his Beep's expression. 'But regardless, they won't thank me for having a long lie down or hot, sweet tea, a chat with the chaplain or whatever it was you were about to suggest. I've got a murder scene to inspect.'

FORTY-ONE

Kate Muraski and Barbara got back to the ship about forty minutes before it was due to leave Helsinki to find a bottleneck at security. Anyone who had been ashore was subject to full screening upon their return. As many people had brought souvenirs, from rock sculptures at the eponymous church gift shop to limited edition bottles of vodka or lakka, bought from the government-run Alko stores, there was quite a line. Muraski tried not to breathe on anyone as they shuffled forward. Barbara had insisted they try a Salmari vodka cocktail 'for old times' sake'. Barbara's old times, that is. It was Koskenkorva Viina mixed with Turkish Pepper salty liquorice. It seemed a desecration of decent vodka to Muraski, who was still struggling with an aftertaste so persistent it made kippers look like transient visitors.

When they had joined the queue on the gangway, Muraski was aware that something had occurred. There was a nervous twitter about the line, people talking intently to complete strangers. Phone screens were also being held up for others to examine.

'This could be trouble,' said Kate from the side of her mouth. They had expected the lines to move smoothly.

'Stick to the plan.'

'I have a bad feeling about this.'

'Oh, hush. You lot at Five are such pessimists.'

But as they stepped off the gangway and into the security area, Barbara suddenly uttered a small cry. 'Can I look at that?' she asked the woman next to her, who was clutching that day's *Daily Telegraph*.

Barbara held up the broadsheet. There was a picture of a ship called *Rapide* on the front. Underneath, an alarming headline: BOMB THREAT TO BRITISH LINER ON MAIDEN VOYAGE.

She turned to Muraski. 'No wonder the internet has been down. They didn't want to alarm us.'

Muraski, though, was trying to digest what she was reading. Some kind of ransom demand had been made. Celebrities on board. Business people. Disaster for Anglo-American Lines. Experts say looking for any explosive device on a ship is like searching for a needle in a haystack. Others claimed that it could be a bluff, pointing to the cases of George Duke-Cohan, a schoolboy who closed four hundred schools in the UK and caused a US-bound flight to be evacuated, or Andreas Dowling, who claimed he had placed devices in the Houses of Parliament and at the US Super Bowl. Muraski knew there were many, many more. For some reason, certain twisted people loved a bomb hoax.

How easy is it to sink a cruise liner? see Page 5.

Obviously, *Thetis*'s owners would rather passengers didn't know about this incident. Being on a ship with three thousand other people was an act of faith that nothing would go wrong. You didn't want newspapers reminding you that every man-made form of transport was vulnerable to disaster and catastrophe. A big steel bathtub was no exception. She assumed all the major cruise lines had done something similar and gone 'technical' on the internet. But there was nothing they could do to stop people connecting when ashore.

Then she read the line:

Sources close to the MoD claim that a highly decorated veteran of Afghanistan, a leader in the field of EOD [Explosive Ordnance Disposal] is included in the team despatched to intercept the *Rapide* in a storm-tossed Atlantic.

Storm-tossed. Wasn't the Atlantic always described as that? Lazy journalism. And what did 'sources close to the MoD' mean? That was the sort of leak that ought to get people sacked.

Then she went back and re-read the section. Afghanistan. Highly decorated. That must cover any number of people. But . . .

'The ATO they've sent?' Muraski said. 'You don't think . . . ?'

Barbara's hand went to her throat. 'Dom? Really? He is back on active duty. Lord . . .'

Another passenger passed along a copy of the *Daily Mail*. It was obviously a later edition. DISASTER AT SEA, it screamed.

An RAF Hercules with all crew and elements of UK Special Forces is feared lost over the Atlantic in a failed attempt to bring the situation on the *Rapide* under control.

The newspaper slipped from Barbara's hands and fluttered to the floor. Muraski watched in horror as the old lady's eyes rolled to white. 'Christ, Barbara. Are you all right?'

'I . . . I can't breathe . . . Pain in . . . arm.' She staggered a little. 'I just need to sit . . .'

As Barbara swooned, a crew member detached himself from the security team and came forward, pushing through the crowd.

'Give her some room,' he said in accented English. Spanish, Muraski thought. 'Please. Step back, please. It's okay, I'm trained for this.'

'So am I,' said Muraski firmly, letting him lower her friend to the steel floor. 'I'll get the defibrillator.'

'You have to punch in the code,' the Spaniard said. 'Seven-nine-two-one.'

Muraski smiled to herself. That Barbara certainly knew how to execute a plan. *I'll make sure you have to access either the first aid box or the defibrillator,* she had said. *Your job is to stash the gun out of sight so we can retrieve it later.*

As Kate entered the code, she glanced over at Barbara, who had started to shake uncontrollably. Steady on, old girl, she thought, you're not going for the Golden Globe.

And then, she realised with horror that Barbara wasn't acting.

*

Ledgard insisted on an audience with Nansen. The captain said he would meet him in his cabin to keep the meeting private. Nansen made it first and helped himself to a large glass of ice-cold vodka from the freezer. Then he poured half of it back. Retreating to the bottle was the sort of thing Jakob would do. Not Harald. He knocked it back in one. Not yet midday, he scolded himself. Yes, and they might be holed or crippled when a more acceptable time came around. He had an overwhelming urge to phone Mette again, to hear her soft, velvety voice, but a rap on the door dispelled the urge.

Ledgard arrived with Shelby, his wife, and Jim, the bodyguard, in tow. Ledgard had shed the Aviators and looked tired, with dark crescents under his eyes, spoiling his slacker persona. 'What a clusterfuck,' he said, slumping down on the sofa without being

invited to sit. The others remained standing. 'What the hell happened to the cavalry?'

'We are trying to establish that. As you can imagine, it might
take some time. Can I offer you something to drink?' Nansen asked.

All three shook their heads.

'So, what can I do for you?'

'We need the internet back up,' said Shelby.

'Basically,' her husband said slowly, as if the effort of speaking
was draining the last of his energy. 'I'm going to have to access
our company computers in London. I need to place the four keys
in different locations and then design a package to deliver to this
BaseHeart to keep him busy for a few hours.'

'Assuming BaseHeart falls for it,' said Jim cautiously, knowing
it wasn't really his place to offer opinions. 'Feeding him phoney
codes is pretty risky.'

'It'll be convincing,' said Ledgard, irritably. 'It will be a while
before he, or whoever it is, twigs it's the equivalent of marked bills.
That's not your concern, Jimbo.'

Even though Jim remained mostly impassive, a slight twitch
around his mouth told Nansen that the bodyguard didn't like
being addressed by that particular name. 'Do you have any idea
who BaseHeart is?' Nansen asked.

It was addressed to Christian Ledgard but Shelby answered. 'Of
course not. It's cyber-extortion. It could be anyone who fancies
their chances of taking what we have earned.'

'Ukraine,' said Ledgard. 'That's where most of these cunts are.'

'So how long do you need to create convincing code?' Nansen
was well aware that they only had three and a half hours until . . .

'Two more hours should do it,' said Ledgard. 'I'll then give
instructions to your Crisis Management Team on what to send
to BaseHeart and then I'll need the internet.'

'I can probably get it in your cabin without making the rest of the ship live, using some kind of local hub,' he said. Nansen wasn't sure if that was the case. But he'd give Alison Reeves of Tech Support that particular challenge.

'We still face a bomb threat,' said Jim, 'whether this BaseHeart bloke falls for the bluff or not. And a deadline.'

'Jim thinks we are wasting our time with fake codes,' said Ledgard. 'But then he is more Action Man than cyber-warrior.'

Jim rolled his eyes.

'He's right, we might still have an explosive device or two to deal with,' said Nansen. 'But the Americans will be here soon.'

There was a sharp edge of sarcasm in Ledgard's tone when he replied, 'Well, fuck me, Captain. Let's hope they have better luck than the last lot, eh?'

FORTY-TWO

Riley didn't want to hang around and watch the Yanks parachute down. In fact, he never wanted to see a parachute ever again. Or a C-130. So while *Rapide*'s tenders waited for the US forces to drop from the sky, he asked Truluck to show him the cabin where the 'demonstration' explosion had killed the ship's security officer.

Once the panels sealing the room had been removed, he asked to have some time to himself. When he closed the door behind him, he sat down gingerly on the corner of the bed, examining, without touching, the shattered body of Jos Swart. His head and chest had taken the brunt of the blast, and there was a crust of dried blood covering the whole area. He would have died instantly. No pain. Isn't that what they always told relatives? *He didn't suffer.*

He thought of Nick, who really had suffered, was in agony, before a Taliban bullet had put him out of his misery. *Look after Trace*, he had managed to shout, before the AK round punched through his skull. Maybe those last milliseconds before oblivion were easier to bear, because Nick had managed to give Riley an instruction.

Riley instinctively looked up when he heard aero engines, the sounded clearly audible over the wind whistling through the shattered window. They were here. The Americans.

The thought of the SEALs' over-water jump reminded him of what they had lost. The mystery survivor had been Kebede, who had a suspected broken collarbone. Capes, Obi, Tremaine, the pilot and co-pilot, navigator and engineer. All gone. The bomber had killed seven people now. Eight including the one before him in the sealed-off cabin.

The thought dragged him back to the moment. Riley put his head in his hands and swore to himself. The aftermath of the Herc disaster could wait. No doubt it would be another log on the bonfire of his sanity. More survivor's guilt.

Haven't used up those nine lives just yet, said Nick.

Must be getting close, though. Very close. Riley reached into his bag, brought out his Lumix camera and began snapping the cabin interior and the corpse from every angle. There would a forensics team deployed after berthing in New York, no doubt, but Riley needed his own record. Who knew what could happen to the ship before they made it there?

The thought of New York made him think of flying home, away from this madhouse. Another one waited for him, of course, in the shape of Ireland, north and south. But he couldn't afford to dwell on Izzy and Ruby. In this game, any distraction, even one concerning his family, could be fatal.

When he had taken shots from every angle he unpacked the Hi-Scan X700 Rover, the 'dog' he had borrowed from Roscoe, promising he would give it a test run. It looked a little like a shrunken, squared-off Henry vacuum cleaner with a far thinner nozzle and was actually a portable Explosive Trace Detection system, capable of detecting various explosives and their residues. Its non-radioactive, ion mobility spectrometry (IMS) source could 'sniff' surfaces and, using swabs, it could also scan hands and fingers to see if explosives had been handled by the subject.

He turned the machine on and the top panel glowed blue. It took eight to ten minutes to warm up. The Rover was not foolproof, but it would detect and analyse tiny particles of GDN, HMTD, Tetryl, TNT and several other explosives. Anything outside its capabilities you could class as 'esoteric' – exotic compounds that ATOs rarely come across.

Time? Under three hours left. Get a move on.

While the Rover electronically pulled itself together, Riley snapped on his non-latex blue medical gloves and set about finding and bagging up the various components of the device that had detonated. Usually he was collecting for Whiz, the army's Weapons Intelligence Section. These he would probably hand over to the FBI's analysis team once they had docked. He assumed the FBI would be involved. There were American passengers on the liner, after all, and the FBI would have state-of-the-art facilities. He had been due to visit one of them, the US Army-FBI Hazardous Devices School in Huntsville, Alabama, on his aborted goodwill tour, but had never made it. He regretted that now. The Americans had kit he could only dream of. It would have been good to snaffle some free samples.

He found the arming switch, still pretty intact, with wires curling from it like tiny entrails. He would give that the once-over himself. It might yield some clues as to what other types of devices might or might not be present on the *Rapide*.

Engrossed in the work, he didn't hear the door open behind him. He gave a little start when the newcomer spoke. 'Jeez, Riley. You're really the best they've got?'

Still kneeling, Riley turned from the waist. He blinked twice, not quite able to believe what he was seeing. It was Cat Cortez, the woman he had stood up at the swanky bar in New York.

And she was the American team's EOD officer.

FORTY-THREE

'Ladies and gentlemen, this is the captain.' He was too tired to include the gender-neutral part. 'I am sure by now you're all aware of the terrible tragedy that befell the aircraft that was part of the operation to place military experts on board. You will also have seen a second group of parachutists arrive and be successfully picked up. They are United States troops, part of the investigation into what exactly happened this morning. I would be grateful if you would offer any assistance they request. They will try not to interfere with you going about your business.' Nansen paused and watched as a heavily armoured US Navy SEAL entered the bridge. 'I have been in contact with the owners and, given the distress caused by events, they have agreed to refund all monies paid out by every passenger so far and will offer advantageous terms on future Anglo-American cruises.'

If there were to be any further A-AL cruises. He knew it wouldn't satisfy all of his clients. There were probably meetings going on at that very moment as groups of passengers plotted how best to put together a class action. There were bound to be plenty of lawyers on board. There always were. Like cockroaches in big kitchens, they were a fact of life.

'I shall be updating you shortly. Thank you for listening.'

He put down the PA handset and turned to the American who saluted smartly. 'Commander Oliver Wang, sir.'

Nansen retuned the salute and held out his hand. Oliver Wang was in his mid-thirties, looking remarkably composed after what must have been a fraught arrival. Or maybe not for a Navy SEAL. 'Thank you for stepping in.'

'My pleasure, sir. It's what we're trained for. I'm only sorry about what happened to the Royal Air Force plane. Does anyone have any idea—?'

'No,' interrupted Nansen. 'It's up to an RAF investigation board now.'

'I thought you might like to see this, sir.'

It was a copy of the *New York Post*. The front page showed *Rapide*. The headline was: DAYLIGHT PIRACY. He scanned the rest. There was a lot of padding and speculation. Irritatingly, they had, however, listed a fair number of the better-known passengers correctly. He put the newspaper to one side, not wanting to think about the situation at A-AL HQ. 'I'd heard the whole world knows. Although I don't know how. What do you need from me, Commander Wang?'

'Your number two has given us the garage space to operate from, sir. I need schematics of the ship sent to our laptops. I would also like one crew member assigned to each of our search teams.'

'We have conducted our own search.' Tetchier than he intended. The tension was getting to him, eating at the public facade he needed to maintain, like those concrete-eating bacteria that attack buildings.

Wang frowned. 'With all due respect, sir.'

The captain rubbed at his itchy right eye. 'I know. Sorry.'

They wouldn't be in the habit of taking anybody else's word for anything. Wang didn't need to spell it out, but he did anyway. 'We are trained in detailed examination of enclosed spaces, we have specialist equipment and Lieutenant Madison, our EDC.'

'Yes, of course. You must see for yourselves.'

'Do you think any of the people involved in this are on board, or could devices have been planted before you left England?'

'I have no idea. But would you want to be on a ship that you have seeded with bombs? It's possible that all this is being done by remote control or, more likely, timers, given our position.'

'Agreed. The one device that did detonate—'

'Is being examined by a British Army ATO as we speak. He survived the disintegration of the Hercules.'

'So I heard.' Wang's eyebrows indicated his surprise that anyone got out of that crash alive. 'I've sent Cortez, our bomb tech, to assist him. I'd also like to post one of my team on the bridge at all times.'

'If you really think that necessary. We are quite secure up here.'

Wang's expression suggested that, in his opinion, that simply wasn't the case. 'There's secure and there's secure against armed Bravos. Hostiles, that is. I don't think your set-up qualifies as the latter, sir. My guy won't get in your way. It would make me more comfortable.'

'Very well.'

'Sir.' It was Javid, the Officer of the Watch. 'Mr Chamberlain on the satellite phone.'

'Excuse me a minute, Commander Wang.'

It was a brief call. Nansen tried to keep himself composed, but it was hard for him to convey the situation down the line. When he had hung up, Nansen looked at his watch. One hundred minutes until the deadline was up.

'What is it, Captain?' Wang asked.

'We've just had another communique from BaseHeart. The blackmailer.'

'And?' Wang asked impatiently. He knew very well who BaseHeart was.

Nansen couldn't hide his frustration when he spoke. 'He knows we are going to send him fake codes.'

Wang ran a hand back and forth over his buzzcut. 'If you'll excuse me, sir, how the fuck did that happen?'

But Nansen had no answer. There was a leak somewhere.

'Sir?' It was Javid again.

'Yes?' Nansen asked, more brusquely than intended.

'There's a riot breaking out on deck five.'

FORTY-FOUR

Greggs hurried out of Whitehall and headed for the old-style red phone kiosk he knew stood in a side street not far from the National Gallery. Remarkably, it still worked, being mainly used by tourists as a photo backdrop and only occasionally by rough sleepers as a *pissoir*. By the time he reached the box, he was convinced he was in danger of a heart attack. What the hell was wrong with using burner phones, like every other ne'er-do-well?

He leaned against the ageing metal frame, resisting the temptation to put his forehead against the cold glass. These past few months had been a steep learning curve. In his darkest moments he wondered if the police, MI5 and the rest knew what went on out there. Just how lawless the world had become.

He had made discreet enquiries about how, exactly, his compromising images might have made it onto the open market – after all his tormentor had claimed he had paid 'good money' for the photographs. This 'package', the material that might one day find him in his garage sucking on the end of a hose running from his Ferrari's exhaust, had probably been auctioned off on ExBay, a Dark Web site. That was when he was a nobody. But when someone wanted a vulnerable figure in the Cabinet Office and COBRA, it had been taken off the virtual shelf, dusted off and sold on to

the man known as BaseHeart. He suspected the entire *Rapide* project had been put together like that. Want a bomb-maker? Look
on ExBay. Need a crew member who is in serious debt? Look on
ExBay. Want a bent politician?

'I'm not *bent*,' he said out aloud. Gregg had convinced himself
that all he was doing was telling the man things that would be
in the public domain soon enough. No state secrets. Just the
hour-by-hour response to the *Rapide* crisis from COBRA and
Anglo-American here in the UK. No matter how many times
he tried to convince himself of that, he still felt his skin crawl,
as if he was infested with lice or ticks or maggots. He would
need a shower when he got back to the office. Then a run on
the treadmill until the pain blotted out everything else. Then
another shower.

He held his breath and entered the phone booth. He dialled
the new number he had been given and waited. It answered on
the fifth ring and spewed electronic gibberish into his ear for a
few seconds.

'Hello?' he asked, when the racket stopped.

'Well?' The Dalek voice once more.

'Nothing to report. The American SEALs are on board. The
ship is being searched again.'

'What about the fake Black Key?'

'Well, I suspect they won't bother now. They are scrabbling for
a response. But Ledgard is a private citizen. They can't force him
to take any course of action. And they don't want to give in to any
demands themselves, even if they could.'

The laugh at the other end sounded like a static storm. 'Of
course they won't.'

Not for the first time Greggs wondered what this man's game
was. He didn't seem bothered that they weren't going to pony up

the Black Key. 'You won't really sink it, will you? With all those people on board?'

The silence lasted a long time and Greggs couldn't read it at all.

'Look,' Greggs continued. 'You promised me my material. I don't know what else I can do. I'm not due to attend another meeting until tomorrow, by which time your deadline will have passed.'

'You could insist on attending tonight's briefing.'

How did he know about that? Greggs allowed some irritation to show. 'You don't know how COBRA works. They know there is a leak. They've sent in the heavy mob from MI5. We are all to be interviewed.'

A pause on the other end. 'I will send you a parcel. It will contain all the images printed off so far plus instructions on how to find the original files on the dark web and permanently delete them.'

A wave of relief swept over him, triggering something close to elation. 'Thank you.'

'Given the nature of the contents, I suggest you open it somewhere private. You don't want Jessica looking over your shoulder, do you?'

The thought of his wife seeing those files made Greggs feel like he might throw up. The elation ebbed away as quickly as it had arrived. 'No. Indeed.'

'But in return I want you to get yourself into the next COBRA session later today. I don't care how. You'll think of something. It'll all be over soon. You can go back to your normal life. I will text you the next number to call.'

The line went dead.

Greggs left the box, unaware as he walked back north, that he was being watched by BaseHeart, who waited until he had turned the corner before dismantling and disposing of the pay-as-you-go-phone he had used. He would indeed send Gregg a package when this was all over. But it wouldn't contain photographs of the politician and his young 'friend'. It would be much more final than that.

FORTY-FIVE

It was less a riot than a sit-in, or rather a stand-in. A decent number of passengers – a hundred or more – had taken over the Cameron Mackintosh Theatre and were refusing to move. Nansen accessed it by a curtained side entrance, parted the drapes, and examined the auditorium. Very few were seated, most were on their feet declaiming loudly, pouring metaphorical petrol on already inflamed emotions.

It took some scanning of faces for him to spot the ringleader, a small man with a shock of ginger hair and a pale, white face that was so crunched in displeasure, he reminded Nansen of a knuckle of pork. He was standing at the front of the theatre, leaning against the railing of the small orchestra pit like he owned the place.

As Nansen walked out from his vantage point and towards him, a wave of hostility broke over him as the protestors became aware of his presence. It was a disgrace apparently, a betrayal, a matter for lawyers. He should resign, walk the plank, kill himself. A lot of the comments appeared to be propelled on a wave of spittle.

What was driving their fury? Not the death of brave men who had come to help. No, the fact that the internet continued to be down.

Nansen let it wash over him, until he reached Knuckle Face. 'How can I help, Mr ...?'

'Finnegan.' American. Boston, perhaps, thought Nansen. 'You can start by explaining this screw up.'

Bodies were pressing close to his back and Nansen felt a jab between his shoulder blades. 'Can we go backstage, Mr Finnegan, so we can talk in private?'

There were howls of derision and anger as they walked onto the stage and disappeared into the wings.

As soon as they were out of sight of the crowd, Finnegan spoke. 'People are angry, Captain. Very angry. There's talk of storming the Communication Suite and turning the internet on ourselves.' A low hum of anger reached them through the safety curtain. 'We can all smell bullshit, Captain. I think you better level with us.'

Nansen thought for a moment before answering. Obviously, he didn't like the implied threat. But perhaps it was time to dole out some truths, a few crumbs of veracity. Nansen lowered his voice as he became aware of stagehands working in the gloom behind him. He took a deep breath. Let it out. Time to jump feet first. He hoped he wasn't misjudging the man.

'Mr Finnegan. The ship is subject to a bomb threat.'

'What?' The little colour in the man's face drained away. Now his skin looked like mottled Italian marble. 'There's a what?'

'There's a claim that there is a bomb on board. It's a blackmail attempt.' Nansen grabbed the shorter man's arm and squeezed, 'And if you don't calm this down and tell everyone that all is in hand, I am going to lock you in the brig, which we use for unruly passengers. Which, you won't be thrilled to hear, is below the waterline. Now, please, Mr Finnegan, let me do my job. And not a word of what I just told you.'

It could have gone either way, but Finnegan, still shocked by the revelation, just nodded. Nansen let the man go and he walked back into the main auditorium. He listened to Finnegan address his fellow passengers.

'Okay, listen up. The captain has just told me . . . everything is under control. No need to panic. Wi-Fi will be available as soon as possible.'

A murmur of something like relief rippled across the crowd.

'But then . . . He then told me . . . that there's a bomb on board!'

Oh, fuck.

FORTY-SIX

Catalina Cortez, born of Puerto Rican parents in the Bronx, was a tech with the PAPD EOD unit and was qualified in dealing with devices placed in many different situations – trains, planes, automobiles and, of course, ships. Riley could see it made perfect sense. He just wished the Port Authority and the US authorities had sent someone else. Anyone else.

'Look, I—' Riley stuttered.

She snapped back, sharp as a whiplash. 'We're workin', okay? Can the personal shit till later. Or never, all the same to me.' She paused. 'But I'd like you to know I ended up partying with firefighters that night.'

Riley didn't know how to answer. He began to mumble an apology.

'You dumbass. 'Course I fuckin' didn't. Firefighters aren't my thing. But it might have come to that, thanks to you. Though my guess is you don't get many FDNY joes in that bar. Thirty bucks for an Old Fashioned? What's old fashioned about that?' She took a breath. 'Right, my guys are setting up in the garage prior to the stem-to-stern search. What we got here, Riley?'

He ran through the likely scenario. 'Straightforward. The ship's security officer, an ex-Special Forces South African, found the bomb and thought it looked simple to disarm, or so I'm guessing. He flipped a switch or cut a wire and . . .'

'Welcome to *Gunther von Hagen's Body Worlds*,' she said as she looked at Swart's flayed face.

'Who?'

'Forget about it.' As she reached into her daypack Riley wondered what had possessed him to skip that date – if that's what it was – with Cortez. She was wearing an olive-drab one-piece, cinched at the waist, which accentuated her figure, whether it was intentional or not. She was tall, five-eleven, he guessed, and her face was usually framed by a mass of black curls which she had tamed with a hairband at the nape of her neck.

Cheesy as a ripe Camembert, pal. Don't objectify the lady.

Fuck off, Nick. Riley couldn't recall seeing him in a *This is What a Feminist Looks Like* T-shirt. Dead *and* a hypocrite.

Cortez extracted and pulled on a similar pair of medical-grade gloves. Her words were softer now, the Bronx edge softened by concern. 'You okay, Riley? I heard . . . you know, afterwards, after you stood . . . after you left New York. What happened in the UK. I heard about your family. Rumours, but I got the gist. I'm sorry. Must have been tough.'

Riley nodded. 'Yeah.'

'But you okay now?'

'More or less.'

'I hope it's more, buddy. Because I don't need some moping Limey screw-up as my only partner.'

Riley laughed. 'Tell it like it is, Cat.'

'Always, Riley.' There was a twinkle in her eye he couldn't quite decode. She pointed at the Rover. 'What's that?'

He explained about the machine.

'And what's it doing now?'

'Warming up.'

'I hope you didn't buy that on your own dollar.' She pulled out a device from her bag, a black oblong about the size of a walkie-talkie. 'They shrunk them. And look, On ...' The machine emitted a beep to show it had detected traces of explosive, which was hardly surprising. 'Off. You don't have to sit on your ass while it waits for the tea to arrive.'

'Does it swab?'

Cortez shrugged. 'You can't have everything.'

'No,' said Riley. 'Where would you put it?'

She laughed at the old joke, pulled on a face mask, and got to work, helping bag up all the fragments of the device they could find, working gingerly around the body, trying to ignore the musty smell already rising from it – and shooing away the tiny flies circling the ripped flesh.

'I hear you brought along an EDC as well as that gizmo.'

'We did. That had its moments. Got full bomb suits, too. You know us Yanks. We never travel light. If we could've figured a way to get an LDV down, we'd have brought that too.' This was a specialised, custom-built explosive ordnance disposal vehicle – a big truck, basically, something like the Babcock some of the British units used. Only much larger.

'You seen this?' Riley asked.

He passed over the remains of the Casio and she held the transparent bag up to the light. 'Weird. You notice?'

'Yeah. It's not been wired in. The timer was a dummy.'

'Which suggests . . . what?'

'It was a simple on-off switch, like a victim-operated switch.'

'Yup.' Cortez suppressed a sneeze. 'You know what? I think

we'd better get him bagged and tagged as soon as we can,' said Cortez. 'Before it starts pumping out cadaverine and skatole.'

Riley knew they were two of the main decomposition gasses but he didn't think putrefaction was imminent, not given the ambient temperature, although he agreed the body ought to be taken to the morgue, and soon.

After they had a stack of evidence bags, numbered, with their location in the cabin noted on a plan drawn by Riley, Cortez sat down, unhooked her face mask and stared at the corpse. She switched on her sniffer machine and held it near to the bags. It started to screech an alarm.

'PETN and RDX. Is that what you got?'

Riley nodded.

Cortez picked up the bag containing the switch and turned it over in her hands. 'You got some swabs for WALL-E there?' She asked, nodding towards the Rover.

'In my kit bag.'

Riley watched as she tore open a bag of swabs, ran one end over Swart's hands and fingers, then placed it into Rover's orifice. The mysterious internal workings whirled for a few seconds and a read-out appeared. Cortez gave a low whistle. She repeated the procedure on the left hand.

'Pretty high,' she said. 'Very high. This guy has been handling RDX and PETN.'

'He might have put his hands up to protect himself.'

'He might. If he was The Flash. C'mon, Riley, you know how much time you have to react when one of these fuckers blows.'

'Just playing devil's advocate.'

'Well, don't. You wanna know what I think?'

She's going to tell you anyway, said Nick.

'Go ahead.'

'Your guy here. Swart, is it? He didn't come across a bomb and try and make it safe. No security guy I ever met is that dumb. And I've met some dumb ones in my time.'

'Which means . . . ?' asked Riley, getting to his feet and stretching stiff limbs.

'Swart was the perp who planted the damn thing in the first place. He died arming the fucker. Maybe he was *meant* to die.' Before Riley could object to her hasty analysis, Cortez started stripping off her gloves. 'You know what, I'm starving. I could eat an angry skunk. You think there's any gedunk on this tub?'

'You can eat later. First we gotta tell the captain or Truluck,' he said.

'About what?'

'Your theory about Swart.'

She gave a deep-throated laugh. '*My* theory until it's proved right. Then it'll be *our* theory. I guess we should tell him. And your cops. They need to do deeper background checks on Swart. Known associates and all that shit.'

'I would imagine they're on that already. COBRA is involved, which means all the security services. But someone should question any of his pals on board. See what they know.'

'And if there is any link to the blackmailer.' The radio on her belt squawked. She pressed receive. 'Cortez.'

'Wang. I don't know where you and the Brit are right now, but get your asses to deck eleven. Lieutenant Madison just found something else.'

FORTY-SEVEN

Barbara was sitting up in bed in a private room in the ship's medical centre. She had just polished off a tray of food and was beaming ear to ear when Kate Muraski arrived.

'Well, this is better than the NHS,' the old woman said.

Muraski doubted Barbara had ever been in an NHS hospital in her life – she struck her as more Bupa than local health trust – but let it pass. 'How are you feeling?'

She waved a hand in a stuff-and-nonsense gesture. 'Oh, fine. Doctor Raja thinks I might have had a drop in blood pressure. Nothing to worry about. Just a reaction to that headline, I suppose.'

'You frightened the crap out of me. No, really. Are you confined to bed?'

A cloud passed over her face. 'Don't be ridiculous. We are on this damn cruise to find out if Dom's been lied to. I am not aborting that mission now. Any news on the crash of the plane that was carrying Dom?'

'I lost the phone signal when we left port. But I pulled some defence of the realm nonsense with the captain and got permission to call Thames House. I spoke to Oakham. He wouldn't say much over an open line. The plane did crash. Several dead, at least. But Dom's okay.'

Her face collapsed into relief, revealing the forced jolliness as a pantomime. 'Thank God for that.'

'He's on *Rapide* now, along with a contingent of US Navy SEALs.'

'And how long until the deadline runs out?'

'Just under two hours. Look, Barbara, it's bloody hard to sink a ship that size. It has to be a bluff. Or a hoax. Well, probably not a hoax.'

'Why do you say that?'

'There has been a fatality. One of the crew members. Blown up while trying to defuse a bomb.'

Barbara frowned at the news. 'Isn't that Dom's job?'

Muraski nodded. 'The bloke probably YouTubed it. No, sorry, not funny.'

'No,' said Barbara prissily.

Muraski suddenly realised how tired she was. There was a cabin above her with a nicely made bed. The thought of a deep, uninterrupted sleep made her yawn.

'So, how did you get on?' Barbara asked. 'With our parcel?'

'In all the fuss, I just had to walk around the metal detector.' The original plan had been to stash the weapon in the defibrillator cupboard or first aid box and retrieve it when the ship was at sea. But Barbara's performance was so convincing – mainly because it was genuine – that she hadn't had to resort to it.

'Where on earth did you get the gun from?' Barbara had gone off alone for close to an hour during their shore time in Helsinki. She had returned with a handbag that was significantly heavier than when she had left.

Barbara gave a mischievous grin. 'Please don't question me any further. I'm a tired old woman.'

When it suits you.

'Obviously I'm more fragile than I thought. Collapsing like

that. About the gun. I'm hoping it won't come to using it. I really do. But if it does, then . . .'

'Barbara, we're not an assassination bureau. I shouldn't have let you talk me into helping with that. I don't know what I was thinking. You can't go around shooting foreign nationals. Especially not Russians. And extra especially not in Russia. And most definitely not former KGB colonels.'

'Why not? They poison ours. Blow them up with, it seems, absolute impunity. Possibly abduct and kill them. Perhaps they really were responsible for whatever happened to Ruby and Izzy. Well, I'm not having it.' The determined set of the jaw reminded Muraski that this was a woman, apparently, who once disposed of a troublesome husband. 'We'll see what's what when we dock in a few hours, I suppose, by which time we'll also know what's happening on *Rapide*.' She unfolded her arms and rolled her shoulders. 'And there's nothing we can do to change either of those things. It's a waiting game which, I am sure you will agree, is the hardest part of our business. Poor Henry thought so. He could be a bag of nerves. But that does nobody any good.'

She gave an indulgent smile, reached out and touched Muraski's wrist. 'Also, you've done your part, getting the Browning on board. Stand down, soldier. Enjoy the ship. Go and eat. But before you toddle off, ring and get me a cup of tea, will you? There's a sweetie.'

'No. Fuck off.'

Barbara looked genuinely taken aback. 'I beg your pardon?'

'No. I have had it up to here with your evasions and obfuscations. I want to know exactly what your intentions are once you are ashore. And I want you to tell me about Rory.'

'That's ancient history.'

Muraski stepped in closer and Barbara shrunk back into her

pillow. 'But it isn't to you, is it? Because you keep making sly allusions to what happened to him then ducking my questions. What took place in Finland somehow defines you and you want me to know that. But like a good spy you don't give up secrets easily. Very well. No truth, no tea.'

Barbara gave a mirthless laugh. 'That's your idea of a threat?'

Muraski shrugged. 'It's all I've got.'

Barbara let a few seconds tick by before she nodded her agreement. 'Then sit down.'

Muraski did so. Barbara's voice took on a wistful tone and her eyes glazed slightly, as if she really was seeing the past play out before her.

*

They were running agents through Finland that year. Fashions come and go in espionage as in everything else. Berlin was out of favour after a couple of incidents at the wall. The Czech border was far too risky, because most of the local agents had been turned. Hungary, similarly, had very little infrastructure left that SIS could trust. But Finland, it seemed, was like an open door.

Although SIS knew not to trust easy invitations.

There were several things going for the country as a conduit, though. A long, wild, mostly unprotected border with Russia. Properly equipped, you could walk across, the biggest danger being the odd bear. There were plenty of Westerners around, thanks to a boom in mining and metal exploration. Gold, nickel and platinum deposits were scattered across the north, just waiting for the big mining companies to locate them. Which meant aerial surveying. Which gave MI6 access to planes.

The one Rory Little was curled up in as it hammered through the night sky was a de Havilland Beaver floatplane with amphibious capability—it could set down on land or water. It was flown by Frank Lyall, a veteran of Squadron 161 (Special Duties), the outfit based at Tempsford in the Second World War that had used Lysanders to infiltrate agents into occupied Europe. Lyall had been dropping SIS people into dangerous environments for twenty-five years.

Alongside him upfront was a younger man, Brian Walsh, who was operating the box of electronics that would detect Russian radar sweeps, just in case they were noticed as Lyall crested any of the ridges between them and the landing point.

Next to Rory in the rear was Jim Harpenden, the agent to be inserted. Waiting for them, if all had gone well, was Alex Kranz, who was to be pulled out and debriefed. He would have had a long and potentially hazardous trip from St Petersburg to the rendez-vous. Even so, Lyall would wait thirty minutes, no more, before he taxied out into the lake and took off again.

'I've got contact from starboard,' said Walsh, looking at the dials of the Decca XIII radar detector. 'Strong.'

'That'll be Radio Engineering Base Solka. How long till the next turn?' Lyall asked, even though Rory was fairly sure the man knew the answer. Lyall was that kind of pilot.

Walsh consulted the chart on his knee. 'Four minutes thirty-two seconds.'

'What can you do?' asked Harpenden.

Rory answered. He had done this run often enough to know the ropes. 'The Russians might not notice us. They're mostly looking for B-52s loaded with nukes coming over the Pole. We could be a flock of geese.'

'And if they do notice us?'

Rory slapped Harpenden's knee. 'They'll scramble a couple of MiGs from Alakurtti airbase. Or send a chopper in from air army base at Olenegorsk.'

'Port. Weak.'

'Unit 28278 Radio Technical Unit Air Defence radars,' intoned Lyall.

'Stronger.'

'Let's hope the operator's gone for a whizz,' said Lyall. 'but I'm taking her down. I suggest you don't look out of the window for a while, gentlemen.'

'Two minutes fifteen to the turn.'

'Roger.'

Rory heard the engine note change and felt the Beaver drop. He did look out of the window, of course. In the silvery moonlight the endless pine forests looked alarmingly close. He knew that there were ridges ahead of them way higher than their current altitude. He glanced at Harpenden. He had his eyes closed. Wise man.

'Port gone.'

'Good.'

'Starboard gone. You going to pull up for that, Skip?'

Rory decided best not to look at what Walsh could see. The nose came up and the Beaver began to climb.

'Starboard again. Weak.'

Skimming over the hills and ridges were equivalent to putting your head above the parapet to a trench in WWI. You just hoped a sniper wasn't watching and waiting.

'Ten seconds to new heading. Nine, eight, seven, six . . .'

'I've got it,' said Lyall. Rory completed the count in his head and the Beaver dipped a wing.

'Nine thirty and then approach.'

'No more dog legs,' said Lyall. 'Straight down the valley. There's a gap in the hills where they'll pick us up, but it's so brief that, with luck, Solka will think it's atmospherics. Unless Solka is speaking to Unit 28278.'

Rory sometimes wished Lyall wouldn't think aloud.

They ran on in silence, broken only by the robotic radar warnings from Walsh, but soon enough there was a silver finger of lake ahead and Lyall brought the Beaver in low, until they were beneath tree top height and streaking past the rows of trunks at what seemed like reckless speed. But the Beaver lost momentum and slumped closer to the water before hitting it gently enough to almost be a kiss, sending up what looked like sheets of molten chrome past the windows. Rory smiled to himself. He knew from other landings with different pilots how difficult that was to do.

The engine cut to a low drone and Lyall nudged the front towards the small pier. He turned to his passengers. 'Welcome to Russia, gentlemen.'

*

They rowed to the pier in an inflatable, because Lyall was worried about snagging a plane float on the underwater rocks. As Rory dug his oars in, he heard a whine, building as it bounced through the trees. An unsettling lower note boomed over the water, like a ghostly bass drum.

'What's that?' asked Harpenden nervously.

'Probably a Mil helicopter,' said Rory. A Hip or a Hound in NATO parlance. Troop-carrying. Searching for them.

The noise faded and there was just the rhythmic splash of the oars as they sank into the ink-black water. 'There,' said Harpenden.

'What?' asked Rory.

'Torch flash. Hold on. T . . . R . . . I . . . O . . . Trio? Is that right?'

'Yes.' He put his back into the stroke, and within two minutes he was tying up the inflatable and scaling the metal ladder. He reached down and grabbed Harpenden's kit bag, then stood back as the agent came up. He could feel the man's anxiety. His breath was coming fast, clouding the air.

'The worst bit is almost over,' Rory said, lifting the spy's bag and walking him towards the treeline. They had just stepped onto solid land when the two enormous spotlights flicked on, turning night into eye-squintingly bright day.

'Fuck!' yelled Harpenden and turned to run. Rory grabbed his arm and yanked him to a stop.

'Stay still, you fool. They'll shoot you before you've gone five yards. Leave this to me,' he said with a quiet confidence, although inside he was wondering what the hell had gone wrong. 'Stay here.'

As he approached the dark curtain of the woods he could just make out figures moving between the trunks and the glint of the dull metal they were holding. Soldiers. Russian soldiers. A silhouette detached from the group and walked into the light. He was pointing a Makarov pistol at Rory's chest. The Englishman raised his hands. Time to deploy his Russian.

'Captain.'

'Tell your pilot to come ashore. And any other passengers.'

'Can I have a word?'

'We're having a word. You are a British agent. You and your friend are under arrest. As will be your pilot and his plane impounded.'

He thought he heard a faint splash. A fish jumping, perhaps. More likely Walsh ditching the radar detection gear. Nothing yells 'spy' like a device designed to spot when the Soviets have 'eyes on'. Rory was surprised that Lyall hadn't cut and run. That was the protocol. Still, he was glad that Lyall was made of tougher stuff than most. This could still be salvaged.

'I think we must be lost. We are fishermen and hunters.'

The captain laughed. 'Oh, you are lost. So very, very lost.'

'If we can just have a talk over here. Those lights are giving me a headache.'

The captain hesitated and looked over his shoulder, as if worried about what his shadowy squad would think.

'I am unarmed.' Rory unbuttoned his coat and held it open. 'And what tricks can I pull?'

The captain nodded and the pair walked into the semi-gloom out of the direct beam of the lights and Rory began his pitch. This was a terrible mistake on their part. A fine was due. In dollars. They had the money in the plane.

The captain was unmoved. So, Rory told him what the real score was. That they were actually on the same side.

'I see,' the Russian said. 'Then I should find an excuse to let you go? So you can continue your mission?'

Rory nodded. 'If you don't want to be posted to some closed city in the east for the next twenty years.'

'You disappoint me, Rory Little.'

It was like a slap in the face, the use of his name. How could he know his identity? Unless, unless . . . No, nothing computed.

The Russian captain spoke, English this time, and louder than before. 'It is as you thought.'

He had addressed someone in the woods and he waited as that person crunched over pine needles and twigs and finally came into view. Wrapped in a fur coat, her face set somewhere between sadness and anger, was a familiar figure. Barbara. His wife.

*

They shared a cigarette while the spotlights were packed away, both of them leaning against the trees out of earshot of the soldiers and Harpenden.

'How long have you known?' he asked, passing the cigarette over.

'Not long. Six months, perhaps.'

'Six months? Christ. You were slow on the uptake.'

It was intended to needle Barbara, but she remained impassive. 'How long have you been in their pocket?'

'Since forty-six.'

'Why?'

'The usual story. I was a naughty boy. A very naughty boy. Not sex, money. You wouldn't remember Thumbscrew. It was an SOE circuit that I supplied cash and weapons to. Except Thumbscrew had been folded up within a day of arriving in France. I kept it alive. Pocketed the cash, sold the weapons. The Russians had proof of my crimes.'

'Christ.' And then she laughed. 'It never changes, does it?'

'Their schemes?'

'Human nature,' she said. For a moment she wondered if Rory had actually betrayed Thumbscrew in order to further his embezzlement scheme. She decided she didn't want to know the answer. He would probably lie anyway.

'How did you get on to me?'

'We suspected when you started picking people like Harpenden to go in. That man's no field agent. But he could be turned. Sent back as another mole. You have something on him, I assume?'

A nod. 'More fraud. He forged his mother's will to pay off debts.' He took the smoke back and waved a hand. 'All this, though? Rather elaborate. I take it we aren't in Russia?'

'No.'

'This isn't my lake?'

'No. It wasn't hard to find something that looked the same in the dark. We had to build the pier.'

'And the soldiers?'

'Finnish, doing a little war games exercise. They do them a lot. Your "Russian" captain was a nice chap called Timo Salo, from the state intelligence agency. And the helicopter? The Finnish army has a couple of Mil-8 Hips they use just to make the games more authentic. Oh, and all the radar tracking was just a bit of theatre. Lyall hasn't been picked up by anyone.'

'I'm flattered.'

'By what?'

'That you went to all this trouble. For me.'

'Don't be flattered.' There was an undercurrent of disdain in her voice. 'It was the only way to convince certain people you were — are — a duplicitous bastard. *Good old Rory? No, you must be mistaken.*'

'So, what happens now?'

'I fly back with Lyall.'

'And me?'

'You stay here. I mean in Russia. You'll make it to Moscow eventually. You and Kim can have tea together.'

He flung the stub of the cigarette into the darkness. 'I was never part of Philby's lot.'

'That's something, I suppose.' The moon had come out from behind the clouds and she could see his face now. The shadows gave it a devilish cast. It felt appropriate. 'The truth is we can't afford another big blow up like Burgess, Maclean, Philby. The Yanks are already reluctant to trust us with super-sensitive information. I can't say I blame them. We have to pretend you never sold us out. So, this is it. Goodbye. It's about eight miles to the border post at Silvenko.' Barbara reached into her pocket and extracted what looked like a pocket watch. She tossed it over and he plucked it from the air. 'Compass. Head north-west of here. You have good shoes on. There by dawn, I would imagine. If you aren't picked up by a patrol before that. I suppose you have a speech prepared for the local KGB people.'

'Barbara—'

'Don't!' she snapped, angered by the tenderness in that one word.

'You don't know what I'm going to say.' His eyes showed sadness and hurt, the lame puppy dog that he could do so well.

'But I do, Rory. That it was nothing personal. That you always loved me.'

'Well, that sort of thing. You were always too clever for me, Barbara.'

She gave a huff. 'But not sly enough. And Rory, it's always personal. Always. Now get going.'

'You are quite the most beautiful—'

'Fuck off, Rory.'

He nodded, put his hands in his pocket and walked towards the protective blanket of the forest. His head was held high and he began to whistle. It was the chorus from 'The Man Who Broke the Bank at Monte Carlo'.

At that moment, Barbara knew that Rory could never go quietly. He wouldn't slip into a discreet retirement. He would shoot his mouth off eventually, spill the beans at some bar or function. Sooner or later, the Americans would discover that the Brits had had yet another mole. More embarrassment would ensue, questions about whether Six could be trusted.

Rory had gone six or seven paces when Barbara pulled out the little Beretta and shot him twice, once between the shoulders and then, as he stumbled forward under the impact, in the back of the head.

She waited a few moments until the twitching stopped. When Rory was finally still, Barbara uttered a single word: 'Bastard.'

Then, without a backward glance, she turned and strode towards the pier to catch her floatplane home.

*

'Jesus,' said Muraski when it was clear the old lady had finished.

'Hhmm. I am ashamed to say that I had a bit of a wobble after that. I returned to Helsinki and locked myself in my room with a case of local vodka. I think the intention was to drink myself to death. London sent someone out to pull me out of the bottle. Henry. He convinced me I had had no choice in the matter. That Rory had cost so many lives . . .'

The sound of a sob coming from Barbara shocked Muraski.

'Sorry.' She gave a loud sniff and then blew her nose. 'As I said, all ancient history.' She had slumped back slightly, her chest rising and falling with some effort, her reserves drained by the tale.

It didn't seem all that ancient to Muraski. During the telling she had been there with Barbara in the forest, had felt the crushing weight of the decision to execute Rory. That's what it had been. Not murder. An execution. 'It was very brave of you,' she said at last.

'Brave?'

Muraski nodded. Now she knew what the story meant, what it was meant to convey. In modern parlance: *don't fuck with me. I will do anything to get to the bottom of what happened to Izzy and Ruby. And, if required, I'll kill anyone who gets in my way.*

She stood and gave Barbara her warmest smile. 'I'll get that tea.'

FORTY-EIGHT

Lieutenant Madison was a rather handsome Belgian. He was sitting in a corner of the Flying Carpet glass box, looking very pleased with himself. So pleased, in fact, that he had taken a large dump to celebrate, which a disgruntled SEAL was busy cleaning up. Like Madison, Wang, the commander of the Navy SEALs unit, standing next to the EDC, also looked quietly satisfied.

Riley had worked with EDCs – Explosive Detection Canines – before and was mostly impressed with them. He couldn't recall the exact figures, but every handler seemed keen to tell you that a dog's sense of smell was something like forty times greater than a human's. People have 6 million olfactory receptor cells; dogs have about 300 million. Around 35 per cent of a dog's brain is assigned to smell-related operations; humans hover at 5 per cent.

He nodded to Jason Truluck, the man who had pulled him to safety from the Atlantic. Wang and Riley introduced themselves, and Riley knelt down next to the dog. He knew that, in the absence of speech, the EDCs were trained to sit when they sensed something untoward. Cortez, meanwhile, took Truluck to one side, no doubt to brief him on their suspicions about Swart. As she spoke at machine-gun speed, Riley turned his own attention to the glass floor around Lieutenant Madison's paws.

He could see the mechanism that would be used to extend the glass box out of the side of the ship in calm weather or in port. The floor was not hermetically sealed; there were ventilation holes drilled in it, probably to allow the escape of air when the pistons deployed. There was nothing untoward he could see. Apart from an inch of blue wire.

'Cortez,' he said, indicating she should join him.

She excused herself from Truluck, crossed over and crouched down beside him. She peered down at the machinery and the few centimetres of blue plastic-coated wire. 'That's crap finishing for a new ship.'

'Or someone has added a little surprise to the proceedings.'

She ruffled the dog's neck fur and a tongue shot out in appreciation. 'And the lieutenant here thinks something is off.'

He stood and walked across to Truluck, who was speaking into a radio. Riley waited till he had finished. 'We might have something here,' he said.

'Right.' Truluck lowered his voice. 'Do you buy that idea? That Swart had something to do with this?' He was obviously still grappling with what Cortez had told him.

'You knew him?' Riley asked.

'Not well, no.'

'Well, we think it's worth a punt. Everyone is bribable, after all. It's just a matter of price. Did he have any close friends on board?'

'We haven't been a company long enough for real friendships to emerge, as far as I can tell. I'll speak to his people, his deputy and so on, see if anything was amiss.'

'Good. Now, how do we get into the mechanism that extends this thing?'

'The deck just below. Karun Roy is your man. Chief Engineer.'

'Can you get him up here?'

'Sure.'

Riley went back to where Cortez was still kneeling, looking down at the suspect wire. He spoke to Wang.

'Did your man here do the whole of this box?' He meant the dog.

'Yeah,' the American said in his surprisingly deep drawl. 'That was the only spot that got a reaction. Why?'

'I don't like the fact we could see that wire. It's too easy. Too careless. Are the rest of your guys still looking?'

'Of course.' There was just a hint of irritation that Riley should suggest they would give up on the first hit from their EDC. 'No stone unturned and then turned again.'

'Glad to hear it. Okay, do me a favour?'

'What's that?' asked Wang.

'Give his nose one more turn around here and then the rest of this deck and then the one below.'

'We've done that.'

'I know. But this could be a tricky fucker. Indulge me. I agree with Madison, something doesn't smell right.' Riley glanced over at the dog, still enjoying the attention from Cortez. 'But he hasn't earned his Bonio just yet.'

FORTY-NINE

BaseHeart unwrapped a Pret sandwich and took a bite, stealing a guilty glance at his daughter. 'Soon be over,' he managed to say with a full mouth. 'Then back to a diet. Only a matter of hours now.'

What he thought of as Operation Black Key was still on a course, if not *the* course to a successful conclusion. The Hercules disaster could not have been predicted. Nor the subsequent deployment of the Americans. He couldn't have foreseen that. Except he had, after a fashion. He had created a whole sequence of 'If A, then B' playbooks, all leading towards the same conclusion. A lot of money in his banks. He would bleed this beast dry.

He took another huge bite of cheese and pickle and glanced at the clock. Time was running out. Eighty minutes left. Still, there was no word from Greggs and COBRA. But that committee did not keep regular hours.

BaseHeart put the sandwich to one side and broke open the packaging on a pay-as-you-go phone. He powered it up and inserted the headphone/microphone earbuds. Onto the mic he clipped the Taiwanese-made 'Deceiver', an electronic device that would scramble the audio profile of his speech. He set the degree of distortion so that it would not sound inhuman, but if anyone were to tape him, the voiceprint would no longer match his regular speaking voice. It was a precaution he only took with journalists, who might tape the conversation, and nervous politicians he was blackmailing. For the latter he used the kind of timbre that made Greggs think he was dealing with a pitiless automaton. Which, in one sense, he was.

He looked at a second screen, which was showing the FTSE 100 index and a screen-bottom tickertape of other share prices. He hit a number on the computer keyboard and a pop-up screen appeared. It was a list of journalists. A red line was through several names, those he had already fed stories to. He scrolled down and selected three candidates. He quickly narrowed it down to Hamish Stewart, Senior Investment Commentator for the *Financial Times*. People sat up and took notice of him.

He cleared his throat and practised his opening lines, conjuring the plummy tones of the public-schooled, a voice that would automatically put any *FT* journalist at ease. *One of us,* it said. 'Hello, Mr Stewart. You don't know me. My name is Johnson. Max Johnson. I think I have a story for you.' A story you need to put on the website, he thought. They couldn't wait for the old, doomed dinosaur of the print edition.

He looked at the wall clock. Should he call him yet? Timing was of the essence. He had to hit the markets just right. Perhaps he should wait an hour or two.

A second burner phone on his desk rang. He picked it up. It was Greggs. News from COBRA, no doubt. Good news, he hoped. More tinder for the fire.

FIFTY

This, thought Captain Nansen, is what they mean by an angry mob. Well, not a mob, exactly. But a hostile audience. Once Finnegan had let the cat out of the bag – an act that almost earned him a fist in the face from Nansen – the captain had put out a message over the speakers, and via a letter delivered to all cabins, that a meeting would be held in the grand ballroom. This was the captain's least favourite public space on the ship, rebelling against the clean design aesthetic in place elsewhere on *Rapide*. Its centrepiece was a giant chandelier, studded with Swarovski crystals, and there were gilt cherubs, red velvet swags, ormolu light brackets and silk panels. It was like a cross between the Palace of Versailles and Blackpool Tower ballroom, with perhaps a touch of the Paris Opéra.

There must have been close to a thousand people in the overwrought room, not every passenger, but almost. A full house. So full, there weren't enough chairs, so many were standing at the rear and sides.

Some had split into cadres, with an obvious leader – usually a male – and those were the ones who could smell big money in this crisis. Compensation was a word he had already picked out of the general hubbub. Those pockets gave off a sense of greed and entitlement and outrage. The others, the amorphous majority, had a whiff of anger and anxiety about them. Some also exuded the unmistakable aroma of hard liquor. Nansen might have to consider closing the bars or putting a cap on drink purchases. Booze and cruises made for volatile bedfellows at the best of times. Add fear of dying into the mix and it made for a very unstable threesome.

What do you expect me to do? part of him wanted to demand. *It's a shit show. But it's not a shit show of my making. Suggestions from the floor welcome.*

Or maybe not.

The captain was sitting at a desk on stage with Jason Truluck and Rashmi Fonseka, the Guest Security Supervisor who had been Swart's deputy. She still had red eyes from crying over her boss's horrible demise. Nansen had questioned her closely about Swart, but she hardly knew the man. If the bomb people's theory was correct — and Nansen had his doubts — then the idiot probably acted alone. He had, of course, alerted Anglo-American about the notion that Swart was a bad actor and they were going through his background with the proverbial fine-tooth comb.

Several members of Fonseka's security staff were patrolling the room looking for those who decided the embargo on filming the event didn't apply to them. There was a surprisingly large number who thought that the right to keep and bear cell phones was actually the 28th Amendment in the US Constitution. There had already been some heated exchanges. Finnegan, Mr Pork Knuckle, was there, arms folded, glaring at him. Nansen was still tempted to put him in the brig, but the damage was done. He had gambled on getting him onside and failed.

His eyes fell on Christian Ledgard, whose leg was pistoning up and down. He was there with his little coterie – Shelby, bodyguard and his chums Ben and Amber X, who had kept a low profile

KIM HUGHES

since it transpired that their friend was the unsuspecting engine driving this situation. Ledgard himself had a face like a dropped pie. Once the fake code ruse had floundered, Anglo-American had asked Nansen to pressurise the man to at least go through the motions of releasing the real Black Key. He had refused and Nansen could hardly force him.

Nansen looked at his watch. Fifty minutes until BaseHeart's time was up. He had best get a move on. He tapped the microphone to make sure it was live and leaned into it.

'Ladies and gentlemen.' There was an unfortunate howl of feedback, but it did the trick. The room settled and the audience turned to face him expectantly.

'And others. Thank you for coming and thank you for your patience. I know you have lots of questions.' Many hands shot up, waving like a fleshy field of wheat. 'But if you will bear with me, I would like to make a statement. I promise you it will give you the facts as we know them.'

Truluck flashed him an *is-that-wise* look? The Royal Navy had imbued in him a need-to-know attitude. And civilians didn't need to know. But this wasn't the Royal Navy. Nansen was involved in a tricky PR campaign and he was well aware that in one sense, he held the future of Anglo-American in his hands. No wonder he was sweating.

'Afterwards, I will take questions from the floor.'

He was as good as his word. He gave them the absolute unvarnished truth, as much as he knew it, about the destruction of the Hercules and the deployment of the US forces. He explained that the ship was being re-searched, public and crew areas first, but it might involve cabin-to-cabin too. He held back about the demand for the Black Key codes, because that was at an impasse and he didn't want Ledgard to be the subject of threats, coercion or abuse.

268

There was a brief, almost stunned silence when he had finished. Then the hands again. He pointed to a woman in the front row, who was wearing a tracksuit accessorised with pearls the size of Slazenger 7 golf balls. 'How easy is it to sink the ship?'

A murmur of approval of the question went around the crowd. Many nodded, as if they had been about to ask the same.

'Extremely difficult. The US Navy SEAL team has gone over every inch of *Rapide* below the waterline. Commander Wang is confident there are no devices that could threaten the ship.' He raised his voice to cover the swell of volume building from the crowd. 'And if it did happen . . .' He cleared his throat. 'If it did happen, the ship is very well designed. I am not going to tempt fate by saying "unsinkable", but I am confident *Rapide* would come through any, uh, incident.'

'Are there enough lifeboats?' someone shouted.

'Please, if you could wait till I point at you.' He selected a young, smartly dressed man. 'Sir?'

'Are there enough lifeboats?' he asked, to some laughter.

'Yes,' said Nansen. 'With capacity to spare. All exceeding SOLAS specifications and regulations. That's Safety of Life At Sea. All have quick-release systems and the ability to be launched in a 25-degree list, or heel as we call it.' The QRS was a vast improvement on the old-fashioned davits system, which had to be swung out before the lifeboat could be lowered. On the QRS the davits were rigid girders extended out either electronically, hydraulically or, as a last resort, by hand. Once occupied by the passengers, and with the steel beams holding the hoist ropes extended, the boats could be in the water in a matter of seconds. But Nansen didn't want to get bogged down with technicalities. 'If you're worried I suggest you all check your lifejackets are at hand and re-familiarise yourself with your muster station.' He pointed into the audience once again. 'Yes. In the white top.'

The man stood. His polo shirt was stretched over an ample belly and he spoke in a southern drawl. Texan? Nansen couldn't tell. 'Is it true that some details of our situation have leaked to the press?'

Nansen nodded. The A-AL press office had been inundated by calls, texts and emails from worried friends and relatives, to the point where the comms systems had all crashed. 'Unfortunately, yes. It isn't helping.' Nansen pointed towards the back of the room. 'Madam—'

'Excuse me, sir,' the Texan continued with exaggerated politeness. 'Ah have not finished. If that is the case, our loved ones must be mightily worried.' A grumble of approval built and ebbed way. 'So, should we not be given the Wi-Fi back, if only for a short time, so we can reassure them things are in hand?'

The grumble turned into something of a roar. Nansen waited. 'There is no easy way to put this. The technicians on board are concerned that any device might be triggered over the Wi-Fi network.'

A flash of fear ran through the crowd.

'They have also asked me to disable the Bluetooth, for similar reasons, so the apps will stop working.' Now shouts went up. It was as if he had told them he was turning off their pacemakers. 'Do not worry, there are manual options for most things. Sir? To my right. Blue tie.'

This one stood, too. He spoke with a slight Spanish accent. 'I'd like to discuss compensation packages.'

'I am afraid that is a job for our lawyers.'

That didn't phase him and he started to lay out his terms. Nansen let him run. He wouldn't be making any more promises, no matter how vague. Head office had made that clear. He found himself pondering, yet again, what the aftermath of this fiasco would be for his career.

'When will we reach New York?'

This was the moment that Nansen finally returned his full attention to the proceedings. 'As you can see, the weather has improved and our speed has increased accordingly. But . . .' Here we go, he thought. 'We're not going to New York.'

He held up a hand as the crowd reacted, anger and disbelief jumping from group to group like wildfire.

'Please. It has been decided it is more practical to divert to Halifax.'

'How does bloody Halifax feel about that?' English, northern accent, corpulent red-faced man at the back.

'I'm sorry?' Nansen asked. Did he think he meant Halifax in Yorkshire?

'Look at your history, man. Back to 1917. In Halifax harbour the SS *Mont-Blanc* collides with a Norwegian ship. The French vessel is full of explosives. The lot goes up. Two thousand dead, seventeen thousand injured, no docks left.'

We are not full of explosives, he wanted to say, and it was reckless to suggest that. Nansen tempered his response. 'Hardly the same situation.'

'Halifax?' a woman in the front row shouted. 'It's the middle of nowhere. Worse. It's Nova Scotia!' She said it like he was suggesting colonising Mars.

'I think we should put it to the vote,' said the Spanish guy. 'Decide whether we want New York or Halifax.'

Nansen leaned into the microphone again and spoke softly. 'I am all for democracy in most situations, but this is my ship. You can vote on what to have for dessert or what songs the band plays. Everything else is my decision. I'm the captain.'

271

There was a scattering of applause. He had made another omission there: they could vote for America all they liked, but the New York Harbor Authority would not allow *Rapide* to sail to its designated berth at Pier 90 nor at the Brooklyn Cruise Terminal. Not while it might be a 'live, ongoing threat' as they put it. It would be quarantined at a 'safe anchor point' for full inspection and boarding by the FBI, ATF and a raft of other agencies. It was probably going to be quicker putting in at Halifax, given the reams of red tape awaiting them in NYC.

'We will be docking within twenty-four hours. We are also now within fixed-wing aircraft cover from Maritime Forces Atlantic. Soon, we'll be in helicopter range, too. A frigate has been diverted to escort us into port. I'm sure you agree, the sooner we disembark, the better.' Even if they could have continued to New York, the atmosphere on board had already curdled. There was no chance of business as usual There goes the hip hop burlesque show, he thought, albeit with little regret.

He caught Ledgard's eyes and wished he hadn't. The man looked as if he wanted to kill him. His wife, too, was about as attractive and inviting as a bear trap at that moment. Clark and Amber X appeared to be more sanguine and had placed themselves some way from the Ledgards.

'The company has already chartered various aircrafts to fly you on to New York, after clearance by the authorities.' Which meant the anti-terrorism branch of the Canadian Army and the Royal Canadian Mounted Police. It was going to be a slow process, but not as tedious as docking in the United States. 'The company will also, of course, pick up any extra transportation costs.'

No doubt as soon as Ledgard could get back on his computer, which still had limited outside access, he would try to find an air freight company to take his cars down to the start of his precious

rally. Which might cost a small fortune. He could drive it in fourteen hours, batteries permitting. Which would save A-AL a lot of
cash. So he added a caveat.

'Within reason.'

'We should take to the lifeboats!'

'No . . .' began Nansen.

'They're telling us to stay behind . . . We'll all die out here.'

Truluck stood and with a voice that embodied hundreds of
years of Royal Navy discipline, bellowed loud enough to drown
out the babble. 'There are armed guards on the lifeboats. Because
that is not the best option. We have experts on board who will
bring this situation under control. Comparisons with the *Titanic*
are less than helpful. You need to have some backbone, ladies
and gentlemen.' He waited a beat. 'Or however you identify
yourselves.'

Nansen spoke from the corner of his mouth. 'Armed guards?'

Truluck covered his microphone and lowered his voice. 'Not
yet. But we don't want a stampede towards the boats, Skip.' He
addressed the audience again. 'You have as your captain the best
in the business. I suggest you give him your trust and support.'

Nansen felt a little of glow of embarrassment on the back of
his neck as well as a prickle of guilt that he ever doubted Truluck.
He looked down at the desk as a folded piece of paper was passed
to him by Jon Capelli, as he said, 'Your brother insisted we give
you this.'

He flipped the note open. It had one word on it. He had trouble
focusing. He needed sleep, but there was no way he was going to
get that anytime soon. He blinked and the letters sharpened into
something so unexpected that he almost gasped.

Reptilicus.

It generated a little stab of fear inside him, a memory of

an ancient terror that he hadn't experienced for a long time. *Reptilicus.* He took a deep breath, ready to deploy his best brook-no-argument *basso profundo*. The note, with its sense of warning and childhood dread, meant it was time to bring this meeting to a close.

FIFTY-ONE

The door providing access to the machinery that extended the Flying Carpet was set back in a small recess off the main passageway on deck ten, which had been cleared of those passengers not at the general meeting on deck five. The door could be opened by an alphanumerical pad or swipe card. Cortez and Riley were only too aware that either could be wired up to detonate a bomb. For a few minutes Riley, Cortez and Karun Roy simply stared at the steel door, pondering what little surprises might be waiting on the other side.

Roy was a small man, just over five feet, and spoke with a nervous energy. Spoke too much, in fact. Once Riley had extracted as much information about the door as possible – one handle, swung up to unlock, opened outwards, step down once inside – he had decided they needed some quiet.

'I have an access card,' Roy said.

Riley thought about this. He had two objections. It was simpler to wire up a swipe device to detonate a bomb and it would be harder to activate from a safe distance than a keypad.

'No,' he said to Roy. 'We are going with the keypad. But the card reader: would a computer keep a log of who had accessed this room?'

'Probably, yes. But not the keypad. It's just there as a secondary electrical circuit backup. In case the swipe fails.'

'Can you check for us? And if there is any CCTV footage of this corridor here?'

'Yes. But it's been down for a few hours now.'

'Down? Why?'

He explained about the fire in the CCTV server system cupboard.

Sabotage? Riley wondered. 'Well, we'll take a look when we get a chance. In the meantime, can you check and get us the log of those who have been in? We're fine here.'

As he reluctantly turned to go, Riley asked: 'Karun. What's the code?'

'Seven-nine-zero-one-hash.'

When he had gone he asked Cortez: 'Suit up?'

'Whoever goes down there and punches in the code should.'

'Not going to be much use if that door comes off its hinges.'

'No,' she agreed. 'You got a robot?'

'No.'

'We have.'

'Of course you have.' He thought for a minute. 'What kind?'

'The L-11.'

The Lockheed 11 was a lightweight model, mainly used for remote inspection. It's manipulative functions were limited. 'Bit of a toy,' he said. 'No offence.'

'Offence taken,' she said, as if he had insulted a family member.

'All we need is an expandable antenna, like a selfie stick. Have to be, say, two metres long. We could tap in the codes from around the corner.'

'Although the one doing the tapping should also wear a bomb suit,' she suggested.

'By the book, Cortez?'

'By the book, Riley.'

'Yeah, well, I'm not much of a reader. A suit'll slow us down.'

'Your call.' She nodded at the long black sausage of a kit bag she had dumped down the corridor. 'Got an extendable probe in there that could work. From a safe distance. Kinda.'

Riley reached into his pocket. 'Heads or tails?'

Cortez hesitated. 'Heads.'

He flipped the coin. 'Heads.'

'I'm up then,' she said.

'Best of three?'

'Fuck off, loser.'

It was no use pulling the *I'm-a-man-I'll-do-it* macho routine. Cortez was a star graduate of the Redstone Arsenal Academy at the Hazardous Devices School. She had done courses in chemistry, physics, robot control, basic electronic countermeasures, manual defusing and more. But that didn't mean he was going to let her waltz in blind.

'We should drill the bulkhead first,' he said, 'Offset from the door frame. Put a FERRET in.' This was an inspection camera. 'Make sure there's no party tricks.'

'Good idea.'

Riley looked at his watch. Forty minutes left until the deadline. 'Best get a move on, eh?'

*

Three minutes later, Riley, ear defenders on, was kneeling at the door, putting a three-centimetre circular hole cutter in the chuck of his high-torque cordless drill.

'Bigger,' said Cortez, who was standing back in the main passageway, peering around the corner.

'What?'

'You need a bigger hole.'

'Why? The FERRET will go in there.' The inspection device was a small diameter, semi-rigid flexible tube, like a larger version of an endoscopy camera.

'Trust me. Give me three inches. Four would be better.'

Can you make do with a solid eight? Riley bit his tongue on the standard army-issue response to her request. Best not. In silence he used a size ten bit to punch a guide hole through the metal wall and then took out a four-inch circle of metal with the round cutter. 'Camera?'

Cortez held up a small case as she approached him. 'Got it.'

She knelt, unclipped the case and from it extracted what looked like an oversized wristwatch that reminded Riley of a giant 1970s Seiko. 'Monitor and controls,' she said, as if that explained anything.

'More toys?'

She ignored him. Next out came a spindly little object which appeared to be constructed out of matchsticks that had been painted with black Hammerite. There were two other sections that clipped on to complete the unit, the latter consisting of four tiny rotors sitting on a frame.

'Jesus,' he said. 'Is that a drone?'

'Of sorts. It's called a Hornet. It's our eyes.'

Cortez stood and fed the delicate mechanical creature through the hole, her small hand sliding through easily. She offered the wrist with the controller strapped to it to Riley. 'Press the red button.'

He did so and heard a high-pitched whine from beyond the aperture he had made. Cortez withdrew her hand and began to swipe and press on the screen on her wrist. A small but very clear image of the world beyond the door appeared.

'How is it back there in the Stone Age?' Cortez asked him with a cheeky grin.

'Bit bored with the taste of mammoth.'

For six minutes, just about its flight time thanks to the small battery, they used the Hornet to examine the far side of the door for wires or infrared beams. There was nothing untoward they could see. That didn't mean it was safe to just barge in.

When they were as satisfied as they could be, Cortez landed the drone on the floor inside and switched off the monitor.

'We go manual now?' he asked, looking at his watch. Twenty-seven minutes left off the deadline.

'Fine with me.'

They took up position either side of the short corridor that led to the door. Cortez took the left hand side, the extended metal probe in her hand. Although she had agreed to ditch the whole bomb suit, she had put on a visor to protect her face, in case shrapnel should start flying. They both knew that if the door was wired to blow, it would release a pulverising mixture of heat, gas and metal fragments. The visor would help her eyes and face, but the chances of Cortez being able to withdraw her arm in time were fifty-fifty, depending on what type of circuit was used. But she could withdraw it a lot quicker without a bomb suit weighing her down. At least, that's what they hoped.

'How come you got this gig?' he asked. 'Navy SEALs got hundreds of Operators of its own.' Seven hundred or so bomb specialists was what he had heard. Although many of them were employed on US Navy ships. Any vessel that carried weapons or aircraft had to have at least one bomb-tech on board in case of mishaps.

'It wasn't because I heard you were on it,' she said. 'In case you were wondering.'

'I sort of guessed that.'

'Between you and me? The Norfolk Virginia mobile det would have been used, but there was a crash and fire on one of the big carriers. A fully armed F-35. All hands on deck. Literally. So, they came for me.'

She extended the probe and tested its weight when held out horizontally.

'So, you seen any action lately?' she asked him, her words muffled by the visor.

He assumed she meant in his professional rather than private life. 'Just some relic from World War Two. You?'

'This is about it. Seven-nine-zero-one-hash, right?'

'Right.' Then: 'Hold on.'

'What?'

Riley stepped across the opening of the recess and lifted her visor. He felt her tense a little. 'Watcha doin'?'

He pulled a handkerchief from his pocket and wiped the inside of the plastic face shield until it was clear once more. Misty visors were one of the more mundane problems with the job, but they could cause big trouble. You want to be able to see clearly when you are gambling with your life. And pressing buttons from a distance.

'I don't need a half-blind partner.'

'Copy that. Time?'

'Twenty-five and counting.'

Riley went back to his previous position, flat to the wall. Cortez swung herself into harm's way and, using the telescopic steel rod, punched in the door codes and then swung back. They heard the lock bolts withdraw with a *thunk*. They waited. After a pause, they clicked back again. No bang.

All they had to worry about now was the handle. And the doorframe. Both could be hot-wired.

Cortez took off the visor, jutted out her jaw and blew some air over her face. Together they moved into the short corridor and examined the door itself and where it met the frame. Being a new ship, the paint was fresh and unmarked. There were no scratches or chips that looked worrying. The handle, Karun Roy had told them, clicked up into the 'open' position. Then you simply pulled and the door opened. Or so they hoped.

When they were satisfied that they had inspected it thoroughly, Cortez put the face protection back on.

'Maybe use the robot for this part?' she suggested.

'Can you leave off about the bloody robot? Just because you brought it doesn't mean you have to unpack it.' Riley knew from bitter experience that, like all machinery, the 'wheelbarrows' sometimes let you down, especially the small, highly portable models. Although every now and then they had the irritating habit of saving your life. But not here, as he explained: 'Look at this door. It isn't your average domestic number. Your L-11 doesn't have the strength or versatility to lift that lever, let alone pull the door open. Not in the time we have left.'

That's about twenty-two minutes, pal.

I know, Nick, I know.

Just sayin'.

Like that helps. 'Sometimes you have to stay in the Stone Age,' he said.

'Okay, better ideas welcome,' Cortez said.

From his bag back in the main corridor Riley fetched a length of fine nylon rope. 'We use this, eh?'

'Worth a go.' She walked over, took it and hooked it onto her belt. 'Stand back.'

Riley stayed where he was while Cortez walked towards the entrance to the machine room as slowly as if she were approaching an IED in Afghan in a full bomb suit. Not that she had ever served there, but she would have been taught at HDC that you never rush. You measured every step. Pace, stop, look, pace, step right, stop, step left. Everyone had their own little sequence. On paper it would look like one of those old-fashioned ballroom instructions for the foxtrot or waltz. What it was really doing was trying to make sure this wasn't a dance of death.

'Okay, punching in the code. Let's hope it's not a two-step we are doing here.'

'I doubt it,' he said. Although he didn't know why. It was possible to rig the explosives so that the first punch of the code, the test one, didn't trigger anything. That the second inputting of the numbers was what initiated the blast. Or a timer was set up to start counting down for a few minutes after the initial code entry, blowing up when the techs came back to gain entry.

'Code in.' Out in the main passageway, still pressed to the wall, Riley thought he could hear Cortez's heart thumping in her chest through the comms. You can never purge all the fear entirely. Your body was telling you it was time to cut and run. The logical thing to do. The instinct – or one of them anyway – that all ATOs are trained to suppress. Then he realised the thumping in his ears was his own heart.

'Handle up,' Cortez yelled. 'Still here.'

'Glad to hear it.'

Cortez reappeared, rope gripped in one hand. She rounded the corner to take her out of the direct line of fire and gave a tug. There was the rubbery plop of a seal breaking and then the faintest of creaks followed by a clang. New hinges, well oiled. Cortez took off the visor, shook her head and peeked around at the now-open door.

'We must have less than twenty minutes,' she said.

Eighteen, mate. Eighteen.

'About that,' said Riley. 'Let's have a quick shufti at that door-frame, shall we?'

She gave a croaky laugh. 'That sounds kinda rude, Riley.'

'It isn't. Come on.'

Seventeen minutes.

FIFTY-TWO

Clive Greggs slumped in the chair in front of the unlit fire in the main room of his house in Chelsea, a glass of whisky in his hand. He didn't particularly like the drink, but an over-generous pouring of a decent single malt felt like the last resort of a scoundrel. That and a revolver.

It was getting dark, but he left the lights off. He felt like hiding from the world. He could hear someone in the kitchen. Jessica? Or Xanthe? He was too weary to call out. The COBRA session he had insisted on attending had drained him so much that Pearman had sent him home after asking if he was unwell. Not unwell, he had felt like replying. *Sick.*

Sick to his swollen stomach. How could it have come to this? Being a puppet of some unknown nutter. Going against everything he had stood for in his political career. All because of a youthful indiscretion. Well, not so youthful. That was part of the problem. The only youth on show was . . .

He let out a yelp. A tongue of pain licked down the back of his leg. Sciatica. Probably from sitting on his fat arse for hours on end in meetings. He rubbed at it, to little avail. God, he was crumbling, mentally and physically. He reached down with some effort, undid his laces and shucked off his George Cleverleys.

Pulling himself out of the chair with a grunt, he padded in stock-inged feet over to the drinks trolley and poured himself a fresh medicinal dose of whisky. He reclaimed the armchair with a sigh and sipped his drink.

Not for the first time, he wondered what his options were. To confess? But surely that moment had gone. The time for that was when the little worm with the Dalek voice had first tapped him. Now Greggs had leaked information from the Cabinet Office, he was beyond the pale. Excommunication and worse lay ahead. He saw his political life rapidly falling apart, like a jigsaw in reverse as he lost pieces in rapid succession.

And he hadn't yet faced up to what would happen to his imme-diate family. Jessica had been a loyal loving wife, an asset to his career. But when friends and acquaintances had strayed in one way or another, she had peeled away her civilised veneer to reveal the she-wolf beneath. He always assumed it was a display of what would happen if he ever went beyond 'window shopping' as she called his occasional stray glance.

Goodbye to the house in Ascott-under-Wychwood, and with it long lunches at The Swan. Farewell the Ferrari, although he could live without that boy's toy, he supposed. But maybe even the Range Rover and the Merc would go. Oh, and the half share of the villa in Umbria.

More whisky.

He could always take what used to be known as the honourable way out. But how? He had already thought about the old exhaust pipe suffocation – he had read that was the best method – but he couldn't imagine him actually doing it. Poison? Gunshot? Hanging? Leaping from a tall building?

No, no, no. The thought of the puzzled, bereft children and the anguish that it would mean for his wife stayed his hand. He wondered how long it would take for him to simply drink himself to death. That would at least give them time to adjust.

The door opened, the main light flicked on and a plate holding a cheese and tomato sandwich the size of a house brick entered. It was followed by a long, skinny arm and then a matching frame, topped with long, blond hair, roughly tied back into a ponytail.

'Hey, Dad.'

Greggs started in shock. It was Maximillian – Max – his son, taller and more tanned than he remembered, radiating the energy and confidence of the invincible young. All the acne had long gone, and the slight moon-face had been replaced by something more chiselled. He even made the ponytail look half decent. His son, he realised, was strikingly handsome.

'Max, bloody hell, I thought ... You were in Colombia last I heard. Weren't you going to Mexico?'

Max took the other chair and examined his sandwich as if it were a piece of art. Then he looked up and smiled. 'Change of plan.'

The wolfish grin told Greggs that the change involved a girl.

'You were meant to be away for a year.'

'Sorry to disappoint,' he said and took a hefty bite of the construction.

'That's not what I meant. All okay?'

A nod was all his son could manage.

'No trouble?'

A shake of the head this time.

'Good.'

Greggs wondered what his son would do now. He had deferred university for the year-long South America trip and had managed five months, in which he had asked for 'funds' or 'a loan' on four occasions. He doubted that Max had returned because he was too embarrassed to ask for more. That would never have been on the cards. So, unless he left one step ahead of the police or drug dealers, he had come back thanks to the pull of some sort of holiday romance.

Greggs took another slug of whisky and felt a quiver of needles land in his big toe. He groaned.

'You all right, Dad?' Max finally asked, once his mouth had emptied.

'Yes. Well, no. Not really.'

Max looked taken aback, as if that answer was both surprising and unacceptable. He didn't want his father to have deep problems or issues. Just deep pockets. 'Oh. Sorry to hear that. What is it?'

Max took another shark-sized bite from the sandwich and Greggs realised he wouldn't be speaking for some time. Before his higher brain centres could stop him, words began to spill from his mouth.

'Max, I've been a very foolish man.'

FIFTY-THREE

You don't just walk into a 'hot' room. The clock might be ticking down, but fools rushed in and stood on a pressure plate that put two contacts together and . . . So you fear to tread, even if time is running short. You look for plates and you look for gossamer-thin wires or a passive infrared detector or switch that will detonate a device if the beam is broken. You let it soak, as they said, before you crossed the threshold. And you do it every time, in every doorway and exit, every car and truck. It's how you stay alive.

So they killed time, sweated the space before they entered, all the time scanning the threshold for any nasty surprises.

'So is what I heard true?' she asked by way of conversation. 'About the shit that went down before they got your wife—'

'Ex-wife.'

'—and daughter?'

'I don't know what you heard.'

'Then enlighten me.'

So he did, much to his own surprise, almost as a series of bullet points, from the Nottingham bomb through to the disappearance of Izzy and Ruby. He managed to keep it together, externally at least. But every word, especially towards the end, seemed to burn a hole in his guts.

'Fuck, man. That's bad,' she said when he had finished.

Bad didn't begin to cover it. 'Yeah. You know what's odd? I feel their absence like I'm dragging a big rock behind me all the time. How can nothing weigh so much?'

She had no answer for that.

'Time?' he asked.

'Let's let it soak a tad more.' She spoke the next few sentences so softly, he had to strain to hear. 'I do know how you feel. I lost a kid. Almost at term. I went out on a call. Eight months pregnant.'

'You worked that late?'

'Not officially. One of the teams asked for my advice. There was what they thought might be a WWII mine in the harbour at Port Newark. Just come and take a look, we'll do the rest. They didn't want to wind up the Navy EOD guys.'

'Never really off duty, eh?'

'No shit. But I never made it to the harbour. Got hit by a truck, rear-ended, in the Lincoln Tunnel. Went into the trunk of the car in front. Bang. Airbags didn't deploy. Transpired they'd been turned off. I didn't even know you could do that. Turn 'em off. But the one careful driver before us must have done it. So, I was trapped.' She mimed having a large belly. 'Concussed. Broken rib, fractured ankle. I survived, the baby didn't. End of story.'

Not quite, he sensed. After a while she gave him the coda.

'Ray, my husband, blamed me. I should have said no to going out. Which turned out to be a rusty barbecue, you know, with the lid? I killed his son going to look at a fuckin' Weber grill. You know what he said? We, us, the people in our business, we're like bullfighters or old-time racing drivers or barnstormers. That we're half in love with death. The romance of it anyway.'

There might be some truth in there, but he didn't want to admit it to Cortez. Or anyone. It was a familiar question for an

ATO: how the hell can you do what you do? And why? Riley had never come up with a convincing answer. 'There's no romance when our game goes tits up. We don't even get to drive a fancy car or wear tight trousers and a little jacket like matadors.' He pointed a finger. 'The bomb suit does not count.'

'Right. Nobody ever said to one of us, "Hey, why don't you slip into your sexy work gear, let's do some cosplay."' She gave a lung-busting sigh. 'Not like firefighters. Anyway, five years gone since the divorce, water under the George Washington Bridge.'

For a few seconds, the only sounds came from the creaks and pops of the ship.

'Clear?' he asked, checking his watch again. She had used up four precious minutes. Only twelve left. 'Got to be by now?'

Cortez didn't reply immediately. He saw her mouth tighten, creating a few lines on her cheek. He knew she was remembering other doors, other corridors, other bombs, where maybe things hadn't gone so well for someone, wondering what they could have done differently.

'I reckon,' she replied eventually. 'I'm still point, Riley.'

'Be my guest.'

Some gentleman.

It's called being woke, Nick. Things have changed since you checked out.

Cortez went in first. Riley counted to ten and followed.

They were looking at a room full of unfamiliar machinery, a lot of metal pipes and levers and hydraulics.

The core of the room was a large electric motor that powered the pistons that extended the Flying Carpet along the rails it ran on. Riley did a quick visual, searching for anything that looked like it didn't belong. He couldn't actually see the room above, there being a metal shield over most of the ceiling, so the drinkers in the cocktail bar, which is what it was when retracted, didn't have to look down into the working nuts and bolts of the extendable space. Why spoil the magic?

'Riley. Come here.'

Cortez was standing below the spot where Madison had sat down. There was a steel track on either side of the base of the glass box, with captive wheels inside. These guide rails ran above their heads. On the track on the right hand side, one of the wheels had a slack piece of blue wire running from it, the one they could just make out from the floor above.

Neither of them said a word as they took in the path of the wire and what it led to. Once more, Riley consulted the Omega. Six minutes.

Now he started to sweat.

FIFTY-FOUR

When they were children, younger than ten, anyway, the Nansen brothers, Jakob and Harald, stumbled upon an old monster movie on TV. Normally, their mother would have turned it off, fearing nightmares. But this one was different. The creature in the movie didn't raze downtown Tokyo, trash the White House or climb the Empire State Building. No, the target for the massive regenerated reptile was Scandinavia. Not, unfortunately, Norway, their home turf — it was always somehow invigorating to see your own back-yard monstered — but the Danish countryside and landmarks of Copenhagen, including the Langebro Bridge.

Reptilicus, their codeword for when their father was, like the pre-historic dinosaur, on the rampage. The warning could be written on paper or in the steam on a window or shouted or whispered or sometimes simply mouthed, silently, eyes wide with fear. It always meant the same thing: trouble is coming.

So seeing it told Nansen that something serious was up with his brother. Something that he could not ignore. It wouldn't be to do with their father. Could it be about their mother? No, it was more likely to be about Jakob. As he hurried from the meeting, questions, yells of anger and howls of derision ringing in his ears, he clenched his fists in anticipation of being furious with Jakob once more. If he was using their shared childhood code merely to get his attention, the captain swore he would cut his brother dead. After he had sold whatever of Jakob's possessions he needed to repay their mother.

He entered the radio room and asked the two duty operators for some privacy. He could have made the call from the bridge, but he had a feeling he didn't want witnesses for this. His nerves were already ragged, it wouldn't take much to push him over the edge. His head was swimming with fatigue.

He used the satellite phone to call his brother's cell phone. Lord alone knew how much this was going to cost. Jakob picked up on the second ring.

'Can I please speak to Captain Harald Nansen as a matter or urgency?' He sounded breathless. An image came into Nansen's mind of Jacob in New York, tie pulled down, his face glazed with sweat, cigarette in his mouth, tumbler of liquor in hand.

'It's me, Jakob. Are you okay?'

'Yes, yes. Everyone is fine.'

'Good,' he said with some relief.

'Listen, you know I've been trying to make good some of the losses we've made? The company, I mean.'

'What have you done now?'

'Nothing. Well, not exactly nothing. You heard of the Bourseul Exchange?'

'Boor who?'

'Bourseul. He invented the telephone.'

Nansen thought that was Alexander Graham Bell, but he sensed Jacob wasn't in the mood for pedantry. 'Go on.'

'Well, it's not exactly above board.'

'Jakob—'

'It's not illegal, either. You know regulation has trouble keeping up with technology. Think of it as an underground Bloomberg. You have to pay through the nose to access it, but when you do . . .'

'I can't give you any money, Jakob. I asked you not to involve the family in any of your schemes. I don't know if you heard that I am in the middle of something myself.' Nansen's eyes went to the clock. Six minutes. He felt a tightness in his chest.

'Of course I heard! That's why I sent you the message, you idiot. *Reptilicus*, remember? I needed your attention. Just shut up and listen.'

'What's this Boursin or whatever it is got to do with *Rapide*?'

'Bourseul. I'm trying to tell you, Harald. The bomb threats. I know who's doing this shit to you and I know why.'

FIFTY-FIVE

The blue wire that Riley traced led to a square piece of plastic. It was sitting between two spring-loaded terminals which, if the non-conducting material inserted between them was removed – by, in this case, the extension mechanism moving – they would touch each other. That completed a circuit, powered by a battery pack, which led down to det cords on top of two containers the size of Calor gas cylinders on the floor. So far, so day one of bomb college.

Except there was also a black box.

It was slightly larger than the kind of transformer you might get on a TV plug. Wires went into it and came out. Riley took out his camera and snapped every inch of the whole set-up.

'You know, unless they got an H-bomb in those babies, this isn't going to sink any ship,' said Cortez, pointing at the cylinders.

'You still wouldn't want to be on top of it when it went off.'

'True enough.'

From his day bag he took a glue gun and squirted the rapid setting and non-conducting liquid over the terminals, effectively welding the material in place. While he was doing that, Cortez stripped an inch from the wires leaving the battery pack and connected a resistance unit onto them using crocodile clips. It was like an electrical roadblock, designed to reduce the juice that could reach the detonator assumed to be attached to the det cord, thus making an explosion unlikely.

'You want to see what's in that?' he asked her, pointing to the ominous black box.

Cortez considered it for a moment and leaned in, close, as if she could see around the back. It was resting inside the steel conduit which guided the Flying Carpet's wheels, so it was impossible to see the rear plate.

'X-ray?' he suggested.

'No time.'

She was right. Portable X-rays were useful but set-up would take too long.

'Could there be a trembler in there?' She was speaking out loud. She already knew the answer, but he gave it anyway.

'Not sure you'd use a tilt or trembler switch on a ship. Too likely to get movement that would set it off prematurely. Especially in the Atlantic.'

She flashed him a smile. 'Here's hoping.'

From her bag she extracted a hand-held tool the size of a small electric razor and two pairs of green-tinted safety glasses. She passed one of them to Riley. 'Put these on.'

'What is that thing?' Riley asked

'I forgot. You guys are still using saws, huh?'

The American bomb techs always did have the latest gear and the irritating habit of boasting about it. 'What is it?'

'A laser.'

'Oh, come on,' he said. 'You don't get hand-held lasers.'

She shrugged and moved a dial on the machine. Next she took a sucker on a stubby plastic rod – it looked like one of the darts that fired from kids' toy guns in lieu of bullets – from her pocket and placed it on the side of the metal rectangle.

Finally, she pulled on a pair of thicker gloves over the blue medical ones and placed the business end of the device so it was a few millimetres from the surface of the box. She flicked the 'on' switch and the machine began making a clicking noise. Then she pressed what was obviously the 'fire the laser' button. He was expecting to see the bright beam of light, but instead a thin red line came from the rubber cowling. It was now making a rapid pulsing sound.

'That's not going to cut it. You need three hundred watts to melt metal,' he said.

'That's the aiming beam. The actual laser is gated so it pulses incredibly fast. Femtoseconds or some such shit. It's virtually invisible once you have those goggles on. Welcome to nanotechnology.'

She moved the device along in a straight line a few millimetres away from the edge of the box, leaving a ragged cut in its wake and rivulets of melted steel and black paint. Sparks and gobbets of hot metal raced through the air whenever she hit impurities and he took a step back. Now he understood the heavy gloves; Riley noted with approval how steady her hands were.

'Aren't you in danger of melting what's inside the box?'

'This was developed from dental lasers. It has adjustable cutting depth.'

'I gotta get me one of those,' he said. The laser had caused a lot less vibration than the mini circular saw he often used.

As she reached the last centimetre, Riley moved in close again to stand behind her, reached in and held the stalk of the sucker, so the newly freed section wouldn't fall away. She turned off the laser, rested it on a nearby pipe and took off her gloves. While she waited for the ragged metal edges to cool, Riley checked the resistance of the panel and peered behind it as it gently came away, checking if there was anything attached to the other side. Like a pull-wire.

Cortez took a pencil torch from her top pocket and shone it through the ragged gaps she had made. He rested his head on her shoulder to get a better view.

'Riley, you're breathing in my ear,' she said.

'Sorry.'

'Worse than the damn dog. Anything?'

'No tugging that I can feel.' Which meant no wires were attached that might trigger a detonator.

'Pull out the left side a little, can you? Easy now.'

He did so. She shone her pencil torch into the crack and gave a low whistle.

'I'll be damned.'

'What?' he asked.

A playful smile flickered over her face.

'I think you're in for a surprise, Riley.'

FIFTY-SIX

BaseHeart looked at the burner phone sitting next to his keyboard and frowned his disapproval at it. Next he watched the giant Rolex timepiece on the wall of the grubby basement office he had rented off Gray's Inn Road – the clock was a copy of the ones used on Formula One tracks – until the hand moved round and showed seven minutes to the first deadline.

Back to the burner, which remained mute. What was Greggs playing at? COBRA must know by now that the first bomb had been found and the threat neutralised. Or maybe they hadn't located it? No, it was as obvious as a wart on a witch's nose. They had to have discovered it and rendered it safe.

He had waited long enough. Greggs had let him down. He had to take a gamble. Had to spread the good news when he was not at all certain that he had good news to convey. No matter. In the end it would all come together, whatever had happened on *Rapide*.

'Time to grasp the nettle,' he said to his daughter's portrait.

Using a second disposable phone he dialled Hamish Stewart from the *FT*. The man answered immediately, his voice reminiscent of Andrew Neil, slightly strangulated Scots. His manner was similar, too, brusque, to the point, take-no-prisoners. 'Stewart here. Yes? What is it?'

What is it? As if he wasn't about to make his day.

'Mr Stewart, I have a source on board *Rapide* that has just told me something very interesting. You know *Rapide* . . . ?'

'Of course I know *Rapide*. Who is this? And how can you have a source? It's locked down.'

He ignored the request for identification. 'The captain is still communicating with the owners and with COBRA. It's a very leaky vessel.'

He explained that a device had been located and made safe. That the ship and its passengers were safe and the crisis over. That was all he had to cast on the waters for Stewart to bite. As the journalist began to bombard him with questions, BaseHeart gave a curt goodbye and hung up.

It was, of course, all a lie.

Rapide was still in great danger. But this fake news item was the 'dead cat', and Stewart was one of his instruments of delivering it to the markets, the others being social media, financial news feeds and share tip sites, including 'grey' ones such as Bourseul.

BaseHeart was almost done with Operation Black Key. But there was another detail to take care of. He picked up a second burner and dialled. It was answered right away. This voice was raspy and he could almost smell the cigarette smoke over the ether.

'Yeah?'

'Boban. It's me. How ya doin', buddy?'

'Me' to Boban had an American accent. BaseHeart liked to compartmentalise his contacts.

'Yeah, okay.'

'You busy at the moment?' Boban worked for Oktane, the international job agency for his kind. His kind being hired killers.

'Not really.'

'In which case, I have a job for you. Usual terms.'

'When?'

'Tonight.' He held the phone away while the man had a cough-ing fit. BaseHeart heard a deep rattling in the chest. He was no medical man, but it sounded serious. He put a thumb over the microphone. 'If you live that long.'

Boban hawked and spat then cleared his throat. He could at least have held the phone way. 'Twenty per cent bonus. Short notice.'

BaseHeart could well afford that, but it always did to barter with these Balkan types. Before Oktane, Boban had been a member of the *Cikali*, the Jackals, a paramilitary unit active in Kosovo in the late Nineties. Their job was ethnic cleansing of Albanians, by any means necessary. It was there he began to think of human life only in terms of monetary value. 'Ten.'

'Fifteen. And the same for Rado.' This was his driver.

'Done. I'll send the details over. Oh, and Boban . . .'

'Yes?'

'Don't overstep the mark this time, eh, buddy?'

'When do I ever?'

Padstow, BaseHeart thought, but decided it was best not to pick another argument over that. 'Call me when you're done.'

FIFTY-SEVEN

Riley reached over and pulled the rectangle of metal that the laser had cut away. It gave easily. There was nothing attached to it. Inside the box was empty, save for the wires that ran straight through without a break. No circuits, diodes, resistors, no blinking digital countdown clock. All that was in there was a folded piece of paper, like a fortune cookie or a wrap of cocaine. That was what Cortez had glimpsed through the cut.

She put the right hand glove back on as protection, reached in and fetched it then handed it to Riley. He unfolded it, swore softly, and showed her the word written on it in blue ink and blocky capitals.

BOOM!

'What the fuck?' said Riley. 'Boom?'

'They can't be serious.'

Underneath was a fragment of a sentence in smaller, lower case letters: *bleed the beast.*

Riley wanted to screw it into a ball or tear it into a thousand pieces, but he stayed his hand. Evidence.

'You okay, Riley?'

'Why?'

'The look on your face. Like you want to bite someone's head off.'

He tried to relax his features, purge the fury from his expression. 'Not yours. I just don't like being played for a cunt.'

'Who the hell does? Gimme that, I'll bag it.'

He did as he was told.

'What does *bleed the beast* mean?'

'I dunno. Let's get this sorted,' said Riley. 'And then we'd best check the rest of the room again. Get Karun Roy in to be certain everything is where it should be and there's no unwelcome guests. The note might be to lull us into a false sense of security. Maybe someone is trying to fuck with our brains.'

Cortez took out a pair of snips from her bag. 'Brains? I'll just pretend I'm cutting his balls off.'

'Hold on.'

'You gonna mop my brow this time?'

Riley went over the circuit one more time, looking for a link to a secondary device, perhaps an anti-handling device they might have missed. Nothing. Not unless there was a pressure-release system of some kind under the cylinders. Which is why he wouldn't be lifting them in a hurry. But, given the relative crudity of the set-up, he doubted there was anything that sophisticated lurking beneath them.

'Okay. I always wanted to say this. Can't believe I never got the chance.'

Cortez looked as if she was beginning to doubt his sanity. 'Say what?'

Riley watched as the second arm of the watch swept towards the deadline. One minute. He pointed to the circuit. 'Cut the blue wire.'

303

FIFTY-EIGHT

A jubilant Engineer Karun Roy, apparently thrilled that the bomber's deadline had been passed, joined them in the search of the machine room. He brought two things with him, apart from a foot-wide grin. One was Kebede, the other survivor from the Hercules. He had finally been given the all-clear by the ship's medical staff. He still looked shaken and there was something in his eyes that hadn't been there before.

Riley shook Kebede's hand and they exchanged a look that carried everything they couldn't yet vocalise. He introduced the captain to Cortez and they greeted each other with a nod. It was no time for small talk.

Roy's second delivery was the news that the room had been accessed by Swart's card. Then an addendum. It had been used twenty minutes after the security man had been blown up in the empty cabin.

'Which means . . .' said Kebede.

'We have at least one other bomber on board,' said Riley.

Roy's grin contracted somewhat.

'This device we found,' said Cortez. 'It wasn't the work of a serious bomb-maker.'

Riley turned to Kebede. 'It was designed to be triggered by the extension of this.' He pointed to the Flying Carpet above them. 'But that was never going to happen till the ship docked.'

'I don't understand,' said Kebede.

'We think the bomb was meant to be discovered,' said Riley. 'It also seems as though the bomber was going through the motions. He or she didn't want anyone to die.'

'Swart? Last time I looked he was pretty dead.'

'Yah, shit man, bombers fall out, just like thieves,' said Cortez. 'That might have been personal.'

Kebede frowned. 'I think you're just guessing. But you think there could still be something else on board?'

Riley showed him the note.

'But the deadline passed,' said Roy. 'We're safe. Aren't we?'

'*A* deadline passed,' said Riley. 'They lie, these scumbags, you know. Let's ask the SEALs to keep looking.'

Karun Roy had another piece of news from the bridge. 'I thought this was just belt and braces. But we might need them after all. The Canadians are sending out what they are calling a High Risk Search Team and another bomb tech. They will rappel on board once we're in chopper range.'

'The passengers are certainly getting a show,' said Riley. 'And the Canadians are good.' He assumed they would not only do yet another search alongside the Yanks, but also match up passengers and luggage before disembarkation. Which was going to take a while.

'I can't see anything amiss here,' said Roy, waving an arm to indicate the machine room. 'I think it's safe to assume that was the only device in here.'

'In that case, I need a shower,' said Cortez.

'Me too,' said Riley. She shot him a look daring him to make a crack about doubling up to save water. Which was unfair. It had barely crossed his mind. He was mainly thinking of the way he had sweated getting into that room. And his skin still smelled of rubber from the dry suit, despite showering.

'Can you take me to your guys first?' Kebede asked Cortez. 'I'm not much good as a one-man band. I'd like to contribute something.'

'I'll take you down to the garage,' she said. 'They've set up there. I'll introduce you to Wang.'

Roy and Riley watched them go. 'My gear is apparently stowed in a crew cabin.'

'I'll show you. I warn you, they aren't as, um, plush as the passenger cabins.'

Riley yawned. It wouldn't matter. His body wanted all the adrenaline he had used up paid back. He was in biological debt and needed sleep, but it would have to wait.

They took the lift down to the depths of the ship – below the waterline, Riley noticed, then tried to ignore the fact – before walking through narrow passageways, past the bustling kitchens, and down one more level to a warren of cramped cabins, apparently decorated with sickly green paint left over from the MoD's Cold War stock. Roy looked in on several of them before they found Riley's, indicated by his Bergen sitting on the top bunk. 'Have I thrown someone out of their berth?'

'Don't worry about it. They'll be hot bunking. You've got a shower and sink. Lavatory along the passageway.' He gave a grin. 'All out of en-suites, I'm afraid. There's a lifejacket under the lower bunk.'

'Thanks. I'll clean up. Then I guess I'd better brief your captain.'

'He'll be glad to meet the hero of the day.'

The words had a very hollow ring to Riley, but he just gave Roy a thin smile in return.

When the engineer had left, Riley stripped off his clothes and dumped them in the corner. He had fresh kit in the Bergen that had survived the drop from the Hercules and had been rescued with him by Truluck's tender crew. He held out his hand. There was a distinct tremor. Fatigue and strain. And trauma. You don't fall out of a doomed plane without consequences. Shit, he had enough trauma in his head to keep a team of shrinks going for a year.

And it's not over yet.

No, he agreed with Nick, it's too neat. The jokey note was designed to lull them into a false sense of security.

Riley stepped into the shower and ran it hot enough to be almost unbearable. A rapid sequence of images began to flicker in his head: an empty street in Padstow; a devastated shopping mall; a steel box belching gas at Arsenal; Izzy, Ruby; a flaming, falling engine; a black wave trying to engulf him; the face of Norwell, pale and puffy . . .

BOOM!

BOOM?

And what about *bleeding the beast*?

'Whoever you are, whatever you are, you are a fuckin' *cunt*!' he yelled into the spray. Not big. Not clever. But it helped.

Riley turned the water off and vigorously dried himself until his skin glowed red. It didn't help calm the twisting in his guts, the feeling he was missing something, that this twat was jerking his strings, making him dance. Hero? Don't make me laugh.

There was clean underwear in the Bergen, protected in plastic, and he had just pulled a T-shirt and boxers on when he heard a fist hammering against the door of the cabin.

Riley yanked it open, ready to yell at whatever unfortunate

was thumping on it. It was Cortez and she managed to stifle any surprise or curiosity at his state of undress. 'Get your pants on, Riley. Madison's found something else.'

I fucking told you so.

FIFTY-NINE

'C'mon, Dad, it was just a blow job.'

Clive Greggs shifted uncomfortably in his armchair. His face was glowing bright red and so hot he was sure he could rent it out to the national grid next time the wind farms failed. It had taken all his willpower to tell his son the whole sordid story – well, edited highlights – and here was his son as calm as an aged Catholic priest, long past shockable, familiar as he was with the full scope of human foibles. He felt an odd sense of pride in the young man.

'Fetch me a refill, will you?' he asked, waving his empty glass.

'I think you've had enough for now, Dad.'

'Probably right,' Greggs conceded. His head had grown heavy and his chin was sagging onto his chest. 'Where's your mother again?'

'I told you. The opera.'

'Ah, yes. Back soon?'

'Soonish. It's one of those that goes on for days.'

'Will you tell her?'

Max shook his head. Good lad, he thought. Then the sting: 'No, but you will.'

'Don't be ridiculous.' The words slurred slightly.

'And then you'll call the police.'

What came out of him next was more animal than human, the sound of a cornered fox.

'Look, you need to get this off your chest, or you wouldn't have told me. Would you?' Max crossed over in one stride of his long legs and crouched down in front of his father. 'For my generation, what you have done is nothing. I know people of both sexes who think of blow jobs as little more than a handshake.'

'Really?' Greggs was genuinely surprised. In his day it was the Holy Grail of sexual encounters. And if she swallowed, that was the bloody Ark of the Covenant.

'With an added risk of STDs, obviously. What's so funny?'

'Nothing. Just you, that's all. Child is father to the man, eh?'

'In this case, yes.'

'But the police. I can't . . . I've betrayed . . .'

'What have you done, exactly?'

How to dress this up? 'I leaked some information from meetings. To an interested party.'

'What sort of information? State secrets?'

'Good Lord, no'

'Insider trading?'

'That sort of thing, yes.' He held up his glass. 'Just a splash. Please?'

Max shook his head in disapproval, but stood and fetched a few millimetres, barely enough to wet the bottom of the tumbler.

'People recover from political setbacks and scandals. Look at Clinton. Johnson, for God's sake. Look, Mum'll be back soon. Why don't you go for a walk? Clear your head. Think what you're going to say and how.' He took the whisky off him. 'You won't need this. It's going to be a long night.'

'Yes.'

310

Greggs let himself be pulled to his feet.

'I've got some emails to send. Unless you want company.'

'No, no.' Greggs gave his son an awkward hug. 'I love you, Max. I'll do better, I promise.'

Greggs went into the hallway and slipped on an overcoat. The autumn night might have a bite to it.

'I won't be long.'

No answer. Earbuds probably in already.

He opened the front door and stopped. There was a figure standing there. For a second, he thought Jessica must be home, but then the hooded man raised a silenced pistol and shot him twice in the face.

SIXTY

Captain Nansen asked to see the Ledgard party in his cabin once again. They trooped in with an air of pent-up aggression mixed with fatigue and took their places around the table. Jim, the body-guard, hovered in the background.

'No Mr Clark?' Nansen asked, looking at the empty chairs. 'Or, um, Ms X.'

'Nobody's been trying to blackmail them,' said Shelby irritably. Nansen sensed a falling out. But it was Christian Ledgard he had mainly wanted to see.

'As you know, a device has been found and neutralised. The deadline has now passed.' Nansen had made a tannoy announcement to that effect. 'We have had no further word from BaseHeart.'

'So that's it?'

Nansen hesitated. 'We are pretty certain that there are no more bombs.'

'Pretty certain?' asked Shelby. 'I'm pretty certain I'm not pregnant, but I couldn't rule it out.'

A sly smirk crossed Jim's face, which disappeared before anyone other than Nansen could spot it.

'Just because you haven't heard from this BaseHeart character, it doesn't mean he's given up,' Shelby said.

'Which is why a Canadian search team is on the way. To make absolutely sure we're clean, another sweep with fresh eyes.' He didn't mention the BOOM! nor its mysterious aphorism *bleed the beast*. The only reference they could find to the latter was a Mormon cult that aimed to defraud the government, aka The Beast. Maybe it was as simple as that – Ledgard was The Beast to be bled dry. He had passed the information on to the authorities in both London and New York, just in case this extortion really did originate in Utah and BaseHeart turned out to be a fundamentalist Latter-day Saint.

'So why are you telling us this in person?' asked Christian Ledgard.

'You've seen Klondike's share price?'

'Of course I've seen my fuckin' share price. The moment news got out that I was on this shittin' ship, it went through the floor.'

'And now both you and *Rapide* are safe?' asked Nansen.

'That'll take time to hit the news feeds,' said Ledgard. 'The moment it does the HFT boys'll be all over it.' The High Frequency Trading, he meant, the ones who used algorithms to react to information in fractions of a second. His brother was a mine of acronyms.

'But your feeling is?'

It was Shelby who answered. 'Investors are like a cross between a sulky teenager and a lemming. It will probably bounce back. We'll end up worth more than when we started.'

'I would like you to bear this in mind. I suspect the bomber or bombers knew damn well you wouldn't hand over the Black Key. But what they did know was that your shares, and probably those of several other CEOs on board, would fall. My brother knows about financial markets. He said if anyone knew what was happening in advance, they could bet against the shares falling, then, on the good news that you're not dead, rising again. Is that correct?'

'Yes,' said Christian Ledgard. 'It was why Apple kept news of Steve Jobs' illness quiet. Why there was radio silence when it was believed a plane carrying Bill Gates had crashed. Jesus, what a sick fuck. Just for, what? A few hundred thousand? A million? Two?' He stood up. 'I need to call my people, Captain.'

'My brother, who is not unfamiliar with the dark side of the web, is a member of a "black tip" site that advises its members of unusual trades worth looking out for. Not always legal ones, it seems. It told him both Anglo-American and Klondike were being shorted. This BaseHeart character knew you were on board, Mr Ledgard, and figured out someone was betting on the market panicking when news got out about the bomb.'

'It's never a bad bet,' said Shelby.

'My brother suggests it might have been a FLID. Is that right?' In fact, Jakob could have been talking Mongolian for all it meant to the captain.

'A what?' asked Shelby. 'That's a new one on me.'

'A Front-Loaded Investment Device,' said Ledgard. 'It's basically an anonymous group of investors clubbing together in somewhere like Vanuatu to work as activist investors, with a legit company as the Trojan horse. They use EDSs – Event-Driven Strategies – to manipulate the market.'

'An EDS like a bomb on a boat containing various CEOs?' asked Nansen.

Ledgard laughed, a harsh bitter sound. 'Well, it's not meant to be that extreme. But they do cross the line, so the SEC and FCA are about to shut them down. Creating an EDS will be illegal.'

'But it takes time, right? This is what my brother said. Regulation is always one step behind innovation.'

'Or thievery,' added Shelby.

314

There was a banging on the door and it swung open. It was Karun Roy. 'Sorry to interrupt, sir. There's been another development.'

'You mean another bomb?' asked Shelby in alarm.

Roy ignored her. 'You might want to come down.'

'Where?'

'The garage.'

The Ledgards exchanged horrified glances. 'Please tell me it's not my fuckin' car!'

SIXTY-ONE

The dog, despite the best efforts of his SEAL handler, wouldn't budge, it seemed, until at least one ATO turned up. When two turned up, he finally relinquished his position.

The SEALs had made the garage into their operating base, and Riley could smell the testosterone they had pumped out into the already putrid air. He had once been very cynical about US Special Forces, with their high fives, hooyahs and *Beavis and Butt-Head* level of banter, but having seen them in both training and action, he had revised his opinion. They weren't quite as calm and efficient as the Brits when things went tits up – improvisation wasn't their forte – but they were formidable opponents.

He and Cortez stared at the spot where the dog had been sitting. Wang, the SEAL commander, was at their side. 'What do you think?'

'Pull your guys out, just in case,' said Riley.

'Seconded,' said Cortez.

'Whose vehicle is that? Do we know?'

'The Ledgards'.' It was Jason Truluck. 'Captain's on his way down.'

In among the dozen cars that occupied part of the hangar-like garage, Lieutenant Madison had positioned himself at the side of the expensively customised Land Rover Defender, right next to the inflatable shroud that was designed to protect the bodywork in case of flying objects during the voyage. How the hell the dog could sense anything through that was a mystery to Riley.

'I think we remove that overgrown lifebelt,' suggested Riley, 'and see what's what. Maybe use your little playmate.'

There was a commotion from behind and Riley turned to see Nansen trying to hold back the Ledgards and their bodyguard. 'Hey, hey,' he said. 'This is now a restricted area with an active EOD investigation going on.' He turned to Wang. 'Can you get everyone to just fuck off?'

The American winced a little at the bluntness. 'Sure.'

'Keep the captain back, too. But can you stash the owners of the vehicle somewhere safe?'

'In the brig?'

Riley wasn't entirely sure cruise ships had brigs. Besides, they had no grounds to put them in chains. 'I think anyone who had anything to do with this vehicle should be confined to quarters. I'll need to swab them, see if they handled explosives. Maybe you can put some of your guys outside their cabins.'

'Hooyah!'

Riley did his best not to roll his eyes. 'And you, if you don't mind,' he said to Truluck. 'Best not be here while we set up.' Or if anything goes wrong, more to the point.

Truluck nodded but showed no sign of moving.

'Well?' asked Cortez.

'Sorry. I've just realised something,' Truluck said.

'What?' asked Riley, impatiently.

'I'm not sure. I'd better check before I say anything.'

'What's it about?'

'The Ledgards,' the sailor said. 'As I say, let me check, I don't want to make any wild accusations.'

'What's below here?' asked Cortez, stamping on the steel deck.

'A whole lot of pipework and conduits and then it's the Atlantic, pretty much.' Truluck gave a grim smile.

'Marvellous. Can you get me the keys to that?' Riley asked, nodding at the Defender.

'They'll be in the quartermaster's safe. Give me five minutes.'

After everyone had left, they took some time looking at the modified Land Rover. It was basically a pimped-up, steroid-injected, re-engineered version of the old army, expedition and agricultural workhorse, with a more powerful engine and far superior brakes, soundproofing, steering and suspension. And a far larger price tag than the normally used Defender. Riley had heard they went for upwards of a hundred and fifty grand.

'Jeez,' said Cortez.

'What are you thinking?' asked Riley.

'We use the robot,' she said. 'Unless you got any better ideas?'

'No. Hands on again, Cortez. Mark One Eyeballs. Best way. I think I'll give it a once-over with the Rover, too. And then maybe try your other little playmate.'

'Will you stop saying that?' she said.

'What?'

'Playmate. You sound like Hugh fuckin' Hefner. It's a fuckin' robot, not a pin-up.'

'Sorry. I meant the sniffer, not the bot. Just want to be sure we've got an explosive device in that Defender. See if the machines agree.'

'The dogs are rarely wrong.'

'I know. Just a hunch.'

She poked his arm. 'Riley. Tell me what's going on in that tiny dickwad brain of yours.'

'Two things. One, the dog might have got the scent of cocaine. I hear rich folks like a bit of powder.'

'Yeah. But, shit. Think about it. Bringing cocaine into America from the UK? Come on, man. Ice to Eskimos.'

'You could be right.' It couldn't be hard to get gear in the US and the chances were the quality would be better. Not that he had ever tried any. Even at his lowest, booze was Riley's drug of choice.

'And the second?'

Riley walked around the vehicle before he answered, feeling the atmospherics, leaning and peering through the windows, looking for telltale signs of booby trap or IEDs. He got nothing from it, no tingles, no squeeze of the guts. The Land Rover felt cold, unthreatening.

'The car isn't wired to blow at all. But it has traces of PETN or something in it that the dog picked up. So, then we know how they got the explosives on the ship in the first places.'

*

Truluck delivered the keys to the pimped-up Land Rover Defender and then, sensibly, made himself scarce. Cortez and Riley cut away the rubber buffer with knives, revealing the naked Defender, secured to the deck by a system that looked a variation of the hated yellow parking clamps. While Cortez laid out the kit she would need, Riley did a proper 360 visual on the 4WD, peering in every window, getting down and examining the underside, both with the naked eye and a mirror-on-a-stick. Like Cortez earlier, he didn't wear a bomb suit because it gave him more flexibility. You get on the ground in one of those things, it takes all your effort to get back up. As far as he could tell, the vehicle was clean – everything in its right place.

'Shame it's a two-door model,' he said to himself. If anyone was going to put in tripwires and the like, they tended to boobytrap the driver or passenger doors. Sometimes both. Going in the rear doors was always safer.

'How's it looking?' Cortez shouted. She had moved back to a safer distance, as was SOP, and her voice rang harshly as it bounced off the bare metal surfaces.

'Benign.'

'What do you mean, fine?'

'I said benign. Nothing suspicious yet.'

'Almost done here.'

'Just going to switch on your playmate.'

'Can you fuck off, Riley?'

He wasn't sure why winding her up gave him such pleasure. Maybe it was because he liked the sound of anger in her voice.

Grow up, Dom. You aren't pulling pigtails in the playground now.

Maybe blokes never grew out of that. It just evolved into something less physical. Or maybe insults and needling were a very British way of flirting.

As he walked to the rear of the Defender, Cortez's handheld sniffer gave a little whoop of alarm. 'Not coke then,' he said.

'You got a reading?'

Riley checked the read out. 'Low.' He walked around the other side of the 4WD. Once more a feeble alarm sounded. Of course, that could just mean the explosive had been well wrapped in some material that wasn't porous to the volatiles that common explosives gave off.

He selected a large screwdriver and moved to the front of the car. He inserted the blade beneath the 'Twisted' brand nameplate and levered it off. He shone a torch into the exposed cavity. He could just make out the cable of the bonnet pull. He then took a pair of needle-nosed pliers and yanked on the metal wire. There was one advantage of working on factory-fresh cars: everything was still nicely oiled and greased. The bonnet popped up like an eager puppy.

Riley took a step back and with it a deep breath. He had to keep the oxygen flowing. He ran a quick survey of his other vital functions. Heartbeat steady, palms dry, plenty of saliva, mood: focused and calm. He'd do. Riley moved back in and ran his fingers inside the gap created by the bonnet releasing. Nothing.

As he touched the catch that would allow him to reveal the engine compartment, Riley felt a prickling over his body, as if he were covered in fine filaments, like the nerve net of a primitive sea creature. Hadn't felt that in a while. Not since . . . Afghan? Out in the wind-blasted desert, the sun on his neck, stretched out, painting the sand, brushing away the rough particles to reveal the pressure plate and its lethal corona of wires, death sitting on your shoulder waiting for the misstep. Adrenaline coursing through his veins, heightening all his senses, because, ironically, the closer you got to death, the more alive you felt.

He pushed the spring-loaded lever back with his fingers. Paused.

'You okay over there?'

'Tingly.'

'Yeah, I get that too.'

The electrical storm playing over his skin said one thing: *easy, now.*

Riley lifted the bonnet in increments, scoping the inside as it was revealed, until he could use the metal rod to lock it in place. He spent some minutes looking at the pristine engine bay. Nothing stood out as extraneous. No suspect leads ran to or from the battery. He used a 13mm spanner to disconnect the live terminal, wrapped it in insulating tape and then attached it to the bulkhead, out of the way. Now, if anything nasty had been plugged into, say, the interior light, it was neutralised. As long as that car battery was the only power source.

'Okay. I think we should unlock it.' Again, this needed the human touch: robots were pretty useful, but dealing with locks wasn't in their prime directive. Sometimes you can't beat an opposable thumb.

'I'll do it,' said Cortez.

'I do believe it's still my turn at the sharp end. You just stand by with a mop and bucket.'

'You're sick, Riley,' she said, a half-laugh in her voice at his fatalism.

He looked down at the key fob. It was an electronic one — something of anathema to fans of the original Defender he would imagine — with a green button for open, red for closed. He wasn't going to touch those. But a lot of drivers didn't realise that many apparently keyless cars had a hidden key in the beeper unit, in case the battery died. The Defender certainly did. He pulled out the metal shank with its pattern of cuts and collars. A walk round the vehicle confirmed that there was a lock only on the driver's side. Riley crouched down before it.

He checked the shakiness of his hand. Minimal. Then he inserted the key into the barrel under the door handle. He was gambling on nobody bothering to put an anti-handling device in the mechanical lock. There were far simpler ways to kill him, if they wished. Even so he left the key in there for a few moments before turning it.

He held his breath and rotated. Click.

Wait.

He let the air out of his lungs and wiped his forehead. Barely a sweat. 'Okay, door unlocked.'

'Good work.'

Next: open the fucker. And hope there's no tricks he hadn't spotted.

Operation Certain Death.

Yes, Nick. Again.

He reached out for the handle. His fingers almost touched metal. And the atmospherics changed. The air grew dense around him. That ATO sixth sense, the one that had kept him alive in Afghan, kicked in. 'What the fuck?' he asked himself.

There came a low rumble, vibrating through floors and walls, followed by a powerful blast that blew out the lights in the garage. As he stumbled through the pitch black, trying to put some distance between himself and the Defender, there came the gurgling rush of freezing, pitiless seawater greedily pouring through distorted metal plates.

SIXTY-TWO

'Oh. I thought I told you that you needed a visa for Russia?'

Barbara flashed Kate Muraski a disingenuous smile and carried on cutting up her bacon into postage-stamp-sized pieces. They were breakfasting prior to arrival at the docks that gave access to St Petersburg. Outside was cloaked in a fluffy mist, which made the dining room feel like twilight. Whatever quirk of the weather that had brought the fog had also delivered a mirrored calmness to the sea.

There were few other passengers up for food at that hour. The previous night had been a Come As Your Favourite Book or Author Party in the main ballroom. Judging by the amount of booze consumed most passengers appreciated works such as *Hangover Square, Fear and Loathing,* the *Patrick Melrose* novels, Dorothy Parker and Charles Bukowski.

Kate picked at her avo on toast and, trying not to sound petulant, said: 'You didn't tell me about the visa. You told me you could access the city with just a boarding card.'

'Ah, well, that *used* to be true,' Barbara said. 'But they've tightened up, apparently. The Russians, I mean. Especially for British vessels. The usual pettifogging.'

Sometimes Barbara's vocabulary was positively antique. 'That's ridiculous. We've come all this way and we can't go ashore?'

'Well, the landing card allows you to go on the organised tours. Of which there are several. I think you should see the Hermitage at least. It'll explain why they had a revolution.'

Muraski realised what the old woman was suggesting. That she work alone. 'You've got a visa, haven't you?'

Barbara gave one of her gnomic smiles.

Kate felt a flash of frustration. 'I thought I was part of this. Here to help.'

'Believe me, you have a part to play. I need to get ashore without being tailed.'

'Is that likely?'

'This is Russia. I want to see the colonel without a party of FSB on my back. Ah, Edith.'

Barbara waved her doppelganger over. Muraski had already been introduced to her. She might look like Barbara, but she was the antithesis of the spy: vanilla yoghurt to her chilli-spiked hot sauce. Her late husband had owned a chain of builders' merchants, left her well off, two children, Tokyo and Houston ... blah, blah, blah. Edith was nice enough, but Muraski had a good idea why the kids had decided to change continents.

Edith sat down and pleasantries were exchanged before Barbara dropped her bombshell. 'Edith, I'm still feeling a little weak after the, um, incident. I'm not sure I could face all that tramping around those endless corridors ... would you mind terribly accompanying Kate around the museums?'

'I'd be delighted,' she said, fixing Muraski with an indulgent grin. 'We'll have fun, won't we, dear?'

Muraski smiled back at Barbara's chosen decoy for shore leave. How long had she been setting this up? she wondered. Edith had been put in place, unwittingly, to act as a distraction, to fool those not paying attention that she was Barbara, while Barbara did ... what, exactly? 'Oh, yes. So much fun,' said Muraski.

Edith turned back to Barbara. 'But what are you going to do all by yourself?'

'Oh,' said Barbara airily, 'I'm sure I'll think of something.'

SIXTY-THREE

The high-pitched honks screeched through the garage, sounding like an animal being tortured. The flashing lights that came in sync with the racket strobed across the space. Riley could intermittently see the distorted giant shadow of Cortez cast on the wall, like Orson Welles in *The Third Man.*

It took a second for him to piece together what had happened. There had been a detonation. But not in the Twisted Land Rover. Because if there had been, he wouldn't have dry feet. Or maybe any feet at all. However, he had felt the air in the garage compress. And his ears had popped. Something had blown nearby. The explosion had triggered the car alarm on the Koenigsegg, which was the honking sound. It cut dead as quickly as it had started, just as a string of emergency lights on the ceiling flicked on. They looked like several strings of illuminated pearls.

'Riley! What the fuck did you do?'

Riley looked down at his feet again. Still dry. But he could hear water. Whatever device had detonated it wasn't in the garage, but a compartment close by. A ship's alarm started, seven long blasts and a short one. Then the PA:

'Muster stations! Muster stations! Please proceed to your designated muster stations with your life jackets. If you cannot access one, jackets will be provided,

327

including for children. Do not return to your cabin to pick up belongings. This is not a drill.'

Riley threw caution to the wind, jogged back over and opened the door of the Land Rover.

'We ought to get out, Riley.'

'Give me a minute.'

Riley slid into the driver's seat and began to check the door storage bins and then the glove compartment. Nothing. Just a stack of official-looking insurance forms. He grabbed those.

'I've got my gear. I'm going,' yelled Cortez. 'You coming?'

'I'm right behind you.'

Riley and Cortez both headed for the exit. They didn't need telling that they were below the waterline. Drowning was another way to go he didn't much fancy. The main lights came back on. Riley assumed that was a good thing.

Truluck was standing at the doorway, waving them on.

'Are we sinking?' asked Cortez.

'Unlikely,' was the less than reassuring reply. 'Nobody else in there?'

'No,' said Riley.

Truluck pulled the door shut behind them and sealed it with the lever. They stood to one side as crew raced by, heading for whatever stations they had been assigned. It was like watching a river in surge, threatening to sweep you away, thought Riley. Truluck spoke into his radio. 'Garage cleared.' He turned to Cortez. 'And in answer to your question, no. There's some hull damage next door. It's been isolated. It'll flood but we can balance the ship using the anti-roll tanks.'

'What's in there?' Riley asked, shouting over the alarm. 'The flooded section?'

'Laundry. Nobody was badly hurt. Follow me, we'll have to

go up. I need to help organise the passengers.' Riley could only imagine the scenes above their heads. They had been promised no more bombs and now this.

'Are we abandoning ship, then?' asked Cortez.

'That's up to Captain Nansen.'

Riley had another concern. The confusion caused by the explosion might just be the perfect cover. Although for what he wasn't sure. 'I need to find your guv'nor. Commander Wang.'

'Why?' asked Cortez.

'Because we have to arrest whoever owns that Land Rover in there,' he yelled. 'That's the key to this whole shitstorm. Fuck, can't someone turn that off?' He was certain the alarm would only add to the rising sense of panic. It certainly wasn't helping his disposition. 'And . . .' Riley hesitated. Something had changed, something he had sensed even through the incessant racket filling his head.

Truluck knew exactly what had happened. There was no vibration through their feet. 'We've stopped.'

'What does that mean?' asked Riley.

'Once the passengers are at the muster stations, we'll be manning the lifeboats. We are abandoning ship.'

SIXTY-FOUR

The first taxi driver in the rank at the port on Vasilyevsky Island suggested a price so high – five thousand roubles – no amount of bargaining would reduce it to something reasonable. Barbara threw him a well-timed insult and moved on to the next in line. She had waited twenty minutes to pass through Russian immigration and customs, which was incredibly speedy by their usual standards, but had nevertheless tested her patience. Of course, there was another reason she was concerned about the delay.

She hadn't mentioned to Kate that her visa and, indeed, the passport it was in, were not in the name of Barbara Clifford-Brown. She might be an espionage dinosaur, but there was always a chance someone had a computer that reached back to the Mesozoic Age. She had needed cover, just in case. Which also explained her wig, a bob in a colour she thought of as post-post-menopausal.

She felt a twinge of guilt about sending Kate off with Edith. But she was working on the premise that to anyone watching, one old, grey-haired biddy looked much like another.

She had hung back while the coaches had drawn up on the dockside and were loaded with passengers, then transported into the city and to its attractions. She hadn't warmed to St Petersburg on her previous visit. The wide, impersonal boulevards, the obscenely opulent palaces and over-elaborate churches. She far preferred Moscow. Of course, that could just be the difference between working in a place — especially as an agent — and being a mere tourist, which she had been when she and Henry finally visited St Petersburg. She wasn't actually very good at tourism. She hoped Kate enjoyed the Hermitage tour, though. Despite her antipathy to the city it was a must-see, and the French impression-ist collection was first rate.

The second taxi didn't have an obvious meter — there were plenty of freelance cabbies as she recalled — and she moved on, wondering if perhaps she shouldn't have asked Kate to book one using an app, as the guidebook in the ship's library had sug-gested. She tapped on the window of the third, a silver Mercedes, and when it lowered she barked out the address and demanded a decent price. The young man at the wheel looked shocked, whether at the destination, her accent or the sharpness of her tone she couldn't tell. But he pointed at his meter, indicating he would charge whatever it showed (not always a given) and she climbed into the rear.

It was a forty-minute drive to the Pushkin district, heading south and avoiding most of the tourist spots. The cabbie took her over the bridge and they plunged straight into dull suburbs that were in stark contrast to the opulence of Nevsky Prospekt and its surroundings. Another twenty minutes and the tower blocks and just-as-grimy low-rises dropped away and greenery appeared in the shape of parks and a funfair. There were houses, too, and those high-rises that were visible over the treetops were well spaced out, the facades free of the black tear stains that ran down the concrete of their brothers and sisters in the centre.

'Pushkin!' the driver announced proudly.

Barbara simply nodded, not wanting to engage. She shifted her position on the seat, wishing she had found a more comfortable hiding place for the Browning Hi-Power that was digging into her hip.

SIXTY-FIVE

Truluck was keen to see the captain, but Riley delayed him for one minute while he quickly shuffled the papers he had taken from the Defender. There had to be something in there that would help. Some clue, a tell, a hint. Proof of ownership, service records. He would take anything. He thrust a piece of paper with the A-AL heading at the sailor.

'Is this something?' he asked, his voice frantic.

'No. It's just a safety notice for cars in the garage. How much fuel they can have in them and so on,' said Truluck. 'Look, I'm needed elsewhere.'

Riley hadn't finished. 'Or this?'

'They're just insurance and import papers for the vehicle,' the sailor replied irritably.

'Riley,' said Cortez. 'Calm down. Let the man be.'

'This?' Riley ignored her and waved a handwritten piece of paper that had been hidden between the forms under Truluck's nose. Then Riley looked at it again. The ink was very similar to that used on the *Boom!* note, as was the blockiness of the letters. 'What does that mean? Fuck's sake, it must be something.'

'Let me see,' said Truluck calmly. His brow furrowed as he read out the numbers and letters. 'S, ART6.'

'Meaning?'

Truluck's demeanour changed in a heartbeat. 'Christ. It's an abbreviation from the deck plans. Starboard side, anti-roll tank six.'

'What is it?'

'Somewhere we can flood to stabilise the ship.'

'Would you go in there? I mean do crew members routinely go inside?'

'No, of course not . . .'

'Will it be filling now?'

'Possibly,' said Truluck. 'It's all computer controlled. But to counteract the laundry bomb, it might flood.'

Certainty hit Riley like a punch to the face. 'Then that's where the next bomb is,' he said.

SIXTY-SIX

If Pavel Brodsky was surprised to see Barbara Clifford-Brown on his doorstep he didn't show it. His house was a small, neat gingerbreadish cottage on the edge of a small wood. It was almost like a miniature dacha in the suburbs. There was a VW Passat parked outside and a bicycle chained to a metal post. Pavel himself was unshaven, dressed in voluminous jeans – an unwise fashion choice for a man of his girth – and a collarless shirt.

'You should have phoned, Barbara,' he said, as if she had just been passing. His breath sounded slightly laboured. He was carrying too much weight for his frame, Barbara thought. Shame. He had once been Nureyev-lithe. But then, they had all changed for the worst, those that were left.

'Would you have baked me a cake?'

'I might have done,' he said, warily.

'It's an old English expression. Tea will be fine. Do you still do Turkish? In a *çaydanlık*?' This was the double-stacked kettle essential for an authentic brew of *rize* tea.

'I do, I do. Come in.' He indicated the interior with the cane he had been leaning on. 'You are a wonderful surprise, Barbara.'

We'll see about that, she thought, as she walked down a short corridor and into a living room. It was filled to the point of bursting. Every wall surface was covered in paintings, photographs and stuffed animal heads, including a bear. There were cabinets containing models of Soviet-era warships and jets. One corner was crammed with silver and gold samovars and shisha pipes. Somehow room had been found for a baby grand. There was soft classical music playing from an old yet obviously much-loved Radiola Rigonda, the state-produced 'household electronic device' that was the equivalent of the western radiogram. The whole place reminded Barbara of the Pitt-Rivers museum in Oxford, curated by someone incapable of throwing anything away.

'Have a seat,' he said. 'You must forgive me, I had to move from a much larger apartment to be out here. For my lungs.' He thumped his chest. 'Doctor's orders.'

Barbara sat in a brocaded wing-backed armchair, her handbag resting on her lap. One of the wall shelves held a small glass-fronted case of medals. She recognised a platinum Order of Lenin, the blue-ribboned 'For Distinction in Counterintelligence' medal and a 'For Distinction in Special Operations' with crossed swords. There were half-a-dozen others that she wasn't familiar with. All in all, quite a collection.

Brodsky saw her staring. 'A lifetime's service, all reduced to one dusty box.'

There wasn't a speck of dust on the case or a smear on the glass. 'One that speaks volumes. I don't take sugar in my çay.'

'Ah yes. Five minutes.'

'Take your time. It shouldn't be rushed.'

His eyes narrowed momentarily, as if he had read something into that innocent remark.

'I'm happy just taking this all in. One gets so used to rooms decorated from . . . What's that ghastly Swedish place? IDEA?'

'IKEA,' he corrected. 'We have three of them here.'

'Really? Three? Is nowhere safe? Anyway, it's wonderful to see some character for a change. I shall just sit and luxuriate.'

He returned five minutes later with a circular silver tray holding two glasses of dark tea and a plate of spiced biscuits. He laid the tray down on a cushioned footstool and moved it so it sat at her feet.

While Brodsky had been fussing in his kitchen, Barbara had unclipped the Browning from her undergarments and, with a sigh of relief, placed it on the arm of the chair. Brodsky had given no sign of noticing the pistol but, of course, it would have been the first thing he clocked on his return.

He took one of the glasses and sat on the sofa. She waited for hers to cool a little. She tried one of the biscuits. It tasted like Christmas.

'I was sorry to hear about Henry.'

'I hope you aren't going to feed me the same bullshit you forced on my grandson.'

'I wouldn't dare. What would be the point?'

'So, no talk of rogue elements.'

'Well, it's partly true.'

'The thugs at his hotel. They were designed to make sure he had disposed of the document you gave him?'

He nodded. 'A little crude in retrospect.'

'Disappointing, Pavel.'

'I don't have the resources I once had at my disposal. Ah.' His eyes widened. She could almost see a lightbulb go on over his head. 'The gun. It came from there?'

'Helsinki, yes. When Dom had taken it from his attackers at the hotel, he put the Browning above a ceiling tile in his room. I pre-booked the same room before leaving the UK. Dom told me to count five tiles from the left wall, six from behind the bed. It was exactly where he said, sitting on a metal crosspiece. And here it is.'

'You came by ship then.'

She nodded and smiled, an acknowledgement he could still put two and two together.

'You wouldn't risk an airport.'

'No'. She picked up her tea, blew on it and sipped through pursed lips. 'Very good. You haven't lost your touch.'

'Nor you.'

'One thing you can clarify for me. When you met Dominic. How did you know Henry was murdered by an injection under his nicotine patch? That wasn't in the public post-mortem.'

'I'm a spy, Barbara. An old one, true. But it isn't beyond me to get hold of the *other* post-mortem report. I suspect you don't believe that there were rogue elements at work.'

'Your rogue elements? An old man, put out to grass, who wants to prove he can still mount an operation, still strike fear into the West, still get rid of this government's enemies, even on foreign soil. The men who killed Henry. Were they your *ospis*, Pavel?'

A heartfelt sigh. 'Originally, yes. A small number of people drawn from Unit 29155. But they really did go rogue.' Barbara made a noise that suggested she thought 29155 was rogue and rotten to its core. 'Thought they knew better than the old man back in Russia about how to achieve their aims.' He reached over and put his glass back down on the tray. Her hand moved a few millimetres towards the gun. But he leaned back and raised his palms briefly to show he had no intention of pulling any stunts. 'Are you here to kill me, Barbara?'

She drank some more tea, using her more arthritic left hand, keeping the right free. 'That rather depends.'

'On what?'

'Your answer to the next question.'

SIXTY-SEVEN

Riley carefully descended the ladder that led from the sliding watertight door down into the darkness of emergency anti-roll tank six. It was a cavity in the skin of the ship, maybe ten feet wide but as tall as a four-storey building, designed to fill with ballast water to help stabilise the ship should something catastrophic happen on the port side. As indeed it had.

The space smelled of oil, metal and something close to sewage. The air was filled with the mournful sound of the water sloshing against the metal sides as the ship wallowed. It reminded Riley of those abandoned forts in the Thames and the decommissioned North Sea rigs that he had trained on. He glanced up and his head torch caught the pale ovals of Truluck and Cortez's faces, looking down at him from the access hatch above. They seemed a long way away.

'You okay?' asked Cortez.

'How deep is that water down there?'

Truluck answered. 'Karun says it barely pumped any in before I called him. Tanks five and seven fill first.'

Riley reached the point where the ladder disappeared into the ink-black water and hesitated. There hadn't been time to kit up in a dry suit again, so he was wearing a set of the crew's one-piece oilskins, designed more to protect sailors soaked by waves on deck than submersion. He stepped off the ladder and gasped as the cold numbed his legs.

Although he had on his head torch, its narrow beam was swallowed by the space, so from his belt he unclipped a more powerful handheld torch and began to play it across the surface of the water. He wasn't even sure what he was looking for.

Something that doesn't belong.

Me, he thought. I don't belong here.

He sloshed through the two feet or so of Atlantic, examining the walls, playing the beam as methodically as he could. He was shivering already, the water sucking the heat from his core, despite the oilskins. As the ship rolled, the motion meant the filthy liquid tugged at his legs, threatening to topple him. Death by hypothermia or drowning was the menu for the day. It wasn't much of a choice.

It should have leapt out at him as incongruous. He almost missed it. Who needs a fire extinguisher in a ballast tank? As he got closer, he added a codicil to that. Who needs a fire extinguisher with holes drilled in it?

'What you got, Riley?' asked Cortez.

'I think it's a flotation trigger,' he said through chattering teeth. The idea would be that when the tank was filled to compensate for the flooded laundry, this bomb would deploy.

Inside the fat red cylinder, which looked as if it was resting on top of the water, would be something similar to a ballcock in a lavatory cistern, or rather, given the size, the float chamber in a carburettor. Except instead of cutting off the flow of water or fuel, the buoyant sphere would move an arm that would close an electrical contact and . . . as BaseHeart wrote, *BOOM!*

'Be careful,' warned Cortez.

Riley waded over to the wall where the fire extinguisher sat on its bracket. The device itself wasn't large enough to cause significant damage to *Rapide*. Not by itself. It had to be connected to something else to be a real threat.

A sudden shiver caught him by surprise, so powerful it hurt his ribs. He knew he didn't have much time before he started shaking violently. He refocused on the device rather than his plunging body temperature.

The whole set-up was safe as long as the water level didn't get any higher and raise that float. He was just probing beneath the surface for wires when he heard a sound like his grandfather gargling and felt the push and pull of swirling water on his legs.

Someone or something had opened the stopcocks to anti-roll tank six. The Atlantic was coming in.

SIXTY-EIGHT

BaseHeart was in his basement, waiting for the Bouncing Cat, when the news about Greggs broke. He did not consider himself a vindictive man. On the other hand, he did not like people taking him for granted or playing him for a fool. Or, like Greggs, letting him down by refusing to attend any more COBRA meetings. Bit late for him to grow a pair of balls, he thought. Sooner or later, he would settle any score. Ask the Johnsons. The *Evening Standard* and *The Independent* both broke the news almost simultaneously. The former had gone with 'DANDO-LIKE DOORSTEP ASSASSINATION OF TOP CIVIL SERVANT'. The Indy went with 'MASKED MAN GUNS DOWN GOVERNMENT MINISTER IN FRONT OF FAMILY'. No doubt that would be corrected soon. The Cabinet Office was ministerial all right, but Greggs was no minister.

He picked up the picture of his daughter and spoke to it. 'Looks like Boban earned his money last night, eh?'

He set the frame back down and BaseHeart sent a coded message which would instruct one of his employees to send the file containing the incriminating evidence about Greggs to the *Sun on Sunday* and the *Daily Mail*. It would be routed to appear that it came from Qatar. Soon, stories would appear that Greggs was trying to blackmail certain people with details of the party where he had indulged himself in the incriminating photograph. None of it would stand up to too much scrutiny, but that wouldn't matter. It would take root and establish itself as fact in some corners of the internet, where it would reside forever. The half-truths and lies would serve to muddy the waters.

BaseHeart felt his stomach rumble. It was some time since he had eaten. And then the news flash he had been waiting for. An explosion on *Rapide*. The captain had clearly switched on the ship's internet because the wires were humming with the news.

It was the bouncing cat he had been waiting for. The idea was simple. The news that *Rapide* was the subject of a bomb threat had caused the share price of Klondike, Anglo-American Lines (and many other companies associated with cruising) to plummet. Then, with a bomb discovered and disarmed and the deadline passed, markets responded by sending the prices back up. But the news that a device had exploded would cause the graph to drop again. The 'dead cat' was the share price, of course, and the bounce the temporary blip upwards before the crash became fatal. In markets, pre-knowledge was power. And he had known that explosion was coming.

He took the hard drives out of the two computers and placed them in a case. He would dispose of them later. He unhooked the Rolex wall clock and put it in a carrier bag. He rather liked it and it would be a shame to lose it. He also picked up the picture of his daughter, gave her a brief kiss, and slid it into his jacket pocket.

Everything else could burn. Including the furniture shop above the office. He opened the metal locker next to where the clock had been and turned on the timer that sat on one of the blocks of plastic explosive strapped around the sides of the Calor gas cylinder, like an inanimate suicide vest. Thirty minutes. Enough time.

Next he splashed petrol from a red plastic container over the desk and the keyboards and monitors. Satisfied that it would obliterate all useful indications of his presence to even the most diligent of forensic officers, BaseHeart went in search of a decent meal. *Pasta a la Norma*, he thought.

SIXTY-NINE

Riley watched in horror as the water rose over his knees. His torch picked out the bubbling fountain where the sea was flooding in. As he stepped towards it, his shin banged against a low, hard object. He let out a groan, which wasn't all to do with pain. That, he knew instinctively, was the main charge. And given where it was placed, he assumed it would be a shaped charge or something similar, designed to punch down through the hull. He reached into the water and touched metal, walked his fingers along it, estimating dimensions. It was a metal framework of some description. He would come back to that.

'Truluck!' he yelled.

'He's gone to close the sea cocks,' shouted Cortez. 'He says they're computer controlled. Must be a malfunction. Can you get to the flotation trigger?'

Riley moved to the extinguisher and made to lift it from its bracket. Get rid of the firing switch and he'd be quids in. Except it didn't move. It was welded in place. He tried again. 'Won't budge.'

'Get out, Riley.'

He looked at the ladder then at the water level. 'Never make it. It'll be moving the float before I'm halfway up.' Never get to find out what happened to his little girl, either. The thought hit him like a runaway train. Fuck, no. He wasn't going to die down here or halfway up a ladder.

He tried to put his finger into one of the holes in the casing of the extinguisher, designed to allow seawater in, but they were too small for his digits. It was best not to poke inside anyway.

'Catch.'

Riley looked up. Cortez was leaning into the hatchway, arms into the void, her hands clasping something.

'What's that?'

'The laser.'

You'll never catch that.

Riley half stumbled until he was under the hatch. He clipped the large torch back onto his belt as he raised his hands. Nick could be right. Riley had a great history of dropped catches on the sports fields of England. He raised his arms.

'Go.'

He saw her hands unclasp but he couldn't see the device as it fell away. He stared up into the thin beam generated by his head torch. Nothing. And then there it was, spinning down, over to his right. He lunged for it, made contact, felt it slip from his grip into the water, then, like his grandfather tickling a trout, he managed to come up beneath it and snatch it into the air. He hoped the fucker was waterproof.

Cortez had used gaffer tape to fix a pair of goggles to the body of the laser and Riley stripped it away as he sloshed back to the extinguisher. He found the power switch and flicked on the little machine. It began its clicking sound, like an electronic cicada.

'Turn to ten on the dial,' Cortez yelled.

'Isn't there an eleven?'

'Hurry up, Riley. And don't look at the light without protection.'

He did as he was told, put on the goggles, held the rubber cowling against the top bracket and, with shaking hands the colour of alabaster, pressed the central button. The aiming beam played over the metal, which instantly began to sag as the pulses quickened. The water was now halfway up the cylinder. He hoped the float was at the top.

The bracket fell away and Riley turned the laser off and pushed it into his belt. He pulled at the cylinder and it came free at the first tug, almost sending him backwards into the seawater. He heard a rattle inside and remembered that a ballcock/carburettor flotation tank could work as a trembler switch as well if shaken too much.

He held up the extinguisher at shoulder height, keeping it vertical. Now he could see the thick black cable that ran from its base and disappeared below the surface. It was probably several separate wires, wrapped in layers of insulating tape. So the flotation device acted like an on/off switch, initiating a larger device under the water.

'How's he doing with those pumps?' he shouted.

'I dunno, Riley. Hold on.'

Hold on? The water was climbing above his waist with indecent haste. The black cable that ran to the submerged explosives was as taut as he dared make it. And his chilled muscles were already fatigued.

Riley used his feet to search below the churning surface trying to locate the main charge. His toecap touched something hard. He traced its shape as carefully as he could, keen not to snag any wires. Lifting the extinguisher with one hand, he thrust the other beneath the surface and briefly re-examined the submerged device.

'Fuck,' he said softly to himself, clutching the extinguisher with both hands now.

'What?' asked Cortez.

'It's a metal frame. I think I know what's in the centre. A shaped charge.'

'Fuck,' she agreed.

They were both familiar with shaped charges. They consist of a metal cone, normally made of copper that, on detonation, becomes a jet of super-heated plasma, like a volcano exploding, but more focused. The old phrase 'hot knife through butter' could have been invented for shaped charges.

As the water level rose to the bottom of his ribs, Riley's arms began to vibrate uncontrollably with the strain and the cold. 'In a bit of trouble here,' he admitted.

'Hey, Riley.'

'What?' His chest constricted as the inky seawater lapped against his diaphragm. The Atlantic was coming in faster than ever. Now it was at the base of the elevated extinguisher. His biceps began to scream in pain as he lifted it higher. '*What?*' he shouted again.

'I've got an idea. Hold on, I'm coming down.'

Cortez managed the ladder like a pro, Riley thought, sliding down with her feet on the outside of the verticals. As if a firefighter had taught her the fast descent technique.

She hit the water and let out a string of profanities.

'Sorry, I couldn't find the heater.'

'Fuck me, Riley,' Cortez gasped as she waded over.

'That would be very difficult at this temperature.'

'You really are a Neanderthal, you know that?'

Cortez reached him and put a hand under the extinguisher, taking some of the strain off his arms. 'This isn't the return date I was expecting, Riley.'

'Nor me. There's a cable running. From the bottom. Of this.

Or a bundle of wires. It goes to the shaped charge, if that's what it is. We can't ...'

She picked up the thought. 'We can't just cut it. No way of knowing if it's a collapsing circuit.' Her speech was also becoming staccato as her chest muscles constricted and her jaw clenched from the cold. And she didn't have a survival suit on.

'What's your idea?'

'We turn the shaped charge over,' she said. 'So it doesn't fire through the hull.'

Riley gave a laugh that hurt his chest. 'That's an idea? That's suicide.' It was what they had called Operation Certain Death back in Afghan. A one-way ticket to oblivion. 'We'd have a choice of being scorched to death in the air or broiled like a lobster under water or probably both.'

Cortez nodded. She had been well aware of that. 'You got anything?'

'Have you got any Gunk?' he asked. It was the substance that Riley was hankering after when he was dealing with the Second World War bomb. It was a non-conducting resin would set fast and seize up the float.

'What?'

'That instant-setting stuff you use to lock mechanisms solid,' he explained. 'We could pump it in here.' He nodded at the extinguisher. 'Nobble the float.'

'Right. In the kit up top, yes.'

'You want to get some? I'll be okay.'

She let go of the cylinder, hesitating to make sure he had taken the weight, and turned to head back to the ladder when there came the high-pitched whine of an electric motor. They both stared at the watertight door as it slid smoothly on its rails and closed with a soft click. Their head torches picked out the smooth metal wall surrounding the now-sealed aperture. There was no internal release. No handle. They were trapped.

*

Riley swore again. 'Okay, we go with Plan A.'

'Remind me.'

'We turn the charge over. At least we'll save the ship.'

'And probably nobody will know about our sacrifice,' Cortez said.

'Only the Good Lord,' said Riley. 'Maybe it'll get us in the speedy boarding lane at the pearly gates. Can you hold this?'

Cortez took the extinguisher from him and held it above her head. Riley was relieved he had a taller-than-average partner on this one.

He pushed over to where he had located the main charge, filled his lungs and ducked down into the water. The torch stayed on, but the water was opaque and he could barely make out the rectilinear metal cage that held the copper cone. He braced himself as best he could, gripped the far end of the frame and pulled it towards him as he rolled it, so as not to yank the wires from the cylinder Cortez was holding. As he did so, one of his hands touched a circular metal disc. A quick feel confirmed this was where the lead from the extinguisher was connected to the main charge. He let the cage drop and stood into the air, blinking to try and clear his stinging eyes.

'Done?' she asked, the effort of holding up the flotation trigger showing in the sinewy cords standing out in her neck.

'Not yet. I've got the detonator. Big brass circle. There's two protruding lugs on it. Like on a fire hydrant. So you can grip it. I think it unscrews.'

'It'll be booby trapped.'

'Maybe. What have we got to lose? Can you do another minute or two with that?'

She nodded.

Riley filled his lungs again and went under once more. He used cold fingers to locate the circular plate again and gripped the lugs to try and turn it. The disc didn't budge. He used both hands and every ounce of strength he had to give. No movement at all.

He surfaced again and spat out water. 'I might be mistaken about it unscrewing. Stuck tight.'

'Tricky bastard,' she gasped.

They were tricky bastards . . .

'Thank you,' he said, diving into the waters again. His hands had lost almost all feeling now. It was like his fingers had been replaced with sausages, swollen, almost useless appendages. He located the detonator cap once more and, counter-intuitively, pushed it clockwise. It rotated smoothly. Left-handed thread. Just like the slyest of Nazi bomb designers liked to use. Nothing new under the sun, he thought. Or the waves.

Riley's eyes felt like they had been squirted with acid and his lungs were beginning to burn. He needed air, but he had to resist the urge to surface. He had to act calmly and very slowly. Three full turns and what he had assumed was the detonator was free from its housing, however this was somewhat bigger than he had expected, about the size of a toilet roll tube, but made of metal.

It's got to be a booster, Riley thought to himself. Often explosive boosters were used to enhance the detonation wave between the initiator and main explosive charge. An extra kick up the arse for the big one.

Now he had to withdraw it from the back of the shaped charge, as gingerly as he could. He pulled, feeling for any resistance that might suggest an anti-handling wire. No snagging that he could tell. The detonating charge gave and came away in Riley's hand. Now effectively a lump of High Explosive with no means of initiation, the shaped charge could be ignored for the moment. Satisfied, Riley kicked upwards, breaking the surface of the water and began wheezing and coughing like an asthmatic sea lion.

'Got it,' he yelled. 'Booster.'

'I'm . . . I'm slipping here.'

He watched as the extinguisher started to slide through Cortez's frozen fingers. Riley pushed through the water, lifting the detonator charge clear of the surface as he did so. Three big splashy strides got him to her side. He caught the falling flotation trigger as it touched the water. He lifted it again, feeling something pull in his deltoids. He quickly wrapped the trailing wire around the body of the larger cylinder, binding the booster to the side as he did so. With all the strength he could manage to summon from frozen, protesting muscles, he launched the combination like a torpedo through the air. Then he lunged at Cortez, pushing down on her shoulders and making sure he was on top of her and they plunged beneath the water.

A heartbeat later an explosion erupted above them, sending razor-sharp fragmentation hissing into the water around them. The overpressure concussed off the internal walls of the ship's hull, creating a deafening bass sound that was amplified through the water. They were buffeted as if they were wallowing in surf. Riley surfaced into a tank filled with wisps of smoke and the stink of consumed explosives. He reached down and pulled Cortez into the foul air.

'Christ,' she spluttered. He wondered if he would look quite so good with snot streaming from his nose. She wiped it away with her sleeve. 'Riley—'

'I know, I know. I should have let you go on top. I'm a caveman, remember?'

She tried to smile with blue lips, but the shakes took her, wracking her body. Riley reached over and pulled her close. They heard the high-pitched whine of the door's motor at the same time as a heavier throbbing resonated through their bones. A pump. The waters around them began to swirl in a new way, draining rather than rising. He held her tighter, waiting for the shudders to stop. Over her shoulder he could see Truluck in the doorway.

'I'm not interrupting anything am I?' the sailor asked.

'Put the kettle on, mate,' Riley replied through teeth that were chattering like castanets. 'I could murder a brew.'

SEVENTY

Abandon ship.

Not a phrase any captain ever wants to utter. Leaving your ship is like abandoning your soul, your pride, your dignity. Your whole purpose in life.

So Captain Harald Nansen had not and would not give that order. Not without a metaphorical gun to his head. He looked out from the bridge at the ragged line of lifeboats standing off *Rapide* on the starboard side, knowing there was a mirror image on the port, and wondered if he had done the right thing. And it was not a total abandonment, he told himself, more a partial evacuation.

He had ordered all passengers into the boats, along with two crew per vessel. They would stay out there on, thankfully, far calmer seas than they had been through (although he had no doubt there would be many uneasy stomachs in the boats), while there was any possibility of further explosions. There was an empty passenger ship out of Halifax that was several hours away, two tankers and a cargo ship closer than that, although with less potential for taking all the passengers on board. But needs must.

In the meantime, a Canadian helicopter with a contingent of Joint Task Force 2 Special Forces on board – including yet more explosive experts – was en route. It would be refuelled in mid-air and then arrive to deliver a fresh team. They would carry out yet another bow-to-stern examination of *Rapide*, but he appreciated that the Canadian government needed to be seen to carry out its own searches and precautions. Certainly, with the passengers gone and a skeleton crew on board, cabins could be examined more easily.

The captain had spoken to Jakob again who suggested something called the dead cat bounce, a strategy to create peaks and troughs in share prices that could be exploited. It was all a combination of witchcraft and alchemy to Nansen – mysterious rituals that had no place in a sailor's world.

He had, of course, informed his masters of Jakob's theory but all he got back was a feeling of helplessness. The various global financial markets had an inner momentum and twisted logic all of their own. *Rapide* and A-AL were just puppets, and some murderous bastard was jerking their strings.

Erik Santos, his number three, came up to report. He laid a clipboard on the table beside the captain. 'Lifeboats all report everything calm. Passengers are warm and there is plenty of food and drink. Although there have been some requests for alcohol.'

Nansen laughed at that and shook his head. Given the amount some of them had drunk in the last twenty-four hours, he wouldn't be surprised if the DTs would set in for some of them if they stayed out too long. 'Of course there have,' he said. 'Thank you, carry on. Oh, and Erik. Make sure you check in with them every twenty minutes.'

'Yes, sir.' Santos picked up the clipboard and left.

Nansen gripped the edge of the instrument bench as his head swam a little. The combination of lack of sleep and no food was taking its toll. He called down for a sandwich and a coffee, just as Truluck appeared on the bridge. His face was etched with worry and he looked grey and drawn. Nansen wondered if it was like looking in a mirror, if he too was showing the physical toll of the crisis.

'Well?' Nansen asked. 'How are the ATOs? And how did they stop the damned bomb?'

'Warm and changed. We owe them some thanks.'

Truluck explained about the bomb set-up in the anti-roll tank and the flotation trigger. 'We drained the tank and the bomb has been made safe by Staff Sergeant Riley and the American Cortez.'

'And they think that's it?'

'They hope so.'

'Don't we all? And the Ledgards?'

'Christian and Shelby are still in the Owner's Suite, demanding to know why they aren't out there.' He indicted the bobbing lifeboats.

'What's happening?'

'The ATOs are swabbing them. So far, Clark and Amber X have been cleared and Reece, the mechanic.'

'And the bodyguard?'

'Well, there's no sign of him, which is . . .' He banged his forehead with the heel of his hand. 'Shit. In all this, I forgot . . . shit.'

'Jason? What is it?'

'I'll be right back. Christ, I hope they didn't wipe it.'

'Wipe what?'

Truluck told him about the salacious CCTV footage he had ordered destroyed. The couple having near-as-dammit sex and the possible identity of those people on the tape.

Nansen frowned, wondering how significant it was. *Very,* came the answer. 'I think you'd better tell the bomb people. Quick.'

Truluck, though, was already on his way.

*

'I thought the CCTV was out?' asked Riley, massaging one of his still-aching biceps. He might have had another hot shower but he wasn't convinced that he would ever feel warm again.

'Not all of it,' replied Truluck. 'Besides, this one of the couple pre-dated the fire in the CCTV racks.'

They were in an empty cabin opposite the one that held the Ledgards, Cortez and Wang. Truluck had pulled out Riley, telling him he had some news. The ship, stripped of its forward momentum and with the asymmetrically filled ballast tanks, was wallowing and each had to brace against the wall as she pitched and yawed.

Riley shook his head to clear it, trying to process what Truluck was telling him.

'Just run this by me again. The CCTV operators took footage of two people playing tickle the tonsils—'

'And more,' said Truluck. 'It was quite a passionate clinch. It might have gone further but someone disturbed them. It's not unusual by any means. The slap and tickle, I mean. There's usually a compilation made at the end of the cruise season of the juiciest footage and shown at the crew party. It's pretty harmless fun.'

'Unless you're the one caught on camera. But you don't have this charming scene?'

'No. I ordered it wiped.' The words were clouded with regret and self-recrimination.

'But you recognised the couple?'

'I am ninety per cent sure it was Mrs Ledgard and her bodyguard.'

'Who we can't find.'

'Right. I've asked every lifeboat to check if Jim Varney is on board.'

'Jim Varney?' The name carried with it the corrosive shock of bad memories.

'Yes, that's his name. Why?'

'There was a James Varney . . . Used to be SBS. But it can't be the same one.'

'Why not? Don't a lot of former SBS guys go into security?'

Riley nodded, conceding the point. 'They do.'

'If it's the same one, why would the name ring a bell? You worked with him?'

Riley's mouth was dry. He helped himself to a glass of water. 'I was there when he screwed up a training exercise a few months back. I was an observer. Christ, it was a mess. You know the Thames forts? Well, he had had engineers rig up a flash-bang to scare the life out his men, not knowing that a stash of oxygen and acetylene cylinders for the welders was being helicoptered in and would be stored close to the explosives. The bang was much bigger than he expected. People died. Two ATOs among them. Bomb disposal guys. Jesus, it's why I ended up here instead of . . .' He didn't want to think of Ireland or Ruby or Izzy just yet. 'It was hushed up. MoD don't like people to know Special Forces can be fuckin' idiots like everybody else.' He drank the rest of the water.

'Would you recognise him?' Truluck asked.

He thought back to that wind-scoured beach in Kent and the black shadows launching a RIB into the waves. 'I never saw him,' Riley admitted. 'Except as a distant figure on a beach in a bala-clava. Can I make a call to London?'

'Sure. Why?'

'I know someone who runs a security agency.' Scooby could get him details on Jim Varney's history and current employer. Like the ATO mafia, the Circuit was also a very tight-knit group.

'What now?' Truluck asked.

Now he needed some of the skills his grandmother possessed. 'I'll go back in with the Ledgards. That was useful information, by the way, thank you. The CCTV stuff.'

'Is it significant, do you think?'

'I reckon, but I'm not sure in what way. Shelby wouldn't be the first bored, rich woman to have a fling with her bodyguard. But given that Varney is missing and had access to the Land Rover . . .'

'You've swabbed them?' the sailor asked. 'The Ledgards?'

'Yes,' Riley replied. 'No traces. We had the dog sniff them. Nothing.'

'But you still think the bombs came in on the Land Rover?'

'I do, until a better option presents itself. We need to find this Jim Varney. Eliminate him from our enquiries, as they say.'

Truluck's radio gave a buzz and he answered. The voice that crackled out the speaker sounded panicked. 'Santos here. The captain just collapsed.'

'I'll be right there.' He looked at Riley. 'Sorry. Emergency.'

'No kidding. Christ. Does that make you captain?'

'Acting, at least.'

'Sorry, that sounded . . . insensitive. I hope he's okay. But if you're the boss, I need your permission.'

'To do what?' Truluck asked.

'Blow something up for once.'

Truluck looked genuinely shocked at the idea. 'What? Why?'

'I need to make the Ledgards think it isn't over yet.'

*

Despite his protests that he was perfectly fine, Captain Nansen was helped to his quarters by Sajiv and Santos. They had already brought Dr Courtney back to the ship from the lifeboats. When he had passed out on the bridge, Nansen had caught his head on the edge of one of the desks. There was a tear in the skin and a livid bruise and the medic set about dressing it while the captain sat at the glass-topped table in his living area.

'You may have some concussion. Someone should stay with you.'

'I have not got concussion,' said Nansen irritably. 'It was a glancing blow. I fainted, that's all. I didn't eat until half an hour ago.'

Courtney took his blood pressure and declared it a little low. He shone a light in his eyes but saw nothing untoward in pupil reaction times. 'I should pop back every twenty minutes.'

'I'm not on suicide watch,' the captain snapped. 'I just need some more food and for this shambles to be over. I've got food in the fridge.'

'And drink plenty of water. You may have been dehydrated.'

'Yes, yes. I'll be fine. Truluck will hold the fort.'

The doctor began to pack his things away. 'I'm not surprised you fainted. If I say the word "stress", then . . .'

Nansen almost bellowed his response. 'Then I'd hang you from the yardarm. You do not put that in your notes, you understand? I don't want that on my record. '

'As you well know, we don't have a yardarm. And that was a passing, informal comment. None of this is official, as far as I am concerned.' The older man sighed. 'You know, I've been on a fair number of cruises in my time. Never one like this.'

Nansen barked a laugh. 'I don't think any of us have. How is morale out there on the lifeboats?'

The doctor smiled. 'Surprisingly good. There are those who look upon it as a great adventure. Of course, there are others who . . . Well, you can imagine. The Americans in particular. But that is the way of the things. However, your crew appear to be doing a grand job of keeping spirits up. Of course, it'll be different once the passengers are on dry land.'

'Well, look on the bright side. There'll be plenty of material for your second volume of memoirs.'

'Yes,' the doctor agreed, with an expression of fleeting pleasure, before he appreciated the captain might not be entirely serious. 'But our prime concern is getting you well.'

'I will be fine. Tell Truluck and Santos to let me know when the Canadians arrive.'

'I will. We can't do much until then, anyway.'

'Except fret.'

'No fretting, Captain. That's a doctor's order. I'll pop back later.'

'Don't make a fuss.'

The doctor just raised his eyebrows, zipped up his medical bag and left. Nansen breathed a sigh of relief now he was alone. He thumped the glass table, making the vase of flowers jump up. He felt a flush of shame and embarrassment. Skipper keels over from stress. How would that look to any future employer? Because there was no way he could keep the incident quiet. Too many witnesses.

There was no doubt that there would be numerous enquiries and that he was unlikely to come out of the process unscathed. After all, this could change the future of cruising forever. From now on CEOs would retreat to private yachts and jets, putting an even thicker bubble around themselves.

Nansen got up and walked on slightly wobbly legs through to the galley section. In the fridge was a plate of smoked salmon. He extracted it, tore off the cling film and went back to the table. He ripped sections off and ate them with his fingers. Mette would be appalled. He would phone his wife as soon as all his strength returned. Maybe he should take a nap. He could set an alarm. He yawned. Stress? He was just tired.

His body went rigid when he felt the gun barrel touch his neck, cool and impersonal. Cold as death, he thought.

'Don't say a word, Captain. I'm not going to hurt you. I just need somewhere to lay low. I thought I'd have this room to myself for a while, to be honest. Your place being on the bridge in a crisis and all that. But you're here now. All you have to do is exactly what I say.'

Nansen turned his head slowly so he could see the gunman with his peripheral vision. He had suspected as much from the voice. It was Jim Varney, the Ledgards' bodyguard.

He was about to say something when he heard and felt the unmistakable thud of another explosion.

SEVENTY-ONE

Barbara Clifford-Brown had moved her right hand so it rested on the butt of the pistol. She was well aware that her reflexes weren't what they used to be. Nor were her fingers, which sometimes sparked with the pain of arthritis. That was why she preferred the lighter modern polymer pistols such as the Walther PPQ to the bulky steel-framed automatic next to her. But, with the barrel of the Browning pointing right at Brodsky's chest, she was certain she could pull the trigger before he could launch himself out of the chair.

Fairly certain.

She wasn't fooled by the cane. Yes, there was a limp, but Brodsky's body was still dangerous. In his youth he had moved like a feline. It had been a joy to watch him walk into a room, a tomcat prowling his territory. Without the pissing, obviously. He was bulkier than that now, but Barbara suspected he could still manage a turn of speed.

'What is the question, Barbara?' Brodsky asked. 'Neither of us have much time left in this world.'

'Some less than others.'

'Oh, come on. You have years in you yet.'

'I wasn't talking about myself.'

Brodsky managed a wry smile. 'I know. You know, I could track down those men and women from Operation *Reznya*. The ones who, shall we say, exceeded their orders. They murdered poor Henry. I could arrange an accident.'

Barbara shook her head. 'It won't bring him back, Pavel.'

His head shook slowly, as if propelled by a great sorrow. 'Nothing will. Not even killing me.'

She lifted the gun now. The safety was already off and she had racked a round in when Brodsky had been in the kitchen making the tea. The weapon felt heavy in her hand and she let the arm of the chair take some of the weight.

'That's not what this is about, Pavel. It is about the living. It's about my grandson. Dominic Riley.'

'I told him we had nothing to do with his wife and daughter. It is the truth.'

'And I am not sure I believe you.'

'How can I convince you?'

'You can tell me who was responsible for their abduction. Dom thinks it was the Irish.'

'And you don't?'

'Like you, I still have some residual influence. I sent a couple of our lads out to an oyster place where George O'Donnell, the IRA bomber, was enjoying a plate of molluscs. They leant on him. Heavily. They reported back a 99 per cent certainty that he had no idea what they were talking about. Not that he was upset to learn of Dom's misfortunes. But he had nothing to do with the events in Padstow.'

'You told him this?'

'My grandson has been rather elusive. And I only got the report shortly before we set sail for here. I had intended to lay it out for him in person. I still hope to, God willing.'

'Don't bank on God helping you.' Brodsky suddenly looked animated. 'Barbara, I'm afraid you have had a wasted journey. I'm also sad that your powers of deduction are waning. You have been asking the wrong questions. Not who abducted them. Not why. But how? How did they know where to find the wife and daughter? That's where the answer lies.'

'Don't talk in riddles.'

'I'm not. I don't know who did this to your grandson, but I am damned sure I could find out. The answer to your question is right under your nose, Barbara. You haven't considered the matter properly. Just as you hadn't considered that a man like me has made many enemies over time. Not just you. And that it might have been considered worthwhile to install a panic button or two in my house.'

She was aware of sound and movement down the hallway to her left. Cursing her stupidity, she turned and made the mistake of moving the Browning in an arc as she did so.

The two heavies who had come to take her in interpreted this as an aggressive act and had no hesitation firing their own weapons, filling the room with noise, smoke and blood.

SEVENTY-TWO

Riley made the call to Scooby from the comms room beneath the bridge. He wasted the first few minutes bringing his old friend up to speed and trying to get past Roscoe's astonishment that he was the ATO on *Rapide*.

'I assumed you were in Ireland,' he said. 'Dealing with that shit in Fermanagh.'

Riley resisted the urge to ask: *what shit in Fermanagh?* It wasn't important at that precise moment. But he felt a stab of guilt at the reminder. He *should* have been in Ireland, looking for Izzy and Ruby, but for *Rapide* and the maniacs threatening her. 'I wish,' was all he said in response. 'Listen, Scooby, how long would it take you to do a check on someone on the Circuit?'

'You hiring?'

'I have an X-ray somewhere on board and I need to know who and what I am dealing with.'

'Ten, fifteen minutes.'

'Great. His name is Jim or James Varney. I think he might have been SBS. You need a description?'

'Maybe not. It's not a common name. I'll make some enquiries. You'll call me back?'

'I will, thanks.'

366

He hung up. Truluck poked his head in. 'You okay?'

'Yes. Although I'm afraid I've blown up the basin in one of the cabins.' He had used a length of det cord to make what sounded like a big blast, but had in fact only caused superficial damage to porcelain and glass. But he hoped it had done the trick and jangled some nerves among the Ledgards. Especially the wife.

Truluck shrugged. 'In the scheme of things . . .'

'How's the captain?'

'Doc says he'll be okay. Just needs food, water and a rest.'

'Is he still on board? The doctor? Not gone out to the lifeboats?'

'No, he's here. He's waiting to check on the skipper again.'

'Can you fetch him?'

Truluck looked puzzled. 'Sure. You hurt? Or in pain?'

'No.'

'Then may I ask why you need him?'

Riley didn't like being questioned about what he was up to. He felt it was bad luck to spell out his intentions. Besides, it might all go to shit. 'Tell him I want to give blood.'

Truluck realised he wasn't going to get much more. When Riley called Roscoe back, he answered immediately. 'Dom, what the fuck have you got yourself into?'

Riley really didn't like the sound of that. Unlike his namesake, Scooby was not prone to being spooked. But he sounded it now. 'You tell me.'

'Okay, yes, he was Special Boat Service. Resigned, but in reality canned for a hazing that went wrong.'

'Some stunt where a couple of ATOs died, yes?'

'Correct,' confirmed Scooby. 'But that's not the part that concerns me.'

'It concerns me if it was deliberate. If it was a way to winnow the ranks of available ATOs in SBS even further.'

'Well, that's possible, I suppose. But after he got out, he did indeed go on the Circuit. Within a month he'd been snapped up by Oktane. You heard of them?'

'Nope.'

'Initially it was a bunch of guys who put themselves up for hire after the Balkan wars. Mostly ex-White Eagles and Šakal. They were mainly muscle for drug gangs, sex traders and people smugglers.'

'They sound charming.'

'They are. But a couple of them had bigger ambitions. You ever see *The Wire*?'

Riley had seen some of it in Afghan, but he was sensing a fork in the road and a big Diversion sign. 'Scooby . . .'

'Okay, Okay. Stringer Bell, one of the drug guys, realises that selling crack is like selling any other commodity, subject to the same market forces. So, he goes to night school to do a business course. The Oktane guys did something similar. They decided they could be like the Google or Uber or Amazon of the security and black information world. Right now, they are in the early disrupter phase. Cheap prices, good service. I'll be lucky to be in business in two years. The thing is, they've never forgotten their roots. Beneath the smooth surface and the data trading, there's always the bubbling threat of violence if you cross them.'

'And Varney is working for them?'

'Yup, he's on their books. And there's something else.'

'What's that?'

'They always work in pairs.'

*

'You look like shit.'

'That,' said Riley, 'is the general idea.'

Cortez shook her head. 'You're just playing games. You sure that this chum of yours has it right? About them working in pairs?'

'I don't know. But he's in the business. I trust him.' They were in a cabin two down from the Owner's Suite, one that was merely opulent, as opposed to the mini-Versailles that the Ledgards were in. He was in an armchair, facing the door, so that he would be the first thing that anyone who entered would see. 'You want to go and get her?'

'Sure. You want me to stay while you chat?'

'Yes. Best have a witness. And a female presence.'

She walked over and crouched down next to him. She smelt a whole lot nicer than he did, that was for sure. 'What if there is someone else out there?' She pointed a thumb at the doorway. 'Busy planting bombs? Then your little ruse won't work. Will it?'

'We'll see. But I'm pretty certain she is a key component in of all this.'

Cortez stood again and sighed. 'Okay, one rich bitch coming right up.'

Riley heard the commotion coming from the Owner's Suite, particularly Christian Ledgard's objections. He sounded like a whining, frightened child being deprived of his mother. He had a surprise or two coming. But eventually, the door to the cabin opened and Shelby Ledgard was ushered in by Cortez. Her face looked gratifyingly shocked when she caught sight of Riley.

'Jesus . . . Are you . . . are you all right? Fuck. Is that your blood?'

Riley touched his face, which had a spray of red spots across it. 'Some of it. The rest of it belongs to the two crew members who died when that bomb your boyfriend wired went off about ten minutes ago. I think you must have heard it.'

She didn't say anything, just worked her jaw like a guppy.

'Sit down,' he instructed.

Cortez guided her over to a second armchair and eased her into it. She then stepped back, out of Shelby Ledgard's line of sight. Riley waited. The cogs were turning. She would respond eventually.

'What boyfriend? What the fuck are you talking about?' she demanded. The Righteous Indignation Defence.

'Either Jim Varney is your boyfriend or you have a particularly interesting employer-employee contract. Let me explain. One of the ship's officers showed me a little film of you and Jim.' Well, not exactly *showed*. But Truluck had marked his card well enough. 'In it you were . . . how shall I put it?'

'Making out?' Cortez suggested.

'That'll do.'

'So?' Ledgard asked.

'So your boyfriend is in the frame for the whole catastrophe. The explosives were transported in his . . . or your, technically, I suppose, Land Rover. We had one man killed initially and now, two more.' The lie tripped easily off his lips. Nobody had died, not in the past hour at least.

'Jim had nothing to do with that. He's not a killer.'

Riley laughed at that. 'He's a trained Special Forces soldier. And now he's an employee of Oktane. Does that name mean anything to you?'

'No, of course not. Jim is employed by us.'

'And does Mr Ledgard know about your arrangement with Jim?'

A scowl distorted her features. 'You fucker. You can't blackmail me.'

'But you can blackmail an entire shipping line?'

'You've got the wrong end of the stick. I don't know who planted the bomb that just killed two people and did . . . that to you. But it wasn't Jim.'

'Where is he?'

'I don't know.' She blinked away tears. 'I just want to be off this fuckin' ship.'

'When you will be arrested,' Riley said flatly, as if it were inevitable. In truth, he had no idea which agencies dealt with extortion and murder on the high seas.

She shook her head in disbelief. 'In your dreams. On what charge?'

He smiled. 'Oh, it'll be as long as your arm, I'm sure.'

Anger flared in her eyes, blasting the tears away. 'What right have you got to question me? You're not a policeman. You're not even ship's security.'

'No, Jim killed him, remember? His face reduced to a pulp, like something from a butcher's window.'

'Fuckin' abattoir,' muttered Cortez.

'Would you like to see?' asked Riley.

'We could take you down to the morgue?'

'Or look here.' Riley proffered his camera. 'See what you did?'

'Because you messed them up good. Bombs do that. We should know, me and Riley. Let's see … how many people you killed altogether?'

'Look at it,' insisted Riley, standing and moving towards her. Shelby turned her face away.

'Is it eight? Nine?' asked Cortez. ''Cause the plane's all on you, honey. If it wasn't for you, those guys wouldn't have been doing acrobatics out there. Is it ten?'

'More now,' said Riley. He shoved the camera with its image of a mangled Jos Swart at her. 'Look. Look, what you and your boyfriend did. Look, for fuck's sake!'

Shelby spun to face him. 'Nobody was supposed to die!'

The air in the room thickened, so that Riley found it hard

to breathe. Had he heard right? *Nobody was meant to die?* Was that a confession?

As if to confirm it, Shelby Ledgard put her face into her hands and began to sob, her shoulders shaking. Cortez raised her eyebrows in what Riley hoped was recognition that he had been right about her, right to bluff her that people were still dying in explosions.

'Who else is in on it in your party?'

'Nobody,' she croaked. 'Amber was beginning to suspect something was going on with me and Jim. And then she caught us . . . she's hardly spoken to me since. But she thought it was just another fling with the staff. Christ, she could talk. Two-faced bitch. And Ben is an idiot . . .' She stopped, head cocked to one side at the intrusion of a new sound.

The suite's solid surfaces began to thrum. The windows emitted a high-pitched whine and rattled in their frames. Riley turned to look out to sea, in time to see the dark shape of a helicopter flash by, temporarily blocking his view of the lifeboats.

'The Canadians,' he said.

The racket subsided as the chopper moved off, no doubt to turn and do another recce fly-by. As the noise diminished there came a new unmistakable sound. That of a gun being discharged.

SEVENTY-THREE

'Was that your doing?' the captain asked as the noise of the explosion faded.

'No,' Varney said, his face puckered in worry. He moved around the table and sat at the far end, well out of reach of Nansen. He laid the gun down and ran a hand through his hair. 'I just need time to think.'

'Not going to plan, then?'

'Shut up!'

'I think this BaseHeart screwed you. While you're stuck here, running out of options, he's banking the money made from the share collapse and the bounce that you engineered with your bangs.'

'I told you, *shut up.*'

Nansen decided it best to back off a little. The bodyguard was a mass of ragged nerves, unpredictable and dangerous. They sat in silence for a while. 'Was Swart involved in this scheme of yours? Did you kill him?'

'The fool killed himself.'

When he didn't elaborate, Nansen said: 'You know, the doctor will be back in a while to check on me.'

Varney touched the gun, a Sig-Sauer, as if to remind Nansen it was there. 'And you'll tell him you are fine. Just resting. If you try anything else I'll shoot you both.'

Nansen said nothing in reply. The man had the air of a cornered animal. He could smell the sourness of it, like stale sweat. Minutes ticked by before he spoke again. 'So, can I have a few guesses? I think this started out as a way to make money out of Christian Ledgard. You and Mrs Ledgard? You became lovers?' Of course, he thought to himself, sex and money, the toxic binary combination behind many a crime. 'But I seem to recall that there is a pre-nup between the Ledgards, which would leave Shelby penniless should she run off with her bodyguard. Well, you know. Down to her last million or two. But somebody came up with a way to make money from Klondike by manipulating the shares. Was it you? Shelby? A third party? BaseHeart, I suppose, is the most likely candidate. You're told there would be harmless bombs just to keep up the blackmail masquerade. But Swart . . . ?'

'I knew nothing about that.' Varney scooped up the gun, walked through to the kitchen area and helped himself to a beer from the fridge. He drank it with his left hand, the Sig held loosely in his right. 'He fucked up.'

'How on earth do you think you can get off the ship?' Nansen asked, genuinely curious about the man's next move.

'There are a million ways.'

'You haven't got a million of anything, Jim. It might be best to give it up now. If you really had nothing to do with Swart you can always claim to be an innocent dupe of a criminal mastermind.'

'Fuck you.' Varney waved the 9mm in Nansen's direction. 'I'm trained in things you people wouldn't believe. I can get out of this.'

The confidence rang hollow but the captain didn't challenge him. He was busy cocking an ear to a fresh sound. 'Helicopter,' he said. 'It must be the Canadians.'

Varney nodded and moved towards the panoramic window as the *whup-whup* sound grew louder. That's when Nansen made his move.

SEVENTY-FOUR

Kate Muraski headed back to *Thetis* with something of a guilt complex. After four hours in the Hermitage on the official shore excursion she never wanted to see another opulent room covered in gold leaf again. Similarly, she was all arted out. It was like a ghetto for paintings, all these great portraits and landscapes herded onto crowded walls, where each lost their individual impact and culminated in a sensory overload.

Or, possibly, she just hadn't been in the mood for it. Having Edith yacking in her ear the whole way hadn't helped.

Back on board, after giving Edith the slip, Muraski knocked on Barbara's door, but there was no reply. Not done yet, then. She had to remind herself that Barbara had been playing the spy game since well before she was born. She was a trooper, a survivor.

In her own cabin she failed to notice the envelope on her pillow until she had showered. Some spy she was turning out to be. Her name was written in ink in a neat cursive that betrayed only the slightest shake in the hand of the author. Barbara. She must have paid one of the stewards to deliver it while Muraski was listening to the guide drone on about the armour in the Knight's Room.

She sat on the bed, twisted a towel around her head and ripped open the envelope. Inside was a single sheet of paper, written in the same hand as her name had been, but less precise. This message had been scribbled in some haste.

Dear Kate,

First of all, let me say how much I have enjoyed your company these last few days. It would have been unbearable without you. As you correctly realised early on, my whole aim was to see Brodsky and get the truth from him, something my grandson failed to do. Still, it isn't his field of expertise, is it?

If you are reading this without me then I am still not back. If I am not on board by the time the ship is due to sail, tell the purser I have had another funny turn and am being kept in for observation on shore. I don't want it to wait for me. It would be a waste of time. Now, if this comes to pass, you can do one important thing for me. Get hold of Hector at Six on the number written on the back of the envelope as soon as you possibly can. Memorise the number and then destroy it, as we melodramatic old spooks like to say. Don't save it in your phone.

Tell him this: the asking price was too high. We have withdrawn from the sale. Please advise on alternative.

He'll know what that means. Do not worry about me. But if you don't want to continue the voyage in my absence (if that is what transpires), I suggest you fly home from Tallinn, the next port of call. I have left my card details, so you have no need to worry about the bill. Needless to say, please dispose of this letter.

Take care, Kate.

Barbara had signed off with a flourish of curves. She read it a second time. *The asking price was too high.*

What did that mean? She stripped off the towels from head and body and began to dress, unable to shake the feeling that she knew exactly what the message meant. That Barbara was dead. Or worse.

SEVENTY-FIVE

Riley pointed a finger at Shelby Ledgard. 'You stay here. Do not move. Understand?'

Ledgard nodded her consent. Cortez was already out of the door, sidearm drawn, racing down the passageway past the Owner's Suite towards the captain's quarters. Riley ran after her. 'Hold on!'

'Keep up!' she said.

She stopped and sniffed the air like Lieutenant Madison. 'In here.' She thumped on the door. 'Hello! You okay in there?'

Riley caught up with her. 'Stand back, I'll kick it in.'

She gave him her best withering look, raised the Glock and gave Riley just enough time to put his fingers in his ears before she fired two shots in the door jamb, where lock met wood. She gave a sharp kick and it swung back. Riley went in first and stopped dead, trying to make sense of the scene within.

Captain Nansen lay spreadeagled, like a starfish, a bright bloom of blood still growing across his chest. His eyes were open, staring at the ceiling.

A few metres towards the windows was Jim Varney. He, too, had suffered damage to his upper torso, although not from a bullet. Sticking out from just below the sternum was a long pole of dark, ancient wood. Varney had been harpooned. Nansen had tossed a harpoon straight into his chest.

What, really? What do you think this is? Moby fuckin' Dick?

'Jesus Christ,' muttered Cortez from over his shoulder, looking at the skewered figure before her. 'Is he dead?'

'I reckon.'

But Varney's eyes flickered open and, working on the instincts of a fading brain, he raised the Sig in his hand and fired, the boom filling the room. As he twisted away under the impact and began his fall to the floor, Riley had one terrifying thought as the first fires of pain flared.

Gutshot.

SEVENTY-SIX

The FSB is like a nation within a nation, with its own housing complexes, hospitals, stores and schools. It was to one of the hospitals that Barbara Clifford-Brown was sent. At least, she assumed it was. Even in Russia, turning up at a regular medical centre with gunshot wounds would cause a stir. She was also in a well-equipped private room, clean and bright that she imagined was a cut above the accommodations on offer in the state versions.

All this took quite a while to sink in, as she kept drifting out of consciousness from whatever drugs tried to keep hold of her. Her right hand was throbbing and she managed to raise it. It was encased in plaster. With her left she explored her scalp. There was a large dressing on the side and rear of her skull. They had shaved a large patch of her hair off. Perhaps the wig would have a second use now. She found herself feeling remarkably sanguine about that. It was possible the drugs had blunted her emotions.

Barbara had trouble recalling the final moments at Brodsky's house initially, but it was slowly coming into focus. Both FSB men had fired. One of the bullets had smashed into her gun hand. The sudden, burning agony had caused her to pitch forward, which meant the second round, no doubt aimed at her temple, had skidded along the back of her head, ploughing a bloody furrow.

Brodsky fussing over her, shouting at the men for being idiots, demanding an ambulance, that much she recalled, albeit as if viewed through muslin. She had passed out after that.

She took a deep breath as a spear of pain travelled from wrist to elbow. A dull ache had begun to colonise her skull. She closed her eyes and lay back, one thought before she sunk into the blackness.

Kate will be worried.

*

Barbara awoke to the sound of a trolley. It was being pushed by a young nurse who was dressed in the kind of starched whites that in Britain now only existed in *Carry On* movies. As she watched, the pains returned and she let out a groan.

The nurse was busy preparing a tray of food, but at the sound from Barbara's lips she came over and asked, in Russian, if she was in pain.

'Yes. I am now.'

She put a cool hand on the old lady's forehead. 'I shall get the doctor. But you must eat also.'

'I'm not hungry.'

The nurse smiled, as if everyone said that. She was pretty, her face scrubbed pink, with red hair, attractively slanted eyes and high, prominent cheekbones that suggested Slav blood. 'You must eat and drink, grandmother.'

Babushka? She would have laughed except for the fear of the pain it might cause. It was meant affectionately, but it was because she was a grandmother that she had ended up in that predicament.

She placed a lap tray over Barbara and lifted the cloche off a plate. It was a stew of some description and even the smell made Barbara heave. 'I can't.'

The nurse poured a large glass of water. 'I shall fetch the doctor.'

As she turned to go, Barbara asked: 'I think someone has taken my mobile. Can I make a phone call, please? It's important.' Why it was so urgent she couldn't quite grasp. It was just a churning in her stomach. A feeling she had information to impart. Something to do with what Brodsky had said just before his thugs had shot her. But it would come back, she was certain of that. 'I'd be very grateful.'

The nurse shook her head firmly. She looked as if Barbara had asked for the Bolshoi Ballet and the Marinsky Orchestra to come in and entertain her. 'There are never phone calls for patients. It is forbidden,' she said and swept out of the room as if she had never been so insulted in her life.

*

'Keep still.'

Riley had passed out from the pain, he reckoned. He was on the floor, staring up at ceiling tiles. Something soft had been slid under his neck, a towel or a cushion. Someone was kneeling next to him. He could smell citrus.

A dull throbbing worked its way up his side, settling around his neck before making a jump to his temples. His mouth was dry. He licked his lips.

'Keep still,' the doctor said again as he heaved into view.

'How's Cat?' Riley tried to turn his head. Something spasmed in his side.

'We're dealing with her.' This was Truluck. 'Stay still, Riley. You've been shot.'

Riley was no medical man, but he could have come up with that diagnosis. 'How's Cat?' he repeated, his tongue thicker, heavier than before.

'I've given you something for the pain. You'll be fine.'

'No.' Riley tried to sit up. Hands pushed him down. 'No morphine.'

Truluck came in close, speaking softly into his ear. 'You remember what happened?'

Speaking became more of an effort. 'Yes . . . Captain?'

'Captain Nansen is dead. So is Varney.'

'Ha . . . Cat?' he managed for the third time.

'Emergency blood transfusion. The bullet passed through you into her.'

Gutshot.

Oh, God, no.

'How . . . Will she . . . be okay?' Slurring now, his lips out of his neurological control.

'We don't know. American and Canadian medics are working on her. They seem to know what they are doing.'

They'd be better at gunshot wounds than the ship's doc, that was sure. Riley closed his eyes, felt the tug of the warmth coursing through his veins. He snapped them open again. 'The Canadians . . . here? Now?'

'They are. We're going to move you soon. We can get you to hospital on the mainland using their chopper if we hurry.'

'Ca . . . ?' he could no longer manage the final consonant.

Truluck squeezed his shoulder. 'Her too . . .'

But even as he succumbed to the blandishments of the drugs, the promise of warmth and dark and peace, Riley could hear the unspoken part of his sentence. *If she makes it.*

PART FOUR

SEVENTY-SEVEN

Kate Muraski had excelled herself. She had gone one step beyond last time, when she had taken him down a hidden conduit between airside and landside. This time, Riley was asked by the flight attendant to wait until everyone else had deplaned. As he looked out over the wing of the Air Canada 787 Dreamliner, he saw a black Range Rover pull up on the tarmac next to the Boeing. He instinctively knew it was for him.

She was waiting next to the rear door as he walked down the steps, trying to hide how stiff he was. He felt like he had aged two decades in the past week since he had been shot. Life was slower, more painful. So were the memories.

She opened the door as he approached her. 'Welcome home, Riley.'

'I've got luggage.' He had put it in the hold, not wanting to trust his stitches by shoving a bag in an overhead locker.

'Don't worry, we'll get it. VIP treatment. Try not to stare if you see any pop stars.'

'I don't know what any pop stars look like. Madonna, maybe. Lady Gaga if she's wearing meat.'

'You really should get out more.'

He laughed and immediately regretted it. 'This is what happens when I go out.'

Muraski watched him climb into the back seat, again trying to mask his lack of mobility. She reached across to get the seatbelt. 'I've got it.'

She remained leaning over him. 'You okay, Riley?'

As he clicked the buckle home, he breathed in the clean scent of her hair. He had spent too long in artificial, air-conned atmospheres. 'Pretty much.'

'I'm sorry about . . . you know.'

He nodded and then looked away, staring at the back of the immobile driver. *Nobody was meant to die,* the woman had said. And, Riley reminded himself, in an ideal world – a fair world – Riley should have been in Ireland, looking for his former wife and daughter, not fucking about on the high seas. And people did die. Swart first, the captain, Varney and then, very nearly, Cortez. Not to mention those on the Herc. Those deaths, ultimately, were down to Ledgard and Varney. *They work in pairs,* Scooby had said. But which had been the pairing? Varney and Shelby Ledgard or Swart and Varney? He'd probably never know. Maybe they did threesomes sometimes.

Varney's bullet had passed clean through Riley's side, creating a deep, bloody channel, but hardly slowing at all. It had then slammed into Cortez's stomach. As he went down, Riley had seen her clutch her abdomen and heard her cry out. The already deformed 9mm round had spun as it tore into her, acting like a scythe, a bloody harvest through her internal organs. She lost a lot of blood very quickly. She was still in hospital in Halifax, the same place where he had been patched up, with a tiny chance of a full recovery. When he thought about her, full of tubes, wired up to blinking and beeping machines, lost in an induced coma, his skull buzzed as if it had been invaded by a swarm of bluebottles.

Somewhere on this heartless planet a man with the code name BaseHeart was on some offshore tax and criminal haven, counting his money. Riley's guess was he had played everyone for chumps. There was never any intention for Varney and Shelby to get away with anything. The true crime was being played out in stocks and shares. BaseHeart had won that game. The bombs were simply a means to an end. Even the shaped charge that had been in the ballast tank was unlikely to have actually sunk *Rapide*. They were simply designed to keep the ATOs on their toes and the cycle of danger/no danger leaking to the media. The threat of explosions was the tool he had used to manipulate markets. Was it insanely clever? Or just insane?

Muraski joined him in the back and slammed her door. 'There's people who want a word with you.'

'So I hear.' MI5, MI6, the army, Counter Terrorism Command, even FBI's London legat, they were all queuing up to talk to him. He was pretty sure, given the callous disregard for human life and cruel duplicity of those involved in the scheme, he hadn't screwed up. His job would be to make sure none of the organisations tried to make it seem that way. When people die, there's always a cry for someone to blame.

'Look, my lot want first dibs, if that's okay,' said Muraski. 'Thames House. Just an initial chat. But we can call by your flat first if you wish?'

'Yes, thanks. I need a change of clothes.'

'Okay, Phil – thanks,' she said to the driver. They pulled away and drove to the entrance of the VIP lounge, where the driver hopped out to fetch his luggage.

'Customs? Immigration?' he asked.

'Don't be ridiculous,' Muraski replied.

His phone beeped. It was a voice message from Scooby.

Welcome home, pal. I sent the cleaner in for a quick dust. There's milk in the fridge. Tell me when you are up for a jar. You've been through a lot, buddy. You see the Sunday Times? *Three pages. And a big graphic. That fire extinguisher trick. What a doozy. I think you earned your bonus this month.*

Riley texted him back. *Got your VM. Thanks. You don't know the half of it, pal. Up for a jar now, but duty calls. Next day or two tho'.*

'Scooby,' he explained to Muraski when he clicked off. 'He's had the flat spring cleaned.'

'He's a good mate. But he knows first-hand what you've been through. What you're going through.'

'Afghan? Well, his story isn't the same as mine.'

'I know that. But he had a daughter, too.'

'Evie? How do you know about her?'

'I pulled his file last year, remember? When he was helping with the Viper case.'

Riley didn't. The previous year seemed decades ago. 'I know you want to know what went on out there ...'

'It can wait. You'll be sick of telling that story.'

'Has Five had any luck on BaseHeart this end?'

'No. Shelby Ledgard reckons they dealt with two people. A Northern Irish guy and one who sounded like Toto Wolff.' *They always work in pairs.* Mrs Ledgard was still in detention in Canada. She had been interviewed by UK anti-terrorist detectives and an agent of MI5, who had reported the conversations back to Thames House.

'Who's that?' Riley asked.

'Austrian guy. Head of Mercedes Formula One. Quite sexy.'

'Oh.' F1 was something else, along with pop stars, which Riley knew very little about. 'You following the money?'

'The financial wonks are trying to. BaseHeart did a good job of covering his tracks. They reckon they'll get there eventually, but by then the pot at the end of the rainbow will probably be empty. The beast will have been bled.'

Riley yawned.

'Yeah, it does that to me, too. High finance.'

'Sorry. Bushed. Listen, if that theory about BaseHeart being named after some relic of a TV show is right, we should ask Scoob. He knows all that Sixties crap.' He stifled another yawn. 'And my grandmother?'

'Still somewhere in St Petersburg. The Foreign Office reckon they'll be able to swap her for a couple of oligarch visas.'

Barbara was worth more than bits of paper for some foreign crooks, but he shouldn't complain if it was a relatively simple exchange. 'They've seen her? The FO?'

'Yes.'

'And?' he prompted.

'She . . . Well, she was injured interviewing Brodsky.'

'Badly injured?'

'I don't know.'

'Why did she go and see Brodsky in the first place?'

'She thought he lied to you in Helsinki. About being involved in the abduction of Ruby and Izzy. And the death of Henry.' She hesitated and then said it anyway. 'I think she went to kill him.'

'That really wouldn't surprise me.'

'Nor me. You know about her first husband?' asked Muraski.

Riley's mouth dropped open. 'What? No. I thought that was Henry.' How could his grandparents have kept that fact from him?

'Apparently not. Long story. If true. I'm doubting everything she's ever told me now. But it'll wait.'

Riley grimaced as a familiar lance of pain tracked across his lower abdomen. He took out a blister pack of painkillers. Muraski passed him a bottle of water. 'Don't tell anyone,' he said.

'About what?'

'The drugs. We army types are meant to chew on a bit of old leather.'

She laughed at that. The driver returned with Riley's case and placed it in the rear. As they set off again, Muraski said, 'Maybe you should close your eyes for a bit. Going to be a long day.'

'I'm fine.' But he was asleep before they hit the M4.

*

Riley was still groggy from the nap when he arrived at the flat. Scooby had been as good as his word. It sparkled. He could tell that Muraski was surprised. She had clearly expected some sort of man cave, stacked with bits of vintage bombs and decorated with posters for *The Hurt Locker, Face/Off, Juggernaut* and other don't-cut-the-red-wire big clock countdown movies.

'I won't be long,' he said, going through to dump his bag in the bedroom.

'Take your time,' Muraski said.

In the bathroom he stripped off his top and washed his arm-pits and his face. The dressing on his side was intact and he had been told not to shower or bathe for a while. He looked down at it, and again flashed back to Cortez and the frightened noise she had made when she realised what had happened. The bluebottles swarmed. He blinked back hot tears of rage.

Army types don't cry, either, mate.

'Maybe they should,' he said aloud.

Back in the bedroom, he pulled off the rest of his clothes and put on fresh underwear and jeans. 'Fancy a cup of tea?' Muraski shouted.

'Sure.' A proper brew would be very welcome. 'There's fresh milk in the fridge, apparently.'

He was trying to select a top — T-shirt or collared shirt? — when his phone rang. He didn't recognise the number.

'Hello?'

'Dominic? It's Barbara. Your grandmother.'

As if it could be anyone else with that voice. 'Hello. Christ, it's good to hear from you. Where are you?'

'Russia, still. I have been allowed one call. This is it,' she said sharply. 'Let's not waste time. No time for niceties. This is about Ruby and Izzy.'

A bucket of cold water on his face. Goosebumps lighting up his arm and neck. His scalp itchy. The light in the room brighter, sharper. The fatigue pulled away like a magician's tablecloth. He thought of all that lost time, and lost lives, on the ship, felt the familiar roiling rage burst from its pen, telling him he still had work to do. 'Go on.'

'I have had plenty of opportunity to ponder. I have re-checked Ireland and drew a blank. There is no link there, Dom. Brodsky told me I had to think about who knew where Ruby and Izzy were that day. Who could have pinpointed them? Who could have tracked them to Padstow? Not the Irish. Not the Russians.'

That seemed the full pack to Riley. There was nobody else in the frame, apart from a deranged Afghan bomber, and he had been well dead by the time they were taken. 'Brodksy knew who took Izzy all along?'

'No. But he told me how to start looking. Under our noses.'

'Who then? Who did it?'

The voice on the other end hardened, as if to brook no argument. 'I think it was your friend who supplied the bodyguards.'

Riley's mind cycled through the list of people she could possibly mean. The answer was ridiculous.

'You mean Scooby Roscoe?'

'Yes.'

He shook his head, as if Barbara could see him. 'You never liked him.'

'Strange boy. Those voices. Like a demented Mike Yarwood. You wouldn't remember him. But that's neither here nor there. I think he was involved in Padstow.'

'But he lost an operative in the kidnapping. One of the women was killed. Jackie. The other one was lucky to be alive.'

'Perhaps that was unintentional.'

Nobody was meant to die.

'Maybe his women were better at their jobs than the opposition expected. A kidnapping is like trying to tame fire – you never know who is going to get burnt. Look, Dom, I have to be quick.'

His brain was still reeling, as if it had broken from its moorings, spinning away on a flood tide. 'Scooby? It can't be . . . Why? Why would he?'

'Why?' She laughed, a bitter sound. 'I don't know. Maybe he hates you. Maybe he always has. Some grudge you've forgotten about. I admit I might be wrong. This place might have turned my brain to mush. But that's what I think. You know we couldn't find out who dobbed you in to SUPO in Helsinki? Made sure you were arrested? Not Five. Not Six. Did Roscoe know about that trip?'

Watch out for the Finns. The cops, the spooks. They're paranoid.

'Yes, but—'

'I know. Supposition. But you need to be very careful, Dom.'

He didn't answer immediately, still reeling from the suggestion. Scooby?

Shelby Ledgard reckons they dealt with two people. A Northern Irish guy and one who sounded like Toto Wolff.

No, not Toto Wolff. Arnold Schwarzenegger. Not any old Northern Irishman, but Ian fucking Paisley.

He recalled Scooby slapping his belly in the pub. *My only daft idea is to feed this beast.* Beast? Was that a coincidence?

A great abyss opened beneath him. Scooby had taken his family. Scooby, the master of mimicry. He was also . . .

BaseHeart? *Scoob knows all that crap.*

No, impossible. Nice Scooby, his mate from school, who gave him a Rover sniffer that had helped on the *Rapide* operation, had cleaned his flat, stocked his refrigerator. It couldn't be.

Yes it could, pal.

Other phrases came back to him. *You remember the Johnsons? . . . Shot in the face.*

Had Scooby arranged that? Did this all go back to *school days*? Had Riley done something that Scooby had held against him all this time? Did he blame him for his treatment at the hands of the late unlamented Johnsons?

That would mean Scooby had been fucking with him for a long time. Years. And that he would have to be tied in with Oktane if he was this BaseHeart, or worked for the man. But Roscoe was in the bodyguard business. Of course he would know Oktane. And people like him were always on the lookout for ex-SBS or SAS personnel.

Perhaps he hadn't just lost an eye in Afghan, he had lost his mind, too. And if he had, if he was BaseHeart or one of the people behind him, there was no end to what hurt he could pile on Riley.

What did Kate say in the car? He had a daughter? *Had?* No he *has* a daughter. Doesn't he?

Okay, forget the motivation for now. What solid evidence did he have?

The fire extinguisher.

Fuck. The fire extinguisher. How could Scooby have known about that? All such details were classified. They never, ever released actual descriptions of devices for fear of copycats. Not even to the *Sunday Times*. Unless Scooby knew . . . . unless he designed it.

Welcome home, pal. I sent the cleaner in for a quick dust. There's milk in the fridge.

'Dom? Are you there? Dominic?' his grandmother's voice echoed down the line.

He couldn't hear her. The black wave he had been dreaming about broke over him, cold and choking, the pressure on his chest threatening to push him under. Riley staggered under the impact, dropped the phone on the bed and in two strides he was at the door, yelling. 'Kate, don't open the fridge!'

But he was already too late.

APPENDIX

OPERATION BLACK KEY: THE REAL MISSION.

This is an edited version of an article by journalist Robert Ryan first published in *Lifetime (Omega)* magazine in 2018. It is reproduced with the author's permission, who would like to thank Anders Peter Mejer for commissioning it in the first place.

A QUEEN'S RANSOM

It had not been a smooth Atlantic crossing for the *Queen Elizabeth 2*, the world's most famous ocean liner. After leaving New York on 15 May, 1972, it had encountered fierce storms, and the windows of one of the ballrooms had given way, flooding the dance floor with seawater. The grand piano in the salon had come loose and skidded across the floor, fortunately failing to make any human contact. Many passengers, naturally, were seasick. However, by the third day of the voyage the storm had abated somewhat, although the ship was left nosing its way through turgid, unsettled seas towards Cherbourg and Southampton. Little did the captain, 800 crew or 1,438 passengers know, but the inclement weather was only an appetizer for the main course of drama that was to come.

Just after 3pm New York time on May 17, Charlie Dickson, the finance director of the Cunard Shipping Line, the *QE2*'s owner, received an anonymous call. The man at the end of the line claimed that two accomplices, who apparently had little concern for their own wellbeing, had planted six bombs on board the *QE2*. They would go off late the following day unless a $350,000 ransom was paid. Dickson was told there would be further instructions once the cash – in unmarked ten- and twenty-dollar bills – had been gathered.

Dickson hung up and contacted Cunard's HQ in the UK, which alerted Special Branch at Scotland Yard in London, who in turn called the FBI in Washington. William Law, the *QE2*'s captain, was radioed and told of the threat. He considered his options. The ship was 1,000 miles from land. No other vessels were in the immediate vicinity. There was no way to offload the more than two thousand souls on board. Captain Law ordered a preliminary, discreet search of the vessel, while pondering how, when and if to break the news to his passengers.

Eventually the Ministry of Defence was informed of the threat and it was decided there was only one outfit equipped to tackle this extortion on the high seas: the elite, secretive unit of the Royal Marines known as Special Boat Section or SBS.

A Most Secret Service

Unlike its 'sister' unit, the Special Air Service (SAS), the SBS has always had a relatively low public profile – members are instructed not to reveal that they serve in it and it rarely makes headlines. This behind-the-lines commando-style force specialises in covert operations against high-value targets and detailed mapping and assessment of terrain for the arrival of the main force, carried out mainly, but not exclusively, by sea. It is also active in Marine Counter Terrorism. The unit's motto is: 'By Strength and Guile'.

SBS was formed early in the Second World War by Roger 'Jumbo' Courtney, a British Commando officer, and known as the 'Folboat Troop', after the type of folding canoe they used, but it became the Special Boat Section in 1941. It was mainly deployed for reconnaissance missions prior to Allied landings and infiltrating and exfiltrating agents behind enemy lines. It took part in sabotage operations in Crete, Symi and Rhodes. It recce'd the landing sites for Operation Torch in North Africa and Salerno, Italy. The SBS was also highly active in South East Asia, deploying its skills along the Chindwin and Irrawaddy rivers, gathering intelligence and blowing up the odd oil or ammunition dump.

After the war it was disbanded, before quickly re-appearing again as part of the Royal Marines. It was the Royal Marine Commandos, not the SBS, that carried out the famous canoe raid against German shipping in Bordeaux in 1942, filmed as *The Cockleshell Heroes*. That daring mission formed part of the blueprint for the post-War SBS, so it seemed logical to have it operate under RM auspices. Since then it has carried out duties in Korea, destroying lines of communications and oil facilities behind enemy lines, and was on the ground prior to the start of the Falklands War, scouting out landing sites and assessing enemy strength. More recently, SBS teams have operated in Iraq, Afghanistan, Libya and Nigeria.

So how do you become a member of the SBS? Well, the Royal Marines itself is a tough enough nut to crack. Recruit training is the longest basic modern infantry training programme of any NATO combat troops – thirty-two weeks for recruits and fifteen months for officers. It starts with basic physical fitness, then a gym test, and various field exercises. Most of the tasks are completed wearing fighting order of 32 lb (14.5 kg) of Personal Load Carrying Equipment. This is then followed by the notorious Commando Course, which features a nine-mile speed march in full combat gear, an Endurance course over rough terrain – including crawling along through pipes, culverts and tunnels, the Tarzan Course (a ropes/climbing test that must be competed in under thirty minutes) and a 30 mile (48 km) march across Dartmoor. It is believed the drop-out/injury rate is around 50 per cent.

Normally, those who have managed to be accepted into the Royal Marines have to serve two years before they can apply to join the SBS, although these days SBS does recruit from outside the ranks of the RM. The first stage is to attend the five-day SBS Special Forces Briefing in Poole, Dorset, where it is laid out in no uncertain terms what qualifying for the unit will mean.

Once that is completed, those deemed to have the right aptitude and attitude have to undergo yet more gruelling training in diving, demolition, survival training (in Scotland), jungle training (Belize), parachuting (over land and sea), beach reconnaissance, mapping, canoeing, infiltration of ships and oil platforms and the Battle Swimming Test (a 600 m freestyle swim in 15 minutes followed by a 25 m underwater stretch). In all this might take thirty-nine weeks. Like the Marines, it has a high failure rate: at any one time there are only two hundred personnel in the SBS, from the many thousands who apply.

The SBS has undergone some name changes over the years. In 1977 the Special Boat Section was renamed the Special Boat Squadron and ten years later the Special Boat Service. But back in 1972, when the call went out to Major Richard Clifford that he was needed for an unusual and dangerous mission, it was still known as the Special Boat Section.

MISSION: ALMOST IMPOSSIBLE

In 1972 Richard Clifford was the officer commanding 2nd SBS at Poole in Dorset, and on 18 May, he was told to prepare a two-man squad for a parachute drop into the sea, something all his men had trained for. No further details were given. So he selected himself and, as the other half of the team, a man whose skill and calm attitude he respected, Corporal Tom Jones.

They were flown by helicopter to RAF Lyneham, where they met the two other men on the mission, an SAS sergeant and parachute instructor called Cliff Oliver and a Welsh ammunition technical officer (ATO) Captain Robert Hacon Williams from the Royal Army Ordnance Corps. An ATO is better known as a bomb-disposal expert.

They boarded a Hercules C-130 four-engined transport and took off into the kind of foul weather that had plagued the QE2. Amid the turbulence, Williams was violently sick. It probably didn't make him feel any better when the objective was finally revealed. They were to parachute from the Hercules into the Atlantic and be picked up by the QE2, where they would locate and disable any explosive devices planted on board.

There was one snag. Captain Williams had never made a 'wet' parachute jump over water before. And never a military jump with kit, just private civilian ones. Luckily, Oliver, as a veteran instructor, was able to give the bomb man some pointers. Nevertheless, parachuting into the sea is a very tricky proposition, and almost impossible for a novice to execute well. So Clifford decided that the junior SAS and SBS pair would jump first with most of the equipment they would need and Clifford would go out alongside Williams and try his best to make sure the ATO didn't drown.

Clifford checked the time on his Omega Seamaster, a modified version especially produced for the SBS, and highly collectible today. (The SBS Omega Seamaster 300 m watches (model 165.024) were 45 mm in diameter, had solid strap bars that were brazed into place, a circled T overprinted on the dial – to show that tritium was used in the luminous markers – and NATO stock numbers engraved on the caseback. The winder was oversized, so the covert operators could use it while still gloved.) By his calculations they would have precious few hours on the 50,000-ton ship to find any bombs and render them harmless. For the rest of the flight he glanced at his watch every ten minutes, willing the noisy, lumbering plane to get a move on.

Meanwhile, with the Hercules circling over the *QE2*, back in Manhattan, Dickson was handed a letter from the extortionist. He wanted the ransom money dropped off in a blue bag at a telephone booth several miles north of the city at 9.30pm that night. 'Be alone,' the note concluded. 'Any sign of police and you will have a catastrophe on your hands.'

On board the ship, the captain decided to break the news to his passengers that there was a bomb threat and that matters were in hand. Not everybody heard the announcement. Some were in the ship's movie theatre. What were they watching? The James Bond film *Diamonds are Forever*. Which was particularly ironic, because these days you could argue it was 007's old outfit that was coming to save the day.

A Spy is Re-Born

Ian Fleming's version of James Bond was not in the SBS but, like the author, naval intelligence. However, as the character has changed and evolved over the years – especially in the movies – so has his background. A naval career of some description has been a constant. After all, he is Commander Bond. But Daniel Craig's grittier version of the spy demanded a more robust 'origin story' than being behind a desk. So, for *Casino Royale*, the writers created a new 'bible' or 'legend' for Bond, which had him working for naval intelligence in the submarine service aboard HMS *Turbulent*.

Feeling his talents were not sufficiently exploited, Bond volunteered for the Special Boat Service. With the SBS he saw plenty of covert action across the world. Bond was subsequently recruited by the Royal Navy's Defence Intelligence Group and, wanting a more active role in defending the realm, applied to and was accepted by MI6.

The physical qualities that Craig brings to Bond – the close combat techniques, ability to survive in hostile environments, resistance to interrogation – come not from his time not in MI6 but the Special Boat Service

It was the sort of courage and determination that 007 has

in spades that Clifford and his SBS/SAS team were going to need that evening in May 1972. For, when they arrived at the drop zone close to the *QE2*, things could hardly have been worse.

SPECIAL DELIVERY

A long-range reconnaissance plane, an RAF Nimrod, was the first aircraft to appear in the skies above the ship, before disappearing into the clouds. Its job was to maintain ship-to-shore-to-Hercules radio contact. Passengers lined the rails to see what would happen next, as the captain had told them a bomb disposal team was on the way.

The pilot of the Hercules, meanwhile, was telling Clifford that conditions were far from ideal for parachuting into the ocean. The cloud base was at 300 to 400 feet, well below the safe height for a jump. They would be going in 'blind'. On top of that there was a wind gusting up to 20 knots, and there were five- to ten-foot waves.

Eventually, between them, the men on board the C-130 came up with a daring and dangerous manoeuvre. The lumbering transport plane would dive down below the clouds, locate the *QE2* and the tender it would launch to pick up the new arrivals, then climb almost vertically to the required height for the men to deploy their 'chutes. Nobody thought this was a perfect solution, least of all the novice ATO. But neither could anyone suggest an alternative.

The passengers and crew cheered when they saw the Hercules break through the murk, then, its engines screaming, climb again. Robin Woodall was Junior First Officer on board that day (he would later become Captain Woodall). He had taken one of the ship's tenders out and had released a smoke marker to show the C-130's crew wind speed and direction.

Some years afterwards, he recalled: 'The Hercules came in low over the ship, saw where the launch was, making smoke, and then climbed into the cloud with his huge aft ramp open. I was informed by radio that the first "stick" of two had jumped, and the first I saw of them was as they dropped through the cloud ... Then I received another message that the second "stick" of two had jumped, and to pick them up first [This was Clifford and Williams, the ATO]. This we duly did, and got them both into the launch.'

[In real life the Hercules survived the parabolic dive, unlike in this novel.]

There subsequently came a phlegmatic moment that Bond would have been proud of. 'After the launch was hoisted back on board QE2, I took the four men up to the bridge, where all the senior officers were assembled. I thought, what do I do now? So I introduced them all to Captain Law, they shook hands, then [Clifford] peeled open the front of his dry suit, shoved his hand inside, and pulled out a newspaper, saying to our captain, 'I don't suppose you've read today's London Times, sir?"

The ice broken, it was time to set about searching the huge vessel. Eventually they were able to identify a single, suspicious trunk and Williams requested a safe area to carry out a controlled explosion. By Clifford's estimate, there were just 18 minutes to go before the threatened detonations.

In New York, carrying the ransom as instructed, Dickson arrived at the phone booth and waited for the extortionist to make contact. A call came telling him to go to a diner a few miles away, where further instructions would be taped under a basin in the lavatory. These told him to take the cash in a remote spot and leave. This he did. Hidden in the darkness, the FBI waited for the culprit.

On board the *QE2*, Williams's detonation of the suspicious case released a shower of ... underwear and dirty laundry. There were no bombs on the *QE2*, no mysterious accomplices with a death wish. It had been a genuine blackmail attempt but a hoax bomb scare. The ship breathed a collective sigh of relief.

Each member of the four-man team was subsequently awarded the Queen's Commendation for Bravery, which was well deserved. The ransom was never collected from its drop. The FBI eventually arrested a forty-eight-year-old shoe salesman called Joseph Lindisi and charged him with attempted extortion and making threatening phone calls. He was sentenced to twenty years in prison.

The *QE2* went on to enjoy another thirty-six years of crisscrossing the Atlantic. The SBS returned to the shadows. But the outfit quickly made sure that, from then on, it had trained bomb disposal experts in its ranks who could, if need be, parachute into the sea. Just in case.

ACKNOWLEDGEMENTS

After a year of uncertainty, the pandemic has brought the country to its knees. Working from home, the lockdown and various levels of government restrictions have become normality, but through acts of pure selflessness, we have risen to the challenge and pushed on. The NHS, our military and first-responders have given their all in the fight against COVID and our gratitude as a nation could not be higher.

During this period, time has allowed for the second book in the Dom Riley series to be written and what a team effort it has been. It goes without saying this could never have been achieved without the support of some amazing people. Firstly, Julian Alexander, my agent, always there at the end of the phone ready to offer sound advice and who helped guide me through another book. Rob Ryan, an amazing writer and friend who has helped me through the maze of fiction writing and ensured I've come out the other side smiling. Bethan Jones and the team at Simon & Schuster continue to support their writers through these difficult times and have remained true professionals. Finally, my friends and family; their continued support has been solid and they have been there whenever I've needed them. Stay safe.

DID YOU LOVE OPERATION BLACK KEY?

Then don't miss

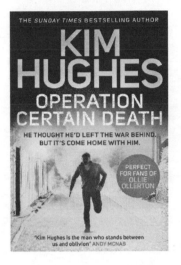

The first thriller in the Staff Sergeant Dominic Riley series from bestselling author and bomb disposal expert, Kim Hughes, GC.

A bomb explodes in a newly designed shopping complex. And this is just the beginning. The bomb-maker has bigger plans in place, designed for maximum destruction. Plans that are personal to Riley — and his family. But our fate is in the hands of a man who has his own demons to face. And they might just push him over the edge . . .

AVAILABLE TO READ IN PAPERBACK, EBOOK AND EAUDIO

SIMON & SCHUSTER